DESIRE UNASHAMED

"Whoever said Scotland was a backward country was a fool. 'Tis a land made for love and desire."

Her cheeks blushed a becoming pink before she lowered her gaze. "It is time I should confess that I . . . found you appealing even when you wore the robes of a cleric."

He raised her chin. "You need never be embarrassed with me," he whispered. When his lips touched hers, he was lost. He could not stop himself from kissing her. His lips moved over hers, and, like a flower blossoming to the sun, she responded eagerly. His hands reached out to caress her arms, her nape, her back. Stroking, touching, tasting, he could not get enough of her essence. She tried, in her innocence, to imitate his movements and he was humbled—and aroused—that her desire overcame her shyness. His hands roamed over her soft feminine curves, pulling her closer into his embrace. He ached with need. At that moment Guy realized that he could never just walk away from this woman. No matter their fate, she would haunt him for the rest of his days.

A PRAYER AND A PROMISE

Marian Edwards

Zebra Books
Kensington Publishing Corp.

http://www.zebrabooks.com

ZEBRA BOOKS are published by

Kensington Publishing Corp.
850 Third Avenue
New York, NY 10022

First Printing: November, 1997
10 9 8 7 6 5 4 3 2 1

Printed in the United States of America

ACKNOWLEDGMENT

To Dr. David Manzo, who graciously shared
his time and expertise.

Chapter One

England 1067

"You want me to do what?" Guy de Bellemare leaped out of his chair, dumping the generously endowed serving maid onto the floor as he glared at the king.

Lying in a heap of half-unlaced tunic and smock, the maid shrieked indignant curses at Guy until William handed her a coin and shooed her away.

After the door slammed shut and the angry woman's footsteps had faded from hearing, the king turned toward the hearth and rested his arm on the mantel. Dressed in the drab colors of a soldier, only his carriage and expression denoted his status as he stared into the bright flames.

"You heard me. I want you to pose as a friar to kidnap a nun from a convent."

Guy shook his head in consternation. "I am not so far into my cups that I do not have my wits about me, sire. I would lay down my life for you, but—"

"Rest your sense of honor. The maid's religious training is more a guise than a true calling. I am told that she fled to the convent to prevent her land from falling into another's hands," William assured, then held out his arm in an expansive gesture. "Besides, if you do me this boon, I will reward you with your own land and title."

Like bait to a starving animal, the temptation dangled over his head. Guy de Bellemare, bastard son to a nobleman, had no other way to gain land of his own. "Are you sure she is not a nun? I may have left the seminary, but I still do hold some things sacred."

"Non. She is no nun. The lady sought sanctuary, together with her brother. She does not wish to marry the man her uncle chose."

"Uncle?" Guy asked, the wine slowly clearing from his mind.

"Oui," the king said, admiration showing in his gaze for Guy's alertness. It was normally a father's place to arrange a marriage. "I do not like being the instrument that must deliver her, but her uncle Aumont has been in my service. When her father fell in battle she fled Normandy for Scotland."

"Who are these warriors?"

"Her father was Hamish of Aumont, formerly known as Hamish Campbell, but upon his marriage he took his wife's name. Quennel of Aumont, his brother-in-law, wants his niece returned, to fulfill a marriage betrothal he has contracted."

Guy was familiar with the names. "Her father was a brave and honorable man, his brother-in-law is not."

"That does not concern the crown."

Nor did it Guy. He cared little for a man he did not know, and for the lady, even less. Still, he could not escape the thought that there was more afoot than he was being told.

"Will you serve your liege lord?" William asked.

With a moan Guy buried his head in his hands. A full skin of wine did not help the thinking process. But he was not so drunk that he would choose to deny his king.

"*Oui*, I will indeed. If she is not a bride of Christ, she does not have the protection of the Church. My conscience is clear. What of her brother?"

"You must bring them both out of the abbey and back to London," the king insisted.

"Is the reason she fled with her brother to ensure his safety? Is he the rightful heir to the estate?" Guy asked.

"Very astute, Guy. Why else would she try to hide her brother? I will offer the boy protection until he reaches the age to face his enemies, but you must return the girl to her uncle. He is her legal guardian," William replied, as if reading Guy's mind.

With little objection to be made, Guy reluctantly gave in. "As you wish."

"I want no trouble from the Papacy. Pose as a priest or a friar and draw her and her brother from the sanctuary of the convent before you reveal your true mission."

"I understand," Guy said, knowing the difficulty of incurring the pope's wrath. "But how will I persuade the lady and her brother to leave the safety of the convent?"

"A convoy of monks has been detained. Such a convoy would be perfect for the lady and her brother to travel to their cousins in Scotland. "It is imperative they not reach Laird Campbell. He is her father's brother and holds family dear. It is rumored he suspects Quennel of foul play."

With good reason, Guy thought, remembering the stories he had heard of Quennel. "Does not Laird Campbell respect your power?"

"The Scots are a rare and strange breed. I would not like to go to war until I am ready. When the time is right, Scotland will come to heel." William took a sip of his wine, then stared over the rim of the chalice.

Guy met the king's gaze. "From what I have seen of the Celts, they will never be conquered."

With a wry lift of the his lips, William agreed. "Then 'tis your good fortune the land I have for you is in Wales. It is a disagreeable territory, but unlike Scotland, the people need only a strong arm, not an invasion."

"I had expected to settle closer to my brother and his wife," Guy said, thinking of the current separation from his family, while doing service for King William.

" 'Tis better to be landed than serve many masters. This will allow you to plan a life," William said with deadly accuracy.

"You are right. 'Tis time I left the battlefields and called one place home." Guy poured more wine in their cups.

"You have tired of war?" William asked with a raised brow.

Guy took a long and thoughtful drink. "I never relished it. 'Twas merely a way out of the seminary."

Humor creased the liege's lips, and his eyes twinkled with amusement. "You would have made a terrible cleric."

A grin slipped naturally in place as Guy spoke. "So Royce said when he prevailed against our mother and rescued me."

"His decision proved fortuitous, not only for you, but also for him," William countered, his expression knowing. "Few men would have used their body as a shield, intercepting a hurled lance meant for another."

When a log dropped in the fireplace, Guy stared at the shower of sparks, remembering that fateful day as he absently traced the ragged scar that lay beneath his tunic. The ugly gash stretched from his breastbone to his side, where the blade had glanced off bone and grazed his rib. "We never speak of it. It was what he would have done for me."

"Oui, you two are close. I knew I had chosen well. As

dedicated as your older brother has been, you will also serve the cause with the same fervor.''

"Though we are both loyal to you, sire, do not confuse us. We are different.''

William studied him, his look measured. "Royce's aspirations are met, but what of you, Guy de Bellemare? What price have you set on your ambitions? What are your dreams?''

Guy had dreams, certainly, but he had not even told his brother of them. He would be damned if he would explain to William. "Whatever they are, my liege, this land will go a long way in fulfilling them.'' He thought it politic to change the subject. "Sire, speaking of my family, have you any news from North Umberland? I am most anxious for word.''

"*Oui,* your brother is the proud father of twins.''

Guy bolted upright. "Twins! Did you say twins?''

The king chuckled. "*Oui.* 'Tis said one boy resembles his ugly uncle.''

Guy ignored the jest and momentarily savored the announcement. "Twins.'' 'Twas fitting. "And my sister-in-law, Bethany?''

"She is well and sends her love and gratitude.''

Guy leaned back in his chair, thankful for the news, proud and satisfied with the part he had played as matchmaker for his brother and sister-in-law. He savored the victory, while ignoring the king's interest. For one moment a tiny hope surfaced before he squelched it. Because Royce had found someone who loved him unconditionally didn't mean he would. Guy had learned a bitter lesson many years ago. Now he expected little from others and was never disappointed. "'Tis a busy half year since I laid eyes on my family. When I see them again there will indeed be more to feast my sight upon.''

William slapped Guy on the shoulder. "I am afraid that

may be some time. It will be years before this country is tamed.''

''Verily, by then there may be no peasants left to pay homage,'' Guy said, remembering all too well the bloody fields.

''I think there will be at least one or two,'' William said drolly, then lifted his cup in the air. ''A toast to seal our bargain.''

As Guy raised his chalice, he wondered about the lady he would betray. No doubt an ugly old crone. *No matter,* he thought, swallowing his wine. He was committed.

They finished another wineskin and as Guy crawled into bed, he suffered the strange premonition that his life would be forever touched by this decision. So strong was the feeling that all the wine consumed could not cloud the impression that he had started on a dangerous path.

Quennel Aumont paced the stone floors of his father's estate in Normandy. Upon his father's death, his sister had inherited the ancestral home, but all his life he had loved this castle and the lands that were governed by it.

Only two little problems stood in his way, and he had taken steps to see those obstacles eliminated. The room still bore the stamp of his sire. When he became master, his first task would be to eradicate any memento of his family. He hated them. Not disliked, but hated. The years had passed with only bitterness and anger to feed his hatred. Now, he could almost taste his revenge.

The tapestries would remain, but the weapons his father cherished and the armor his brother-in-law, Hamish Campbell, used would be tossed into yon field to rust and pit. Home should reflect the master and his taste. Unwanted memories of the past crowded his mind, and the painful headaches began. *God's teeth,* but any thought of his blood brought on the malady that could bed-rid him for days.

He massaged his temples as the door opened and Claude Boleau, the captain of the guard, entered. "My lord, the soldier has returned from England with a report."

"Send him in," Quennel ordered, neither liking nor trusting the seasoned officer who had loyally served the Aumont name.

"As you wish," Boleau said, bowing, then quietly leaving the room.

Though the captain showed no disrespect, Quennel was aware of his contempt. Quennel's misspent childhood still lived in the memories of the old guard.

The doors had barely closed when a knock sounded. A wizened warrior entered and curtly bowed before Aumont. "My lord, the Lady Gabrielle is staying with the Abbess Ambrose. I have, per your instructions, left enough mercenaries to intercept her and her brother, Louis, should they choose to leave."

Quennel turned away from the condemnation in the man's eyes.

"What did King William have to say?"

The soldier cleared his throat. "He is sending a man to expedite the lady's safe return."

"By His wounds!" The curse hung in the air as Quennel whirled around, his face splotched red in sudden outrage. "William has taken my simple request for nonasylum and turned it into a reason to investigate my personal affairs. I will not have it!" He slammed his fist into his palm, then advanced on the messenger. "I want the king's man dealt the same fate as my nephew," he snapped.

"The same, my lord?" the messenger asked, disbelief written on his gaunt features.

Quennel struck the man hard across the face. "Do you have trouble hearing? Death to him!"

"But, my lord, 'tis the king's man," the messenger declared, not bothering to shield himself from possible retribution as he glared at his master.

"What care I for William's authority? He will never know his man died by my command. Make it look like an accident."

"As you wish, my lord." Though spoken evenly, the soldier's words lacked respect. "I will send your orders."

"See that you do. Also, dispatch more men to Britain. My niece and nephew *will* be captured, but only by me."

The man's silence stretched his patience to the limit.

"Send the farmers from the estate," he snapped. "Disperse the men as you see fit to help the mercenaries. And, Channing, if this news reaches the king, I shall know the name of the informer."

"You need not worry about my loyalty, my lord. My family lives on this estate, and as you have already pointed out, their lot, even their health, would greatly diminish if you were displeased with my efforts."

"I am delighted we understand each other."

The man did not respond, though his shoulders sagged lower than when he entered. Bowing his head, he left the room.

With the hem let out, the donated garment fit perfectly. Gabrielle Aumont knelt before the smiling young woman and straightened the folds of her best tunic. "Willa, you will be a lovely bride," she said as tears misted her eyes and she quickly wiped them away.

Abbess Ambrose stepped forward, slipping the silver necklace over the fourteen-year-old's golden mane. As she gently drew the long hair through the chain, allowing the simple cross to slide forward over the tunic's neckline, she said, "Keep this always as a remembrance of your time with us and a symbol of your faith."

"I shall miss you all, especially you, Sister Gabrielle. I am very grateful you befriended me."

"You do not have to thank me." Gabrielle gave a last tug at the pleats as she stood. "It is only a tunic," she said, smiling that her small contribution had given the girl so much pleasure.

" 'Tis not this garment of which I speak, Sister." Her face suddenly grew red, and she spread her hands to encompass the robe. "Though it is truly the loveliest of all tunics, far more beautiful than any of the others you presented me." Her gaze filled with admiration and respect. "But you have given me a gift far more important than I could ever repay. You taught me courage. You were my inspiration."

"Me?" questioned Gabrielle, embarrassed.

"Aye, I was so afraid when Mother and Father died. Then you came to the abbey with your brother, and I learned you had not only lost your parents, but crossed two countries to save your brother. I was ashamed of my fear."

"Nonsense," Gabrielle demurred, feeling again the panic of her flight. "I was not brave. I simply did what was necessary."

The young bride took Gabrielle's hands in hers. "I could not have found the courage." She shook her head. "I never knew a woman, let alone one so fragile and delicate could possess such strength." Willa squeezed her fingers gently. "I pray you will find someone as strong and as good as my Edwin. You should have a shoulder to lean on."

Gabrielle pulled her hands free. "At nineteen summers, I am too old to have suitors," she scoffed.

Ignoring Gabrielle's protest, Willa turned to Abbess Ambrose. "She is no more suited to convent life than I. Talk to her, Abbess."

"Now is not the time to worry about Sister Gabrielle's

future," the abbess said. "Go to the chapel, where Edwin is waiting for you." Mother Ambrose hugged Willa, then hurried her toward the door. The girl turned around and rushed back across the room.

"Willa, you are radiant." Gabrielle enfolded the young orphan in a loving embrace, holding on briefly to a dream that could never be hers, then slowly released her. "Happiness, Willa," she whispered as the bride rushed to the door and her waiting life.

The room receded in a mist, as did the voice of Abbess Ambrose telling her to hurry. She waited, knowing she could neither quicken, nor end the vision. Bright fluffy clouds swirled around her, then dissolved, leaving the image of a lovely field and a couple standing face-to-face. The woman's features cleared, and she gasped to see herself. The man had his back to her, but he was tall, with broad shoulders and a muscular build. Through the veil of rising mist, his hair appeared to be dark. Wisps of white shrouded the man, keeping his features a mystery even when he turned. She stood in a beautiful violet robe and reached up to caress the stranger's face. Then she withdrew her hand, and, before this tall man, she slowly undid the ties of her robe. The material dropped from her shoulders and slipped to the ground, revealing not her undertunic but her naked flesh.

The vision faded and Gabby drew a shaky breath. The Sight was never wrong. She would someday offer herself to a man. Chills raced up her spine at the frightening thought. Would this be the price of freedom? She buried the thought and composed herself. Only those closest to her knew of her Sight, and she could not afford to have her secret out.

Long after the wedding meal and the happy couple's departure, Lady Gabrielle smiled as she passed the sisters in the courtyard. With her hands folded in prayer, she climbed the stairs to her room. Slowly, she walked through the halls. Haste was frowned upon in the abbey. Once in her cell, she carefully peeled off the wimple and head veil that hid her hair and removed the thick wool robe of a postulant. Since her exile, she had carefully considered the religious life. As she folded and reverently smoothed the wrinkles from her clothing, Mother Ambrose's words came back to her. "You must come willingly into God's service. If your vocation is true, there will be no hesitation in your heart or mind." Abbess Ambrose was right, she thought as she slipped into her tunic and methodically brushed her dark hair. She had doubts.

Night bells sounded vespers as she sat at her writing table composing yet another plea, to King William and the Pope to intercede in this family matter on their behalf. Not once in two years had either responded. It was only through the grace of God that both she and her brother had escaped her uncle's retribution thus far.

Louis's life and her freedom would be forfeit if they were captured before reaching their final destination. Even if she fell victim to their pursuers, as long as Louis made his way to the Campbell clan she would be content. And never would she be cowed into one of the abusive unions her uncle Quennel had proposed. It would not be a marriage alliance but a death contract.

Her thoughts drifted slowly to her brother. Louis had thankfully been fostering at the Lemieux castle when Uncle Quennel arrived to be their guardian. If not for the custom which required a young lad to leave his home and board with another lord, giving several years' service in exchange for military training, Louis would now be dead. He had been furious with her for abducting him from his sponsors, but if she had not taken him with her on her escape ... she shuddered. If not for Louis's hurt pride, he would see the right of it.

A shiver went through her at the memory of their dangerous escape. Traveling at night through a war-torn country and hiding just before daybreak, at best, in stables, and at worst, in rainswept fields, it had taken eighteen long months to reach the abbey. Other convents along the way had refused them refuge, fearing William's ill pleasure, but they had found sanctuary here. Still, their journey was far from over. Until they reached their father's clan in Scotland neither of them were safe. Mother Ambrose had heard of a convoy of soldiers, monks, friars, and priests, who were headed north. Gaining passage with the pilgrimage would mark the last leg of their long flight.

"I want to go home," her brother announced sullenly as he threw open her door and stood propped against the doorframe.

Sealing her missives, Gabby drew a deep breath and turned. "Louis, we have been over that a thousand times. Do you not understand? As heir to all of the Aumont estate, you must die for Quennel to inherit, while I am easily disposed of in an unwanted marriage. If he finds us, you will die quickly and I slowly."

"I am a soldier. A man full-grown. I can protect what is mine."

At ten and five summers, he had attained the stature of a man, but he still lacked the maturity necessary to deal with her uncle.

"Uncle Quennel is Satan's servant, truly a serpent from hell. You have never met his ilk before and would be unprepared for his villainous strike. I promised mother on my immortal soul that I would see you reach manhood and attain your birthright: and by St. George I will. You will return home when the time is right and reclaim all that is yours, but to do so before you are ready is to court disaster."

"You always think you know what is best."

His animosity hurt, though she tried to ignore the pain it produced. "That is because I think things through before I act—a practice you might find useful if you ever wish to lead men.''

''I am going to return home now and take Uncle Quennel to task.''

He stood adamant. With the way he held his head and his proud stance, he reminded her of their father. Gabby shook her head, both to deny his idea and to dispel the disquieting image. ''As a man becomes tempered in battle so shall you with a few years of wisdom. Uncle Quennel will only be defeated by brains, dear brother, not brawn. He commands the castle guard. Or did you forget?''

''They will follow me,'' her brother proudly insisted as he approached.

Rising, she met his challenging stance. ''Louis, they will not recognize you until it is too late. My heavens, I barely knew you after four years' absence, and you are my own brother. In all, six years have passed since you left home. How do you expect the guard to see beyond the changes time has wrought? Believe me, brother, the difference is monumental.''

With his fists held tightly at his sides and his shoulders proudly thrown back, he towered over her. ''Then, sister, the changes time has wrought in me should let even you know that I will do as I say.''

''Step one foot outside of this convent and you jeopardize not only your life but mine. Are you willing to accept that responsibility?'' She held her brother's gaze, unwilling to be intimidated by his manner. There were times, such as now, that he was more stubborn than anyone, either living or dead, in their family.

He did not respond but left the room, slamming the door behind him. She released her breath. How she missed the closeness they had shared before this turmoil.

Now he resented her interference, and though she mourned the loss of his affection, she would bear his animosity to keep him safe. She sank back into her chair and hoped, given time, Louis would understand the wisdom of her actions.

Caring for a child was a burdensome task, and she absently wondered why anyone would choose to take it on. Suddenly reminded of her mother, she smiled sadly. Nothing in life was without a cost. Love, though rich with the joy and wonder of life, was also filled with pain and sadness.

A knock at the door interrupted her thoughts. She rose to open the door but a sliver and peeked cautiously through the small crack.

"Abbess Ambrose." With a sigh of relief Gabby threw open the door to her mother's dearest friend.

"I passed Louis in the hall," Abbess Ambrose said as she entered the room. "I expect the stable will be mucked out in short order."

Going from a knight in training to an abbey stable hand had been a blow to his pride. "Did he show you any disrespect?"

"Nay, you are the only one who catches the edge of his temper. 'Tis times like this I suspect you wish you were born an only child."

Gabrielle chuckled.

"You should smile more often, my dear. Perhaps when you reach Scotland you will."

"Have you had news?" Gabrielle eagerly clasped the older woman's hands.

"Your escort will be here within the week," Abbess Ambrose responded, patting her hand.

Gabrielle slipped her arm around the nun's waist and looked up into her warm brown gaze. " 'Tis a blessing the Church sent you to England. Unlike the others, you did not turn us away. No words can express my gratitude," Gabby said, knowing why her mother had always spoken so highly of this woman. "You risked much to help us."

"My dear, I am in the business of helping people."

"A dangerous business."

"Doing God's work has never been easy. But I'm not so noble, my dear. I am merely repaying an old debt."

"Debt?"

Mother Ambrose's expression softened at Gabby's surprise.

"Your mother, God rest her soul, saved my life years ago."

"She saved your life?" Gabby asked, unable to imagine her sweet, quiet mother in a heroic role.

Abbess Ambrose hid her hands beneath her robe, exposing only a mischievous grin as she paced the room. "Aye, Blanchefleur married my intended, the great warrior Hamish Campbell, so I could enter the convent."

"But she loved Father," Gabby declared.

"*Oui,* she did very much," Abbess Ambrose said, confirming Gabby's assertion.

"What of Father?"

"Years later your father confided in me that though he would have been honored to uphold our marriage contract, he had always loved your mother. From that day on I realized that no matter how we scheme, there is a higher hand involved in our destiny."

"Oh, Abbess, 'tis hard to believe such intrigue surrounded my parents."

"Well, 'tis true. Not only would I have been miserable as a wife, but your father, who secretly loved Blanchefleur, would have been brokenhearted bound as my husband. Because of your mother's courageous act all of us received happiness."

"What did she do?" Gabby asked, taken aback by the revelation, and noticing for the first time a gleam in the reverend mother's eyes.

"She went to your father and . . . compromised her virtue.

He was then honor-bound to marry her, thereby freeing all of us.''

"Mother . . . *seduced* Father?'' Gabby asked in wonder.

"*Oui,* she did.''

"Abbess, are we talking about *my* mother?'' Gabby queried, still skeptical.

"Do not look so shocked. Your mother was a beautiful, remarkable woman.''

"I do not doubt it, but Mother?'' she said, unable to imagine her soft-spoken mother as a wanton temptress.

"Do not make the mistake of thinking that quiet people lack passion. It is not necessary to be bold to feel strongly and act fervently on one's beliefs. You are your mother's daughter.''

She hoped not. To be so carried away by emotion frightened her.

Obviously, her terror was mirrored in her features, for Abbess Ambrose gave her a comforting hug. "When the time comes you will be glad you have such passion. Do not be afraid of life, Gabrielle, you must embrace it.''

Morning dawned with Abbess Ambrose, her voice strained, shaking Gabby awake. "Dear, we cannot find Louis. When he was late for his chores, Sister Magdalene checked his room, thinking that he overslept, but the bed was empty, and the covers undisturbed. The sisters have searched, but to no avail. I fear foul play is afoot.''

"*Non,*'' Gabrielle said, remembering his words last night. She threw back the covers, sat up, and reached for her clothes. "He has left.'' Gabby hurriedly dressed, knowing there was nothing for it but to find him.

"Dear, do not leave the safety of the abbey,'' Abbess Ambrose pleaded as she walked with her through the halls of the convent.

"Believe me, I do not want to, but I must," Gabby said, knowing that in all likelihood she would not lay eyes on the good abbess again. She hugged the holy woman, then tore out of the embrace.

"Wait," Abbess Ambrose called out. "Let us offer a diversion."

Gabby turned and listened to the woman's plan. All the sisters would leave the convent riding or walking in different directions. If spies were watching, they would be hard-pressed to follow everyone.

"In case it takes longer to find Louis than you planned, you should leave prepared," Abbess Ambrose said, pressing a satchel of food and clothes into Gabrielle's hands.

Gabby smiled at the woman's ingenuity. If born a man, Abbess Ambrose would have made a very good general.

Fear, anger, frustration, and worry took turns in her mind as she stole out of the convent's back gate dressed in the drab robes of a nun. Her mounting terror conjured horrible visions of blood and carnage as she picked her way carefully across fields with a slow, even tread. A constricting band tightened around her chest, and her heart pounded in her ears, knowing the terrible mental images would become reality if she did not find her brother before her uncle Quennel did. Beads of sweat formed on her upper lip, and beneath her robe the warm rivulets trickled down between her breasts as she recalled their flight, reliving its terror and uncertainty. She drew deep lungfuls of air as the dense forest loomed ahead. The cover of the trees would allow her to move faster and without discovery toward the cottage that housed her transportation.

At the edge of the thick foliage she knelt and covertly checked behind her. Relief soared through her at the sight of the empty field, and she turned and dashed through the brambles and ferns, not stopping until she reached the deserted cottage.

After mounting the horse Abbess Ambrose had waiting for her, Gabby blessed herself, then kicked the horse's flanks. Every minute counted. She could ill afford to misuse even one.

Chapter Two

Louis's stomach growled loudly as he considered his options. He had not brought food when he left the convent the previous night. Each pang of hunger emphasized his oversight, and with his pockets feeling the weight of neither coins nor baubles, he was sorely without means. The sun hung low in the sky and he squinted against the glare, trying not to think of the abbey's evening fare. His sister was right about his lack of forethought, but he would die before letting her know it.

It was for her that he needed to meet with his Norman uncle. Gabby would never know peace until Quennel no longer threatened their lives. Though he reluctantly admired her courage in assuming the mantle of family protector, the image of a tiny woman shouldering such responsibility was ludicrous. Her forbearance and tenacity had surprised him.

He fingered the scar on his arm and shook his head at the memory it evoked. He recalled every detail as if it had happened yesterday and not at the beginning of their flight.

"Gabby, look out," he had shouted to her as the two mercenaries charged forward.

One man grabbed his sister and threw her against a tree. She crumpled to the ground like a disjointed puppet. The assailant then joined his companion, and together they advanced on Louis.

Drawing his sword, he knew a lad of ten and three could not defeat two men. He could hold off one man but never two. As he swung his sword in a vicious arc, he saw his sister stagger to her feet behind his attackers.

"You think two are enough?" he goaded, giving his sister time to take cover.

The men laughed mockingly. "You will be dead in a moment, and then we will enjoy your sister's charms before dragging her back to Quennel."

It was not the words that enraged him but his sister's next move. She grabbed two fistfuls of dirt and motioned her intention. With her loud screech the assassins turned, and she hurled the dirt. The debris blinded one, but only distracted the other.

In the momentary confusion, Louis quickly slipped his sword into the defenseless man's ribs, then pulled his blade free and met the first parry of the remaining mercenary.

After several blocked thrusts, Louis slipped his blade under his opponent's and finished the contest.

As Gabrielle gazed upon the two lifeless bodies her face was ashen, but her shoulders were straight.

"You see, I will take care of you," she said.

Her brother smiled a bit at the memory. She had no idea what would have happened to her had Louis not been there. It was he who must do the protecting. She was frail and fragile, exactly like their mother, save for her mystical ability.

When he left home six years ago to foster at Lemieux's, she was but a young maiden. If time had changed him to her eyes, it was nothing to the surprise he suffered upon seeing her again. She had blossomed into a beautiful lady, and he had trouble reconciling the woman with the playmate of his childhood. Perhaps that was where the problem between them lay. He could not possibly listen to someone who in his thoughts and heart was the girl he had teased in his youth.

He especially resented her edict to use their father's name—Campbell—while travelling in this country. Though Louis saw the merit for the subterfuge, he felt disloyal. The Aumont name dated back to the birth of Normandy, and though Campbell was a proud and noble name, he had been raised an Aumont.

Upon hearing horses, he moved to the side of the road, and looked behind him. A small armed party of monks approached. Excitement replaced depression, as Louis realized this was the expected convoy. He would find compassion and charity in their holy ranks.

The soldiers passed on without giving him any notice. *Arrogant pigs,* Louis thought, bristling at their rude behavior. If they only knew whom they snubbed. But his identity must remain secret. After the soldiers rode by, the monks and friars followed. They, too, passed without even a nod of their pious little heads. Dressed as a peasant and riding a broken-down old church horse, Louis suddenly understood the picture he presented.

"Halt," he shouted, tired of being ignored.

At the imperial summons the last friar in the group pulled back on his reins and turned, staring at him as though he could not believe what he had heard.

"Verily, boy, you need assistance?" The huge man, whose frame seemed more suited to warrior's armor than holy vestments, frowned.

"Aye, I merely wish to ask for some food and lodging."

Louis responded, wary of the friar's intense scrutiny. This cleric had more of a hawk's look about him than a dove's.

"Do you now?" the cleric asked with an arched eyebrow and the beginnings of a smile. "So, you bellowed 'halt'?"

" 'Twas all I could think of." God's teeth! The moment the words left his mouth he knew that his lack of forethought was again rearing its ugly head.

"Relax boy. It worked."

Louis cleared his throat and extended his hand. "Your pardon, friar, I am Louis . . ." His hesitation was telling, and, to cover the faux pas, he rushed on. "That is to say, my friends just call me Louis."

The friar accepted his hand. "Louis? No last name?"

His lapse had been noted. It was too late to offer the Campbell name. "Nay, 'tis not important." Though many did not have a surname, his reservation was an admission he did.

Speculation crossed the man's features, but he tilted his head in a slight bow, conceding the point. "I am Friar Guy."

"No last name, friar?" Louis asked.

"As you say, 'tis not important."

Louis smiled. "I did not know you were allowed to have a sense of humor."

"Humor is not against the Commandments," the friar said. "Wherever did you get the idea that all clerics were dour? Laughter is good for the soul."

"I know several sisters who would frown on that idea."

"How many sisters do you have?"

"Nay, friar," Louis corrected. "I have but one sister, who answered the call to serve God. None of the women in the convent ever jested."

"Ride with me, boy," the friar offered generously as he gestured to the place by his side. "A nun, you say? Well, not many of them have a sense of humor, but then, not many women do. Would you not agree? A lad of such worldly experience as yourself must know that.''

"Aye, but I must confess, friar, I do not understand women,'' Louis admitted, feeling at home in the friar's presence after so long a time spent with the nuns in the abbey.

"Oui, boy, you have the way of it. Actually, neither do I, and I have lived considerably longer than you. They are indeed strange,'' Guy said as he urged his horse into a gentle canter.

"My sister is so bossy. Always frowning and fretting. 'Tis enough to drive a man mad.''

"What is your sister's name, boy?''

"Gabrielle, but I have always called her Gabby. She does come by her name honestly. When she wants to make a point, she talks it to death.''

The friar smiled at that. "Loud and shrill is she?''

"Nay, her voice is whisper soft, but holds a logic a man cannot reason against.''

"Well, I look forward to meeting her. Where is she staying?'' he asked casually. "Perhaps we will stop there.''

"Oh, I cannot travel with you to the abbey,'' Louis protested, suddenly alarmed.

"Why ever not?'' Friar Guy asked.

"Because, friar, I had a falling-out with her,'' he replied ashamed, but afraid not to admit the truth to the cleric.

"I see. Well, you still have to travel a ways with us for food. Do you not?''

Louis instantly relaxed. "Aye, that would be all right.''

By nightfall Gabrielle saw the glow of several campfires in the distance. She dismounted and advanced carefully. Peering through the dense foliage she caught the color and shape of the religious robes in the firelight, and whispered a heartfelt prayer for deliverance. All day she had the feeling of being watched and followed. Tired and exhausted, she trudged toward camp.

Several soldiers walked about, and to her eye it seemed more a military camp than a pilgrimage. But the attacks on travelers had increased, precipitating the need for such force. A posted guard challenged her, blocking her path. As he towered over her with his sword drawn and pointed at her chest, terror surged through her. Before she could explain a monk intervened.

The cleric, a short balding man, greeted her with a smile, "What may we do for you, daughter?"

"I have journeyed all day," she faltered, noticing the guard still held his weapon in a threatening position. "A rest and a little supper is all that I ask."

He stretched his arm, pointing toward his companion sitting at the campfire. "Please, join Friar Guy by the fire, warm yourself, and rest. We will gladly share our meager fare with you," he offered.

As the guard sheathed his sword and walked away, relief swept through her. She knelt before the monk and kissed his hand. "Your generosity and kindness to a stranger during these hard times are a credit to your order."

He helped her up and reached for the horse's reins. "Daughter, difficult times are when charity is least present and most needed."

Her eyes stung with unshed tears, and she waved away the monk's help. "Thank you, friar," she said, leading her horse to the tie line. While attending to the beast's needs, she gathered her composure.

When she walked to the edge of the firelight she studied the younger cleric, whom the monk had called Friar Guy. His size surprised her. Most friars were small of stature. This man's bulk and height were like those of a robust warrior, not an enlightened scholar of holy manuscripts. The sight of a hulking man in dark robes sitting by the fire after a day fraught with anxiety was enough to reawaken her apprehensions. She tried to bury her unwarranted trepidation, but his image struck a familiar memory, one that refused to fully surface. The vague feeling left her unsettled.

Drawn, despite her fears, to the welcoming glow of the fire, she held up her hands and warmed them. Without speaking, Friar Guy poured her a cup of mulled ale. A thick woolen cowl was drawn over his head, forming a hood which obscured his features. "You have a good heart to take care of your animal's needs before your own," he said in a deep, rich voice that sounded too masculine to belong to a man of the cloth. Then he turned with her ale.

She let out a gasp as the firelight illuminated his features. They were so arresting, so perfect, that they literally stole her breath away. Her face burning at her reaction, she accepted the ale, lowered her gaze, and took a seat.

" 'Twas merely what any good horsewoman would do," she replied softly, unwilling to meet his scrutiny.

"True, but generally the horse's care is left to a servant."

She nodded as she blew on her ale and watched the steam rise. "My name is Sister Gabrielle and I have come in search of my brother, a lad of ten and five summers. Have you seen him?"

"I may have." Firelight danced across his high cheekbones as he slipped the cowl back. Blue-black highlights in his ebony hair flashed to life, then faded to darkness as his head tilted, and he met her gaze. "Today I met a young lad who was tired and hungry. He rode with us, sharing our supplies while contributing lively conversation."

Her heart raced at the news. "I must find him." She leaned forward. "His life is in danger."

"And he needs you to protect it?" The cleric raised an eyebrow as he offered her a plate of food.

Gabby set the plate aside, her hunger forgotten. "In a

manner of speaking. I am all he has. I must see to his welfare.''

The cleric shook his head. ''Sister Gabrielle, no wonder he resents you. He is a man, yet you treat him like a boy.''

She squared her shoulders. ''He is a man indeed, but like any inexperienced person, he needs time to be seasoned.''

The handsome friar grinned, showing even white teeth and a twinkle in his eyes. ''He travels with us still.''

''Thank God,'' she whispered. ''I worried my brother had fallen into a trap.''

''Is that why you came looking for him yourself? If he is in danger, are you not also?'' the shrewd friar asked, looking at her with an intensity that made her feel vulnerable.

''Aye, but I am the elder sister, and though he does not depend on me, I have sworn on my immortal soul to protect him.''

The friar's deep, indigo eyes widened, but remained centered on her. '' 'Tis the vow of a soldier, not a woman, and surely not one entering the service of God.''

She held his gaze and took a deep breath. ''I cannot break my oath. I promised my dying mother.''

Understanding flashed across his features, softening his expression. ''Put your mind at ease, Sister, Louis is in yon tent, resting.''

A thick lump rose in her throat as she looked toward the tent he indicated. ''Louis,'' she breathed, rising, but the friar's hand grasped her shoulder and gently pulled her down.

He pointed to her plate. ''Eat first. 'Tis a sin to waste food.'' At her hesitation, he smiled. ''I promise you he is not going anywhere tonight.''

She picked up her plate and moved the food around. ''Tired is he?''

''*Oui.* I fear he was ill prepared for this journey.''

''Not thinking ahead is a failing of his,'' she said, taking a small bite of meat. Though plain, the fare was surprisingly good, or perhaps her hunger made the simple meal seem like a feast.

"And what, pray tell, is your failing?"

Chewing thoughtfully, she chose her words carefully. "I trust people too much," she said, holding up her hand to forestall his objection. "Often, to my sorrow, I find those I believed in are capable of base actions." She sighed, remembering the folly of her nature. "To my dismay, friar, I have repeatedly found that though we are made in God's image, there are evildoers among us; yet like a dull pupil with a lesson never learned, I still continue to believe in the goodness of my fellowman."

The friar's cup paused an inch from his lips as he stared at her. " 'Tis not a vice but a virtue," he declared.

A wry smile slipped over her lips. "Tell my brother that. He is convinced that my beliefs will get us killed."

"I see." Friar Guy stroked the dark stubble on his chin, then glanced away. In that instant, with the light dying, his shadowed face looked dangerous, and she felt her stomach roil.

As quickly as his menacing image appeared it vanished, making her wonder if she had imagined it.

"As I understand it, Louis suspects every stranger to be a foe and is surprised when they are a friend. You accept every stranger as a friend and are disillusioned when they are a foe."

She grinned. "You understand perfectly, friar."

"In time Louis will learn that faith can bridge the chasm between one's belief and one's behavior," he said, reminding her that nothing was truly impossible.

His comforting words filled her with hope. "It will truly be a miracle, friar, when my brother's outlook agrees with mine. On that day there will be no need for either of our professions."

He chuckled. "There are those who would consider that heresy."

"Do you?" she asked, suddenly wary.

"*Non.* I consider it refreshing."

She chuckled. "I told you, I am a trusting soul."

"Still, the prudent course would be not to share your ideas with those individuals who are less tolerant of change."

"Rest your fears, friar. No matter what my brother thinks, I am not unaware that powerful men, both religious and political, direct our futures. But I am not important enough to come to their attention." She leaned forward to see his expression more clearly in the waning firelight. "I can no more change who I am than they can change their ambition. All I can do is take care of myself and my brother."

"You have chosen a difficult task."

"I know." She sighed and leaned back. "You would not be the first person to think I am witless."

"I understand you very well," he declared, solemnly. "In fact, I wish I did not," he said, standing and pointing to the tent. "Now, would you like to see your brother?"

They walked through the camp, sidestepping sleeping soldiers and monks, to reach the tent. Friar Guy placed his finger to his lips before he tossed the flap up, revealing her brother sleeping fitfully on the ground. His head lolled back and forth, and he mumbled words that made Gabrielle cringe.

The perfectly accented French hung in the air.

"Your brother led me to believe he was Scots," the friar said flatly.

"Actually, we are both," she said trying to minimize their Norman heritage. "With a Scottish father and Norman mother, we have lived in both countries."

She knelt beside her brother and shook him. "Louis, wake up," she urged, fearing the secrets he might impart while asleep.

Slowly his eyelids opened. The beseeching look in his eyes tore at her heart. Something was desperately wrong.

"Louis?" she repeated, taking in his disjointed movements and the glazed sheen in his eyes. Had he been given something? Panic assailed her. They had been captured.

Time hung suspended between heartbeats as she turned on the friar. She had foolishly trusted him because he appeared to be a cleric. Fear and rage lived in her soul while her fingers curled tightly into her palms. "Do you wish to tell me why my brother is drugged?"

The friar seemed unaffected by her question. His self-control destroyed hers. Impotent fury surfaced as she raised clenched hands. "Judas," she cried, attacking him.

He took hold of her shoulders. "Cease," he commanded. Ignoring his demand, she pounded out her frustration, unable to stop.

Pulling her against his chest, his hands slid down her back, crushing her attack in a tight embrace until her struggles diminished. Held firm she felt the rhythm of his breathing as his lips grazed her ear and he spoke in a low calm voice. "Sister Gabrielle, I know you are frightened, but I did not drug your brother. He overindulged in the ale. I thought it best to return him to the abbey."

Trapped against his chest, his words rolled like thunder in her mind. Had she heard right? She tilted her head back to see his face. "Truly?" she whispered, wanting desperately to believe him.

He was silent for a long moment. In the silvery moonlight his eyes were strangely piercing. She gasped, recalling a disturbing memory of her Sight. In many a haunting vision deep indigo eyes, had stared through the mist at her. These were the same blue-black eyes. She was sure of it. Like a prey captivated by a predator's gaze she was unable to look away.

Finally, he nodded and relief washed over her. If the man

were a soldier, he could have laid her low with one blow. That he did not retaliate convinced her he was not an impostor.

"But if I was not a cleric, but someone else . . ." he said, pointedly.

A shiver went up her spine and her stomach tightened. It was uncanny the way he divined her thoughts.

Suddenly, she was aware of how intimate their bodies were. Pressed tight against him, his holy robes offered no barrier to the hard muscles and strong physique they covered. Every breath she drew held the musky scent of his body, nor could she ignore the errant lock of hair that slashed across his forehead in a roguish manner. He did not at this moment remind her of any friar, nor did he have a pious mien. He looked like a man, one who had tasted and enjoyed the pleasures of sin. Her nerves tingled with excitement. He had her at a disadvantage. Danger bells sounded within her, pealing out a warning she dare not ignore.

"Are you all right?" he asked.

She could not look at him. The genuine concern in his voice embarrassed her. The attraction had been in her mind, not his. She pushed out of his arms.

"Forgive me, friar," she said curtly to cover up her awkwardness. She scrambled into the shelter and knelt by her brother. The friar remained at the tent flap, watching as she tended her sibling. The noxious fumes of ale assailed her nostrils as Louis reached out to her.

"Gabby, you left the convent?"

"So it would appear," she said dryly, combing her fingers through his messy hair.

"God's teeth, Gabby. You were supposed to go to Scotland," he moaned.

"Louis," she admonished and shook her head in relief and frustration. He was no worse for his overindulgence.

The friar's story was true; her brother did not seem frightened of the cleric.

"We will leave now," Louis said, reaching for her hand and missing.

"Nay, we will stay and travel with the good friar." She stressed the word *good* and was surprised by the cleric's raised brow.

"I tell you, I am going to meet our uncle Quennel and put this problem to rest," Louis insisted.

"How? With your blood?"

"Nay, with this." Her brother flung his arm wide to demonstrate an imaginary sword blow.

"We will consult our uncle Alec in Scotland. He will help us. And brother, he is a master warrior. You could learn much from him. If Uncle Alec feels you should ride in alone and face forces that would easily outnumber an army, then you will have my blessing," she said wryly.

The boy turned to the cleric, apparently willing to forgo his argument in favor of eliciting support. "Women," Louis said despairingly. "They will be the death of me. I have found they make little sense. You cannot live with them, and I am told, it is not worth living without them."

The friar looked at Gabrielle from her veil to her boots in a strange appraisal. "Of earthly pleasures I would not know."

Though he uttered the words with conviction, they did not ring true. And if they were, what a shame. Never had she met a more sensual man.

She had spent too much time in a nunnery.

Chapter Three

Pale yellow and orange light streaked above the horizon and across the sky, chasing the greedy fingers of night away. While birds chirped and men stretched sleeping muscles awake, the memory of the little nun played in Guy's mind. He could not forget the look on her face when she found her brother sotted. Though he had seen the face of fear on hardened soldiers, he had never expected such terror in a woman's eyes. Her expression would haunt him long after they parted company. She needed a protector, and part of him wished it could be he. He thought of the Bible verse of the lion and the lamb, lying together, then quickly discarded the mental picture. Determinedly, he turned his thoughts to another direction.

"My lord." Ferragus's voice startled him. "We will not be able to break camp just yet."

"Why not?" Guy turned, following his man's gaze over to the tent. "Is the good sister not ready?"

"She begs a moment to say her prayers."

Guy ran a hand through his hair. How was he, acting as a friar, supposed to hurry a nun from her devotions?

"Very well, Ferragus, I will see to it. Have the men ready when I return."

Guy walked over to the tent. Morning benedictions indeed. An ugly question entered his mind. What if the woman was not merely taking refuge in the convent as the king thought, but was sincerely intent on being a nun? Taking a deep breath, he pulled the flap open.

His breath caught in his chest at the angelic vision that met him. She knelt in the middle of the tent, with eyes closed and head bowed, clasping folded hands close to her chest. Her whispered words of worship drifted in the air, soft and lyrical. "Please, Lord, protect those I love. My brother is so young. I wish I were stronger, so I could do this myself. Keep him in Your thoughts. Ever Your faithful servant, Gabby."

Guy was touched at the realization that she had asked for others' well-being, and not her own.

She turned and started upon seeing him. The expression in her wide violet eyes revealed her embarrassment. "Forgive me, friar, I did not know you were there." Her hand drifted from her throat, and she rose gracefully.

He silently cursed William for a fool. This woman was exactly what she represented herself to be, a nun. "We are ready." He extended his arm for her to precede him.

"I was just asking for a little divine help," she whispered.

He nodded, inhaling a subtle hint of flowers as she passed by him. "I am sure our journey will be blessed. You need not worry for your safety," he said, wishing he hadn't noticed her fragrance. He escorted her to the horses as soldiers quickly dismantled the tent.

"God will protect us," she said, allowing him to help her mount. "After all, He directed us to you."

Guy forced a smile, almost wishing God would indeed

take a hand in her destiny. Then his conscience could return to an uninterrupted slumber. He turned and noticed her brother watching him carefully. Before daybreak, while the others slept, he and Louis had shared a hot cup of barley water, and a confidence. The boy might be at odds with his sister, but he cared deeply for her. Guy was not the only male who thought the lady needed protection.

As the sun started its climb in the cloudless blue sky, he headed his small band north. Deeply he inhaled the crisp air, tasting the fresh, clean, bite of fall, and relishing the brisk chill of the season.

"Ferragus," he said to his second-in-command "have the men stay alert and sharp. The chance for attack increases the closer we get to our destination."

The man nodded and veered his horse around to pass the word down the ranks.

Guy turned, looking back down the column. He watched Ferragus ride back the full length of the line. Satisfied his orders were carried out, his gaze wandered over the nameless faces of the king's men, until he found her. She rode with her brother, safely tucked in the middle of the procession. Since this morning, like a lover's lingering kiss, the memory of her delicate scent played about his mind, teasing his thoughts and tormenting his concentration as he performed his duty.

Ferragus chuckled as he reined in his horse beside Guy. "She is a pretty little lady. The men trip over their own feet while watching her. But if you keep staring back at her with that leer, she will know you to be a fraud."

"Keep your own counsel, Ferragus."

"As you wish," he said, clearly unimpressed by the order. "Is Lord de Bellemare waiting up ahead?"

"*Non,* I do not wish to involve my brother."

"Then why are we heading north toward North

Umberland instead of turning back to London?'' the king's soldier asked.

Guy stared down Ferragus's insolent expression, then pointed to the horizon. ''Ahead there is a fork in the road. Scotland, where Sister Gabrielle and Louis wish to go, is straight ahead, but we will travel the branch heading west. That road slowly circles southward toward London.''

''What if the boy questions our direction?''

''Tell him the road winds and will eventually turn north.''

''Why bother with this deception?'' Ferragus persisted.

''Because a prisoner who is unaware of his capture offers no resistance,'' Guy said, unwilling to admit that the thought of tying up a woman and a boy turned his stomach.

''I would not suffer such trouble to deceive them,'' the soldier groused.

''That is why the king chose me,'' Guy said.

''The king chose you because of your seminary training, not because you have proven yourself on the battlefield better than I,'' he scoffed.

''Think what you will, but the fact remains I am in charge and you will follow my orders. I want you to ride ahead, and if you see any sign of trouble, report back,'' Guy ordered.

Ferragus's eyes narrowed. ''You could send another soldier.''

''You wanted field experience,'' Guy said, dismissing the man.

Ferragus's face turned bright red, then he whipped his horse's flank and galloped away. Guy winced that the soldier had so little regard for his mount or his assignment. As the soldier disappeared over the ridge, Guy's glance wandered back to the petite woman in dark clothes. She wore the raiment of a postulant, her face framed by the white wimple and black habit. The coarse robes concealed her shape, and the mystery of her hidden form played on his mind. He wondered what color hair lay beneath the thick woolen veil.

The memory of her gaze returned, how, like an opening into the soul, her eyes had revealed a wholesome purity that plagued him. Her exquisite eyes, which were neither blue nor black, but rare violet, held an expression of trust that disarmed his defenses. Captivated by her spell, he had almost given the game away.

She was far too winsome to be wandering about. He had thought her some old crone, but nothing could be farther from the truth. Indeed, her fair face could only be described as incomparable. He wondered about her betrothed's identity and what manner he possessed to cause a woman to flee. Perhaps the maiden was shy. She was so demure and delicate, no doubt she feared the physical side of marriage.

"God's teeth," he swore, catching himself softening toward her. He had to steel himself against such charitable emotions.

Gabby felt the cold north wind bite into her woolen mantle. They had broken camp and were headed toward Scotland. The friar in charge had advocated skirting the abbey to save time, and she had agreed, knowing Abbess Ambrose would send their belongings on. They were already miles from their campsite.

Louis was riding with her, watching the monks and friars. "They are not like any group of clerics I have ever seen," he said, absently.

Still thinking of the handsome friar, remembering his arms around her when he had tried to calm her fear last night, she turned to Louis with a start. "What did you say, brother?"

"They do not seem to be holy men," he replied, looking speculatively at her.

"Louis," she admonished, "the Lord works in mysterious ways. Do not be so suspicious. They are not Quennel's men, or we would not be having this conversation. We are safe with them. Soon we will be on Uncle Alec's land.''

'' 'Tis still several days from here.''

"I know, but I am grateful it will end our long journey. Our prayers have been answered with this pilgrimage." She sighed, knowing that the Saxons' defeat by King William put Scotland on guard. "I would not like to ride through Scotland to reach our kin unescorted. The Scots are nay a friendly breed, now.''

"You should have stayed at the abbey," he said.

His curt dismissal hurt, and she reached out to him, touching his arm. "I could not let you go alone. Besides, we are both in danger," she said, holding his stare until his gaze lowered.

"I know, Gabby, but it makes me feel like a child to have my sister fretting over me.''

"Louis, you are all the family I have left," she said, swallowing the pain of that admission as she lifted her chin. "Until I draw my last breath, I shall worry about you.''

He shook his head in mock despair. "I pity your husband and children.''

"I fear there will be none," she said, thinking of Bayard de Bellemare, the horrid man whom her uncle Quennel had chosen for her.

She felt Louis's hand on hers. "Do not worry, sister. I would die before I let our lecherous uncle hurt you.''

"Do not speak of your death," she pleaded.

Before Louis could respond a loud cry rent the air, causing pandemonium as a band of outlaws fell upon them. Shouted orders passed through the column as one man took charge in the confusion. Gabby recognized Friar Guy's voice issuing the commands, and marveled as battle-hardened soldiers jumped to his bidding. Within seconds he had a solid line of defense formed.

Suddenly another wave of attackers swarmed from their hiding place, outflanking them.

"Lord, help us," Louis whispered.

Screams of injured men resounded around them as Gabby's brother drew his sword and stood ready, his features hard and expression fierce. The monks were at once overwhelmed and though the armed soldiers accompanying the caravan fought well and hard; the sheer number of the attackers made their defeat preordained. Suddenly, Friar Guy appeared at their side, wielding his oak staff to keep the vandals away. "Boy, remember our talk this morning. Ride now. Head for the ridge!"

When Gabby hesitated to join her brother, the friar smacked her horse's backside as the outlaws surrounded them. An assailant's grasping fingers grazed her shoulder, his long nails raking long scratches down her arm in an attempt to stop her. Tears blurred her vision at the stinging pain. Though she struggled, the clenching grip latched on to her wrist, but a sharp rap from Friar Guy's staff saved her from falling. Her horse broke through the circle and panicked, galloping heedlessly away from the fracas. It took all of Gabrielle's skill to ride across the rocky terrain while weaving through the heavy underbrush close behind her brother. Heart pounding, she wanted to look back, but could not.

As the hillside fell away they forded a river, then charged across a valley and up the far side of a ridge. She thought she heard the sound of pursuit, but soon the noise of the battle and horses receded.

Cresting the ridge, Louis slowed his horse to a walk and carefully picked his way down the far slope. Halfway to the bottom of the incline he dismounted and instructed her to do the same, then he pulled back a tangle of vines, revealing a cavernous opening.

"Louis, how did you know of this place?" she asked

when he led her into a damp, musky cave. She gave a slight shiver as the dank air chilled her. Though primitive and inhospitable, it afforded them a safe haven.

"Friar Guy told me of it. Before you awoke we discussed the possibility of brigands. He warned me if we were attacked to head for the safety of this hidden cave." He took her horse's reins and led both mounts to the back of the cave.

"I pray God he is spared." Gabrielle remembered Friar Guy's sacrifice and bowed her head, offering a silent prayer for his safe return.

"I should think he will be—he is a magnificent fighter."

"But a man of the cloth cannot draw blood, and he stands against overwhelming odds."

Louis did not respond—there was nothing he could say. Instead he busied himself making a fire and organizing their provisions. As though the mantle of responsibility came naturally to him, he took over. Gabby bit back her objections and sank gratefully to the floor. Exhausted, she watched him, and for the first time relaxed. It was nice having someone take care of her for a change.

Louis handed her a cup of hot barley water sweetened with honey. She wrapped her hands around the warm mug. "Though I hate to linger in this area, we cannot abandon the good friar."

He shook his head. "We should not wait! Friar Guy said if he failed to show by nightfall, we should strike out for Scotland and our Campbell clansmen."

"We will wait." She took a deep sip from her cup. "Even though logic would dictate our haste, I cannot leave the cleric." She turned, staring into the eyes so much like hers. "And neither can you."

"Aye, you are right," he admitted. "We will wait. 'Tis the right thing to do."

"Honor is not a weakness, brother. I am proud that you,

like our ancestors, have a chivalrous nature.'' She acknowledged for the first time his status as an adult and her faith
in him.

Though he beamed like a child, he suddenly seemed so
much older, wiser. Was it a trick of light or could it be that
he had indeed grown? Perhaps it was time to see him as he
was, not as she wished him to be.

''What is it, Gabby?''

She shook her head. ''You remind me of Father.''

Louis smiled. ''I am pleased you think so.''

''God, how I miss our sire.''

''As do I, but we must see to ourselves.''

''Aye, we must. How far are we from the clan?'' she
asked.

''Two days, maybe more.''

''Then *when* the friar returns,'' she said, optimistically,
''we will be off.''

At dusk Louis attended the horses while Gabby spread
her cloak over the dirt floor. With resignation she snuggled
down into the thin folds of wool and rested her cheek on
her arm. She had no sooner closed her eyes and drifted off
to sleep when the vision came. *Blood oozed from the cleric's
chest. His dark handsome features twisted in pain. Her hands
were red-soaked and slick as she worked frantically to stem
the flow of blood oozing from the wound in his chest. His
eyelids fluttered open and those incredible dark eyes, as
deep blue and mysterious as the sea, focused on her for but
a moment, then his lashes drifted down.*

Suddenly, a thick mist covered his image and she awoke
with a gasp. A clammy moist film clung to her skin as she
lay confused, wondering whether she should tell Louis of
her vision.

By the mouth of the cave, Louis sat guard, his silhouette
clearly defined in the moonlit night. As though he could
feel her gaze on him, he turned.

"A nightmare?"

"Aye," she responded, deciding not to share the dreadful premonition. If it were true—and her sight had never before been wrong—they would know soon enough.

"Go to sleep, sister. I will wake you when I need rest."

Unable to shake off the strong feeling of foreboding, she lay alert for the next two hours, awaiting her turn to stand guard.

When Louis's hand touched her shoulder and his weary voice whispered her name she arose quickly. Giving him her warm spot near the dying embers, she took her position by the cave's mouth.

Exposed to the breeze, she shivered. Wrapping her cloak around her and huddling deep within its folds, she sat down, drawing her knees to her chest for warmth against the night chill. Smothering a yawn, she gazed out into the night. The silvery shapes of the landscape glimmered and swayed with each cloud that drifted across the moon. The eerie vista of wavering shadows seemed alive and demanded all her concentration. During the next hour her eyes tired of staring at the flickering shapes, and she nodded off several times, awaking with a start to hear Louis's heavy breathing, denoting his exhaustion.

The moon was low in the sky when a twig snapped a short distance from the cave. She froze, every muscle tense. Straining her senses she listened carefully while peering out into the moonlit night.

Slowly, a shape took form among the shadows. It was no apparition floating over the ground, but a dark figure stealthily weaving his way through the trees and bushes.

"Louis," she breathed, trying to awaken her brother without giving their position away to the intruder.

Unable to rouse Louis, panic rose in her throat, but her soundless scream died to a sigh of relief when the cleric's outline appeared in the clearing. Moonlight washed over his features, and she gasped. In the silver light his strained expression looked hewn from stone into a frightening, grim mask. With slow and measured steps, he approached, pulling his horse behind him. His tattered and mud-encrusted robe brushed her arm as he trudged past her, dragging his oak staff. Silently walking to the back of the cave, he unsaddled and tended to his horse. Then, still not speaking, he unlaced the belt from his waist as he walked, and dropped his water bladder and food satchel to the floor. Stepping free of the pile, he kicked off his sandals and rolled up in a blanket by the fire.

"Are you injured?" she breathed.

A shake of his head met her inquiry. What a relief. For the first time her vision had been wrong.

Though the man needed his sleep, she could not contain her curiosity. Scurrying over to his side, she touched his shoulder. "What of the others?" she asked.

"They are dead," he said, laying his arm over his eyes.

She drew a ragged breath. "I will pray for them."

"These were not brigands, but Normans sent by a man called Quennel Aumont." He lowered his arm and peered at her. "Are you familiar with the name?"

"Aumont was my mother's name. The man is my uncle."

"He sent his men to waylay you," he said, rising up on one elbow to face her. "I do not think they were sent to rescue you."

"Nay," she said. A handsbreadth separated them. And though the fire had died, the embers still glowed, bathing his face in a soft golden light that presented a breath-catching picture of his perfect features, from ridiculously long eye-lashes to his full, beautiful lips. Suddenly aware of her wayward thoughts, she lowered her gaze, unable to hold his scrutiny. "They would have killed us."

"Why would an uncle do in his own?" he asked. Though

softly spoken, his question held more command than concern.

She swallowed, forcing back the trepidation his inquiry caused. "For land and wealth. I am an irritant, easily disposed of in marriage." She looked over to her sleeping brother. "But Louis is an obstacle that cannot be overlooked. He must die in order for my uncle to inherit."

"Do you play me for a witless fool, mademoiselle?" he scoffed. "Your maternal uncle is not in line to inherit. The law is clear: 'twould be your paternal uncle who is entitled to the estate."

"Nay, the marriage contracts were drawn up to ensure that the Norman land stayed in the Aumont family. My father received compensation for the bias contract."

"So, it is your uncle Aumont who seeks the wealth, not your uncle Campbell?"

"Aye. Uncle Alec is not filled with greed, but with love of family."

"How would you know this?"

"My brother and I have stayed with his clan many times before."

His eyebrows lifted. "Normans living among the Scots. 'Tis highly unusual."

She chuckled at his surprise. "Aye, but it has given us an insight many never have."

"What is it you have learned from the Scots?"

Gabby looked him straight in the eye. "Courage, friar. I have learned courage."

"That you have, mademoiselle," he said, then without another word turned over to his other side to seek his rest.

Guy listened to her move back to the cave's entrance, thinking he had never known such a woman as she. After the attack he no longer doubted her determination to reach Scotland, nor her motives. Her uncle would indeed kill her brother. Thank God William had agreed to protect the lad.

And Gabrielle? She would soon have a husband ... of Aumont's choosing.

He had left Normandy over a year ago for the conquest of England. But he was familiar with the better houses at court.

He took a deep breath, then asked, "Who has you uncle named as your betrothed?"

The silence stretched out in the cave, and just when he thought she was not going to answer him, she said, "The man is a sadistic brute, the worst tyrant in Normandy. I do not wish to sour my mouth with his name."

Her words pricked his conscience; he would be responsible for her future life of misery. Uncomfortable with the mantle of guilt, he dismissed her description as an exaggeration, reminding himself that her fate was none of his business. He had a task to perform, and he could not let anyone interfere with his duty.

"Good night, Sister Gabrielle."

After a moment of silence her musical voice floated over to him like a spring breeze. "Friar, I am not a nun yet, merely a postulant."

Her sweet honesty was like a light against the darkness of his deceit. He cleared his throat. "*Oui,* I know. Have you decided to dedicate your life to Jesus?"

"We all serve God. I am unworthy, but I try to do His work. Alas, I fear my calling is not genuine."

The innocence in her humble explanation stained his soul. It was bad enough that this woman's face mirrored an angel's, but to know she also had the heart of one tore at the very fiber of his honor. If only he could just deliver her to William and be done. But without an escort they were prey for any clan that thought them fair game. It would be a tricky journey.

"Friar, may I ask you one more question?"

"Of course," he said cautiously.

"Do you believe God protects the righteous?"

"A good Christian must." Guy rolled his eyes. Of all topics to discuss, why this, and for God's sake, why now?

"I agree, with all my heart. But of late it seems betrayal has been our constant nemesis. It would be nice to fall asleep without worry and fear. I have not known a restful sleep since my father died."

Shame filled his being. Knavery held one drawback he had not anticipated—self-loathing. Unable to stand one more moment of her goodness, he rolled to feet.

"Seek your rest, Sister Gabrielle. Tonight you need not fear for your life. You have my solemn vow that I will protect you and yon lad with mine."

"Thank you, friar, but 'tis not necessary. My brother's watch is due soon."

"I insist," he said, brooking no argument.

When she reluctantly went to her blanket, he silently chuckled. She asked no help and perhaps did not trust him to watch over her charge. She was a stubborn lady indeed, but one who would not let his senses rest. He was not so blind that he could not imagine the lovely body beneath the robes.

He cut his thoughts short. She was not his concern, but William's. And the king could do as he pleased with her. Guy wrapped the blanket firmly around his body and walked to the cave's mouth to keep watch. By God, he had just given his word to her, and he would keep it. Tonight they would not have to worry. Never had he felt a greater need to succeed. For some reason her approval and thanks meant the world to him. It should not matter, could not matter, but as he paced back and forth at the cave's entrance he knew that it did.

She made him recall the long-forgotten images of what he wanted in this life. For one moment he allowed his thoughts to cover the ground that was lost so many years ago, then banished the dream to the nether regions of his mind. Some things were too painful to look at, too painful to want.

He looked out into the shadowed landscape. It was going to be a long night.

Suddenly a hand touched his arm, and reacting instinctively, he grabbed the wrist, turning to meet his foe. He relaxed when he saw Louis.

"Friar?" Louis asked.

"You startled me," Guy admitted, sheepishly.

"Sleep, friar. I will stand this watch."

Guy smiled, acknowledging the boy's consideration. *"Oui,* you will help these tired old bones catch the rest they need to ride the day's journey tomorrow."

"Friar, 'tis a long way to my uncle's, and I would entrust you with my sister's welfare."

"What say you?" Guy asked.

"I mean that if something should happen to me on the journey, give me your vow you will not let her fall into my uncle Quennel's hands."

Guy bit back a hiss. He could no more vow that than he could admit he was an emissary of William's.

"I have more than once tonight given my assurance, first to your sister, and now you. Do you doubt my honor or my wits?"

"Your pardon, friar, but I worry over her. She has no one except me to protect her. Though she would not admit it, she is vulnerable."

"You are forgiven," Guy said, feeling the bite of his conscience. "Mind you, watch for any disturbance. We are not among friends."

He walked to his spot by the dying embers and stretched out before the soft glow.

"Good night, Friar Guy. Sleep well," Louis's voice drifted back.

Guy smiled. "Aye, I will." Pulling the blanket up to his neck he acknowledged that he had made a decision. He could not just deliver this young man to William. Their Scottish relatives were close. He would see the boy to his uncle Alec, where he would reach manhood in safety. It would certainly make Gabrielle's abduction more difficult, but he would find a way. He was sworn to deliver the girl to William. Interrupting his mission to suit himself was the only way he could live with his conscience. He knew the boy would be safe in Scotland. He could not vouch for the Norman court. Too many men were greedy bastards—the analogy bothered him. Was he not also a Judas? Delivering an innocent woman to the wolves for a reward. He rolled over, angry with the disturbing truth of his thoughts.

Bright sunlight filtered into the cave, and Guy opened his eyes to find two Norman mercenaries standing over him with weapons drawn.

" 'Tis only a friar," the first soldier said to his cohort.

The other man, who held Louis in a tight-fisted grip, did not take his eyes off Gabby. "Let's have done with the boy and then enjoy the charms of this maiden. Or you can have the boy while I enjoy the lady."

Guy watched Louis's face. His anger was justified, but he would have to learn to conceal it better. Self-control was a warrior's strongest weapon, but that would come with time. These soldiers were purposely taunting him.

Making a sign of the cross, Guy rose to his feet and folded his hands in prayer. The soldiers foolishly did not fear a man of the cloth. He caught Louis's eye and was impressed with the clear gaze and intelligent look. The boy was going to make a move, and, when he did, Guy would have to be ready.

Louis called to his sister. "Do not be afraid, Gabrielle, these men will burn in hell for their evil deeds."

With tear-bright violet eyes, revealing far too much of her emotions, she held Louis's gaze. "Forgive me, brother."

The soldier holding Louis leered at Gabby, his frank appraisal causing her to blush and turn away. " 'Tis useless to ask forgiveness of the boy. But if you are nice to me, I might let you live."

Louis moved then, his fist crashing into the assailant's mouth. Guy took his cue and started to fight. Out of the corner of his eye he saw Gabby wielding his oak staff against the man attacking her brother. The two were a formidable team. He ducked then, dodging a fatal blow by inches, and realized any distraction would cost him. He had his hands full fighting the soldier and could not let the man draw his sword. In his pose as cleric he was unarmed, and could only defend himself. His fist crashed repeatedly into the soldier's face. The man staggered back, and Guy charged him. Suddenly, the glint of a shining blade in the enemy's hand caught Guy's attention, and he leaped out of the way.

The soldier's malicious laugh cut through the air along with the lunging stab of his dagger. Guy's honed reflexes, like second nature, came into play, allowing him to escape injury by neatly sidestepping the blow. With a shout, the attacker charged forward, repeatedly slashing the knife in vicious arcs. Guy agilely avoided several knife thrusts before one gashed his chest and arm. He desperately tried to grab the arm that wielded the knife, but the soldier was well trained and strong. Another arc sliced the skin of his shoulder and ribs. Liquid fire raced through his body. Guy felt his strength wane as the blood gushed unchecked from his injuries.

The Norman soldier dived at Guy. Guy staggered back, but caught the brigand, holding the hand with the knife upright as they crashed to the cave floor. Momentarily, Guy's grip weakened. The blade slipped from his hold and shaved a bloody line across his neck. Pain shot through him, and with it a surge of energy that enabled him to parry the next attack and push the weapon away. Guy knew he would not have the strength to hold off another assault. But even as he thought it, the man suddenly, slumped on top of Guy, heavy and unmoving.

He barely had the strength to push the man off. As he eased the body from his chest he blinked, unable to believe what he saw. Sticking there in the center of the soldier's back was a lady's dirk.

Avoiding his gaze, Gabrielle knelt beside him and shoved the soldier completely out of the way in order to inspect Guy's wounds.

"You? You saved my life."

"Aye, 'twas necessary, friar." Her voice quavered, and she drew a breath. "You are a good fighter, but the man had the best of you."

Guy shook his head to deny it, and felt a wave of dizziness swarm over his senses.

Her voice was fading, and he reached out, gripping her arm to hold on to the only reality around him. Soft and sweet, her violet gaze now held his, offering comfort and serenity as he slipped into an abyss of darkness.

" 'Twill be the only way," she insisted.

"I do not want to leave you," Louis replied.

"You must. The friar is injured and cannot travel. Uncle Alec will help us."

"You will be alone," he said regretfully.

"Louis, either you or I must travel for help. We both know I would be an easy target. Go now. I will fare well."

Though torn, Louis reluctantly kissed her cheek. "I wish

we had a choice. But the good friar saved our lives. Courage is not repaid by cowardice. I shall return soon.''

''Hurry.'' She handed him his reins and watched as he rode off into the hazy mist of midmorning. ''Godspeed,'' she whispered, then, with a heavy heart, returned to the injured friar.

He was a big man. Lying there in a pain-induced faint, he reminded her of a felled tree. She tried to undo his cowled tunic and knew after several failed attempts she would have to cut the blood-soaked robe from his body. She removed her dagger from the dead soldier's back, wincing as she wiped the blood free of the blade. Swallowing the bile that rose in her throat at the thought of disposing of the corpse, she returned to the cleric and sawed through the rough-hewn seam of his robe. Carefully, she peeled back the brown wool while wiping the blood away, and was amazed at the breadth of his chest, lashed by corded muscles that were as hard and solid as a breastplate. She noticed the many scars that covered his flesh as she mopped the blood up with a coarse edge of his robe. This man must have seen much of war before he entered God's service. His body was like a well-honed weapon, not plump like the clerics she had known.

Guy groaned, immediately drawing her attention to his face. His black lashes lay closed, but from the deep creases by his mouth and radiating from his eyes, she knew he suffered even in his state of sleep.

She looked at the gashes again, assessing what each would need, then stoked the fire and reheated the water Louis had boiled yesterday. While the flames grew, she looked for the herbs she would need. Without her sewing and embroidery bag, she worried over how she would sew the wounds.

When the steam began to rise from the pot, she pulled her mantle free and broke off the clasp that held the broach together. In her hand lay a fine sharp metal rod with a tiny hole for the catch. She could use it as a needle, but where would she find thread? There was only one answer. Removing her robe, she drew the soft smock over her head and quickly redonned the coarse wool tunic. The undergarment's smooth material slipped through her fingers as she carefully picked the tiny thread free from the delicate lace border and hemline she had painstakingly joined together. With the thread finally removed, she ripped the smock up into strips. Taking a deep breath, she washed the wounds, wanting to be done before the friar regained his wits. It would be terribly painful without spirits to dull the senses.

When the water boiled, she lowered the thread and needle into the liquid. Though she did not understand the need for this, she had seen Abbess Ambrose use the method. If it was good enough for Abbess Ambrose, it was certainly good enough for her. How she wished she had paid more attention to her studies.

Though she had been taught how to tend the sick, she had never personally done so. No matter. The man would surely die if she did nothing, inexperienced though she was.

Everything in readiness, she looked heavenward. "Please, God. I try not to ask too much of You, but this is one of Your own. Please give me the skill to help him."

With that prayer uttered, she started to work. The moment she pierced the flesh of his chest, his muscles twitched and constricted into thick bands. Her fingers stilled over the wound as she waited until his trembling stopped. She released her pent-up breath. "Lord, this is harder than it looks."

Suddenly, she understood the fortitude and strength of Abbess Ambrose. Taking a deep breath, she started again, ignoring the spasms in his muscles. She could not help hurting him; it was necessary to stem the blood flow. His chest wound was the deepest and bled profusely. With every tiny stitch of her needle she felt as though it punctured her own flesh. When he grimaced with the pain, a soft moan slipped past her lips. She knew she would never make a good healer. It seemed to take forever to finish closing the gash on his chest, and, without resting, she stitched his arm. The muscle in his upper arm was huge. The bulk of his limb was far larger than her own waist.

She wondered again how a man of war had turned to the Church. For there could be little doubt that the friar had once made his life by the sword. Too many scars and overdeveloped muscles attested to the fact. Tying the last stitch on his arm, she bathed both wounds, then bound them with ripped strips of her smock. Thankfully, his neck needed only a bandage. Throughout the tedious process he moaned, but mercifully did not awaken.

Once through with her task, Gabby again looked heavenward. "Thank You," she whispered.

Her gaze drifted to the injured man. The campfire lit his face and she was struck again by his uncanny good looks. Leaning over him, she covered his chest with the blanket her brother had left behind and could not help but admire his size and strength. The male body up until now had remained a mystery to her. Over the last few months she had watched Abbess Ambrose stitch and attend ill nuns or village women in childbirth. But this was not only her first time treating an injured person, but the first time attending a man. The experience was totally unnerving, and had taken all afternoon. She prayed she had done an adequate job.

Exhausted, she wanted nothing more than to lay her head down but knew she must bury the two mercenaries. Strength born of raw nerves enabled her to drag the bodies out into the waning daylight, where she found a spot of soft earth. The moon was high in the sky when she placed the last stone on the shallow graves and covered the mounds with brush. It was her Christian duty to say a prayer, but she could not find it in her heart to utter one word on their behalf.

Darkness, black as pitch, filled the cave when she returned. Stumbling over to the campsite, she rebuilt the fire. Bone tired, she nestled down beside the friar, ready to drop off into a healing sleep, but her conscience pricked her thoughts. She could not rest until she checked the friar's condition. Rising up on an elbow, she leaned forward to inspect his wounds.

Gingerly, she lifted the robe and blanket to reveal his chest and arm. Removing the white strips, her fingers encountered the coarse hair of his chest as she gently but thoroughly inspected the area around the wound. Replacing the bandages and well satisfied with his condition, she was about to cover his chest when a moment of curiosity captured her imagination. She would surely never be given such an opportunity again. Upon hearing the smooth cadence of his breathing, she quickly glanced to his face to confirm that he still slept. She should be ashamed of her brazen action, but in truth her conscience bothered her naught. Quick, she must be quick! With two fingers she lifted the corner of the blanket and his robe, turning them back so she could satisfy her ignorance about the male body.

Lord have mercy! She did not believe it—could not believe it!

She could not believe the size of his manhood. Her nurse-maid had somewhat explained the process of mating. But she had to be wrong; this truly would not fit. Never! A woman would be ripped asunder if she were to mate with the friar. Ah! Now she understood why such a virile man became a friar. How unselfish. To dedicate himself to the Church rather than fornicating with such a weapon made her esteem for him rise even higher.

Guy lay still, unable to move. If God intended him to do penance for his impersonation, He could not have thought of a better atonement. How he ached! This indeed had to be his strongest test of moral fiber. Never had he imagined it possible, but he felt ready to burst. That the beautiful, innocent maiden was curious about him had at first been a boost to his pride; but now he felt the nick of a double-edged sword. There was nothing worse than the pain of arousal without benefit of relief.

He felt her snuggle close to him as she drew the blanket over her shoulder and rested calmly by his side. Several minutes passed until her breathing assumed the rhythm of sleep.

He studied her flawless beauty and again wondered if there were any way he could spare her her fate. It was not just her fair face or comely figure that intrigued him, it was the whole woman. She did not have any idea how much she played havoc with his senses. That she admired him and was attracted to him only piqued his interest further. But any relationship between them was forbidden. He had best remember that—and would, once he composed himself. She rolled away in her sleep, and he tried to sit up. How his chest hurt. He examined the neat tiny stitches. She must have sewn on his flesh half the night.

Ever so slowly he moved his arm to ease the tightness. He had known worse injuries; in time these would cause him little trouble. Lying back down, he wondered where her brother had gone. It was clear Louis had left; only two horses stood tied by the back of the cave. Wonderful. They were alone. Which meant he could take her back to London and her betrothed.

The thought soured in Guy's mouth. How could he betray her after she had saved his life? He tried to think if there was another way. Telling William she had died was a possibility, but the maiden would have to be willing to go along with the deception.

Somehow he doubted Gabby would. Odd. He thought of

her as Gabby. But even as the name sounded in his head, he knew he would never think of her as Gabrielle again.

Even though it was ridiculous, he fantasized about rescuing her.

Chapter Four

Guy lay on his back, staring at the rock fissures in the ceiling of the cave. Once again he mentally traced every crack, crevice, and line above him. A week of inactivity had driven him to distraction.

The wound on his chest itched. Absently he tried scratching it, but encountered Gabrielle's soft bandages. A hint of her fragrance still clung to the fine material that bound his injuries. The delicate scent teased his memory, but he could not identify it.

Just then Gabrielle entered the cave, wearing a smile fresher than sunshine. Her eyes sparkled, and he suddenly noticed that the contours of her lovely shape stood outlined without the added weight of her smock. He groaned. She had become far too pleasing to the eye. To his dismay, he realized that not a moment passed without her filling his thoughts. Her sweet, innocent sensuality drove him to the limit of his endurance.

"How do you fare, friar?" Her voice cheered the gloomy

silence. She moved to the fire and poured him a cup of barely water.

"You would make a fine dungeon master, mademoiselle. I will heal faster if you allow me to have some exercise," he said with mock sternness.

Her soft laughter filled the air. "Restlessness is a good sign."

"Idleness has never set well with me," he begrudgingly admitted as he accepted the cup.

"Ah, the devil's tool," she said, leaning forward to adjust his covers.

"What?" he asked, distracted by her scent.

"Laziness is the devil's tool," she prompted.

"Oui," he said, chastising his lapse in concentration. But each hour spent in her company made logic impossible. She stole the very thoughts from his mind. "Forgive me, Sister Gabrielle. I am a very poor patient."

" 'Tis understandable, friar," she said as she stood and walked to the mouth of the cave. "We all have other things on our mind. Waiting is never easy." Sadness seemed to return as she searched the outlying area.

Guy leaned forward, setting his untouched tea on the ground. "When did you expect Louis's return?"

"Yesterday," she replied as her gaze again swept the distant horizon.

"How far is it to the Campbell land?"

"Louis said several days' journey . . ." Her voice trailed off.

"Mayhap the delay was necessary."

She turned around, displaying a smile that did not quite reach her eyes. "Aye, I am sure of it. He probably had to avoid clan raids or the poor Saxons fleeing Britain."

He heard the disapproval in her voice.

"You, a loyal Norman, do not approve of the conquest of Britain?"

She shook her head and sighed. "Too many have suffered for one man's ambition."

He held his side as he sat up. " 'Twas necessary. In the end, it will be for the best."

"Strange you should think so. Did not our Savior teach us to turn the other cheek?"

Guy frowned. He had underestimated her intelligence again. Her uncommon beauty tripped him up. Unlike the dull-witted but comely maidens who filled the court, this woman possessed a keen mind. *"Oui,* that is so, but we have brought Christianity, order, and law to this barbaric land."

"Have we, friar? What gives us the right to dominate this land or these people? Violence can never be justified."

"We cannot understand God's greater design," he said, repeating the Church's explanation.

"God's design, I do not question. What we are talking about is man's design. Specifically, King William's greed."

Her reasoning impressed him, and also pricked his conscience. "Mayhap you are right."

A smile teased her lips, mirth peeking out from the corners like a child playing at hiding. "Why, I am amazed you admit it." Her chuckle was soft, musical. "It has been my experience that men do not admit their faults."

"Non, Sister Gabrielle, I am far from perfect. No more so than you."

She bowed her head.

He seized this opportunity to act the part of a cleric, though he thought the words would choke in his throat. "Only our Savior was free from sin. We are human, and temptation surrounds us."

"True, friar," she admitted, glancing back at him, her face pale. "I am indeed in need of the Almighty's help."

He shifted, trying to see her expression. "What sins trouble you, child?" he asked.

When she avoided his gaze, he suddenly knew she was remembering the life she had taken. "Sister Gabrielle, God understands and forgives. You took a life to save others."

Her eyes widened, confirming his suspicions. "You do not understand. I am not worthy of His grace."

"Soldiers are forgiven. Why would you be less deserving?"

Tears glistened in her eyes as she choked out, "I felt no remorse, friar."

"But you do now," he said, seeing her distress.

"Aye, I pray for forgiveness."

"Then put your mind at ease. You must first learn to forgive yourself, in order for your spirit to heal," he said, knowing the pain she suffered.

She shook her head. " 'Twill be hard."

"God is far more generous with forgiveness than His children," Guy replied, wanting to take her in his arms and soothe the pain, but knowing he could do neither. Still, he started to reach out his hand, then winced as the taut skin around his wound pulled against the stitches.

Concern instantly creased her brow. "Let me check your wounds, friar."

He took a deep breath and shook his head. *"Non,* 'twill be all right."

"Please, friar. I must check that the wounds remain dry. If fever sets in, you could die."

She was right. Yet he found it increasingly hard to remain indifferent to her touch.

"Very well."

With a slight smile at his hesitation, she bent to remove the bandage on his chest. As she neared, the fresh, clean, sweet scent of spring filled his senses. It seemed incredible but in autumn she smelled of violets. Never again would he be able to pass a garden and not think of her.

Her teeth caught her lip as she efficiently peeled back the

bandage. Such a combination of innocence and courage intrigued him. He did not like that.

Her fingers probed the edges of the wound with featherlike strokes. " 'Tis good. The color is pink and healthy."

She rebandaged his chest. Every time her fingers grazed his flesh his muscles tensed. By the time she peeled back the bandage on his arm, a fine sheen of perspiration covered his brow.

Then she glanced up at him and, suddenly, their gazes locked and held. She had the most incredible eyes. A rich, dark, velvety shade which appeared neither blue nor black, but fell somewhere in between. Violet was not only her scent, but also her eye color.

A man could forget his mission while gazing into those bewitching eyes. Guy tore his gaze away. He would not. As a man of honor, he was bound to his king by his word. "Thank you, Sister Gabrielle."

"Friar, is something amiss?"

"Non," he lied. " 'Tis the time of healing that disturbs me, nothing more."

She shook her head. "You are like Louis." She patted his arm and he closed his eyes, enduring the liquid fire her touch sent racing through his veins.

"I will see if I can find some more supplies in the saddle pouch. There was enough in mine to make soup, but precious else."

"There is sacramental wine and medicine in my satchel," he ground out between clamped teeth.

A smile lit her eyes. "I wish I had known you had such supplies before I attended to you."

He was not surprised she had not touched his belongings. "Sister, would you now fetch me a clean robe and the wine?"

She dragged the whole pouch over to the friar. "Rest, friar, I will be back later."

"Where are you going?"

"There is a river not far from us. Louis discovered it when we arrived. I will fetch some fresh water and perhaps even fish."

"Fish?" he scoffed, knowing they needed food, but wishing to keep her safe.

"*Oui,* fish. I am quite adept at fishing. You will see. Our fare will be fish tonight."

"If not, my lady, what then?" he questioned.

"Then, dear friar, we will dine on good friendship and conversation, while fasting for our soul!"

When she had not returned at sunset, Guy slipped a knife into his boot, grabbed his oak staff, and struggled to his feet. Sweat broke out on his forehead, and he took several deep breaths to stem the dizziness. Though he fought the nausea, his thoughts whirled. What in God's name kept her? The possibilities were endless, and all of them disturbing. Holding his side, he limped to the cave's opening. With his forearm braced against the granite overhang, he stared out in the waning light at the landscape.

Nothing.

He would have to look for the little nun. Sighing deeply, he pushed away from the cold wall and left the safety of the cave. Moving with the gait of a warrior too far into his cups, he staggered forward into the brush and struggled through the tangled undergrowth. Though it was only a short distance from the brambles to the forest, the effort cost him dearly. A light purple sky stretched over head when, exhausted, he leaned against a tree. Angered by his weakness, he closed his eyes, resting a moment to gather his strength. In the still darkness he heard the living, breathing soul of the forest. The scratching of small creatures foraging for food or scurrying to safety, the flapping wings of birds as they flew through the trees, and the frantic cries of animals calling their mates combined in a familiar sound that permeated the night. But one sound stood out above all the others, and his eyes snapped open. A man's voice. Guy immediately crouched low and waited.

In the gathering darkness, a twig snapped loudly as two men passed within several feet of his position. "I tell you we must find them. I will not face Aumont or his temper with bad news." Though they spoke in French, the cut of their tunic and the mode of their hair identified them as mercenaries.

"Is it really worth the promised amount?"

"Misgivings, Stanislau? I care not for the girl or her brother. 'Tis rumored they spent so much time in Scotland they would barely recognize their estate in France."

"Hun, you believe Aumont's lies to salve your conscience. War, I understand. But bringing mayhem to a woman and a boy?" Stanislau shook his head and sighed. "That is different, and I have no stomach for it."

"We have a job to do." Suddenly, the soldier's whole demeanor changed. He placed his finger to his lips, silencing his companion as he drew his sword, the silver blade fairly glowing in the moonlight.

Guy groaned inwardly; he too heard the sound of fallen leaves rustling as someone moved toward them. Gabrielle had returned.

Outside of her footsteps, the woods were strangely devoid of all sound. The animals were quiet and the wind still, as if the forest had suddenly gasped. Guy lay in wait, his hand fingering his knife. He would kill two men today, and in his weakened state he would need the element of surprise.

The moon hung just above the horizon as Gabby traced her way back to the cave. Shadows flickered across the path, and the screech of an owl startled her. Taking deep breaths, she tried to calm her racing heart, but her imagination conjured danger behind every tree or bush. Determined to ignore her apprehension, Gabby softly hummed. The reassuring sound of her own voice helped chase away the loneliness and fear.

She had tarried overlong at her chore rather than admit defeat, and now must hurry. Though the answers to her problems evaded her, thankfully the fish did not. Two trout hung from her line.

All day the cleric had preyed on her mind. In the middle of her every task the image of his dark blue eyes, so intense and mysterious, would appear. The memory of his smile and the sound of his laughter filled her thoughts. Heat burned her cheeks whenever she recalled the friar's muscular chest and arms. Perspiration dotted her forehead as the recollection of what lay beneath the blanket surfaced. Some of the memories fairly scorched her. Never had she known a man who could make her this unsettled. It was strange, that a man of the cloth did not bring her peace.

Lord! What was she thinking? She lusted after a friar. Shame filled her. Doused with cold reality, the memory of his strong, bulging muscles faded from her mind.

She stopped and drew a deep breath. Her arms ached from carrying the fish and pouch of water up the incline. She needed to rest and hesitantly scanned the area. When there was no sign of intruders, she sank to the ground and dropped her burdens. In a minute, when her strength returned, she would climb the rest of the way.

She closed her eyes and relaxed for a few moments, but soon her sense of responsibility had her back on her feet. As she wound her way up the path a strange sensation seized her. Suddenly, her skin chilled, although the weather did not warrant it. Unbidden and unwelcomed, she experienced the familiar warning of her gift—*the sight.*

The woods fell away in a flash and she saw blood and the face of a stranger twisted in agony. His eyes bulged, and his mouth gaped open in a frozen scream. The vision only lasted the space of a heartbeat, but the image was seared into her mind. She shook her head and blinked as an involuntary shudder passed through her. Then, just as abruptly, she instinctively knew. Her vision would occur here and now.

All the moisture in her mouth dried, and she could not swallow. Danger! The warning screamed through her senses, but to survive she must appear unaware of the peril.

Good Lord! She had left the friar alone. *Pray God he is safe.* It was bad enough that she might lose the day, but for an innocent man, a man of the cloth, to die because of her would be unforgivable.

She struggled up the last few yards leading to the cave and the hair on the nape of her neck rose. Shifting the water pouch to her shoulder, her hand closed over her dirk so tightly, the hilt bit into her palm. Friar Guy depended on her.

The bushes up ahead by the end of the path rustled, but the cool night breeze had died out moments ago, leaving the woods still. The confrontation was at hand. Though fear twisted her insides into knots, she forced a strained whistle from parched lips and pulled her dirk from its sheath.

The air sizzled, charged with the tension felt before a storm, and her heightened nerves felt every tiny shock and jolt of friction.

The bushes rustled again. Her stomach lurched at the sound, and she stopped. Suddenly, a man charged out of the foliage, heading straight for her. Panic seized her as she heard an ungodly scream. Her gaze halted on his face—the exact image of her vision. She stood paralyzed. Suddenly the assailant pitched forward, his arms stretching wide, a look of shock on his face. He fell facedown in the dirt, a dagger embedded in his back, and died at her feet.

Stunned and relieved she looked toward the bushes as the friar staggered out. *Good Lord!* He had killed a man.

A man of the cloth shed blood?

"Friar!" She ran up and put his arm around her shoulder, offering her strength. When he accepted her help, she noticed yet another soldier lying dead upon the ground.

"He was also a disciple of Cain, sent to kill you and your brother. I heard the men talking when I came to look for you," he gasped, out of breath.

"To save me, you killed."

He inhaled deep lungfuls of air. "Do not fret, Gabrielle, I can bear this sin because it saved your life. 'Tis my conscience and my worry, not yours."

His wound had reopened, and he looked about ready to collapse. "Do not faint," she said.

"Faint?" he asked with indignation, yet his face was pale and his movements disjointed.

Blood soaked through his bandages, and he leaned heavily on her, his weight nearly knocking her over as they stumbled up the dark and rocky path. The sound of his breathing was labored when she finally managed to get him inside the cave. Falling to his knees, he dragged her to the ground with him. He groaned once, then fainted.

Slitting his robe and removing the soiled bandages, Gabby gasped at the damage the fighting had done. Blood poured out of the ripped-open wound as she tried to stem the flow. "God help me," she breathed. She swallowed at the bile rising in her throat. His wound had to be seared—a nasty task, and up until now, one she had avoided.

Her hands shook as she placed her dirk in the fire. Quickly she rummaged through his sack and resurrected the sacramental wine. She took a healthy swallow, drew a deep breath, then took another swallow. "I cannot do this," she whispered, tears stinging her eyes.

If you do nothing, the man will die, her conscience warned. She closed her eyes and swallowed another mouthful of liquid fire. *The friar will probably die anyway.* She drew another gulp of courage, then made the sign of the cross in front of her chest before reaching for the red-hot blade.

The friar did not seem aware of her, but when she held the glowing blade over the gaping chest wound, his eyes opened and his hand seized her wrist. Though glazed with pain, his blue eyes held such intelligence, expressing his need without words. Then, as if he had reached into her soul and found the reassurance he needed, he closed his eyes and released her hand, giving her his unspoken approval to continue. His body went slack, and she knew he had fainted again. She took a deep breath. There could be no doubt, his midnight blue eyes were the ones that haunted her visions. It was not so much their color but their expression—that intense scrutiny and farseeing look. She glanced heavenward, and whispered, "Lord help me, what does this mean?" But there was no answer.

Searing his skin was unlike any experience Gabby had encountered before. When her blade touched the open cut, the skin crackled and shrank away from the glowing steel. She winced, feeling his pain as though it were her own. Although the horrid smell of burnt flesh nauseated her, she drew the knife down the length of the wound until she had finished the task. He lay still and unresponsive while she bound his wound with the remaining pieces of her smock. Even slumbering, his features were drawn from the ordeal. Tears rimmed her eyes as she completed her ministrations, then gently pulled his robe up to his chin.

He had damned his soul for her, and a deep sadness filled her. She was responsible for a man's loss of salvation. Now as he hovered between life and death, there was nothing she could do for him but pray.

He moaned, and she softly drew her hand down his cheek. "Shh . . . Sleep," she soothed. Continuing to caress him, she openly studied him. Strength was stamped in every line and angle of his face. Even now, while he slept, she felt his power and magnetism.

Gabby shook her head. It was a sin for her to have such thoughts. Still, she could not deny them. No doubt they were caused by her heathen Scottish blood. Though Scots were a good and honest people, they did not let religion restrict them. Her uncle Alec would smile, and say, " 'Tis normal, lass, to be attracted to a braw man."

Aye, but the friar was braw. He had an honest look about him, and he was strong and courageous as well.

Closing her eyes, Gabby forced herself to think of their survival and remembered her father's favorite saying. *"Do what you can, lass, and leave the rest to God."*

The two soldiers the friar dispatched to hell would have to be hidden. They would be missed, and others would come to look for them.

Standing up, Gabby shuddered. The thought of disposing of two more bodies made goose bumps cover her flesh. She glanced back at the friar and sighed. "Keep him in your care, Lord, until I return," she whispered, then slipped out of the cave.

When a cloud drifted over the moon, she made her way down the path. She found the first body by tripping over it and landing sprawled on the dead man's chest. Her hands were sticky and moist with what she knew was his blood. Gasping, she scrambled off the corpse and roughly rubbed her palms on the ground, fearing the stain of death would never wipe off. Her skin still stung from the harsh scraping when she yanked the dagger free and laid it aside with the attacker's sword. Slowly she dragged the body to the cliff and pushed it over the edge. A splash sounded when it hit the river far below. Her back ached horribly, but she welcomed the pain. It diverted her thoughts from the gruesome task as she walked back up the trail for the other assailant.

She hoped the river would carry the bodies far downstream. The bodies, if discovered, would delay or lead the searchers in another direction.

At first daylight, she would come back and erase the drag marks from the ground. All traces of the crime would have to be concealed to protect their hiding place.

Exhausted, she walked down to the river and washed her raw hands and arms, scrubbing to rid herself of the dirt and grime. Finally she turned and walked back to the cave, picking up the weapons on the way.

She changed her clothes immediately, throwing away the bloodied habit and putting on her other. She wanted to rebuild the fire but, after today's attack, did not dare. Shivering, she huddled next to her patient for the night vigil. She reached out and brushed his hair from his forehead, feeling his brow as she whisked the strands from his eyes. His skin was exceedingly warm.

"Please, Lord, let him be free of the fever that assails wounded men." She scooted closer to him, placing her arm over his chest as she rested her forehead against his shoulder. Hoping her chilled flesh would cool the heat radiating from her sleeping companion, she closed her eyes. Before long the easy cadence of his breathing lulled her to sleep.

Sometime later Gabby was suddenly awakened by the friar's voice. Half-asleep, she leaned closer to him.

"Bethany," he murmured.

Startled and disconcerted that the friar had uttered a woman's name in his dream, she reluctantly conceded he had led a full life before entering God's service. Still, she hoped the name from his past belonged to a sister and not a lover.

Suddenly, the friar began to thrash about, and she reached

out to grasp his shoulders, trying to still his movements. As her hand brushed his chest, she felt his feverish skin. He was on fire! His lips were dry and cracked, and his head lolled from side to side. His fever had to be lowered. Removing the blanket, she whispered soothing words, but her pleas fell on deaf ears.

She wet a cloth and laid it on his head. His flesh was not hot, but burning. She remembered the Reverend Mother's treatment for fever. The body had to be bathed to lower its fierce heat. "Forgive me, Lord, but it must be done to save Your servant."

She rebanked the fire, then pulled a pan of water over to the man. Taking a deep breath, she peeled back his robe, drawing it carefully across the wounds on his chest, then pulled it down his body. For his modesty, she covered his lower half with the blanket. Still, the amount of flesh revealed was scandalous, and she stared in disbelief at what she saw. Down his arms and chest were scars she had not seen earlier. He had led an extremely rough life before entering the seminary.

Wringing the excess water from the strip of linen ripped from her chemise, she gently bathed his skin. The ridged muscles that ribbed his chest constricted at the cold touch of the compress. He moaned as the seared skin of his wound stretched from the spasm. She was struck anew at the massive chest that held muscles honed to rock-hard strength. He had neither the flabby shape of the overindulgent cleric nor the emaciated form of a self-denying priest. Nay, this was the extraordinary form of a man given to devoted exercise, not prayer.

Over and over, as if propelled by a will of their own, her hands drew the cloth over his flesh, feeling every muscle beneath her fingertips. With each stroke, the heat within her grew, and a smile graced her lips at having the opportunity to touch such a magnificent body. It was the closest she would ever come to knowing a man. That he was half out of his mind with fever told her how wretched she truly was.

Suddenly, he opened his eyes, startling her. But his glazed look did not focus on her.

"Royce," he whispered. "Royce, she loves you."

He grasped her wrist and held on, turning his gaze to her. "Bethany, he does not deserve you." Then he released her arm and slipped back to his dreams—or nightmares. She shuddered at the depth of emotion he sheltered in his soul. He must have loved the woman deeply, and it was also obvious Bethany was in love with Royce.

She did not know what was worse. To have a love and lose it or never to have the chance to fall in love. They were both victims.

She pulled her mind back to the task at hand. What was the next treatment for fevers? Her exhaustion clouded her thoughts. *Remember! Remember!*

She needed to make him drink. He needed liquids, but more importantly, he needed a healing tonic. She had no herbs or potions in her things. A memory flashed through her mind. How could she have forgotten? The friar had medicine.

She reached for his sack, praying it contained the remedy she required.

Unlacing the leather pouch, she tipped it closer to the firelight. Peering inside the soft bag she pulled out some clothing and discovered a smaller pouch at the bottom. Overjoyed at finding a medicine bag, she pulled it free and sifted through the contents. Ignoring a gold medallion and chain, she pawed through the various sacks of herbs. Finding the white-powder, her hand stilled. She recalled Mother Ambrose used a white-powdered medicine. Was this the one? And if it was, how much should she use?

"Lord, I am not skilled in healing. You must help me."

Her soft entreaty echoed in the cave. When silence answered
her plea, she briefly considered doing nothing at all, but
knew if she did, the friar, like the soldiers, would die.

After taking a pinch of the fine powder, she mixed it into
the water. The smell did remind her of Abbess Ambrose's
potion. "If it is Your will to have this man in heaven today,
then nothing I do can matter. However, Lord, he is a good
man, and I think his time here would be better spent helping
his people."

Waiting again for a sign and receiving none, she gently
lifted the friar's head. Although he was groggy and unresponsive, she forced him to take some medicine. The milky-
colored liquid dribbled into his mouth, but slid back out and
down his chin. Holding his head still, she tried once more,
and he finally swallowed a little drink. With a sigh she
lowered his head.

"Lord, life would be easier if You made Your will
known." Then her uncle Alec's words answered in her mind.
"But not as interesting, lass, not as interesting."

She chuckled. "Aye, it would indeed be dull-witted and
lame-jested," she responded, her face suddenly growing
warm as she realized she had not only been talking to herself,
but answering.

She could hear the friar's breathing and gave thanks that
the rattle that often accompanied a fever was absent. If he
remained strong, his body would heal itself. The potion she
had mixed would, she hoped, aid in the process.

Curling up beside him, thoughts of her beloved family
and home wafted through her mind as she drifted off to
sleep.

*The mist parted briefly and the faces were clear. In her
mind's eye, she beheld the striking features and knew immediately that this man Friar Guy spoke to was his brother.*

His face was a harsher version, the planes and angles sharper than Friar Guy's, but the family resemblance was marked.

In her vision, Friar Guy and his brother were talking, but she could not hear their words. When she came closer, their faces dissolved and were replaced by stern, calculating images of William and her uncle Quennel. She screamed and awoke in a cold sweat.

Trembling, she tried to make sense of the dream. Night visions were more difficult to interpret, but one thing seemed chillingly clear. She looked over at the gentle, kind friar, unwilling to believe that the man who had suffered such injuries to save her would, in some way, have a hand in her doom. Fingers of ice gripped her spine. Her uncle Quennel would have his way. Her fate would come to pass, soon, so very soon.

The first rays of dawn streaked across the morning sky, and Gabby's yawn attested to a restless night. Sitting up, she looked over at the friar, and immediately felt his forehead. His brow was cool beneath her touch, and relief washed over her. The fever had broken. "Thank God," she breathed.

" 'Twill be all right. Soon my uncle Alec will come," she whispered, to assure the friar as much as herself.

Though his eyelids remained closed, his hand covered hers, drawing it down to rest against his naked chest.

Heat radiated from him. Not fever, just the flesh-and-blood warmth of a man lay beneath her palm. She felt the rhythmic beating of his heart, and the rolling cadence as his chest rose and fell with each breath. Her fingers tingled from the intimate contact. Touching him drove little pinpricks of pleasure up her arm. She snatched her hand free of his, burying her fingers deep beneath the thick folds of her robe.

"Whether help arrives or not, mademoiselle, I have no fear in my heart."

This was no idle boast. She had witnessed his courage. Either he was very brave or very foolish, Gabby thought. Whatever the reason, he devastated her composure and peace of mind.

"I am not as brave. If my uncle Quennel finds us first, we will not live to see the morrow. I fear meeting St. Peter in this state," she said, tucking his covers more snugly about his chest.

His eyes opened, revealing the bright sparkle of good health. "You could confess your sins."

She stopped fussing with the robe and looked into his eyes. No, she could not tell him of her feelings. It would never do. "Friar, thank you," she said, pouring him some water to ease his thirst. "If I feel the need, I will indeed take up your kind offer. But for now, I shall be content."

"As you wish," he said, studying her over the rim of his cup as he sipped his drink.

It seemed to her that he knew her thoughts, and she felt the warmth of her own guilt creep up to burn her cheeks.

He lowered the cup, and his lips were moist and slightly swollen. When he licked his lips, she swallowed.

The knowing grin that lit his face made him appear more devilish than divine.

Beneath his scrutiny, she endured her embarrassment, while thinking humility was obviously a virtue he had yet to master.

"You know, mademoiselle, a friar never thinks of his confessional as a place to judge or condemn."

" 'Tis not that, friar, it is just hard to confess my sins to someone I know. Somehow being familiar makes the task much more difficult."

"I see. When you are able, then we will proceed." The

reassuring smile he offered her did the exact opposite. There was no way in heaven or hell she would ever confess her sins to this man.

Unable to hold his gaze, Gabby looked away, wondering when her uncle Alec would arrive. Company would alleviate the intimate atmosphere that had arisen between them.

A noise outside caught their attention. The friar placed his finger to his lips, warning her to be quiet. Then he wrapped the robe around his middle, and, though his features twisted in agony, he crawled to the opening.

That he managed to move in his weakened state amazed her. He acted more like a soldier than a cleric.

A twig snapped close to the cave opening and Gabby held her breath.

"Hail, Gabrielle! Come out, 'tis safe."

"Louis," she breathed, and ran toward the opening, but the friar stopped her by clasping her arm.

"It may be a trap."

"Nay, friar, my brother would die before he betrayed his own," she assured, pulling free of his hold and running out of the cave. Louis stood smiling with their cousin Ian as her uncle Alec welcomed her into his waiting arms.

"Thank God," she cried, her voice muffled by his plaid as he hugged her tight. "We had some trouble."

The friar limped out, with his tattered robe draped low around his hips.

" 'Tis clear ye did, lass, but from what quarter did ye feel threatened?" her uncle asked, taking his measure of the half-naked man.

"You do not understand, uncle, this man is a cleric," she explained.

"Is he now?" Alec stared at Guy. "There are braw men and barbaric men, lass, but all of them are men."

Gabby's face flamed, and she looked away.

Her uncle lifted her chin and looked into her eyes. "Dinna

fret, lassie. I know the truth of it. But ye and yon brother are my responsibility. If the Norman king learns ye have left the protection of the abbey, then we will have war, and I canna allow it.''

"I understand, Uncle. Keep my brother safe. If it becomes necessary, I will return to London rather than cause the clan any trouble.''

"Aye, lass, ye are a Campbell. 'Tis proud I am of my brother's bairns. Come, we have a long ride ahead of us, and 'twill do no good to borrow trouble.''

"What of the good friar?"

Uncle Alec's gaze traveled to Friar Guy, and a slow smile bloomed on the Scotsman's face. "I will have the good friar with us," he said, then turned to his man. "Andrew, get a kilt for this man and one for my niece.''

When the soldier left, the laird's gaze returned to Guy. "There is much we have to discuss."

The friar returned the smile, not one bit intimidated by the subtle threat. "I am looking forward to seeing your home, Laird Campbell.''

"Aye. 'Tis a beautiful place, but ye may not think so. Most Normans find my home not to their liking," he said boldly, the insult clear.

"I am not like most Normans," Guy said, then added, "as I am sure you are not like most Scots.''

" 'Tis true, we are unique. 'Twill be interesting to see what similarities we share." The Scotsman looked him over from head to toe, a slow perusal that lingered on his scars and overlooked nothing. Finally satisfied, his gaze returned to Guy's. "A man must know his foe, as well as his friend.''

Guy chuckled softly. "Laird Campbell, I am a man of God and call no man my foe." Though he appeared amused, the irony of Campbell's words had struck their mark. Normans had wounded him, and Scots now befriended him. His mission had gone from bad to disastrous, and he now faced capture by the very man he was to avoid.

He whispered a silent prayer and wondered if God was listening or laughing.

Chapter Five

"My lord, your niece and nephew have escaped," the thin soldier said.

Quennel Aumont stood listening to the returning soldier's report, clenching his teeth so hard his jaw ached.

"They are believed to be in Scotland." The instant the travel-weary messenger ended his summary, he bowed low before his lord.

Quennel's fist crashed up into the man's downcast face, catching him off-balance. The force of the blow knocked the man flat on his back. "This is the news you dare bring me?" Quennel bellowed. The soldier cupped his bloody nose and scrambled from the floor. With rushes clinging to his tunic, he hurried from the room.

"God's teeth, I will see those whelps in hell, especially the girl," Quennel vowed, shaking his hand to ease the sting in his knuckles. "Perrin!"

The young servant ran into the keep's great hall with a

look of wary apprehension on his youthful face that changed
to a hesitant smile when he spied the master. "My lord?"

"Wipe that impertinent look off your face," Quennel
snapped, then slyly caressed the young boy's smooth cheek.
"You may share my bed, Perrin, but not my power. Remember that." He rapped the boy's face smartly, then reached
for the pouch at his waist and handed Perrin a sack of coins.
Walking around the youngster, he paused behind him, laying
one hand on the boy's collarbone as he studied the small,
tight derriere.

"Find someone who can finish the job." Quennel's grip
bit into Perrin's shoulder, holding him still as he moved
closer and fondled the boy's small buttocks. "I do not want
to be disappointed again." Suddenly, his hand slid between
Perrin's legs. "Succeed or else," he said squeezing the
genitals until tears formed and fell from Perrin's terrified
eyes. "Do I make myself clear?" Quennel demanded, releas-
ing his hold.

Doubled over, Perrin fell to the floor, clutching himself
and gasping for air. His face pale, he nodded and crawled
from the room.

Quennel smiled. He loved the look of subservient fear
on a youngster's face and vowed he would see the same
expression on his nephew's just before mounting him.

And his niece. He especially owed her a comeuppance.
Gabrielle had set the alarm that had caused his exile from
his home in Normandy. He touched the bump on his nose.
An ugly break, which had never properly healed from the
blow Hamish Campbell had delivered when he discovered
Quennel sodomizing the servants. He sniffled and wiped his
nose on his sleeve. From that day to this his good looks had
been marred, and his nose dripped constantly.

His lips curled into a sneer. Before Campbell's whelps
met their Maker, he would introduce the boy to the pleasures
of the flesh, while the girl suffered the pain.

He shook his head as hatred poured through his veins. His beautiful sister, Blanchefleur, had wedded and bedded a Scot. A shudder of revulsion rippled through his nerves at the very image. The Scots were so . . . uncivilized. Besides, Hamish Campbell could not be influenced or controlled, and his twenty years in Normandy had been a constant trial for Quennel. Fortunately, Campbell's untimely death had ended Blanchefleur's marriage and Quennel's ill fortune.

Would they ever find out that during the heat of battle it was no foe, but family who had delivered the blow that caused Campbell's death? Now his damn whelps were proving harder to be rid of than their father. Perhaps the instinct for survival grew stronger with each generation.

No matter. If his mercenaries failed in their mission—which was inconceivable—he had still managed to maneuver the king into repaying a boon. He poured a goblet of his favorite wine and downed it without drawing a breath. It was a fortunate position to be in.

He refilled his chalice and this time sipped it, savoring the taste of the sweet nectar as he rubbed his crotch. Leaning back in his chair, he closed his eyes and pictured every road, every boundary of the land he had coveted since birth. His hand slipped beneath his tights and he stroked his organ as he dreamed of full ownership upon his nephew's death. His breathing became labored. His manhood swelled as he squeezed. He needed release.

"Perrin," he screamed, knowing the little catamite had left at his bidding. Damn, without aid he would be in agony.

Now engorged, he worked his rod with both hands. He pumped harder, but without succor. Why was there no one about? He could never fully enjoy this sport without someone to torment. Frustrated, he thought of his sire, that bastard who had left their land to his meek sister in order to protect the people from one he thought was a cruel taskmaster. *Bastard!* He gripped his shaft harder, painfully so, imagining his father's throat beneath his grasp, strangling the very breath and voice from the old man. "Ha," he screamed, as his seed spewed out into the air. He wiped the warm sticky liquid on his tunic, then raised his chalice in mock salute. "Old man, look at your careful planning now. If you wanted to ensure I never inherited your land, you should have eliminated the possibility, as I have done and shall do again to anyone who proves a threat."

Fools. No one suspects me, save my damn niece. Somehow she had seen through every deception. How did the child do it? It almost seemed as though she had the Sight.

It was rumored to run in her father's family. But he had never seen any sign of it in the girl. Yet, she had an uncanny way of foiling his plans. He would have to think on it. Perhaps marrying her off to Bayard de Bellemare was neither necessary nor profitable.

He might want to keep her around to foretell the future. *Non.* Unless he held leverage over her in the form of a loved one's life, Gabrielle would never consciously help him. She was a stubborn chit. Like her father, she had inherited the Scottish curse of being willful, and he'd had a bellyful of that temperament.

Non, his strategy would stand—the boy's elimination and the girl's marriage. His nephew's death was the only way to secure the land. Besides, Gabrielle might be amenable to helping him just to escape the hell her husband would undoubtedly put her through.

Quite pleased with himself, he took another sip of his wine. It was a good plan. He raised his chalice in another silent salute. "To you, old sire. Look what your worthless son has reaped."

Quennel downed his drink, then slammed the chalice onto the table. He felt powerful, and free for the first time since his youth.

Lovingly, he turned the ring on his finger, fascinated by

the rainbow-colored lights that flashed from the rich gems circling the thick band. It was his sire's, and the Aumont symbol of authority, worn only by the ruler. " 'Tis mine now, and I will not hand it over to my nephew. I will rule, and those who oppose me will die," he vowed.

He stared at the topazes, sapphires, and rubies. Though all the gems shone brightly in the firelight, the rubies glowed. The vivid color reminded him of blood. There had been so much blood when he removed the ring from Hamish's finger.

His sire's words when he passed the ring on to his son-in-law echoed in the dungeons of his memory. "Take this ring, Hamish Campbell, and rule with fairness, honesty, and good judgment."

Ha! He would take the ring and rule as he pleased.

Cresting the hill, Gabby brought her steed to a halt when the others did and looked down at the valley. The massive gray castle, sprouting spiraling stone towers and overhanging parapets, dominated the view. A sense of relief and pride filled her at the sight of the Scottish stronghold. Uncle Alec's fortified home assured Louis's safety.

The worry and fear of the preceding months melted away at the sight of Castle Campbell. If the impressive structure of granite and turrets did not inspire security, then the men who guarded it did. Fierce warriors lined the grounds and walked the battlements. No enemy would stand a chance against their numbers. The silhouettes of the huge sword-carrying Scots kindled a deep sense of relief. Home. For the first time in two years Gabby felt safe.

"Dinna fret, lass. If that dandified Norman comes a-knocking, we will teach him to treat his family with respect. I willna let the bastard harm ye," Alec said.

"He would have to be a fool to come calling." There

were tears in her eyes, and she tried to blink them away, but to her shame one slipped down her cheek. "I am sorry."

"Dinna apologize, lass. A woman should not have to bear such burdens. 'Twould be unseemly not to shed a tear or two," he said, a glint of gentle humor sparkling in his eyes. "Just dinna make a practice of weeping," he added.

His image wavered behind a watery sheen. "Aye. I wouldna wanna embarrass kin," she replied, affecting his brogue.

"Pity ye are half-Norman, but there be hope for ye yet." Her uncle chuckled and patted her hand before turning his horse away to join his men.

Louis joined her. "You can rest easy now. Your promise has been fulfilled." He smiled, pointing to the valley. "Look, our journey is over," he said, watching their clansmen ride out from the fortress to greet them.

She took a deep breath of air, filling her lungs with the crisp clean fragrance of the Scottish moors. " 'Tis wonderful," she sighed, and looked past her brother's smiling face only to meet the intense midnight blue gaze of Friar Guy. As usual, his scrutiny took her breath away; nor was it the first time she noticed his regard. She moved her horse over to his.

"I am sorry, friar. I am thinking only of myself. I know the trip has cost you much in pain," she said contritely.

"You should smile more often, Lady Gabrielle. Perhaps now that you are with your family, you will have reason to."

The words were an echo of Abbess Ambrose's. His eyes missed nothing. She could not understand why his concern should disturb her, but it did.

"I hope you, too, find reason to smile, friar."

Suddenly, a grin blossomed on his lips. "I stand chastised, my lady, for my loutish behavior." With a rakish tilt he nodded his head and devilishly met her gaze with an expression that would singe an angel's wings.

Her breath caught in her throat. His smile not only reached his eyes, but lit them with warmth until their dark blue depths actually sparkled. Moments passed before she was able to move or speak.

Ian and Louis rode by, their interruption thankfully breaking the spell. Her gaze latched on to Louis and followed his race against Ian to the castle.

"My brother will have the benefit of my uncle's guidance and counsel," she said, refusing to meet Friar Guy's gaze.

"*Oui,* and from the appearance of this place, Louis will profit greatly from the Scottish knowledge of warfare and soldiering."

" 'Tis more important for him to learn wisdom. I fear Louis's impetuous nature will be his undoing." She turned to him. The moment she met his regard, she knew she had erred.

The laugh lines near his eyes crinkled with mirth. "Your uncle seems capable of offering prudence to a willful youth."

She nodded and, tearing her gaze from his, nudged her horse to follow the entourage down toward the castle.

Guy watched her as he followed. The day was cool and the wind light, disturbing only a few wisps of her long black hair. She drew the wayward strands away from her face, then carelessly lifted the mass of her thick tresses up and over her shoulder.

The long ebony mane shone in the sunlight, so dark and rich in color that it reflected blue-black highlights with every bounce of the horse's gait. He could not take his gaze from her, nor could he forget how her features had softened and the lines of worry eased when she spied the impressive structure before them.

The agony of being her betrayer ate at the very core of his being.

He was, however, truly trapped. He could not disobey an order from his liege lord; to do so would be treason. Cursed! He was caught in the web of his own deception.

Like a Judas priest, he would deliver this unsuspecting lamb to slaughter. The thought sickened him. The promised land and castle suddenly lost their luster. Guy would have gladly dissolved the bargain long ago, but for his pledge to William. A man could not cross a king. Guy drew a deep, cleansing breath, but the stench of his duplicity soured the air.

It was a mark of his wretchedness that he would owe these gentlefolk his very health and repay their kindness with treachery. He wondered at God's great design, then shook his head. Gabby was right. The Almighty had no part in these proceedings. *Non,* this plot was hatched from the minds of men—powerful men. But he forced a smile on his lips as he rode into the courtyard.

Guy grimaced as two big Scots helped him dismount. They lifted his arms over their shoulders and helped support his weight. Pain shot through his gut.

"Have a care," Alec said, wry amusement coating his words. "Ye handle a weak and puny Norman there."

"Have a care, Scot, you defame the Church," Guy responded to the Scottish teasing, unwilling to let this man's aspersions go unchallenged.

"Rest yer wit and flesh, cleric. 'Tis only the good sport of the northern climes. Ye will grow used to it in time. That is if ye live and yer injuries allow ye to laugh."

Gabrielle rushed over to Guy, circling around the men supporting his weight. "Oh, Uncle Alec, I did not think his wounds were that serious. Are they?" she cried, truly alarmed.

Damn. Alec's teasing had Gabby worrying over him, and he glared at the big Scot, who smirked in return.

"Never mind, lassie, he will recover in time. Dinna fret."

When her features still bore the look of uncertainty, Guy reached out and touched her arm. "I assure you, mademoiselle, I am fine. After your tender ministrations, how could I not be? You must forgive your uncle's poor attempts at wit."

"See, lassie! He still has enough spit in him to satisfy anyone."

With a beseeching plea lighting her violet eyes, she laid her hand on Alec's chest, and whispered, "Please take care of him, Uncle. He is wounded."

Guy felt his cheeks warm as two guards stifled a laugh.

Alec smiled, amused by her show of concern.

"Now you know how I felt, friar," Louis teased. "I told you my sister can smother one with her worry and good intentions. 'Tis a pity my mother fell ill when Gabrielle was of the age to marry. Now she is too old to have a husband and children to fret over."

Gabby's expression literally crumpled, her features turning bright red before she lowered her eyes to stare at her boots.

At the men's angry stares, Louis lifted his hands in a helpless gesture of defeat. "What?" he questioned.

"Enough!" Alec snapped, sparing Louis a glare before his gaze softened and traveled to Gabrielle. " 'Tis jesting men do among themselves, sweet lass, nothing more. Louis's training in the social graces must have been sorely lacking, but never fear, I will attend to the oversight. As to the cleric, the man is in good hands. Now away with ye and let us be about our business," he ordered a little gruffly, but still bent to kiss her cheek.

Louis's shame colored his features, as the clansmen looked on the little lass with tender expressions. Whether war-roughed warrior or young lad, Guy realized that none was immune to her vulnerable innocence. She inspired protection.

Gabrielle gave her brother a hug, then turned to her uncle. "Friar Guy, though unfortunately not born a Scot, is still very dear to me," she said.

Guy watched her run up the steps and open the door for them, before calling to her aunt.

"Friar, ye must be a man of great character to win such praise from my niece."

Because she had no idea how black his soul was, Guy thought, and when she did, the truth would break her fragile heart.

"Are ye ready, lad?" Alec questioned, his gaze sharp, searching for any hesitation. "The stairs would be painful. Would ye prefer to be carried?"

"You can carry me when the breath has left my body and not before."

Alec nodded in approval. "Ian, run and make sure yer mother has her healing tray." He pointed to Louis. "Go with him," he ordered.

Sweat beaded on Guy's forehead. He felt pain every time he lifted his leg. Red-hot pokers seared his insides at each step. The horse ride had been uncomfortable, but this was near unbearable.

By the time they reached the doorway only ten short steps from the ground Guy felt as though he had been in the lists. His breath was labored, and he did indeed feel light-headed. He heard a gasp and saw Gabrielle hovering just inside the door.

"Lad, we will have ye on yer feet in no time at all. My niece, like most wee women, worries overmuch. 'Tis a complaint of their nature, but as men we wouldna have it other than it is," Alec said, waving her away as he directed the men, who half dragged, half carried Guy through the great room and over to the pallet that had been made for him by the fire.

"Uncle Alec," Louis protested. "I want no girl crying and fretting over me."

An older woman with a wide girth and ample bosom shook her head in disapproval of Louis's comment, then turned the blankets, back. "Alec, tell yer men to have a care. He is nearly gone from the pain."

"Aye, Mairi." Alec nodded to his men and watched until Guy was lowered to the pallet, making sure his wife was satisfied, before he turned to the boy. "Louis, there will come a time when ye enjoy the attentions of a comely lass. And, aye, ye may even moan and groan when ye feel no pain at all, just to get their attention. I have on occasion used that very device to wring a little loving sympathy from my dear wife," he said meeting Mairi's gaze and chuckling at the becoming blush on her cheeks.

"Uncle Alec!" Louis croaked.

"Father?" Ian questioned.

Alec smiled " 'Tis the war between the sexes that matters most to any soldier. Think on it, lads. 'Tis the only battle ye are likely to lose, but relish the defeat."

Disbelief was mirrored on the two young faces.

Alec laughed as he threw his arms over both their shoulders and pushed them over to the center of the room, saying, "We will talk about this when ye meet a lovely little lass who turns yer knees to weak joints and yer heart to a fast-beating drum."

At the boys' groan, Guy caught Gabrielle's gaze. He extended his hand. "Will you offer comfort?"

She glided to his side as her aunt Mairi checked his wounds. "Soothe your fear. I will not desert you in your time of need," Gabrielle said, taking his hand.

Alec was right. He would indeed groan to keep the lady

near. Already her touch was affecting him. He stared into those violet eyes, and the pain lessened.

"Ye did a fine job, child. Now, he must rest," Aunt Mairi said, reaching for a steaming mug.

Guy was beginning to feel comfortable as he accepted the hot drink Mairi offered to him while Gabrielle fussed over him and all the Scotsmen piled into the room and gathered around the trestle table.

Alec stepped to the head of the table and raised his hands for order. " 'Tis with a sad heart I tell ye that the Norman dog that would kill his own niece and nephew, Gabrielle and Louis Aumont, both of whom are members of our clan Campbell, will no doubt be coming to our land. I say, if he violates our borders, we give him a warm reception."

In unison the men raised their tankards and bellowed their agreement.

Guy shivered as he heard the toasting oath. "The only good Norman is a dead one."

Louis would be safe here. But the real question to ask was—would he? Not if they ever learned his mission.

Alec raised his goblet again. "To our friend, Friar Guy, who saved our clan Campbell members."

Warily, Guy looked around the room. Every warrior's face was turned toward him with their chalices raised, and every one of them was committed to his chieftain. It would be impossible to enlist aid against Alec.

Guy smiled and raised his drink. "To divine wisdom. May He send help to all in their hour of need, no matter if they be Saxon, Scot, or Norman." Guy took another drink of his hot wine, bemused that his subtle reprimand had not shamed but amused them. In fellowship they raised their drinks and with laughter quaffed their brew.

Exhausted, he fell back against the pillow. Gabrielle laid a cool cloth on his brow. Her voice soothingly admonished him to lie still. When he felt stronger he would have to make a bid for freedom. Somehow, he would have to convince Gabrielle to accompany him. He captured her hand again, liking the feel of her soft skin next to his as he laid her palm against his cheek. How? How would he talk her into leaving Scotland? Outside of a royal command, he could not see that happening.

Royal command. Oui, William held the answer. Alec Campbell, though loyal to his brother and responsible for his niece and nephew, might not want to incur a war with England.

But how was he to contact the king? Several ideas swirled through his mind, but none crystallized. Was he feeling the effects of the wine more than he should? Then, it came to him. The wine held a drug. His eyelids weighed as heavy as stone. He tried to fight the effects of the potent drink, but it was futile. He nodded off, only to awaken moments later, feeling groggy and confused.

"Gabrielle," he whispered, unable to open his eyes. Her hand closed over his, and her reassuring touch soothed the fear. Soon he would drift into a deep slumber. A lingering thought pricked through his drug-confused mind. But he clasped her hand tighter, at the pricking thought that the brew might as easily be laced with poison as with a sleeping potion.

King William crumpled the missive from Quennel Aumont. He did not like the tone or the contents. "Demands, does he!" he hissed, his face hot with anger. Well, the girl would be returned, but that would not end it.

Quennel had gone too far. No one dictated to a king. When his supposedly loyal subject realized that a king commanded, not vice versa, perhaps then they would return to a working relationship. "Verdon," he bellowed.

The emissary rushed into the room and bowed low. *"Oui, my liege?"*

"You will travel to Normandy and investigate Quennel Aumont. I wish to know everything about him and his family. How he treats his serfs and the conditions of his estate. Leave nothing uncovered in your quest. I want every detail, past history included. I want to know this man better than I know you."

"Oui, sire." Verdon retreated.

William steepled his hands together. Politics made strange alliances, and he instinctively sensed Quennel Aumont was more dangerous as an ally than he could ever be as an adversary.

Gabby looked over the balustrade to the great hall below, where Guy lay sleeping by the fire.

Her eyes drank in his handsome appearance. She could not get enough of him. With a sigh she tore her gaze away from him and turned to her uncle, who sat at the table drinking his ale. After stealing one more glance at Friar Guy, she slipped down the stairs.

"Uncle Alec."

He glanced up. Upon seeing her, his eyes softened. "What keeps ye up, lassie?"

Gabby twisted her hands. " 'Tis hard for me, Uncle, but the words must be said. I fear my presence will cause you trouble."

He instantly began a denial, but she held up her hand. "Please, let me finish, Uncle. Quennel has a legal right to demand my return. You must, if it is requested by William, send me to London. But under no circumstances can you let him have dominion over Louis. Quennel means to kill him."

"And what of ye, lass? Does he not mean ye harm?"

She lowered her eyes. "I do not know, but Louis stands between Quennel and the inheritance he feels should be his. He would do anything to gain the Aumont birthright."

Uncle Alec took a deep draught of his drink. "Do ye think William will interfere?"

"I believe he will have to. The Aumont family is important and powerful. I would not see you drawn into a battle."

"If 'twas only up to me, lass, there would be no question about protecting ye. But I fear, I must agree with yer judgment. Dinna fret, lassie. Ye have my word, no one will ever harm the lad while I still breathe."

"You are a good and gracious man. Father would be as proud as I to claim you."

" 'Tis true that ye have the Campbell blood in yer veins. But I dinna wish to sacrifice ye to save yer brother. Is there another that we can hide ye with?"

She held his gaze and shook her head. "I have no one else."

Alec ran a hand through his hair and took another sip, obviously mulling over the problem. Suddenly, he slammed his tankard down. "If ye had a husband 'twould end the fuss."

Her gaze darted wistfully to the friar, then returned to her uncle. "Who?" she asked, cautiously, while knowing that anyone would be preferable to the monster Uncle Quennel had chosen.

"Does it matter, lass? Ye would be safe. We could wed ye to a northern chieftain. Then not even William would dare demand ye for fear of involving the Danes."

A smile creased her lips, as hope ignited in her breast. " 'Twould certainly foil Quennel's plans. Would it be possible to arrange a match?"

"I dinna know, lass, but we can try. I will send a messenger tonight."

Gabby threw her arms about her uncle's brawny shoulders

and kissed him soundly on the cheek. "I knew everything would be made right if we made your doorstep."

Guy slowly opened his eyes. Did they say marriage? he groggily asked himself, wondering if he had imagined it or not. Drug-induced cobwebs swirled about in his mind. His mission would be ruined if Gabby were married. He must stop them. Then reality faded, leaving only an image of a lovely face outlined, not in a nun's wimple, but a lace-webbed wedding veil.

Chapter Six

Without a change of clothes, Guy gratefully accepted a green-and-blue Campbell kilt.

Though unusual, he found the Scottish way of dress incredibly comfortable. Long yards of wool were folded into pleats around the waist and held firm by a belt, with the excess material merely thrown over one shoulder. The mode of dress had only one drawback—the draftiness. He wondered, not for the first time, how on earth they stayed warm in winter. But since he would never admit to being less hardy than these folk, he walked around gingerly, his chest wounds visible to all, and watched the castle routine.

Today, claymores and axes were the weapons utilized on the practice field. Louis fell repeatedly before each sparring opponent. No one, not even his cousin Ian, gave him any special treatment. If anything, they were much harder on the lad, no doubt because of his status. Guy sympathized with the boy, but understood the reason behind the harsh discipline. When Alec's men finished Louis's training, he would be an exceptional warrior. Still, Guy wondered if the lad harbored resentment toward his sister, and if so, whether it was the trip to Scotland that raised his pique, or not being able to confront his uncle Quennel. In this, he agreed with Gabby. The boy would someday meet his Norman uncle, but now was not the time.

"Care to try yer hand at our little game, friar?" Alec asked, leaving the field and offering his sword.

Guy knew it would be a sign of weakness to point out that his wounds were not healed; and although his religious status would also allow him to beg off, he could do neither. Smiling at the knowing look in the laird's eye, Guy took the claymore, squared his shoulders, and entered the field.

The Scots were always testing a man's strength and character. He thought that his brother would like this way of life and made a mental note to introduce Royce to the more savage customs of Scotland when he returned to North Umberland.

With effort, Guy lifted the two-edged sword. The weapon was different than the one he was accustomed to wielding. Fortunately, no one would expect a friar to have any training with the weapon.

Alec took a claymore from his clansman, then turned to Guy with a grin. "Dinna fear, friar. I will go easy on ye."

Guy returned the smile. "How kind of you, good sir."

Eager anticipation lit the old man's eyes, and Guy knew this would be an exceedingly hard match.

Still, the blood pumped through Guy's veins with an excited rush he had not experienced in a long time. This was more than exercise and practice. It was challenge to the spirit.

Guy met the first blow easily enough. He preferred to see the man's form before he went on the offensive. Alec surprised him. The laird's sword handling was not aggressive, but more thoughtful and precise. There was a clever brain at work. It would take all of Guy's mental *and* physical skills to match this warrior.

Alec grinned as they sparred, obviously enjoying the test as much as Guy.

" 'Tis surprised I am to find a friar so well skilled in the art of war."

"I was not born a cleric. Before entering God's service, I owed my allegiance to William."

"Aye, ye must have been a passable soldier," Alec taunted.

Guy laughed. "Tolerable I would say. But you be the judge of my prowess." Guy struck out with lightning speed and slipped under the Scot's guard.

The move so surprised the man, it left him defenseless for a second. That was all Guy needed to push the advantage. He arched his sword up and neatly backed the Scot into the wall. "Do you yield?"

"Aye, that I do, lad. I would say ye were more than a passable soldier," Alec acknowledged, his manner not one whit put out that he had been bested.

Guy was amazed at the man's acceptance of his defeat. There were those who would resent being shown up in front of their men. In regard to moral temperament, he mentally ranked Alec with his brother, Royce, and no higher honor could be accorded.

"Ye must teach me that move," Alec said.

"I am in the business of teaching prayers now. I will be happy to have you as my pupil if you will attend church this Sunday."

Alec laughed. "Aye, I will be there, but dinna expect a saint from this sinner. I am a man and enjoy a man's appetites."

"As am I," he agreed.

Alec looked at Guy strangely. "I canna figure ye out, but I will. I canna credit a man such as ye entering the Church."

"Perhaps I grew tired of death and dying."

"Aye, that can sour any man. But I think, in yer case, 'tis a mistake to enter the Church. Ye no more belong behind holy walls than I."

"We will see. Each man finds his destiny."

"Aye, that is true. But in case ye havna noticed, I am not the only one who thinks yer talents are being wasted."

Guy blushed crimson.

Alec slapped Guy on the back. "Never mind, lad, 'twill all work out. I say we dinna waste words talking about it when time will see it done. Let us be away for some tasty fare. Ye have earned it."

At the mention of food young Louis came running up, eager to join his uncle.

Not ye, lad. I am not satisfied with yer practice, and ye will stay out here until ye get it right."

Disappointment assailed the boy's features. "But Uncle Alec, I am starved."

"Then ye will no be dallying. Better to be hungry then dead. See to yer lesson, lad."

Alec turned to Guy as they continued on into the castle. "Do ye think I was too hard on the lad?"

"*Non.* Someone who cared about my welfare once behaved as harshly to me." Guy chuckled. "At the time I hated my brother, but now I appreciate the sacrifice he made." Stepping to a trestle table and lifting the flagon, Guy poured two ales, handing Alec one.

"Ye have the way of it. A man canna enter into the world expecting it to be loving and giving like his kith and kin. Life is rough, and if ye are to survive, ye must be as strong. My wee niece has a soft heart—too soft. Although she wouldna agree."

"I have noticed she is fiercely protective of her brother. What happened to make such a fragile lady take on the sole responsibility for her family?"

Alec ran the back of his hand across his mouth, wiping the ale from his beard. "Her uncle Quennel. I swear on all I hold holy, if that man sets one foot in Scotland, I will strangle him with me bare hands and have no remorse for it."

"You do not mince words, Alec Campbell."

"Nay, I never found the need to, nor could I. I willna apologize for what I said. No doubt, I will burn in hell for all time, but I willna mind the fires if that scourge is there beside me."

"What did the man do to incur your wrath?"

"He is less than a man. The greed in his heart for Gabrielle and Louis's inheritance is as black as his soul. Years ago the hatred began grinding him down into a bitter shell of the man he once was."

Guy could understand what Alec said. Many a man had sold his soul for coin. In fact this analogy hit too close to home. A soldier followed orders, Guy quickly consoled his conscience. Besides, if he refused to do the king's bidding, someone else would.

"Lust for wealth has ruined many a man's soul."

" 'Tis more than their land and estate that he wants. He bears his niece and nephew a personal vendetta. My brother, Hamish, near killed him when—well, 'tis too nasty to relate. Just trust me when I say Quennel hates the children."

"I am a man of the cloth; there is nothing I have not heard," Guy said, leaning forward slightly to invite a confidence.

"All right, but consider this privy information. Little Gabrielle found Quennel trying to use her brother, Louis, and a young servant boy as catamites. Horrified, she ran to her father, who thrashed the daylights out of Quennel. News of Quennel's escapades reached his father, and the elder Aumont cut his son from his inheritance, leaving the estate to his daughter, Blanchefleur, and her line. Quennel has never forgiven Gabrielle or Louis. Though he dinna have time to harm either, his malice has festered through the years.''

"I see," Guy said, sickened by the tale of perversion. Now he understood her fear of Quennel.

"That man has an unholy hatred and blames Gabrielle and Louis for his lot. 'Tis the only way he can live with his conscience.''

"When Blanchefleur and Hamish died their children's lives were in peril?" Guy asked.

"Aye. I have always suspected Quennel had a hand in my brother's death.''

"Why have you waited so long to offer Gabrielle your help?''

Alec barked a laugh. "I couldna intervene until she left England and William's reach.''

"But you did," Guy said, knowing the man had crossed the border to rescue them.

"Why do ye think I saved yer precious skin, friar? I was doing my Christian duty, and none can say nay. I dinna rescue my niece so much as save a man of the cloth.''

Guy refilled Alec's goblet and handed it to him when he returned to the table. Alec took a deep drink, then continued. "On her deathbed my sister-in-law made Gabrielle promise to take care of her brother. After her mother died, the wee lass kidnapped Louis from the castle where he was fostering and safely traveled to England before her uncle could do anything. Still, Quennel recruits whoever will listen to help him.''

Fighting a queasy sensation, Guy thought of William, who would grant his knight, Quennel Aumont, this boon. The king would have to be apprised of the whole picture, especially if Quennel had murdered his brother-in-law. William would never condone such acts. Whatever his liege decided after reading Guy's report, he still had a mission, and would return Gabrielle to London. The thought of his part in this deception sickened him. At least Louis would be safe in Scotland. Thank God he had made that decision; though it was a small concession, it allowed him to sleep at night. Besides, William would not care where the boy resided as long as the girl was returned.

Alec looked at Guy as though he had read his mind. "Ye ken how it is?"

"*Oui,* I do. I can understand your feelings about such a man. Though Quennel would find forgiveness from God and the Church, he would look in vain for your compassion."

"Aye, that be the way of it."

"So be it, Alec. I will not try to change your mind about your Christian duty."

"Ye are a strange one. Until our friar returns, I would ask a boon of ye. If ye say services, then I will keep my word, and be in kirk this Sunday."

Guy smiled. "Then it was worth the sore muscles I will be feeling."

"Aye, lad. I will have Gabby come and bathe the aches away. The girl has exceptional hands."

"*Non,*" he said quickly, then tempered his words. "Though a friar, I am still a man. I do not need any more temptation, and as I am sure you are well aware, your niece would tempt a saint."

Alec laughed. "I am glad I did not misjudge ye, Norman. I think from here out we will be on better footing. Verily, I will send ye the ugliest of maidens. Will that do?"

Guy groaned inwardly. How he used to enjoy bathing with a comely female in attendance.

As the food was placed upon the table, Alec indicated that Guy should sit on his left, a rare privilege indeed.

Lady Gabrielle rushed in just as they had taken their seats. "Uncle, please. You must not be so harsh with Louis."

"Lassie, ye want him to be able to hold his own when

the day comes that he meets that snake, Quennel. Leave his training to me, and do not interfere again.''

Her lip quivered slightly, but she held her uncle's eye. Guy understood why boys fostered at other castles, to forge strong alliances that could be drawn upon in future conflicts. But there was a much more practical aspect. If a mother or sister were to watch the brutal training a lad endured, it would be needless suffering for both.

''Your uncle is right, Lady Gabrielle. You will have to leave this in his hands. Though it seems harsh, every lad who wishes to be a knight must endure the rigorous training, and endure it alone. Your interference will only make Louis's trials harder.''

''I know, but . . . I have always looked out for Louis.''

She looked up at him with huge violet eyes filled with tears, and Guy's heart skipped a beat. How was it possible to feel so strongly about the mademoiselle. It was surely his conscience reacting after what he had heard about her uncle.

''There's a good lass. Fetch us some more wine,'' Alec said.

When Gabby left for the kitchen, Alec turned to Guy. ''Thank ye, friar. She has had her brother's interests at heart for so long and takes her responsibility so seriously that one would think she was his mother. In truth her mother was ill much of the time, and Louis's upbringing fell to Gabby. But she mustna interfere. I would ask ye to spend some time with her to keep her mind off her brother's training.''

''I would suggest you find another,'' Guy said, drolly.

''Nay, it will be good exercise for the both of ye. I willna coddle the lad, nor ye. Think of it as training.''

The Scot was a crafty old devil, and as much as the thought twisted Guy's gut, he had to admire how neatly Alec had maneuvered him.

"In the interest of helping the lass, a friar can do no less," Guy said.

"There ye have it." Alec chuckled. "Good luck to ye, lad."

For the past week, Gabby had worn her nun's wimple and habit. Now that she was to be presented as a prospective bride, her uncle commanded her to wear the kilt of the Campbell ladies.

Standing before the polished metal, she ran her fingers through her hair and shook it free. She had almost forgotten the luxuriant freedom of unbound hair. The reflection of long, flowing hair falling about her shoulders and cascading down her back presented a sensual image that stunned her.

Turning one way, then another, she watched how the soft material of her colorful kilt swirled around and molded to her form. It had been so long since she had worn anything other than drab brown or black that the vivid greens and blues of the plaid made her feel like a spring flower. She smiled and wondered what the friar's reaction would be to her new appearance at the evening meal.

How foolish she had become, worrying over the friar's reaction when she needed to impress the emissary her uncle had invited.

As Gabby carried the rich warm bread to the table the aroma permeated the air. Her gaze caught the encouraging smiles of Louis and Ian while her uncle Alec nodded but not until she chanced the welcoming grin of Friar Guy did she relax.

Alec's guest, Laird Drummond, a giant of a man with Nordic features, grunted his approval when she set down the bread. "There be a good lass. Yer uncle has apprised me of yer fight. Ye must leave the worry to menfolk. Now, ye can keep to yer place.''

Her face stung with indignation. Though the convent had been disciplined, she had never been demeaned. Ignoring her uncle's warning look, she raised her gaze and met the watchful look of the northern laird. ''My place? Where is that exactly, Laird Drummond?'' she questioned sweetly.

''Do not mince words with me, lass. Normandy canna be that different than Scotland when it comes to men and women. Yer husband should be yer first concern, then yer bairns.''

''Has it escaped your notice than I am not wed?''

''Aye, but fret naught, lass. Yer uncle is arranging to change that. I will carry his message north, along with my recommendation.''

Her gaze traveled to her uncle Alec, as she prayed that this hulking, oafish laird was not an example of the prospective bridegrooms.

''Turn around and let me have a full look, lass,'' Laird Drummond ordered.

Her shoulders stiffened. Was she now wares to be sold at market?

''Laird Drummond, there is no need to be coarse with an innocent maid,'' Friar Guy interjected.

''Aye, ye are right, friar. I forget my manners in gentle company. I have been at war too long,'' he said, then leaned closer. ''Besides, she is too narrow in the hips for me. But if the dowry is large enough, the lass doesna have to be, eh?''

Gabby momentarily closed her eyes at the humiliating remarks overheard by half the hall.

In the sudden silence chairs scraped over the floor and Friar Guy's voice rang out in censure. ''Laird Drummond.''

Though her face burned, she opened her eyes and noted the cleric's sympathetic expression as he held Louis and Ian by the arm, preventing them from taking Laird Drummond to task.

Laird Drummond's face flushed red with shame. He stood and bowed to her. "My apologies, my lady."

Though mortified to the bone at the Laird's callous assessment, she would die before she showed the pain of his insult. "I hold no ill will, Laird Drummond," she said, sweeping low into a curtsy to gather her dignity. Upon rising she held his gaze until every pair of eyes centered on him, and he looked away. Then she turned, her head held high, and walked calmly from the great room toward her quarters.

Once out of sight, she lifted her kilt and hurried up the torchlit staircase. Her footfalls barely sounded in the deserted hall, but the silence ended when she reached her room. Like a thunderbolt, the slamming of her door echoed her emotional turmoil through the castle. "Oh Father, 'tis a blessing you are spared witnessing your own flesh and blood the brunt of such boorish humor in your ancestral home."

Tears of frustration stung her eyes, but she refused to shed them. Uncle Alec had allowed that farce to continue, and he never did anything without a reason.

As she had done so many times in the abbey, Gabby began to pace. Abbess Ambrose had called her restless movements disconcerting, and recommended contemplative prayer. But walking helped her think, and allowed her time to get her emotions under control.

Almost immediately, however, a knock sounded at her door. She snatched it open with such force the latch handle slipped from her hand and the door crashed against the inner wall. Two times in as many minutes a loud bang sounded, making her appear the fool.

The cleric stood outside her door, a concerned look on his face.

The heat of embarrassment stole up her cheeks. Could this day possibly get any worse?

"Friar," she said, swallowing the lump in her throat.

"I wish to talk to you, if you have the time. 'Twill not take long, and I think it would be beneficial."

She took a deep breath, wondering what penance he would dispense for her outburst.

"Perhaps a walk outside if you would be so kind as to accompany me?" he asked.

With an inner sigh, she nodded. "I will join you downstairs." There was no way to deny him. It would be churlish to refuse, especially after the way she had answered the door.

With her mantle around her shoulders, she walked through the courtyard, avoiding the clansmen's curious glances as she and the cleric left the stronghold.

When the sun dipped beneath the horizon the sky was awash in deep purples and reds, and the crisp clean air nipped her cheeks. Several minutes of silence stretched out, and each one pulled her nerves taut.

After they walked, the night breeze chilled her. She huddled deep within the folds of her mantle, as the friar adjusted the wool plaid lying over his shoulder.

It occurred to her that she had not adjusted as easily to the Scottish customs as had the cleric. She stole another glance at him in the gathering darkness. He certainly did not look like a cleric. The kilt revealed too much of his muscular chest. As insufficient as a small tapestry hung to hide a wall's imperfections, the dark curly chest hairs failed to mask the scars that crisscrossed his skin. The primitive image reminded her of the texture of his skin beneath her fingers when he lay sick. Her stomach tingled, remembering the wiry thick hair that glistened with sweat when the fever broke and the muscles that bunched and rippled beneath her touch.

"Mademoiselle?" he inquired, raising a brow.

Caught staring, she blurted out the first thing that came

to mind. "I, ah, was thinking of Louis. I am worried about his future."

"Lady Gabrielle, your misguided concern may hurt him one day."

"Misguided?" she questioned, stalling to regain her composure.

"*Oui.* To become a man, he must take the steps alone. You cannot do this for him."

"You are right, friar."

"I think it would be best if you found some other interest to keep yourself busy."

He was right in more ways than he knew. From now on she would work from morning to sunset and drop into bed exhausted. Then there would be little time for worry—or sinful yearning. "Thank you, friar. I had once thought that you were miscast as a cleric. I can see now that I was wrong. You have been such a comfort to me."

Her gratitude made Guy feel like a hypocrite! Being near to her was a purgatory in itself. The subtle scent of violets wafted through the air, and he closed his eyes, savoring this woman's fragrance. He could not afford to see her as a desirable woman. He had a job to do and a part to play. With determination he put his thoughts from his mind. It was time to broach the subject they had both avoided.

"Your uncle Alec was not being needlessly cruel. There are times you must hurt someone to help them. He was giving you a fair warning of what you may face. With your intellect and sheltered upbringing, I fear you will find the northern climes not to your liking."

"My abominable behavior earlier deserves punishment," Gabby said meekly, lowering her gaze. "It is kind of you to worry about me, friar, but I will do what my uncle Alec wishes. There is not another soul I would trust with mine or Louis's welfare.''

"You are an amazing young woman, Gabrielle," he said.

Her head snapped up. "You give praise when assigning a penance?"

"I think sacrificing yourself for your brother is penance enough," he said. "Don't you?"

Her eyes flashed. " 'Tis not a sacrifice, but a choice. I choose to thwart Uncle Quennel's plans. Louis and I have to look out for each other."

"I understand," he said, wishing he didn't. "I also have a brother. Royce . . . What is it?" he asked at her sudden frown.

"You said his name when you were sick," she said, understanding that it was Guy's brother who Bethany loved.

He smiled. "From your expression I can tell I said more than just his name. Though Royce and I are close, there are times I want to throttle him."

She laughed. "You? Good friar. I thought men of the cloth gave up their tempers when they said their vows."

"Did you?" He took her hand and helped her over a small brook, thinking how her smile lightened his mood.

" 'Tis not temper but pride that is my failing," she said. "I have little hope of ever mastering that fault."

"Pride?"

"You have heard Louis describe me, and know I do not hesitate to speak my own mind."

"You call that pride?"

"What else, friar," she asked.

Intelligence, wit, independence, he answered silently. Of pride he had yet to see a trace from a woman who seemed unaware or unimpressed by her own wonderful qualities.

"I fear if I wed a man like the Laird Drummond, then we will not survive the bedding. One of us would not know our place," she said. Then, as if suddenly aware she had spoken her thoughts aloud, her face turned beet red.

Guy chuckled. Her wit served her well, but would be an asset only to the right man. He feared there were far too many men who would see an intelligent mind as a threat.

"Marriage," he said, trying to maintain an authoritative air, "is a serious business. You will, of course, have to yield in all things to your husband. It is the way of it."

She laughed softly. "Oh, friar, forgive me, but you do not know the way of couples. Men and woman can share, at least my parents did. They loved each other very much, but by no means did my mother yield. In truth, I can remember some very heated discussions between them."

"Do you wish to be treated ill?"

"Nay, you miss my point. Although my parents disagreed, they never did so in meanness. My father and mother held strong opinions; therefore, they often had to compromise. That does not mean my father or my mother respected each other any less. In fact, I think the differences added to their enjoyment of each other."

"You miss them very much."

"Aye." Her eyes pooled with moisture, and she quickly swiped at them.

She looked so vulnerable, holding back her tears, that he ached to wrap her in his arms. Damn this charade.

"So much of my world has deserted me. There are times that the fear and loneliness crowd in on me."

" 'Tis true, you need a man," he said, taking hold of her shoulders. At the trust shining in her eyes, he wanted to crush her against his chest, and kiss the tears from her face. Unable to trust himself, he kept her at arm's length. "You would have someone to shoulder the burden," he went on, "or if you like, share the weight."

"That would indeed be a novelty. But the marriage is

being arranged for necessity, nothing more. I will fulfill the contract no matter what manner of man holds my troth.''

"And will you honor your vows?''

"Until I die.''

"Gabby, I believe you have integrity in a world losing its moral fiber. Is it possible for you to seek another avenue?''

"Nay, friar. Unlike yours, my fate is sealed. I have very little choice in the direction of my life.''

"What do you mean, unlike me?''

"Unlike a man, a woman cannot choose her destiny.''

"If you could make the decision, what would you choose?''

She drew a windblown strand from her cheek and met his gaze.

"If my brother were safe, I think I would choose to marry a man I loved.''

The hairs on the nape of his neck rose. "I did not know there was a man who held your affection.''

"There is no one as of yet, and though it is true that I am long past the marrying age, I dream that there might be one man who would consider me young and fair enough to love as his wife.''

Her wistful look captured him, and he literally shook the image from his thoughts. "That is all you would want?'' he asked.

"Having that, what more is needed?''

"Would you not want riches, so you would never have to be at anyone's mercy?''

"I am an Aumont. I have known wealth, and, in truth, my life would be much less complicated if I were a milkmaid.''

"But you are not.''

"I know. I shall face whatever awaits me and try to make the best of the marriage. Friar, I am no young girl. Though I may be ignorant of the intimate aspect of marriage, I am not unacquainted with the emotion that can either bind two people together in harmony or entangle them in a trap.''

Suddenly he had a vivid image of being tangled with this woman naked beneath the covers. Soft skin and delicate curves filled his senses. His blood pounded through his veins as his need grew. He raked his fingers through his hair, banishing his desire and resurrecting his iron control.

"Friar, does something trouble you?''

He looked into her eyes. Her honest concern touched him, but the innocent sensuality in her gaze drove him to distraction. He quickly glanced back out at the hills and took a deep breath. "Just when I think I have the world figured out, something comes along and puzzles me.''

"Do not let it trouble you, friar. The answer will soon fall into place.''

Not when the answer meant acting on his fantasy. He cleared his throat. "I came to offer you comfort and find myself receiving it. Lady Gabrielle, I pray life gives you all you deserve.''

" 'Twill take more than prayer.'' She turned away.

He had heard the catch in her voice and grasped her shoulders, pulling her back against his chest. "Why will it take more than prayer to see your happiness?''

"I know I must marry a Northern clansman to escape my uncle Quennel. But friar, the chances the man will love me are passing small. I will be no more than a possession.''

He turned her around and tenderly lifted her chin to face him. They were alone, on the moors in the night, and a bright moon lit the grass in a silvery glow. He cradled her face between his palms. "Hope, Gabby, is eternal. You must never lose your faith.''

One lone tear slid down her cheek. "Forgive me, 'tis selfish of me to want so much more than I can have.''

" 'Tis no sin. You have thought of your brother for so long that now your own future frightens you.'' His thumb brushed her wet cheek. Her skin was like the soft petal of a flower.

She moved closer into his soft caress, turning her cheek into his palm. When her gaze met his, the big violet eyes revealed her longing and loneliness, and her silent plea reached out to him. He was going to kiss her even though he knew it was wrong. He lowered his head slowly, allowing her the opportunity to stop him. Apparently, she was as lost to the spell as he.

When their lips touched it was a sweet joining, not a ravenous hunger, but merely an exploration of the senses, as if they were each feeling their way cautiously. As though their natures were attuned long before they had even met, they joined and fit exactly. Slowly, he slipped his arms around her and drew her near.

The moment was innocent, sweet, and perfect. He felt such pure sensations, unspoiled by past experiences, that it was the most sensual experience of his life. And yet it had not been a consummation of anything. It was but a kiss.

Her hand reached up and brushed his cheek. His heart raced, and sweat broke out upon his brow as he reacted to this maiden's touch like an untried squire. The featherlike caresses tortured his self-control. His breathing harsh, he tried to take deep gulps of air, stemming his emotion. The exercise was futile for each lungful taken, pressed every line and curve of her body up against his. The contact seared him, making him want more. The woman had a magic, a presence, that affected him unlike anything he had ever known.

When she shivered in his arms, he knew she felt the same. "Gabby," he whispered.

Moonlight and confusion were reflected in her eyes, and she tried to push out of his embrace. "We should not have done that." Her lips quivered as she drew a shaky breath.

When she met his gaze again her eyes were filled with tears. "I beg your pardon, friar."

With a sigh he released her. "Forbidden fruit tastes the sweetest," he said, trying to ease her guilt. " 'Tis not your sin, but mine."

She lowered her head. "Nay, I am not blameless."

Her honesty tore at his being. He took her arm and started silently back toward the castle.

He saw her to her doorway and curtly bade her good evening. He thought about her destiny. He would deliver her into William's hands and probably spend the rest of his days in damnation for it.

He could not deny his feelings for the maid. Every time they were alone together the attraction grew. If he were to remain whole after this episode, he had best get her to London as quickly as possible.

He lay in bed and thought of his options. He had none. No matter how many times he ran the facts through his mind, the same conclusion arose. He owed William his sworn oath. But unfortunately, he believed he was losing his heart to the maiden. He was caught. *God's teeth,* he thought. *There is no escape.*

"Help me, Lord. It appears I am damned if I deliver her and damned if I do not."

Chapter Seven

The fire crackled in the mammoth hearth of Castle Campbell, and the shadows danced and flickered across the walls in the quiet hour before dawn; the time when all the innocent of the land slept.

Laird Campbell laid the parchment down slowly, staring at it with unseeing eyes.

"What is it, Alec?" Guy inquired from the doorway as he smothered a yawn. The look on Alec's face, combined with the early-morning summons, boded only ill tidings.

"I have received an answer to my inquiries," he said, pointing to the document on the trestle table.

Wary, Guy walked across the room and picked up the fragile sheet. His heart nearly stopped beating when he read the words. " 'Tis an acceptance?" The cold fingers of dread chilled his spine.

"Aye, but I dinna wish to tie the lass to such as he," Campbell said, his eyes full of sorrow as he met Guy's gaze.

"Then refuse."

Alec turned away and moved to the fireplace. "I canna. 'Twould be an insult to refuse the man's suit after I invited offers."

With a sick feeling in the pit of his stomach, Guy asked the question he feared to have answered. "What reservations have you?"

"Sinclair is a rough one. I doubt he would appreciate the gentle flower."

Guy drew a deep breath to rein in his emotions. "Alec, you have a responsibility to her. Your brother would not like her condemned to such an existence."

"Nay, but the alternative is worse."

"You do not know that," Guy said, running a hand through his hair. "Would you sentence her to hell before you knew the fate that awaited her? You would be no better than Quennel, from whom you wish to protect her."

Alec sighed, dejectedly. "Perhaps Sinclair has changed."

Guy swore under his breath. He knew Alec was concerned for Gabby, but he could not credit this. "Surely, there is someone who would marry her and be a good husband."

Shaking his head in denial, the laird met Guy's damning gaze with a frank admission. "I have not yet received another reply. If ye were not a friar I would ask ye."

"Me?" Guy felt his throat constrict.

"Aye. Have ye not noticed that the two of ye are made for each other."

"You have lost your wits," Guy protested, raising his hands in a defensive gesture, then dropping them.

"Have I?"

"Oui, you have. Even if I was not a cleric and so disposed to marry her, I could not protect her. I have neither power nor land."

Alec leaned forward, his gaze pinning Guy's. "Would ye give yer life for her?"

Guy hesitated, then answered, "I would if I loved her."

Alec smiled. "Oh ye love her. Ye just have not admitted it yet."

Guy shook his head. " 'Tis wishful thinking on your part to solve your problem."

Campbell merely poured himself a drink. "I would have ye know I would be proud to welcome ye into the family."

It was a touching admission, and Guy felt the weight of it. "I would be honored to wear your plaid. But I cannot marry the girl. Even if I could, she would not have me."

"Are ye blind, man?" Alec slammed his tankard onto the table. "She canna keep her gaze off of ye."

"You must be mistaken," Guy responded gruffly, though he could not deny the prospect pleased him.

"Sometimes, friar, I wonder if ye are lack-witted on purpose. Gabby's interest in ye is more than one good Christian to another. Why, the lass is eaten up with shame over her feelings for ye. The least ye could do is admit yer attraction to her, if for nothing else but to assure her that it is normal and healthy to feel so."

"You condone it?" Guy asked, taken aback.

"Aye, if it is meant to be, than ye can no stop it. Have ye considered that the Lord works in mysterious ways? That yer union could be by His design?"

"Alec, I swear a Scot can dream up a reason to do whatever he wishes."

" 'Tis one of the reasons others wish to be Scottish."

Guy chuckled. "I wish it were in my power to make things right for all of us. But believe me, Alec, I answer to a higher power."

"Have you ever considered leaving the church?" Alec asked bluntly.

Guy drew a deep breath, intending to deny the possibility, but when he opened his mouth, he was startled by his response. "I might."

"I will hold ye to that, friar."

Guy poured himself a drink, wishing he could tell the whole of it. The subterfuge did not sit right on his shoulders. He had downed half the contents before he could look Campbell in the eye.

Alec refilled both tankards. "Pray other lairds reply. For now, I will meet with Sinclair."

"Take care not to make a hasty decision," Guy warned.

"I wish ye to meet with him also. I value yer counsel, and ye can help judge if this man is suited for Gabby."

"*Oui,* I will attend." While agreeing to be there was his duty, it would help him stop the proposed marriage. He was running out of time. He had sent a missive to William with a traveling minstrel. Hopefully, by now, William would have read the report.

Unless he received help from William, either in the form of reinforcements or legal documents, Guy would have to stop the marriage and find a way forcibly to bring Gabby to London, before she married a Scotsman.

Alec's man, Paden, entered the room, interrupting his thoughts. "My laird, more answers to yer inquiries." He dropped a pouch filled with sealed missives.

The quantity of paper made Guy's hopes fall.

Alec tore through the letters and scanned each response. "We have twenty offers."

"Of those twenty, do any impress you?" Guy asked, cautiously.

Alec took a deep breath. "To be sure, cleric, I am treating Gabby like me own daughter. Of the twenty, only five would have my blessing, but I will make my mind up after the meetings. I willna rush into things."

Guy nodded. Five might well have been five hundred. He would have to find fault with each and every one. Guy had his work cut out for him. He knew that several of these men were renowned as great warriors. "When will they arrive?" he asked.

"Within a month."

Thank God, Guy thought. He needed all the time he could get. Though it was not only time, but a solution he needed. For at present he had no idea how he was going to convince Laird Campbell that five brave Scottish candidates were unsuitable. It would be easier to spin a fairy tale than blacken a good Scotsman's name. He was beginning to curse William as the devil for giving him this impossible job.

Up until now he had always believed in William's precepts, believed that Norman rule brought the benefits of order and civilization to the unruly. For the first time he questioned his role as a conquering soldier. With an angry shake of his head, he put the doubts from his mind. He could not afford to distrust his beliefs.

Alec put his hand on Guy's back. "Ride with us. I wish to take young Louis on an exercise. The day's events I have planned will test the boy's reaction in the heat of battle."

"You have not told him?"

"Norman, if he were expecting it, he would not react the same."

Guy raised an eyebrow in answer to such a tactic. He was a guest here, and not at liberty to express his thoughts. Besides, the Scottish methods had served them well for many years. In fact, Guy considered them the best warriors on earth. If they ever united, they would be undefeatable.

After a fortnight the castle still felt unfamiliar to Gabby. Though she had visited Scotland many times before, then she had been a guest; now she was trying to be a part of the clan.

The kitchen was across the courtyard and below ground level. Just after dawn, Gabby found her way to the huge room, where her aunt was busy at work kneading bread dough on a trestle table. Several other clanswomen prepared vegetables and fruits, while exchanging stories of their families. Mouthwatering aromas filled the air as meat roasted on a spit in one of the open hearths, while in the other two fire pits, pots of thick puddings and cereals simmered over the flames.

"Do you like cooking, Aunt Mairi?" Gabby asked, rolling up her sleeves.

"I neither like nor dislike it, but it must be done if we are to keep hunger from our door."

The same was true in Normandy, but the servants and not the ladies did the work. Gabby accepted a thick chunk of dough and began to knead it as her aunt instructed. She rather liked the work; the physical exertion felt rewarding and simulating.

In Normandy I was never allowed in the kitchen, nor to go about the grounds unescorted. I find your customs much to my liking."

"We have less to fear here. However, I would like it if ye took along a guard when ye rode. Yer circumstances are different. I am pleased that ye are no' afraid of a bit of hard work. It must be yer Scottish heritage coming through."

A peasant at heart, Gabby thought humorously. If her Norman friends saw her, they would be horrified. But strangely enough, she found the routine of running a castle truly illuminating. "What other freedoms do you have? You must tell me everything," she said, drawing the avid attention of the other women.

"My, but yer are a curious little kitten," Mairi said, sharing a laugh with her clanswomen.

"Please, Aunt Mairi, if you do not tell me, how will I ever learn?"

"By watching and listening. See how yer uncle Alec treats me? I am fortunate; not every woman in Scotland is treated as I."

"Why is that?"

"Because the poor wee man is witless in love with me,"
she chuckled with fondness, as the other women smiled.

"And you him."

"Aye, it has been so since the first moment I laid eyes
on his incredible face."

Uncle Alec, incredible, she thought. Those tough, weathered, features? Good Lord, how could anyone think him
handsome? But that her aunt did was obvious. The poor
woman looked positively, dreamy-eyed when she spoke of
Alec.

"Alec was the brawest man I have ever known. In truth,
I think I love him more today than I did when he asked me
to be his wee bride."

"You are lucky." Gabby drew a deep breath, and carefully
kept her smile in place as she punched the dough repeatedly.

The clanswomen suddenly lowered their eyes to their
chores, and Gabby realized there were no secrets in the
castle.

Mairi's features softened sympathetically. "My dear, love
can flower where ye least expect it. If yer love is out there,
ye will find him."

"Aunt Mairi, you are a dreamer," she declared.

"Aye, that I am, but I believe the world would be a sad
place without dreams." She rescued Gabby's dough from
the harsh pounding, then looked up with a hopeful expression. "Do ye not agree?"

"Aye, I suppose it would. But what happens when all
your dreams and hopes are spent?"

"When that day comes, little kitten, ye are laid in yon
field and have no more to worry about," she said, placing
the dough in a bowl and covering it with a cloth.

Gabby smiled at her aunt's conclusion. Hope did indeed
last a lifetime.

"Now, lass, I have a surprise for ye," Mairi said as she
dried her hands on a linen cloth. "Follow me."

The robust woman was like a day of sunshine—radiant and warm. Gabby followed her aunt from room to room, and thanked her maker that she had found haven with this good and loving family.

As her aunt Mairi bustled through the doors of the master chamber she whirled to face Gabby, not giving her a chance to look about. "Ye must close yer eyes, my dear."

Gabby complied and heard her aunt slam the door shut, then scurry across the room. "No peeking," Mairi commanded as the sounds of soft rustling and swishing could be heard.

"Ye can open yer eyes."

Gabby complied and drew in her breath. Before her, dangling from her aunt's fingers, was the most beautiful kilt she had ever beheld.

"It is beautiful."

"It is yers."

"For me?" she asked, tears misting her vision. "But Aunt Mairi, I already have one."

"And who else would I be giving yer grandmother's kilt to if not to me favorite niece?"

Gabby accepted the kilt, then embraced the woman. "You are too kind. Many other woman would have kept this heirloom for themselves. But not my aunt Mairi."

"Go on with ye," her aunt said, embarrassed by the praise. "Try it on." She shooed her behind the screen. "We must see if it needs adjustments."

Gabby started to undress, remembering the stories of her grandmother, Moire Campbell, who also had the gift. *Suddenly the colors of the rich Campbell plaid faded as the Sight's mist enshrouded her and the murky, fog-covered moors replaced the chamber. Voices she recognized called to Louis. She saw Louis lying on the ground, his face twisted in pain as he whispered her name.*

The vision faded as quickly as it appeared. Gabby's hands

trembled as she reached for the kilt. When her fingers grazed the soft wool, a shout sounded from outside. The commotion grew louder and continued as horses whinnied and the clatter of hooves over cobblestones slowed, then stopped, in the courtyard below. Men's voices, loud and anxious, were raised in excitement.

The hairs on the back of her neck rose. "What is it, Aunt Mairi?" she asked.

" 'Tis sure an ill omen," Mairi said as she ran to the window and peered out. "Ach, a lad is being carried in."

"Who?" Gabby held her breath.

"I canna see."

By the time Gabby raced over to the window and peeked over her aunt's shoulder, the men had already carried their charge inside. Her heart skipped a beat as she retied the ties to her dress. "Quick, Aunt Mairi," Gabby said, flinging the kilt to the bed and rushing across the room for the door. "We must hurry."

"I am coming, child. I have to fetch my healing tray."

Gabby had gained the stairs when she heard her uncle. "Find Gabby and keep her busy."

It was Louis! She half ran, half stumbled down the stairs, making such a racket in her descent that her entrance captured her uncle's immediate attention. Her uncle Alec's face was drawn and his eyes cloudy as he nodded to his son Ian. Her cousin ran up to meet her, but she brushed past him, trying to see over the sea of men gathered around the trestle table. She could hear pain-filled moaning. Every sound sliced through her as she tried to pry her way into the crowd. Alec turned and blocked her advance.

"Lass, go no farther. I forbid it," he said, as Friar Guy joined them.

Terror shot through her veins. "How bad?" she whispered, looking from her uncle into the friar's compassionate blue eyes as her aunt Mairi bustled by her and disappeared into the crowd.

Guy took hold of her arm. " 'Tis not as bad as it looks, mademoiselle. But 'twould be hard on the boy if he could not cry out for fear of shaming himself in front of his kin."

"Please, do not spare my feelings. Tell me what happened," she pleaded, feeling relief from his mere touch.

" 'Twas merely an exercise gone awry. The lad is fine. Just his dignity and his derriere are injured."

"Thank God! What happened?" Gabby asked, both relieved and exasperated now that she sensed the danger was not as bad as it seemed.

"Your brother fought with a thornbush and wound up the loser."

"What?" A slight indentation appeared between her violet eyes as she held his gaze.

"He was thrown from his horse. He landed in a briar patch."

"Oh!" she said, the tension draining from her body. "And, tell me, sir, did the briar patch survive?"

"Barely," Guy said, enjoying her wit, while drawing her away from the crowd.

Taking a deep breath, Gabby let Guy lead her from the castle. Her uncle could see to Louis's injuries. He was right—her brother would indeed be embarrassed.

As they walked through the archway she heard her brother yell out and shivered.

"Put your mind at ease," Guy said, laying his arm over her shoulder and giving her a gentle squeeze.

His comforting embrace sent her thoughts flying, and her stomach roiling. "Aye," she breathed, trying to ignore the effect he had on her.

"Louis will soon be a man."

"I doubt I will ever stop worrying about him. He is all

the family I have," she said, slipping out from under his light hold to face him.

His eyebrow slanted up. "You have your aunt and uncle."

"Aye, but 'tis not the same." She sighed and turned, walking out of the keep. How could she explain the bond that existed between her and Louis?

"You are too kindhearted."

She stopped and looked at him. "Because I care for my brother as any sister would?"

"Not just your concern for your brother. Look how compassionate you were when I was wounded."

"Again, I tell you, anyone would have done the same."

"Is that why we live in a world where armed guards must accompany caravans to protect them from robbers?"

"It is hardly the same thing," she scoffed.

"True. But you are kindhearted," he insisted. "You will simply have to take my word for it."

Staring at his unyielding features, and his growing frustration, she suddenly burst out laughing. "Friar, are we quarreling about how nice I am?"

Guy's laughter joined hers as he placed his palm on the small of her back to move her out of the way of a hay wain.

She felt a tingle clear up her spine from his touch and her cheeks reddened from the momentary contact.

"Will you take another walk with me? I have a need to visit God's church."

"God's church?"

"*Oui.*" He swung his hand in a wide arc to encompass their surroundings. "The wonders of God's world abound, and I need to see the beauty of creation. The wonder and magic of His hand are evident in the simple leaf or the complex mountains, the soft clouds or the harsh sun. His miracles surround us, and their presence helps me work out my thoughts."

She took a deep breath and looked around. The bright

blue sky above, the crisp air filled with the earthy aromas of overturned fields and the landscape painted with the rich shades of autumn filled her senses with the day's texture. "You are right, friar. This is His church. It is lovely. I had not really noticed His hand in the land, but there is reason to give thanks for the sheer beauty."

"I feel closer to God out of doors than in a church," Guy said, then added softly, "Strange that I can tell you these things."

Her heart raced with the intimacy of his confidence.

"You are blushing, Lady Gabrielle. Do I make you nervous?"

"Aye . . . nay," she stammered. " 'Tis strange, but I feel as though every reaction and emotion I have in connection with you is right and good." She lowered her head. "But I know it is wrong. Forgive me."

His lips thinned, then he lifted her chin with his finger. "The fault is not yours, but mine. I have never mastered self-denial, and I fear it is long overdue."

With a quivering smile she met his gaze. His blue eyes reminded her of the sea, dark and mysterious, and though she knew it was forbidden, she wanted to delve into his depths. She cleared her throat. "I hope you will still find me worthy of being your friend." She extended her hand.

The intense scrutiny he subjected her to made her shiver. For a fleeting moment she thought he was going to refuse her offer.

"Friend," he said, grasping her hand. "I would like that."

The moment he touched her, Gabby knew that friendship was a foolish notion. Her fingers trembled and she quickly withdrew her hand. "Friar, you must have had . . . admirers before," she said, sure a man with such virile looks had attracted more women than just she. "What did you do?"

Good Lord, he's actually blushing, she thought.

"I am sorry, friar, I did not mean to pry," she said in an

attempt to save him further embarrassment. "Please forgive me."

The friar cleared his throat. "Do not trouble yourself, Lady Gabrielle. 'Tis of little import."

How kind he was. How thoughtful. "Thank you." No matter how uncomfortable, he was still trying to make this easier on her. He had risen in her estimation.

As they walked he took her hand and enfolded it in the crook of his arm. "Have you given any thought to reentering the Church?" he asked.

She glanced at her hand securely held within the shelter of his arm. "Nay. I am not suited for the religious life. Though I would do my best, I fear I would fall far short of the mark."

He chuckled. "Your honesty is refreshing. There are times when I wonder if I am suited for the life I have chosen."

Remorse filled her. She was responsible for this good man's doubts. "Friar, you do such good works. How could you consider giving up your life?"

" 'Tis nothing to concern yourself about. Everyone occasionally doubts the wisdom of a decision. I have been having these doubts for a long time."

She sighed with relief. Her burden felt much lighter now that she knew she was not wholly responsible for his doubts, though she did not discount the part she played.

"Now, my lady, I am afraid we have strayed to a far too serious topic again. Shall we try for a lighter vein?"

"Aye. That would be wonderful," she said, thinking that anything but the discussion they were having would be a welcome change. Sometimes this man seemed to have more substance than any other she had known, and that, in itself, was frightening.

"When I leave Scotland I shall miss this land and its people."

"You are leaving?" The news hit her like a punch.

"My place is in London. When our pilgrimage is over, I must return."

"Oh, I am sorry, friar." And she was, more than she could ever declare. She had come to rely on him and enjoy his company far more than she should. His departure would leave a sudden and empty space in her heart.

"Do not look so crestfallen. I will not leave for some time."

It was uncanny, but he seemed to read her mind. This man understood her better than even those whom she had known since childhood. Aye, she would miss him, probably all the days of her life.

Guy knew he was in way over his head. He had actually blushed! He was no inexperienced youth. Yet with her, the feelings seemed fresh and new.

And knave that he was, he let her believe in him. This charade was wearing his moral fabric to tatters; and of ethics, he did not have a vast supply.

Perhaps William would make a decision and this fine mess would be taken out of his hands. For the time being, he was trapped. He had no choice but to stop her suitors, then find a way to spirit her off to London.

London. He remembered how crestfallen she had looked upon hearing of his departure. Lord help him, but her sadness had elated him. He truly was a knave.

They came to a bend in the road. "Where does this lead?" Guy asked.

She smiled. "To a secluded place renowned to be popular with the fairies."

A grin split his face. "Let us have a look. I would not miss a chance to see a fairy!"

The glen was indeed a strange place. Huge boulders and tall oak trees looped with mistletoe rimmed the perimeter, but the bushes and trees that sparsely dotted the encircled area seemed stunted, their size small and deformed. Beneath his feet rested a soft carpet of tightly woven grass, not the wild growth that flourished on the moors and fields. He glanced toward her to say that the terrain did not seem to belong to the area and noticed the strange look upon her face.

"Gabby?"

She did not respond. Instinctively, he felt he knew what was happening, but he did not know what he should do.

Though it seemed forever it lasted only a few moments. Then she turned to him, her eyes searching his. "You will have a very hard decision to make, friar. 'Twill be the hardest decision of your life. You will not want to do what is right. But you will."

"How do you know?" he asked seriously.

She shrugged. "I just know."

He sensed her withdrawal. "Do you trust me?"

She nodded her head.

"If you trust me, you will confide in me."

As though weighing his words and testing their strength, she looked away and then back at him. "I did not see anything. They were just impressions and thoughts. You are very worried. Torn between two goals. Is that not so?"

"Amazing. I have heard of the gift, but never witnessed it before." He took her hand in his and found that it was trembling. He lightly squeezed her fingers and smiled. "God has favored you with such a gift," he said, watching the guarded look disappear from her eyes. "How long have you had this unusual power?"

She sighed. "All my life. Sometimes, when it is stronger, I have visions." She looked at him as though searching for approval.

Her violet eyes full of uncertainty melted his heart. "You have not told many people about it, have you?"

"Nay, only my family. My father understood, and my uncle. Bless my mother, she loved me, but was a bit afraid of my ability."

Understanding came from her Scottish side. Not surprising, since they believed in fairies and all the mystical things that others scoffed at.

"I trust my senses. This gift has been a part of me so long that I know what I feel is real. But you do not have to be polite if you feel uncomfortable. I will understand."

"I do not judge you, Gabby. 'Tis not my place. I would no more condemn you than you would have a right to pass judgment on me."

"You truly are an extraordinary man." She took a deep breath. "I should have known you are not one to scream witch and heretic. Tolerance is a very special virtue. If more people had it, there would be less hate and anger in the world. Unfortunately, tolerance is one of the least abundant wonders on God's earth and the most needed."

"Acceptance starts with one person. It will spread."

She smiled up at him. "It has been my experience that people, no matter what their beliefs, are afraid of anything they do not understand."

"True. But there is always hope."

"Aye, friar. But for those who do not share your enlightened opinion I would ask you not to reveal my secret." She squeezed his arm. "Please. Even here there are those who would not understand."

"You have my vow, I will never betray you," he said, to alleviate her anxiety. Suddenly, his lie stabbed his conscience.

To accomplish his mission, that was exactly what he would have to do—betray her.

Chapter Eight

A horrible rumble shook the earth as dirt and rock slid down the hill, sweeping away the grazing sheep along with the children who tended them in an avalanche of mud. Cries of fear and anguish filled the air. White tufts and flailing limbs dotted the murky tide before being churned beneath the flow as half the mountain slipped into the valley. When the landslide ended, only the pasture on the far side of the valley remained untouched.

Gabby bolted upright from her nap. Though a fire blazed in the hearth to ward off the dampness of the storm, she felt chilled to the bone. This was no nightmare but a vision. Perspiration coated her upper lip, and her hands trembled beneath the covers. Swallowing her fear, she pushed the covers back and stood up on shaky legs. She had foreseen the destruction of the village's children and animals. Hastily, she pulled on her clothes. Though she had rarely shared her visions, she could not remain silent. The image of the children being swept away haunted her as she ran through the castle.

Outside, the rain poured without respite and thunder cracked overhead. The booming sound shook the rafters and echoed off the walls as the wind howled around the castle. Lightning flashed an eerie light that sent shadows racing across the walls as Gabby descended the stairs. In the dimly lit hallways, torches burned in iron holders, their wavering flames small pools of yellow light in the gloomy darkness.

Every member of the clan, from wee bairn to white-haired grandfather, was gathered in the main hall for the monthly grievance hearing. Gabby ran right into the hallmoot, weaving her way through the crowd toward the front of her uncle's court.

Disregarding the young Scotsman pleading his case, Gabby pushed past him and faced the laird. "Uncle Alec, you must move the sheep in the valley. There is going to be a terrible disaster."

Alec Campbell's bushy eyebrows arched over a piercing gaze as the hall fell silent. When he stood up and leaned forward over the table, all eyes centered on her. "What say ye, lass?"

"The face of the mountain will slide into the valley, taking the wee children that tend the flock and the livestock. You must act now. You must move them to safety."

At her uncle's silence she whirled around to face the assembly. "I have seen it in my mind."

A murmur traveled through the room. Guy looked warily around. Few of the faces looked accepting of her mystic ability.

"Please," she pleaded, looking as fragile as a tiny sapling amongst a grove of oaks. Her wide-eyed violet gaze searched the room for support as she turned full circle, scanning every face until settling on Guy's. Her silent appeal reached across the room and touched a chord within him. He could not look away. She was lovelier than any woman he had known, and he fought the overwhelming desire to rush to her side.

Alec raised his hand for silence, then turned to Gabby. "Come forward and explain."

With head held high, she stepped up beside her uncle and again faced the crowd. "I have the ability to prophesy. My Sight is never wrong. I have seen a landslide. It will destroy your children, your animals . . . your entire village. You must listen to me."

"Friar, what say ye?" a frightened woman called out.

Slowly Guy rose to address the clan, unsure what he would say. He could feel the uncertainty and mistrust in the room. It was time to discredit her. A witch would not be wanted as a bride, or a clanswoman. With ill feeling directed toward her, his mission would be easily concluded. He opened his mouth, ready to damn her before the clan, then he looked into her trusting eyes. "I have witnessed Lady Gabrielle's gift. She would not warn you unless there was a reason. Mayhap, it would be to your advantage to heed her." He saw her relief and could feel no remorse for his decision. She was not a hardened soldier to be ruthlessly cut down, but a kindhearted woman.

One warrior groused. " 'Tis a lot of work for a whim."

"If I am wrong, you lose nothing but a little time. If I am right, you will save your children and livestock."

The grumbles died under that piece of logic, but there still remained an air of misgiving as the men agreed to move the herd of sheep.

"You must put them on the south pasture," Gabby said, rushing after the men as they filed out of the great room.

A high clansman turned back. "The grass is thinner there, lass."

"Aye, but they will survive there. Do not put them on the east or west hill. For the north end of the mountain will give way and take part of the adjoining hills."

The men bustled out of the castle into the inclement weather. Almost giddy with relief, Gabby twirled around, but her smile faded at the cold look of censure in the eyes of the women and children. Friar Guy joined her. "I think it best if we all say a prayer for the success of their venture."

Gabby readily closed her eyes and knelt for the invocation.

The rain continued all night and still the mountain held.

In the morning the sun shone bright and the valley remained intact. Guy noticed immediately the ill feeling directed at Gabrielle as she walked through the village. The Scots were a superstitious people. Though he hated to see her ostracised, he knew it would work to his advantage.

"My lady," he said.

"Friar, you would speak to the witch?" Gabrielle asked, her embarrassment clear.

"Oui. I believe your intentions were in the right place."

"I am afraid the good Campbells do not agree with you."

"They are afraid, alas. They will not truly turn against you, but if they should, I could always see you to safety."

"Thank you, friar." She glanced at the faces who even now refused to make eye contact. "I will spend today in contemplation," she said, and walked away, her shoulders slumped under the weight of her clan's disapproval.

When the next morning dawned without a landslide, the villagers' animosity grew.

"Witch," a clanswoman spit as Gabby tried to walk through the courtyard.

Mairi cuffed the woman on the side of the head. "Watch ye tongue, or ye be having the flat of my husband's hand instead of mine."

"Please, Aunt Mairi, the names do not bother me."

Mairi patted Gabby's hand. "I know that child, but they bother me."

"Do not worry," Louis began, as Mairi took her leave, but Gabby cut him off.

"Louis, only family or the friar speaks to me. I fear the villagers wish me gone. I have decided to wait a week, and if the landslide does not come to pass, I will leave for the abbey. I do not want to jeopardize our uncle's position," she said.

"Friar," Louis called to Guy, "please counsel my sister. She fears her prediction will bring harm to our family. I am late for practice, or I would stay and argue the matter." Louis bent and kissed her cheek before he, too, departed.

When Gabby met Guy's gaze, her indecision and worry had etched tiny lines by her mouth and eyes. Though he wished to ease the tension, he could not.

"The Sight has never failed before," she said wearily. "Now, I fear I acted rashly in warning the clan."

Guy took her elbow. "Come, we will discuss the matter."

As Gabby turned a little boy tripped and fell before her. She stooped to pick him up, soothing his cries within her embrace. Suddenly, a woman shrieked and ran toward them. "Leave me child be," she screeched, pulling her son from Gabby and hugging him to her breast.

Gabby took a deep breath. "Friar, we will leave on Sunday," she said, as her eyes brimmed with moisture.

"A wise and unselfish choice, daughter."

"I think it best if I remain out of sight today. Excuse me."

Watching her walk away Guy could take little satisfaction from the ease with which he would wrest her from Scotland. Her shoulders suddenly shook, and he knew she had lost her battle to hold back her tears. When she disappeared inside the castle he pivoted to face the villagers. "You should all be ashamed of your behavior." He stared at the clanswomen until they lowered their gazes or walked away. Sunday could not come soon enough. The way his blood pounded, he was dangerously close to exposing his masquerade.

On the morning of the sabbath, a terrible rumbling shook the very ground. The villagers ran out of their cottages in fear. After the terrible noise died and the trembling subsided, the braver of the lot investigated and found the whole north face of the mountain lying in the valley. The south end remained untouched, and the children and livestock were uninjured.

The villagers rejoiced. With loud voices, they stormed the castle, pouring into the great hall and demanding to see Lady Gabrielle.

When Gabby stepped to the banister and peeked over, her hands covered her cheeks, stifling a gasp. Down in the great hall the clan gathered and knelt before her. Even the woman who had screamed witch ran up the stairs and kissed her hem.

"My son would be buried under the mountain if ye had na warned us. Bless ye, my lady. Forgive me for doubting ye."

Gabby reached down and helped the woman to her feet. "Please do not humble yourself so," she said.

"My lady . . ."

"Shh." Gabby cut off a further apology and hugged the woman. "All is forgiven."

Though the crowd was so large it spilled out of the castle and into the courtyard, the room was hushed when Gabby turned and gestured for the clan to stand. "I am indeed fortunate to have your support."

The crowd roared in approval.

Guy stood at the hearth and watched his dreams of whisking Gabby away die under the barrage of admiration. He looked heavenward and gave a wry smile. "You could have waited until after we left Scotland to fulfill her prophesy," he silently gibed.

"Giving thanks, good friar?" Alec chuckled, slapping Guy on the back.

"I talk to God often."

" 'Tis a practice I will take up," Alec said, joining his clansmen in celebration.

Guy drank in the joy on Gabby's face. He could never begrudge her this happiness, no matter his predicament now that the good Campbells would never let such a heroine leave.

He shook his head at his own action. He had never considered himself a fool, but after this chivalrous act he could not deny, that where this woman was concerned, his judgment was impaired. He could not allow such another mistake.

News of Lady Gabrielle's accurate prediction spread throughout the countryside. Her reputation among the Scots rose to dizzying heights, and responses to Alec's request for a husband poured in, assuring a large turnout for her hand. The first potential bridegroom arrived in mid-October and the trees stood as sentinels dressed in brilliant coats of red and orange by the time all the contenders arrived.

The hall was filled with thick brogues that made Alec's Scottish accent seem mild in comparison.

With a reverent look on his young features, Ian turned to his cousin Louis. "These lairds of the North country are indeed well deserving of their reputations," he whispered. "Their victories in battle are, and will continue to be, legends of the Highlands."

Guy's stomach lurched at that piece of information, while Alec laughed appreciatively. " 'Tis a grand gathering indeed. How do I choose among so many fine examples?"

"Why not let the choice belong to Lady Gabrielle?" Guy offered, hoping the man would take his advice to heart.

Louis shook his head. "Nay, Uncle Alec. My sister will not know who is best suited for her."

"I will choose," Alec announced. "But 'tis just as

important not to offend the others as it is to choose the right man. I have decided on a contest.''

''A contest?'' Guy said, horrified by the prospect, while Louis and Ian smiled their approval.

''Aye, 'tis the only fair way. Dinna ye agree, friar? Scots by nature are gaming people. These warriors would relish and abide by a test of strength and valor.''

Guy scanned the crowd of thick-muscled, heavy-chested men. Besides physical strength, every man there wielded great power. A contest was the only logical choice. Reluctantly, Guy met Alec's gaze. *''Oui,* 'tis the only way to keep peace.''

''Aye, now ye have the way of it.'' Alec smiled and slapped him on the back. ''Take heart, friar. The victor of such a contest will be well able to protect Gabrielle.''

Alec then turned to the assembly. Raising his arms for quiet, he began his welcome to the visiting clan chieftains. When the laird spoke, every member of the crowd remained still, listening with respectful silence as he outlined the *wedding list.* Guy silently groaned. Discrediting these men would be impossible.

God's teeth! Somehow he had to find a way to prevent gifting Gabby to the strongest knight. Thinking of her as some brute's trophy nettled his nerves, which did not make plotting any easier.

Only two choices came to mind. He could either kidnap her and make for London now, or enter the lists and vie for her hand. He realized both plans were pathetic, but unlike his brother, Royce, Guy was not known as a great strategist.

He stared at the crowd as the laird finished his speech. Kidnapping was ill-advised at best. It would be impossible to slip past these men with the Campbell heroine kicking and screaming in his arms. *Non,* he would have to fight for her. Being a fair-minded and lusty people, the Scots would understand if the needs of the flesh overcame the needs of the spirit.

Guy had a week to prepare. According to Alec, the contest would begin on the first high tide in November, known as All Hallow's tide, and the matches would continue throughout the day until only one man stood victorious.

Alec lifted his chalice in the air and the men followed suit, cheering. Alec saluted their toast, then turned to Guy and said quietly, "Mayhap, friar, ye might want to enter the lists yerself."

Guy stared into those knowing eyes and remained silent.

"If ye do wish to compete, know that I would consider yer suit a valid one."

" 'Tis an honor you do me, Alec. I will think on it."

"Dinna take too long, laddie. The field grows thicker each day."

"Oui, I can see there are many to vie for the lovely Lady Gabrielle's hand."

"Did ye doubt there would be?"

"Non, though I wondered how many of them would be willing to risk William's wrath?"

"Most of them have ties with the Danes. King William would not like to risk a confrontation, not until he solidifies his position in England."

Guy raised an eyebrow at the Scot's astuteness, for he had a good understanding of politics. "Why would you accept me as a candidate? I am Norman, and an unlanded one at that."

"Gabrielle has a considerable dowry. Once married to a decent man, who has her best interests at heart, she is safe from Quennel's revenge."

"If under my protection, Aumont would never harm her," Guy said, surprised by his own vehemence. There was no help for it; he would have to enter the lists. Once victorious, he could take the girl with him to London and be rid of this trouble once and for all.

William was greatly disturbed by Ancil's report. "Do you have proof?"

"*Non,* my liege. But I believe Quennel Aumont is responsible not only for his brother-in-law's death, but his sister's as well."

"Then issue an invitation to Quennel Aumont to visit my court. I wish to meet this knave."

"As you wish, sire." The scribe took the instruction down.

"And Ancil,"—the king turned, stopping Ancil from securing his parchments—"send a message to Abbess Ambrose. I wish a written report, detailing everything she knows about Lady Gabrielle."

"Abbess Ambrose, my lord?"

"The only way to win this game is to have all the information before the players are in place."

Ancil had begun to pick up his papers again when the king started talking anew. Sighing, the little man regained his seat.

"I also want a missive sent to Alec Campbell. Tell Laird Campbell that the king would be greatly displeased if anything should happen to the Lady Gabrielle. I shall consider her stay a visit, and expect the lady to return when I send for her."

"My lord?" Ancil questioned, wondering why the king was forewarning the man.

"'Tis a political game, Ancil. I want Alec Campbell to know I am aware of everything he does. 'Twill make him wonder what my next move will be."

Ancil bowed and gathered up his work. Holding the papers tightly to his chest he started for the door, only to have the king stop him halfway. "Three more missives. One to Royce de Bellemare. Advise him 'tis time for him to make use of his Scottish ties because I fear Guy is in great peril. He must proceed to the Campbell stronghold and give *Friar Guy* and Lady Gabrielle an escort to North Umberland. Place this in the packet also." He handed the scribe a sealed letter.

"*Oui,* my lord?"

"Also send an inquiry, along with these personal documents I have prepared"—he held up a sealed packet—"to the castle where Louis Aumont fostered."

Before Ancil departed, the king picked up the last missive that a minstrel had delivered. After reading it through, he shook his head. "Lastly, draft a letter to Guy de Bellemare and send it by way of the bishop. Inform him that I agree with his recommendation about the boy. Louis Aumont can remain in Scotland. As for Gabrielle Aumont . . ." William paced back and forth across the room. He needed time to study all the reports before he brought the girl to London. "Tell Guy his orders are not to return directly to London, but stay in North Umberland with the girl and bide his time until I send for him. In addition, tell Guy to use whatever means are necessary, but do not, under any circumstances, let the lady wed a Scotsman." He thumped the table with his fist. "We cannot afford to lose the Aumont dowry."

"Is that all, my lord?" Ancil asked hesitantly.

"*Oui.* Once these missives are sent, seek your rest."

Two of Quennel's half-starved peasants followed the road to the northern climes. Along the way they asked questions of those they encountered, but met with severe resistance. Normans were not welcome in Scotland; they were outlanders.

"What makes you think they have come this way, Soren?" the one with the hideous scar on his cheek asked.

"Because every stubborn Scot has directed us else-where."

"Do you think they will be found at this gathering we have heard about?"

"I am certain of it," Soren said, pushing the loose strands of his white hair beneath his cap. "But we need to dress as Scotsmen, or we will never get close to the girl. In the next shire we must change our tunics for kilts. We will listen and say naught. Once we possess the information we need, our job is half-done."

"I have no stomach for finishing the job."

"Would you rather go cold and hungry this winter? Do you want your family to starve, Evarard?"

"I will do what I must, but I do not have to like it. And for all your bluster, neither do you, brother."

Soren shrugged his shoulders. "We have little choice in the matter."

Gabby looked out the window and marveled at the assembly below. Lairds from all over northern Scotland had crowded the courtyard. Heavily muscled, long-haired warriors gathered in the inner bailey, while curious clansmen waited just beyond the gate. Leaves swirled and whipped about as the wind gusted. Kilts billowed out, showing muscular legs and a knee or two.

"Why, their hair is nearly as long as mine," Gabby breathed. Although the Campbell clan wore their hair long, it was not of the absurd length worn by the warriors below.

Friar Guy, with his Norman style, stood out like a shorn sheep. Her gaze traveled over him. If not for the hair, he could easily pass for one of the northern lairds. His bronzed skin and thick muscles were the equal of any, and a shiver went up her spine at the memory of his warm skin beneath her fingers. As if he sensed her lustful thoughts, his head lifted, and he held her regard. When he smiled at her, her heart tightened and fluttered in her chest.

"Well, my dear, it is time. Shall we let them once again see what they are competing for?" her aunt Mairi asked.

Gabby turned slowly from the window. "I do not like this," she said truthfully. She felt like a bag of grain at auction. Though she brought a rich dowry to her husband, she knew that word of the Sight had spread. The lairds came because she had the gift. All week long the men had rushed to her side if she appeared to take her repast. In truth, their fawning had become so wearisome that she now took most of her meals in her room.

"Now, lamb, dinna fret." Her aunt ran an appraising hand over Gabby's hair, then straightened the drape of her apparel. Once satisfied, she took hold of her hand. "I am sorry it canna be as ye hoped. Courage, lass, Alec will do what is right."

"Such as set me on the steps and call out bids!"

Mairi sighed. "It does seem like we are selling ye to the highest bidder, but yer uncle wants to be assured ye are safe from Quennel Aumont. Do ye ken, every laird out there would lay down his life for ye. There willna be chance of anyone breaching their defenses to do ye harm."

"I am aware of why I must marry. Still, it is unnerving. They look at me with such eager anticipation."

"It is called desire, lass."

Gabby's face flushed with warmth as images of Friar Guy suddenly appeared. "Please, Aunt Mairi. I do not want to discuss such things."

"Has no one told ye about what to expect after ye wed?" Mairi asked, pursing her lips.

"My nurse explained as best she could, but she was not expansive."

"Well, then my lass, I will not be so vague."

"*Non!* I do not want to hear," Gabby said, remembering

with embarrassment how she had peeked under the friar's blanket.

Mairi shook her head. "Ignorance will not serve thee well," she said sternly, but her expression softened when she saw Gabby's real distress. "Never mind, lass. With any of the men out there I would wager ye will not be disappointed on yer wedding night."

"Enough," Gabby pleaded, feeling her stomach turn. How could she admit to Mairi that it was not ignorance, but an unmaidenly curiosity, that made her react this way. "I will learn when 'tis seemly, on my wedding night."

"As ye wish, lass. But by the end of the lists when you face yer intended ye may grow more curious," Mairi said. After making last-minute adjustments to the kilt and pinning another pleat, she held Gabby at arm's length. "There, ye are ready to meet yer fate."

Never in all her life had Gabby felt less ready to meet anything, much less her fate.

Guy watched Gabby walk out into the courtyard, and his breath caught in his throat. Beautiful did not begin to describe her. The sun shone on her hair, lighting the silken black tresses with hidden blue lights. Her cheeks, either warmed by the sun, or all the ardent admiration, were softly colored by a light, becoming blush. She was stunning. As he looked around the courtyard he did not like the gleam in the other men's eyes.

"My niece, Lady Gabrielle," Alec announced to the assembly.

Gabby made a full curtsy before the crowd, and they abruptly stilled.

"God's teeth, she is as lovely as a princess," Ian murmured.

Guy concurred wholeheartedly, and so did every other male.

All but one. "I do not know what all the fuss is about. 'Tis merely Gabby," Louis said morosely.

Guy guessed that the boy was feeling the pangs of separation and did not know how to express it.

"Your sister will miss you a great deal when she leaves," he said to the lad while keeping his eyes on the men being presented to Gabby.

"Aye, that she will. She will not have anyone to boss around," Louis said, unwilling to admit his loss.

Guy smiled at the ploy, but his smile faded as he saw one overly amorous man linger too long at his presentation.

His eyes narrowed as he watched the proceeding.

"What is troubling you, friar?" Louis asked.

When the cleric continued to stare without responding, Ian nudged Louis's side with a sharp elbow. He jutted his chin at Gabby, then the friar. "Love," he whispered knowingly.

Louis shook his head in denial, but suddenly he, too, looked at his sister and the friar in a contemplative way.

Guy was so absorbed in the tableau he did not notice their actions. "Think it seemly that your sister has no champion she knows?" he said.

" 'Tis the way of it," Louis said.

"I will ride for her favor."

"You cannot!" Louis laid his hand on the friar's arm. "You are of the Church."

"I have already decided to leave the religious life," Guy said, drawing a deep breath to gain control of his displeasure as he watched the men filing before her. He could not stand another minute of this fawning.

Louis looked dumbfounded, but Ian merely nodded in agreement.

Guy knew he was courting disaster, but it was done. He

marched forward and bowed before Alec and Gabrielle. "With your permission, I will enter the lists."

Stunned gasps and murmurs of disapproval sounded in the hall at his suit.

Alec held up his hands. "This man has my approval. He, like anyone else, is eligible."

At Alec's announcement, loud challenges issued forth.

"He is a man of the cloth." One chieftain stated what the others only mumbled. A chorus of agreement rose.

"A cleric can renounce his vows." Alec turned to Guy. "Tell them true, lad. What is in yer heart?"

Guy turned to face the men. "I have discovered I do not have a true calling and have followed my conscience. I do not belong in the order. I do, before God and this assembly, publicly proclaim it."

Silence met his oath.

Alec stepped forward and stood beside Guy, subtly, signaling his allegiance. "Does any man object to this suit given in good faith?"

A bark of laughter sounded from a barrel-chested chieftain in the center of the assembly. "Nay. Cleric or not, 'tis all the same to my sword. 'Tis not a contest to the death. If he wants to have a chance, I will not deny him."

His speech seemed to set the tone as others heartily agreed lest they be thought afraid to fight a former cleric.

At Alec's nod, Guy turned to Gabby, whose eyes were round in surprise. Then ever so slowly a soft, beguiling smile spread across her lips. The pure pleasure of her approval made the insanity of his decision worthwhile. Whatever happened in the future, he would always remember how her violet eyes sparkled when she learned he intended to fight for her hand.

Alec stepped forward and slapped him on the back in good fellowship. " 'Tis the right decision."

Guy knew he was right, but a small problem still nagged him. He felt himself crossing a threshold in his life from which there was no turning back. The challenge of the lists bothered him not, but coming under the spell of Gabrielle's bewitching violet eyes terrified him.

Chapter Nine

"Alec, would you lend me the use of a sword and shield?" Guy asked as they made their way through the crowd in the great hall.

"Aye, I would be proud if ye would take my sword and wear my colors into battle," Alec responded, meeting the other chieftains' curious gazes with a nod.

Guy looked down at his blue-and-green kilt. What had Alec expected him to wear?

When he looked up again, he saw a smile teasing Alec's lips.

"My ancestors fought without any clothes. 'Tis an honorable way to fight."

"Not for me. I prefer to keep my backside covered."

Alec chuckled, and slapped him on the back. "Then ye be no Scot," he said, as they joined Ian and Louis.

"*Non.* I lay no claim to that. Though it would seem I am vying to marry one."

"Ye were not meant for the Church. 'Twould be a sin to

force a man into such a life, when he was obviously not suited for it. Why, pray tell, did ye ever think ye were meant for the religious life?''

''I did not, but my family did,'' Guy said honestly before he could stop himself. Why was he telling the truth to these people? They were becoming friends, and that was the worst mistake of all. It would make his mission that much harder.

''Go with Ian and Louis to the armory.'' Alec turned to his son. ''Lad, see Guy is given my finest sword.''

''Aye, Father,'' Ian said, while Louis stared in awe at the honor.

''What about Lady Gabrielle?'' Guy asked, watching her meet the few men left in the line. ''I beg you, do not leave her alone with all those men.''

Alec smiled. ''Dinna fear. I will return to her side.''

Guy followed Ian from the great room, while Louis kept pace beside him.

''Why are you doing this?'' Louis asked, Ian glanced back over his shoulder, a curious light in his deep blue eyes as he waited for the answer.

''Louis, you have much to learn about men and woman.''

''I would rather not know any more than I do.''

''You keep up that attitude, and you are likely to get your wish.''

''What is so special about my cousin?'' Ian asked, as they rounded a corner and headed down a long, narrow hallway.

''Ian, there is nothing sweeter than hearing the right woman say your name.''

''Friar Guy,'' a woman's voice hollered, the words reverberating within the closed hall. Though shrill and grating, Gabby's voice was easily recognized.

Snickering, Louis raised an eyebrow and peered at Guy, who ignored the sardonic grin of his companions and turned to watch Gabby turning the corner in uncommon haste.

''You can't do this,'' she said, nearly out of breath as she skidded to a stop before him, her hair settling like a soft cloud about her shoulders.

For a moment he could do nothing but stare, stunned by her soft, innocent beauty.

Her cheeks were rosy, her eyes as big as violets opening to the sun, as she reached out and touched his arm. "I am honored, but you can't leave the church."

Taken aback by her request, he eyed her sharply. "If I no longer wish to be a friar, it would be a mistake to stay."

She looked about and wrung her hands. "But—"

"My mind is made up." He folded his hands across his chest. "Do you not want me in the lists?"

"Nay!" she blurted out, her face coloring at the denial.

Relief surged through him as she caught her breath. Gazing at her slightly parted lips, he had an overwhelming desire to kiss her.

"I mean, I want you in the contest, that is the problem." Her eyes lowered. "Forgive me, I have fought against my own selfish desires, yet when you are near, my heart beats faster, and when you are not, memories crowd my mind; your image, and the sound of your voice, fill my senses to dispel the loneliness. Though I try to deny the attraction, just the sound of your voice thrills me, and your touch leaves me shaken and tingling. I know how deeply I care, but I never dreamed you would return that affection. To realize you feel the same takes my breath away." She drew in a ragged breath, and her shoulders trembled. "Now that I know you are within reach it will be that much harder to accept your loss when you are defeated."

"Gabrielle!" Louis exclaimed, embarrassed by her assumption.

Her head snapped up and she frowned at her brother. "Louis, I am sorry for speaking so truthfully. But how can a friar hope to match the others? They are hardened men of war."

Guy was not offended, for her honesty was one of the many qualities he prized. He took hold of her shoulder and turned her to face him. Their gazes met, and suddenly this innocent contact was filled with sensual awareness. He felt himself responding to the longing and concern shining openly in her expressive eyes. She moistened her lips, and heat flared through his veins. His heart raced and he pulled her into a loose embrace, her body softly touching his. She lowered her gaze, but he placed his finger beneath her chin and lifted it, refusing to let her look away. "I promise you, I will hold my own in the lists."

She closed her eyes. "I do not want to see you injured."

His heart skipped a beat, and he smoothed back a silken strand of dark hair that brushed her cheek. The touch of her soft skin beneath his fingers tested his willpower to the limit. God, he wanted to kiss her. "I will be all right," he said hoarsely. "Have faith and say a prayer."

Her eyelashes fanned wide. "I will say *many prayers*," she said fervently.

Guy chuckled at her impassioned response.

Tears brightened her violet eyes as she looked up at him. "I must return before I am missed. Good luck, friar."

She started to pull out of his arms, but he held her still. "Under the circumstances, could you not say my name?"

"Guy," she said, and the throaty whisper surrounded him like the veil she now offered. "Please wear my favor, for it is you I wish to see victorious." Her hand touched his cheek. "Guy," she said again. The sound of her voice offered a promise that could not be denied.

He watched her until she disappeared from sight, and still his gaze remained fixed. "You see, Ian. The right woman can say your name and then the music of her voice plays over in your head, whispering to you when you need to hear the familiar melody."

"Then you really do care for her?" Louis asked in awe.

"I really do." Upon hearing his own words, Guy could no longer deny the truth. He cared, and cared deeply.

"Come, I will help you choose your weapon for next week," Louis said, as Ian once again led the way.

Guy chuckled at Louis's serious expression. "You seem to have as little faith in me as your sister."

"You have led a life of prayers and books. In a few days you will meet men who have wielded the sword because their very lives depended on their skill. What would you think, friar, if you were I? Would you hold no doubts?"

"Oui. But before I entered God's house I led the life of a paid soldier."

"Ye were a mercenary?" Ian asked.

"Oui. And I take exception to slurs cast upon my prowess by your cousins. You will see in due time that I am still fit."

"I hope I will, Guy. For if ye are not as capable as ye think, I am not the one who will suffer, but ye," Ian said as he opened the door to the armory and stepped aside.

The lad had a point. Guy's skills were fresher than anyone knew, and he had no doubt he would hold his own. But nothing less than victory would be acceptable.

The armory was more elaborate than Guy had expected. If there was one thing the Scots took good care of, it was their weapons. The size, shape, and quality of every one he saw bespoke the expertise and pride this clan possessed.

Ian walked over to the wall and removed a blade with a blood red ruby embedded in the hilt. "Tis my father's sword," he said, handing it to Guy.

Guy took several test swings. "A fine weapon," he said, then surprised both Ian and Louis by returning it to its place on the wall. At Louis's aghast expression and Ian's studied censure, he explained, "I am honored that Alec would offer his claymore. But as I live and breathe, that sword belongs not in a Norman bastard's hand, but only in the grip of a

Campbell laird." He looked at Ian. " 'Tis the symbol of the clan, and should only be used by you and your father."

At Ian's understanding nod, Guy turned back to the wall and chose another sword. Though Alec's sword was an excellent piece of craftsmanship, he preferred a less elaborate design.

"Guy, 'tis a poor choice," Louis protested.

"*Non.* It feels right in my hand and will serve me well," Guy said. " 'Tis not the weight of the sword that will win this contest, but the strength and speed of the opponent. We will be fighting on foot. If I were on horseback I would have chosen differently."

Louis looked unconvinced.

"Trust me. I know what I am about."

"Friar, I hope the Lord is with you, for I fear you will need divine help," Louis offered. "Thank God, you have a week to practice before the contest begins."

Guy wanted to cuff the insolent pup, but laughed instead. Perhaps the lad was right. In any case, it could not hurt his cause if divine aid was forthcoming. He made the sign of the cross and said a quick prayer.

Royce de Bellemare laid down the king's missive, then picked up and reread his father-in-law's report from Scotland. "Guy, you poor fool."

"What is it, husband?" Bethany asked as she tucked their twins into bed.

"Guy is in trouble," he said, and briefly explained Guy's circumstances. He tapped the report against the table. "I am afraid, my love, that I must go and help my brother."

Bethany crossed the floor and stood beside Royce's writing table. When he leaned back in his chair, she bent over and kissed her husband on the cheek. "Give Guy my love and take care no harm comes to you. Your sons would be greatly distressed, not to mention their mother.''

"I love you, wife," he said, pulling her into his embrace and kissing her with warmth and tenderness.

"I love you, too." She laughed. "With my blessing, go rescue your brother and this woman. I would have a look at the lady who has stolen your brother's heart.''

"Is it his heart or his wits? I must say, I am looking forward to offering as much unneeded advice about love as Guy once foisted upon me." Royce smiled at the thought of his revenge.

"Remember, husband," Bethany said, caressing the side of his cheek, "Guy meant well. If not for his interference, you never would have admitted you loved me.''

"Bethany, I would have died for you, which should have been enough. I would eventually have admitted my love without my brother's prodding.''

Bethany chuckled, slipping off his lap. "Aye, but by then we both would have been too old to enjoy it.''

"Careful, wife, I am not doddering yet," he warned smiling, then returned his attention to the letters.

He re-read the missive and sealed letter from King William, mentally turning over strategies to enter Scotland. "I pray Guy stays safe until I can reach him," he muttered, raking his hand through his thick, black hair. The moment the words left his mouth, he saw his wife grow still.

"Royce?" She turned, her face strained with worry. "Does King William expect trouble?" Bethany asked, coming to her husband's side.

"*Oui*. He also wants me to join up with the Mactavish.''

Bethany shook her head at the gravity of the situation. "That will be more difficult than William knows.''

"*Oui,* I am aware of it. In the morning I will journey to your father's home and convince him of the merit of supporting William's cause.''

Bethany's arms encircled him. " 'Twill take more than words to convince my father."

He hugged her to him and fervently kissed her forehead. "I am aware of how stubborn your family can be." His frown appeared. "My brother's life depends on a united front. I will persuade your father to ride with me. William wants only a friendly show of power."

The mist cleared and a tall, white-haired warrior, his eyes the same unique, blue as Guy's, lifted his bloodstained sword. "You have wronged my family, my sons, and my honor. I must now right the wrong set in motion twenty years ago."

The soldier kneeling on the ground stretched out his arms in supplication. "Mercy, Lemieux. I did as I was bidden by my master."

Lemieux ran the man through with one lunge. Slowly withdrawing his sword, he turned to a younger version of himself. "I have been an idiot, Rule. We must go to Britain. Royce and Guy have been misjudged."

The younger man did not look pleased. "Let the past go, Father."

"If it were you, my son, would you wish me to walk away?"

"Nay, but after all this time, they will not forgive you."

"I must try."

Gabby awoke, bathed in perspiration. She could not recall the whole dream, and the partial memory haunted the fringes of her mind. The ruthless killer of her vision . . . was he truly her beloved's father? Whoever this tall, silver-haired warrior was, he would enter Guy's life soon. She wanted to tell Guy of her strange dream, but her fears could not be shared. Not this time. Tomorrow the contest began. He had enough on his mind.

* * *

On the long-awaited day of the matches, a cloudless blue sky promised a fine day. Many visitors had come to watch the contest, and the village overflowed with commerce and trade.

Since a former cleric was not considered a serious contender, Guy, to his chagrin, was scheduled to fight the lesser-known lairds. He was glad his brother, Royce, warlord of North Umberland, was not there to witness his humbling. Though Guy felt the bite to his pride, he recognized the stroke of luck. No one would know his prowess with a weapon until it was too late. He had practiced in the woods away from the men.

He carefully studied his opponents as Ian imparted important information about each laird. Guy had two contests in the morning. Each one he won, but since several matches were occurring at the same time and his was of lesser import, he drew few spectators.

Around him villagers hawked their roasted meat or baked scones, while children ran exuberantly around the field. With each new match, soldiers gathered at the roped-off area, watching their chieftains fight. Ian pointed out the most powerful contenders, and Guy marveled that all visitors honored their host's rules. Though it was not a fight to the death, many Scots were injured and had to be carried off the field, yet their men remained on the sidelines and did not engage in the battle.

In between contests Guy's gaze strayed repeatedly to Gabby, who sat on a raised dais, watching the affair with her aunt and uncle. She looked strained, and as the day progressed he could see the toll being taken on her lovely features.

After the midday meal Guy had his third match. This one was difficult. His opponent had great skill to eliminate his adversaries and advance to this level in the contest. Guy suffered a slash to his leg before he managed to defeat the laird. His victory made him a finalist.

After Guy's leg was stitched, Ian pointed to the field.

Two great warlords of the North, each sporting long, flowing hair and a great wild beard, faced off with claymores. The red-haired giant looked familiar, and Guy leaned toward Ian.

"Who are these lairds?" he asked.

"Fenrir Gunn, from Caithness," Ian said, pointing to the redhead one, "and Laird Mackay. I'm certain he is the one my father favors."

Guy remembered Fenrir Gunn and frowned; the laird had suffered defeat at Royce's hand not long ago. One could only hope that the redheaded warrior would not recall Guy.

A brutal fight ensued on the field, and Guy waited to see who was victorious. Unfortunately, Fenrir Gunn won the match. If Guy had not declared earlier, he certainly would have done so now.

Guy caught Gabby's anxious look as he passed before the stand to take his place on the field. Lord, but her eyes were expressive, or maybe he was more attuned to them. Her concern was etched into every solemn feature. But even worry could not dim her beauty. When their gazes met and held, he was lost in her spell. Then she moved her sensuous lips and he read the silent words she mouthed: "Be careful, Guy." The memory of her voice echoed in his mind; the soft seductive way she'd said his name warmed his blood and filled his heart. He felt invincible, and touched beyond measure that her concern was for him, when her very fate hinged on the outcome of this contest. Later, he would take her in his arms and comfort her. The thought drove him wild.

The moment the redheaded chieftain raised his sword, Guy's attention snapped back to the conflict.

Though large and strong, Fenrir Gunn was also agile, a deadly combination. He had bested all contestants. But Guy had discovered his opponent's weakness. Fenrir Gunn dropped his left shoulder just before swinging his sword in a downward arc. It was a crucial piece of information that would give Guy the edge. Before the redheaded warrior knew how or why, Guy had scored several damaging blows and blocked every thrust made.

The Highland chief's face turned bright red as he tried in vain to surprise Guy.

The final blow came quickly. When the Scot made a strategic lunge forward, Guy neatly sidestepped the attack, moving out of harm's way to trip his off-balance opponent. Guy had the advantage and pressed it. With his sword poised at the giant's throat, he yelled, "Yield!"

Fenrir Gunn's eyes glowed with hatred. Suddenly a gleam of recognition shone in the red-rimmed gaze. "Ye," he spit.

"Yield," Guy repeated, pressing his sword against the man's flesh. "Do you wish to die?"

Alec rushed down from the platform, drawing his own sword. "Yield, Fenrir," he ordered.

The wind blowing through the trees was the only sound that could be heard.

When the warrior finally grunted, the match was called in Guy's favor before any blood was let.

The crowd cheered as Guy sheathed his sword, and the vanquished laird stood and stumbled back. Amidst the clamorous celebration, the Lady Gabrielle dashed down the field to join her hero.

Alec beamed at Guy, and said, "Will ye wed the lady?"

Guy looked at Gabby's beautiful face and for moments was lost in the wonder and awe of her perfection. "I will."

"Nay," Fenrir roared. He stood only several yards away, pointing his finger at Guy. "He is ineligible. He deceives us."

Guy's stomach twisted. He would not allow himself to be exposed! He advanced on the man before Alec could intervene, his sword drawn. "I have beaten you fairly, Scot. Do you now choose death instead of defeat?"

The redheaded Scot's eyes grew round with fear as perspiration dotted his forehead, and he stilled beneath Guy's soft-voiced threat and sharp-edged sword.

Alec stepped into the confrontation. " 'Twas a fair fight Gunn. How can ye call foul?"

A silence again descended on the field. Gunn looked around, and his face flushed at the open disdain of the clansmen. "Aye, he has won fairly, I willna dispute the fight."

Guy relaxed. He had not been denounced as a fraud. Fenrir Gunn needed his clan's approval more than he feared Guy's threat. But when Gunn turned back, a gleam of cunning shone in his eyes.

"Still, the man deceives us. He is without honor." Fenrir snarled, as Alec held Guy back.

Cries of outrage filled the air.

Fenrir turned to his clansmen. "Hear me! My concern is not for myself but for the lady. I am familiar with this man's family. His brother fought for a maiden's hand and then made her his slave, not taking her for wife until almost a year later. This man is a friar and now would have us wait until the Pope grants him dispensation to marry. Would ye have Lady Gabrielle suffer such an injustice? I have beaten all contenders except this man, who I consider ineligible, and I am willing to wed the lady now."

Several of Gunn's clansmen yelled approval, while the other Scotsmen remained silent.

Alec held up his hands. "Must I remind the good lairds, that all of ye agreed to let the friar compete. He has won the right to take my niece in marriage."

"But when will he?" a clansman shouted. Gunn smirked and folded his arms across his chest.

Guy stepped forward and drove his sword into the dirt. "I have given my word, and I will honor it."

Alec looked around at the clansmen. "Would it satisfy ye if he took her in the rites of our ancestors," he said, stretching his arms out to encompass all the contestants, "so each and every man will know he entered this contest in good faith?"

Guy glanced at the faces of the Scottish lairds. By their expressions they were of one mind. It was little enough to do in exchange for their trust.

" 'Tis done," he said, his gaze returning to his opponent's angry face. "I will undergo your heathen ceremony to put your mind at rest." Then he turned to Gabby, and the vision of her loveliness and innocent, trusting expression dissolved his anger. "I *shall* wed the maiden," he declared.

Chapter Ten

Alec nodded in approval. "Aye, ye have his word on it. Dinna worry, I am here to see it done proper," he said, escorting Fenrir Gunn back to the castle. With Alec's departure the soldiers and villagers followed, until the field was empty of spectators. Guy and Gabby stood alone.

"You fought for me," she said in awe.

"Your uncle was not pleased with the man who was winning."

"You had already entered the lists," she said, smiling. "I do indeed owe you an apology for doubting your skill. Someday, when you wish to talk about it, you must tell me where you learned to fight. It is obvious you are no ordinary soldier, nor in any way an ordinary man."

" 'Tis a wonder when a betrothed thinks her intended is no ordinary man. See that you always have such respect for your husband."

She chuckled at his lighthearted jest. "Aye, my lord. I will give you all the respect you deserve."

Her eyes sparkled, and her lips parted in a lovely smile. He found it near impossible to stop from taking her in his arms and kissing her as witless as she made him.

His heated gaze must have reminded her where they were. "My uncle left us alone. In Normandy 'twould not be allowed."

"Whoever said Scotland was a backward country was a fool. 'Tis a land made for love and desire."

Her cheeks blushed a becoming pink before she lowered her gaze.

He raised her chin. "Never be embarrassed with your husband," he whispered. When his lips touched hers, he was lost. Within their embrace a special union existed. He could not stop himself from kissing her. His lips moved over hers, slanting, coaxing, begging entry, and like a flower blossoming to the sun, she responded eagerly. His tongue stroked her lips before slipping in to taste her nectar, while his hands reached out to caress her arms, her nape, her back. Stroking, touching, tasting, he could not get enough of her essence. She tried, in her innocence, to imitate his movements and he was humbled—and aroused—that her desire overcame her shyness. His hands roamed over her soft feminine curves, pulling her closer into his embrace. Her body melded with his, and he ached with need. At that moment Guy realized that he could never just walk away from this woman. No matter their fate, she would haunt him for the rest of his days.

"Will you always be such an ardent lover?" she whispered, breathlessly.

"Always," he replied, watching a dreamy expression soften her features. When she snuggled farther into his embrace, he cupped her chin and kissed her lightly on the lips. "Gabby, never fear that my feelings for you will change."

She touched his cheek with a reverent caress. "From the

moment I laid eyes on you, Guy, I felt a powerful bond existed between us."

He had, too.

Suddenly, her face reddened, and she lowered her gaze. "It is time I should confess that I . . . found you appealing even when you wore the robes of a cleric."

He smiled. "I also found you appealing, even when you were dressed as a nun."

Her head snapped up, and she looked at him with wonder. "Truly?"

"Truly," he assured.

She smiled brightly before withdrawing from his embrace and pulling on his arm. "Shall we join my uncle?"

"*Oui,*" he readily agreed. As much as he wanted to, Guy could not allow himself to be alone with her. Her attraction was stronger than any he had known. He was the king's knight, he reminded himself.

When they entered the great room, Alec smiled and waved them over to his table. " 'Tis glad I am to have the lists behind me."

"Uncle, did you not enjoy the company?" Gabby gibed while gesturing at the lairds who lined three tables set with the evening meal.

"Aye, lass, but the guests eat more than their share. 'Tis not right to take advantage of my generous nature."

"Hush now," Mairi said above the laughter, " 'twas not that much food and look what it accomplished."

"If Friar Guy had but lost his complacency sooner, then I could have saved the stores in my larder."

Mairi patted her husband's arm. "Never mind, Alec. The right thing was done for the wrong reason."

Just then a castle guard entered the hall and approached the laird. "There is a Norman soldier sent from William at the gate. He begs an audience to deliver the king's message."

Alec nodded. "Admit him."

A deafening silence filled the room, as every Scot awaited the Norman's entrance.

Gabby's eyes were locked on the door, and when she reached her trembling hands toward her chalice she knocked it over. Louis rose and straightened her fallen cup, then placed his hand on her shoulder.

The messenger entered the room and glancing about nervously, made his way to the laird.

"King William sends a missive to the laird of the Campbells." He bowed and handed the parchment to Alec.

The lairds of the various clans leaned forward over their meal as Alec broke open the waxed seal. He looked at the message, then lowered it. "William sends me a gentle warning and requests that I send Gabrielle Aumont to him when he requests her presence."

Lady Gabrielle leaned back in her chair and closed her eyes, as her brother patted her shoulder.

Alec's gaze traveled to Guy. "At least we have time to send to Rome for yer dispensation."

Guy nodded his head. "I will do that today," he said, knowing the missive would be intercepted by William's contact. "Alec, the Church has its protocol. I will have to send the missive through my bishop."

Alec nodded. "Pray that dispensation arrives before the king's summons, but in any case, ye shall wed my niece tomorrow." Alec raised his chalice, as the lairds yelled their approval and joined the toast.

"*Oui,*" he agreed, feeling the king's noose tighten around his neck, as he quaffed his wine. "If William calls her back, I will accompany her."

"Aye. Ye will accompany her as her husband, not her confessor." Alec wiped his mouth on the back of his hand. "I willna let the lass go until she has a protector. I have no fear with the lass in yer charge. Though ye may have to shed some blood on her behalf, I know ye will do the right and good thing.''

That Alec trusted him that much was humbling, and, not for the first time, Guy wondered how he would extricate himself and his soul from this ruse.

Laird Campbell stood and walked over to his niece; taking her hands in his, he kissed her on the cheek. '' 'Tis late, time for rest. Go with Mairi. In the morning I will send for you when the priest arrives.''

She rose and curtsied before her uncle, then her glance slanted sideways, meeting Guy's intense gaze. During the brief instant under his admiring appraisal her cheeks blushed a becoming shade of pink before she turned and accompanied her aunt from the hall.

Guy believed that he held an uncommon affection for the girl. He also could not deny he had fantasized about being with her. For a moment he entertained the idea of disobeying his orders, then dismissed the traitorous thought. No matter how lovely she was, no matter how much he wanted her, he would deliver her to William.

Still, he knew if he ever made love to her, he would lose his resolve to accomplish his mission. He was a man of flesh and blood, not stone, yet he had to deny himself what he wanted most—his wife. How was he to live with her without touching her delectable skin, tasting those delicious lips and burying himself in that delicate body? Hell existed; he knew, because he had found it.

Shortly after dawn Gabby opened the window to her room and gazed unseeingly at the countryside. She had barely slept a wink all night. William's missive had reminded her of the peril that still existed, but she had to put Uncle Quennel from her mind. She drew in the crisp clean air. It was her wedding day.

A soft knock on her door heralded her aunt Mairi as she directed the servants that carried in the bathtub and the water.

Gabrielle could not believe she would marry the man she loved. It was her secret dream fulfilled. So much happiness filled her heart that she feared it would burst. That her love was returned was more than she had hoped. She twirled around the room, ignoring her aunt's indulgent chuckle.

"I will be back to help dress yer hair. Try to contain yer deep disappointment," Mairi said, smiling as she hustled the servants out and shut the door.

Gabby trailed her hand in the water and inhaled the lovely scent of flowers, then slipped off her smock and eased into the tub. Lovely images floated through her mind as she bathed. Slowly she rinsed the soap from her skin, enjoying the decadent feeling of the warm water and mild soap.

After her bath she wrapped up in a large linen sheet while she dried her hair by combing the long strands. It would take hours to dry, but she did not want to braid her hair.

She would take pains with her appearance; she wanted to impress all who attended the wedding. Wanted to please Guy. He thought her special enough to fight for—he had chosen her over the Church! Though she had never believed in a vengeful God, she did not want to tempt fate. Dropping to her knees, she said, "Please, God, do not take this away from us. We could not help falling in love. Though we have broken no laws, I wouldst have Your blessing."

A tear of intense joy slipped down her cheek as she realized that dreams and miracles did come true. "Thank you," she whispered heavenward.

Abbess Ambrose was right. *You must never stop believing, for even in the darkest hour, He listens,* Gabrielle thought. There was a time when she had doubted that. Never again.

She thought of her parents. "Oh, Mother, Father, I wish you could have met him. I know you would love him as I do." She drew a ragged breath. "Now I can only ask your blessing through prayers. Keep us in your hearts always."

She arose, marveling how one man could bring so much peace to her. Guy was the answer to her childhood prayers. Now she understood why from her earliest recollection, she had seen his eyes in the Sight. She would cherish and love him all of her days.

The door opened and Mairi bustled in with a violet gown embroidered at the hem and cuffs with a delicate border of the mistletoe's white berries and green leaves.

Gabby reverently touched the exquisite gown. " 'Tis lovely."

"You must wear this if ye are to be married in the ancient tradition. A Druid wedding is far different than a Christian ceremony," her aunt said, holding the gown up by the shoulders and shaking it out to show how sheer and full it was.

It was so delicate she could see her aunt's form through the sheer fabric. "Why?" she asked suspiciously.

"Because after the ritual, and all depart," she said, toying with the front ribbon and dangling it in the air, "ye simply untie this, and stand before yer husband."

"In my shift?"

Her aunt shook her head.

Gabby swallowed, feeling her face burn, while a curling sensation of excitement sizzled through her at the thought.

"Now, lass, I think it is time we have that wee discussion ye dinna wish to broach before."

Gabby's eyes flew open. "Please, Aunt Mairi, I really do not think that is necessary."

"Nay, I would be remiss in my duties if I dinna prepare ye for what awaits a maiden in her wedding bed. Sit yerself down."

Gabby sat stiffly on the side of the bed and briefly wondered if Guy was suffering through the same talk with her uncle, then dismissed the notion, listening spellbound to her aunt.

A short distance from the stronghold existed a grove devoid of vegetation except for the stand of trees which grew in a small circle. Sparse leaves dotted the limbs, and the low-hung branches were bare, except for the clumps of mistletoe clinging to them. Scottish lairds with swords drawn stood between the rough black trunks, making a solid ring of wood and muscle.

The mournful wail of the pipers filled the air with the music of the land. Gabby shivered as the cold wind slipped beneath her hem and curled up her leg. The heavy mantle she wore over the sheer smock, was not enough to keep away the chill. She bit her lip, slowing her pace as goose bumps covered her flesh.

"Courage," Louis whispered, giving her hand a comforting squeeze as he presented her to the Campbell clan.

Though her heart pounded, she offered a smile and bowed to the villagers gathered to witness the Druid wedding.

A roar of approval rose from the spectators crowding the path, and a clanswoman slipped a garland of mistletoe over her head. Then, in a show of respect, the crowd parted before them. Louis walked her down the path through the ring of men to stand in the middle of the circle before the priest.

The music suddenly died out. Her breath caught in her throat as the men stepped aside. Guy entered the grove from the other direction and took his place beside her. He lifted her hand from Louis's and placed a small warm kiss in her palm before clasping it in his firm grip.

Her heart fluttered, and her flesh tingled from his touch. When her eyes met his, she shivered at the primitive expression in his dark blue eyes. Guy pulled her to his side and stepped before the priest as Louis withdrew to join Alec Campbell.

The priest raised his hands for attention.

"Today we will witness the uniting of a man and a woman." He extended his hands toward the bride.

Gabby withdrew her hand from Guy's, missing his warmth as she placed her palm in the priest's cold grasp.

The Druid priest removed the garland of mistletoe from around her neck. He held the greenery up to the crowd, then wrapped it around her wrist before tying the ends around Guy's arm. The Priest faced Guy. "From this day forward ye will care for and protect this maiden from all, including yourself."

"I will with my life," Guy pledged.

His solemn vow sent quivers up her spine.

The priest turned toward Gabby and smiled a gap-toothed grin. "From this day forward ye will not question him. He is yer life and love. Give unto him all he is due as a good and fair husband."

"I will," she whispered.

"Then lower your heads and receive the wedlock blessing." He lifted his hands toward the sky. "Hear me, I beseech the gods of heaven and earth on behalf of these two before us. We are all one with creation and ask yer blessing on this union. Letting the stars guide their destiny, may this joining be as fertile as the earth, and their love warm their nights as the sun warms their day. Teach them to cherish life and they will learn to cherish each other. Remember to show them the beauty in the world around them so they may never fail to see it in themselves. And lastly, teach them forgiveness, so they may live in harmony forever." He lowered his hands, then removed the mistletoe from their arms, and held it above their heads. "Husband, either claim or reject yer bride."

Guy leaned down and enfolded her in his embrace. The

moment his lips touched hers she felt a charge of excitement streak through her. A taste of delight teased her senses, but the contact was brief, leaving her frustrated. His warm lips merely grazed hers in a show of acceptance to the Druid ceremony. When Guy pulled away, the priest draped the mistletoe on their shoulders, symbolically signifying the end of the ceremony. Without a word, the priest turned to the crowd and signaled the departure with a wave of his hand. Suddenly the music started, echoing through the air as the crowd marched back toward the castle.

Once they were all alone, Gabby turned toward her husband. It would be hard to disrobe right here, but she knew that she must. ''Help me,'' she silently pleaded, longing to be in the security of his embrace. For just a moment she stared into his eyes, searching for some sign that would make this easier, but his return gaze revealed nothing.

Swallowing her apprehension, she slid the heavy mantle from her body with a brave shrug, revealing the sheer violet gown. Immediately the cold air bit into her. With trembling fingers she slowly untied the ties. Though the air was chilled, her cheeks burned. She slipped the long violet gown back off her shoulders and the soft material slithered down her arms and slipped past her hips to pool at her feet. His eyes widened, and his facial features tightened.

She stood before him exposed and vulnerable. A tiny fear grew within her heart, and she lowered her head, unable to bear his disappointment.

''God, but you are lovely,'' he said hoarsely.

A tide of relief washed away all her doubt. Her gaze traveled up his chest to his eyes, which were bright with admiration. Thank God, he truly wanted her. He reached out and enfolded her in his muscular arms. The air was crisp, but she felt deliciously warm in his embrace.

''Alec told me about the ceremony,'' he murmured against her hair. ''I knew this was coming, the offering of the bride,

but I had no idea how moving an experience it would be."
His hands roamed up and down her back, warming her flesh
and sending a tingling current through her. She shivered
with delight.

Abruptly, he pulled away and her fears returned. He
reached down for her smock and, to her consternation,
slipped the gossamer gown around her. With trembling
hands he closed the front and tied the ribbons. Then he
rescued her mantle and drew it over her shoulders.

She frowned, wondering what he was doing.

"You must be freezing," he said, while wrapping his kilt
around them both.

His warmth surrounded her as she nestled closer to him
and looked up. "I cannot wait to be your wife. 'Tis shameless
to confess, but I have dreamed of this moment." She stood on
tiptoes and kissed him, but his lips were stiff and unyielding
beneath hers. Instantly, she felt a chill.

"Guy?" she questioned.

He drew a deep breath and rested his forehead against
hers. "As much as I am loath to do it, I would ask you to
wait to become my wife until we receive a dispensation
and can be married in the Christian faith. Do you find this
acceptable?"

Her spirits sank as she saw the serious expression in his
eyes. She sighed. "If that is what you wish, my lord, but
'twill be difficult."

He cleared his throat, and the sound rumbled deep in his
broad chest. "Difficult, my lady? *Non,* 'twill be absolute
purgatory to hold you in my arms and feel your womanly
curves conform to mine; to smell your intoxicating fragrance
and hear my name upon your lips, and not take you as my
bride.

Joy soared through her as he rubbed her back and shoulders, warming her chilled flesh through her garments.

"Come, we must get you out of the cold."

With uncommon boldness, she wrapped her arms around his neck, not wanting the moment to end. "Will you kiss me, husband? A single kiss to seal our union."

He drew her so close to him she felt crushed against his ribs. "My pleasure, wife," he growled as his lips covered hers in harsh possession. The touch and the taste of his kiss was so primitive, so intense, that she considered pulling away. Then just as suddenly, the texture of his kiss changed, drowning her momentary fear. From rough to tender, his mouth moved over hers, his lips caressing in a velvet touch like the soft warm petals of morning flowers. She moved into the kiss with a deep-throated sigh, her lips gently opening to welcome his stroking tongue.

Strange little currents sizzled through Gabby as she met and matched his every movement, finding pleasure not only in what he did, but what she did as well. His hands molded her body to his by pressing her hips forward. She felt every inch of his muscular form and knew he desired her. Oh, Mairi was right. She could not wait for the wedding night.

His kiss deepened and his hands slipped between them, opening her gown to caress her breast. Desire shot through her at the intimate touch, and she moaned. Of their own accord her hands glided up and down his chest, slipping beneath the linen shirt to rub across his taut, hair-roughened skin. She felt his muscles tense, and knew she disturbed him as much as he did her.

She wanted more, much more. Her kiss matched the depth and intensity of his; her hands devoured his muscular form the same way that his explored hers.

When his lips at last left hers, his breathing was labored. "Lord, *chérie,* I desire you far more than I had ever dreamed possible. We must stop now, or I will not be able to hold back."

"But . . ."

"Please, Gabby, do not move. I need to cool my blood, as do you."

Gabby stilled in his arms, engulfed by disappointment, but also elated that he found her so irresistible. It would be a terrible burden to find yourself married to a person you did not desire. A shy smile lit her face. She was glad that was not the case between them.

The Norman peasant dressed in a threadbare wool plaid turned to his scruffy older companion, Soren. "Brother, we will have to tell Quennel that the friar has beaten out every contender for the girl's hand. As for her brother, I cannot tell whether he is among the boys fostering here or not. The Scots protect their own and none will talk of the boy. Perhaps the laird has sent the boy to another clan."

"What will you do if you discover the boy, Evarard?"

"I am not fool enough to take on the Scots here. That is the mercenaries' job. Quennel wanted us to gather information. Give him the report, Soren."

"I am glad to be leaving this heathen land. I will tell your family you are safe."

"Take care, and steer clear of Aumont's temper when you tell him the disappointing news."

"Oui," Soren said, then looked at his companion curiously. "Would you end the Aumonts' lives if so ordered?" he asked.

"Non. I owed their father my allegiance. If the new master"—Evarard spit when he referred to Quennel—"so wishes, he will have to find a colder heart than mine."

"Coin will purchase his revenge."

"Oui, and the day it does, Hamish and Blanchfleur Aumont will turn over in their graves and their people will know no peace," Evarard said.

"Then why will you not let me give a false report to Aumont?" Soren asked.

"Because if the ruse were ever found out, not only would you suffer, but our families."

"We owe the old master and mistress something," Soren protested.

Evarard bent to his brother's reasoning. "I will think on it. Mayhap an opportunity will arise to help the children."

"Listen to me," Soren begged, throwing his travel sack over his shoulder. "You are respected among our villagers. If you have a plan, they will follow it."

Evarard scratched his head. "I can make no promises." Though the thought of betraying the young mistress and master sat heavy on his mind, unless fate intervened he had little choice.

Chapter Eleven

For a week Gabby spent every morning in chapel before the small wooden altar, giving thanks that Guy had been victorious, while begging for a quick dispensation.

Today Louis joined her for the service, and she could not stop turning to glance his way. Though she had agreed with Uncle Alec's decision to send him to another clan for his protection, her heart was melancholy. She would have no idea where he would be living.

After the chapel had emptied of all the other worshipers, Louis reached over and covered Gabby's folded hands with his own. "What is it, Gabby?"

"Soon we will depart for different homes. You will be off to another clan, and it is only a matter of time before William calls me to London. I have so much to say to you, but I am without any idea of where to begin."

Louis's mouth shaped itself into the sheepish grin that always managed to touch her heart.

"To my surprise, your departure fills me with sadness as

well. I once thought that if you would only leave me be, then I would be at peace. But I have learned that doing what is best for a loved one is not always easy or simple.''

Gabby took a deep breath to dispel the thickening in her throat. "I am sorry."

"For what?" he asked.

"I made a holy vow to protect you. If I seemed unreasonable at times—forgive me. In truth, dear brother, I was terrified."

"I know," he said.

She blinked at his revelation. "It appears the only one I duped into believing I was capable was myself. Oh, Louis, the last thing I ever wanted was to be the head of our family—it was thrust upon me, and I am afraid my poor frame was barely up to the task."

"Nay, Gabby, you did fine. I know I did not make it easy for you, for it bruised my pride to have my sister looking after me as though I were still a babe in arms."

She smiled at his observation. I apologize for sometimes treating you that way, but I cannot regret my actions. I would risk my very life to keep you safe. Someday you will return to Normandy and claim the lands and title that rightfully belong to you."

"Because of your courage that is possible. Mother and Father would be proud. Take care, sister, for you do not realize how good you were at your job. Perhaps, when I have liberated our home, I will seek your counsel on how to run it."

"That I would like," she said, as a sad wistfulness invaded her heart. "So much has happened that I fear our childhood memories will never again yield the joy of the past. I hope you have not been robbed of too much." She took a deep breath and glanced away. "So many things changed when Father and Mother died." Her voice cracked, and for the first time she let loose her grief.

Louis's arm instinctively encircled Gabby, and she turned into his strong shoulder, accepting his comfort.

She cried for her parents, whom she missed, and for the fear and suffering they had endured escaping from Normandy, only to be met with the monumental task of crossing a war-torn England on route to Scotland. All the feelings she had been containing rushed through her, and she cried to the only person who would understand her anguish.

With her tears, years of worry drained away. Louis's safety was assured. He would go to another clan and be absorbed so thoroughly by them, no one, not even she, would be able to find him without permission.

"I will avenge all of our family, Gabby," Louis whispered against her hair. "Do not worry. From this day forward I will carry both the benefit and the burden of the Aumont name."

She pulled away, brushing tears from her eyes. "I am sorry. I am the eldest, and here I weep like this. 'Tis unseemly."

" 'Tis not unseemly. I should have listened to you instead of challenging your authority."

"Do not berate yourself, brother. You have learned a valuable lesson, as have I. Therefore, the experience is not without its profit. I simply never want to learn a lesson so well again."

Louis smiled. "And in the future will you allow your husband to shoulder the burdens?"

His question took her by surprise. "Verily, I would. But I sense a great turmoil within him," she said, speaking her fears.

"No man escapes conflict. But he is a good man and will resolve his problems. His actions have already proven his worth." He patted her hand. "I accept him as my brother as you must accept him as a husband. My wish is for your happiness."

She looked at him, and for the first time saw not the naive youth of her childhood, but a sincere and strong young man—a man not unlike their sire. "You have grown up. I wish I had noticed sooner."

Relief sparkled in his eyes as he gave her a hug and helped her to her feet. "Come. We will be missed."

As they opened the chapel doors a maid met them just outside. "My lady, there is a furor going on in the great room."

"What, pray tell, is the commotion about?"

She lowered her eyes and anxiously twisted her apron. "It concerns ye."

"Lord, but I do not feel up to any more intrigue. Please, you must tell me what I face," she implored, already feeling the knots form in her stomach.

"I dinna know, my lady. I was sent by Lady Mairi to summon ye at once."

"Do not worry, Gabby," Louis said. "I will stand by you and, if need be, bear the brunt of any displeasure."

"Even if it is from Uncle Alec?" she nervously teased, knowing Louis's training had been very exacting.

Louis grinned. "Aye, I have learned how to shoulder responsibility, not shirk from it."

A great serenity filled Gabby's soul as she linked her arm through his. "Then shall we meet the problem?"

"After you, my lady." He bowed.

"Oh no." She chuckled. "I will not precede you. This we do together."

As brother and sister crossed the courtyard, wary looks were cast their way, which boded ill for the coming meeting. Gabby took a deep breath as they climbed the steps to the great hall. When Louis opened the tall, heavy doors, a wall of loud angry conversation could be heard. Alec and Guy were arguing, but there were other voices, too, voices she

A PRAYER AND A PROMISE 187

could not identify. Head held high, she entered the great
hall on her brother's strong arm.

A huge tree trunk burned in the center of the vast hearth.
The roaring fire heated the entire hall, while casting a golden
light upon the chamber. Alec, Guy, Ian, and two strangers
stood in the middle of the room.

"*Non!* I will not ride with you, brother," Guy said, his
face red and stance rigid.

She turned to look at the warlord he addressed, and her
eyes widened. So, this hulk of a man was Guy's brother,
Royce. Though there was a family resemblance, next to Guy,
the harsh-looking man seemed almost homely. In Gabby's
opinion it was easy to see whom God had smiled upon.

Royce slammed his chalice of wine down onto the table.
"Have you lost what little wits God gifted you? What of
your duty to the Church?"

"I have left the Church, Royce. The idea that I would
make a good cleric was ridiculous."

"You did what?" Royce gasped. "God's teeth, Guy, you
will break Mother's heart."

"Mother will survive." Guy crossed his arms over his
chest. "Why have you come?"

"William asked that I give you and Lady Gabrielle an
escort to North Umberland."

"Was it an order?"

"*Non,* he requests it. Had he demanded, I would not have
sought an audience peaceably, but would have attacked this
stronghold."

Gabby winced.

Alec Campbell now addressed the other Scotsman. "Are
ye part of this?"

The barrel-chested, stout warrior turned. "I have to support the man. He married my daughter, Bethany of North
Umberland."

Alec nodded his head in understanding, but a frown

marred his brow. "As of late, Mactavish, we seem to be on the opposite side of the stream more often than not."

No one was paying any attention to Louis or Gabby. Now she approached her husband and said loudly, "Guy, what is happening?"

"Lady Gabrielle, this is Royce of North Umberland, your dear brother by marriage."

"Marriage!" Royce roared.

At the bellow, Louis's eyes narrowed, as did Ian's. Unlike Alec Campbell, the lads had not yet learned to conceal their emotions. Mactavish merely raised his chalice in a silent salute.

"Aye, married," Guy said, calmly to Royce. "We were wed in the ancient way." He raised Gabby's hand to his lips. "My brother comes with an order for me to return to North Umberland."

"Then we will go to North Umberland, husband," she said, though the very idea of returning to England turned her legs to such jelly she feared they would not support her.

Hands clasped behind his back, Royce walked around her as though he were inspecting a piece of horseflesh. "So this is what you left the Church for. She is very tempting, I'll admit."

Embarrassment replaced fear, and Gabby's face burned. Her husband's face on the other hand, was tight with anger. But within those taut lines she saw the battle to retain self-control. She sensed there was a reason he would not challenge his brother here. Louis, on the other hand, did not feel so restricted.

He grabbed the Norman by the arm and spun him around.

"You have insulted my sister and my house! I demand you apologize to the lady."

Dark brows bunched together as Royce peered down at Louis. "Are you calling me out?"

Gabby gasped. Louis's training had improved, but he was not skilled enough to take on this knight.

All sound died in the room as everyone waited for Louis's response.

"Again, I ask you to apologize. My sister does not deserve such an insult."

Gabby's heart skipped a beat at her brother's stubbornness. Her nails dug into Guy's arm.

"Royce," Guy warned, his voice hard. "Do not embarrass me with your boorish ways."

The Norman warlord kept his gaze on Louis.

"You are right, sir, she did not. I apologize. But do not push the matter. I count it done."

Gabby released her pent-up breath, and silently applauded Guy for defusing the situation. Although tempers had calmed, the tension had not eased. She could feel the mistrust swirling in the room, waiting to be released. Her eyes sought her uncle's, but his gaze was riveted on Guy.

"My niece's future is settled. She will journey to North Umberland with her husband. I leave her care in yer hands, Guy," Alec said, then his gaze slowly traveled the full extent of the room.

Though she could not put her finger on the cause, something else was afoot here. She shivered with unease.

"Louis, say yer farewell to yer sister. By evening tide ye will be away," Alec said.

Gabby embraced Louis, and whispered, "I shall miss you greatly, and I have never been prouder of you."

"Do not lose hope—I will regain our lands." He pointedly glanced at Royce, then whispered. "You will always have a refuge."

She nodded, holding back the tears. She knew he meant every word of his promise. She also knew by the time he fulfilled his vow, her fate would also be sealed.

When he released her, he moved to Guy. "You will take

care of her or answer to me. She is a treasure worth protecting. I hope to God you understand that.

With a proud bearing, Louis strode across the room, several strong clansmen falling in behind him. Before stepping
outside he threw Gabby one last look, then he was gone.

"Godspeed," she whispered.

They had barely finished breaking their fast when Gabby
stood taking leave of her relatives. Royce's men had
mounted and by their expression were eager to be away. "I
shall never forget your kindness," Gabby said to Mairi.

Tears gathered in her aunt's eyes as she held out her arms.
"Remember us, lass." She hugged the girl, then moved
aside to give Ian a chance to say farewell.

"Take care, cousin," Ian said as he embraced her. "If
ye should ever need me, just send word."

"I will," she promised, then turned to Alec with tears in
her eyes. "Oh, Uncle Alec . . ."

"Dinna worry, lass," he said, enfolding her in a gentle
embrace. "Ye have kin who would move heaven and earth
to see ye safe." Kissing her cheek, he delivered her to Guy.
"See ye take care of my niece, for she is a rare and special
woman."

Cold gray clouds swirled overhead, and Gabby shivered
at the first touch of winter as snow began to fall in big white
flakes.

Guy rode up next to her and took his place in the column.
"Royce just informed me that there has been a small change
in our travel plans."

"Why?" she asked, noting her husband's unease.

"Mactavish agreed to accompany Royce only if the caravan headed north toward Caithness, where he has business with a chieftain.''

"Is that not Fenrir Gunn's home?" Gabby was alarmed, but hesitant to discuss it with the soldiers riding so close.

"Do not worry about Laird Gunn. I promise there will be no trouble.''

She doubted he believed that, but did not challenge the matter as they rode together and talked.

The trip should only delay them a few days, but by late afternoon the weather had turned unseasonably cold, and Gabby's cheek stung against the biting wind as she tried to burrow deeper into her wool mantle for warmth.

"I am going to ride up ahead and take a robe from the supply wagon," Guy said with a concerned expression.

" 'Tis not necessary, husband,'' she said, trying to brave the elements as staunchly as the men.

" 'Tis necessary. Your teeth are chattering,'' he asserted. When he rode off, two soldiers moved up on either side of her.

The snow fell harder, and soon Gabby could barely see the horse in front of her as she waited for Guy's return. Her fingers felt numb from the biting cold and the horse's reins slipped from her grip. *Suddenly, the white landscape fell away as a vision appeared. Terror gripped her and she tried to yell out, but something restricted her voice. She could not move. She was bound so tight that all she could do was watch. Before her eyes were tired and troubled men, who moved before a campfire drawing lots. She instinctively knew they were deciding who would end her life. Finally one sorry but determined man stepped toward her. He drew his arm back and in his hand glinted a sharp dagger. She tried to swallow; tried to scream, but could do neither. Fleetingly she thought of Guy then . . .*

When the apparition faded blinding snow filled her view. But instead of receding like the vision, her fear increased.

The danger was right here, all around her. Frantically, she looked about for Guy, but she could see nothing beyond the blowing snow. Her stomach roiled. There was no time to warn him.

She cried out, but the howling wind swallowed her voice. Not even her escort could hear her warning.

Panic surged through her. *Stay calm,* she tried to reason with herself; if her sight was restricted by the blowing snow, then so was her attacker's.

She waited, listening, straining to hear any sound that would help her, but the thick blanket of snow swallowed all noise. Her body was on fire with apprehension.

Abruptly, Gabby was jarred as the escort on her right fell to the ground between their horses. Her horse danced to the left, and met no resistance. The guard who rode in that column was missing. She felt a heavy jolt from behind and her horse whinnied and began to prance from the added weight. Icy hands fell against her face, covering her mouth. She screamed and struggled, but no one could see or hear her. Frightened tears streamed down her face as her frustration mounted. She fought, but her efforts only succeeded in sapping her strength.

The assailant held her roughly against him as he snatched the reins. They were leaving the safety of the caravan, and there was nothing Gabby could do to alert the others. In desperation she struggled harder, and managed to slip her mantle from her shoulders and wrestle the cloak free so it could drop to the ground. The wind bit through her thin clothing, but she ignored the cold, knowing she had left a sign for her beloved to follow.

Guy! her mind screamed, hoping and willing him to hear her silent plea. But as seconds passed her shoulders slumped in defeat. Guy could no more hear her than his sight could pierce the blinding white curtain of snow. She was utterly alone.

* * *

Head bowed against the wind, Guy rode back through the snow to offer his little bride another mantle of fur to keep her warm in this unexpected blizzard. After conferring with Royce they had now halted the caravan so no one would be lost. The snow blinded his eyes but he moved down the line with the confidence of a soldier used to such hardships. When he reached the spot in the caravan where he had left Gabby, he called out to her. There was no answer. A niggling of fear wormed its way to his heart. Though she could have left the caravan with her escort to answer nature's call, he doubted it.

Raising an alarm, Guy moved back along the line on foot, and found the two groggy guards. His heart pounded as he listened to their stories. She had been kidnapped!

Like a man driven, he trudged through the snow, inspecting the ground until he found the trail. Her discarded mantle had snagged a bush and only one corner lay partially covered by snow. He applauded her presence of mind to leave such a clue. That its loss would cost her dearly, he would not consider. When he found her abductors, and he would find them, they would suffer.

Slowly the caravan of soldiers walked through the snow following the narrow trail. That the falling snow had not fully concealed the hoofprints meant that the abductors were not too far ahead.

After an hour the snow began to dissipate and soon Guy spotted a light flickering in the distance. He closed his eyes, offering a silent prayer. A campfire burned through the trees. Guy and Royce deployed their men. Crouching, they crawled through the snow toward the dim light.

Guy peered through some ground thickets. In a clearing ten men stood by the campfire. To the other side of the fire sat Gabby, bound and gagged. After drawing straws, one man separated himself from the rest of the men at the campfire and advanced toward her.

Guy leaped up, but Royce held him back. "Wait until our men are in place," Royce whispered.

The soldier stood above Gabby and pulled out a dagger. Guy's heart sank and he pulled free of his brother's hold, but Royce grabbed and held him still. "God's teeth! Look." Royce pointed.

Guy shrugged free of his brother's grip, and stared where Royce had directed.

The soldier drew back the dagger, but before he could use it, a comrade attacked from behind. He fell forward, and his attacker withdrew another dagger. "Forgive me, my lady," he said, reaching down and cutting through her bonds. "I must deliver you to Lord Aumont. I have no choice, but I have no liking for it either. This hired soldier," he pointed to the dead man, "decided to make you this evening's sport. He made us draw lots to see who would use you. He won. I could not allow that, my lady."

She bowed her head as he untied the gag. "Evarard, is it you? Are you part of this?" she asked, rubbing circulation into her wrists.

"Our families are held hostage, my lady. 'Tis lucky we found you and not the band of mercenaries sent by Lord Aumont. This one," Evarard said, removing his dagger and wiping the blood from the blade, "was a mercenary assigned to our group."

"I have already made their acquaintance," she replied through chattering teeth.

Upon hearing the peasant's explanation, Guy breathed a sigh. She would not be harmed. Even so, Gabby looked pale, her body shivering, as she tried to huddle into a small ball.

He watched and waited until all his men were in place and the peasant moved away from Gabby.

The moment the man stepped back to the warmth of the campfire, the Normans and Mactavish's Scots descended on the band. Guy sliced his way through the men to reach Gabby, pulled her into his arms, and held her tight. Her hands were like ice, and he shoved them inside his smock, warming her chilled flesh against his chest.

The conflict ended in a heartbeat. It was a pitiful fight, for the assailants were farmers, not soldiers. When the leader was brought before Royce for sentencing, Gabby tore away from Guy and stepped between the adversaries.

She looked at Evarard the farmer as he knelt fearfully in the dirt, then turned to Royce. "You will not harm him or his men. They could no more stop the tide of events than you or I. They are loyal men forced through fear to do my uncle's bidding."

"Lass, ye canna show them clemency," Mactavish said, harshly.

"Mactavish is right," Royce insisted.

The serfs cringed as Gabby shook her head, cold tears resting on her cheeks. "You do not understand. Their loved ones are being held hostage on our estate to ensure their obedience. If it were you, would you not do whatever necessary to protect your family?"

"What do you suggest, my lady?" Guy asked, his tone more reasonable than Royce's or Mactavish's.

"We must help them. They are but pawns in a game not of their choosing."

At Royce's subtle nod, Guy turned and stared hard at the men before him. "By your lady's generosity you are spared my sword. But remember a man cannot serve two masters." He knelt to shuffle through the dead mercenary's clothes and found a pouch of gold coins. "This should be enough to bring your families to England. I shall have, an estate in Lleyn, and you would be welcomed there." He stood and tossed the coins to the men, before joining Gabrielle.

Gratitude shone in their faces for their lady's clemency and the lord's help. They bowed to Guy. "Oui, my lord. We will."

Guy lifted Gabby in his arms and wrapped her in his own mantle.

"Mayhap you are right, Guy," Royce said. "Few ladies could inspire such loyalty among their serfs. I know of only one other, and recognizing her unselfish nature, I married her. 'Twould seem, brother, we have an eye for rare quality. 'Tis no wonder you dote on her."

"Mind to the business of soldiering, brother. Leave other matters to those who have a better understanding of the softer side of life."

Royce's booming laugh resounded in the still air.

After all the other men had retired for the night, Royce kept watching Gabby across the campfire where she sat on Guy's lap, bundled in a robe. His gaze unnerved her. "Does your brother have to make a point of staring at me," she whispered to Guy, feeling the weight of such disconcerting scrutiny.

"Do not let my brother's faults trouble you, my dear. Royce has always had a dark side. 'Twas our mother's fault, for she did not hide the fact that she favored me," Guy said in an overloud voice.

Gabby blushed to the roots of her hair and, horrified, jabbed her elbow into Guy's side.

But Royce simply chuckled, and Gabby relaxed when she saw how the two brothers enjoyed teasing each other.

"The sad truth is she favored me," Royce countered, "until I rescued you from the sem—"

"Royce," Guy warned.

"Guy, what happened?" she asked.

"Never mind, Gabby. 'Twas a long time ago and I do not like to talk about it. Royce," he said pointedly, "never should have brought it up."

Royce had the grace to looked ashamed. "I am sorry, Guy."

Guy nodded. "Next time, brother, think before you speak."

In turn, Royce smiled at Gabby. "You would do well to remember, Guy only snaps when he cares."

"Do not tell her that," Guy scowled.

Royce winked at her. "I owe my brother for interfering in my own marriage. So, little sister, if you ever need to know anything at all, come to me. I will tell you the truth."

"Royce, I swear, there are times I would not claim you."

As he stood up, Royce laughed again. "You would claim me," he said, then walked away, leaving Gabby and Guy all alone.

Gabby shifted on Guy's lap. "You are as fond of your brother as I am of mine."

"*Oui,* I am." He shook his head with wry amusement. "Even though he is sometimes a big oaf."

"How far is it to Royce's home?" she asked, suddenly aware of her intimate position, sitting on Guy's lap. She shivered at the thought.

Instantly, he drew her closer to his chest, and his hands roamed up and down her back to warm her. She snuggled deeper in his embrace, not at all cold, but feeling a delicious warmth.

"Only a day's ride, but we still must travel north to pick up Mactavish's charge. We will arrive at Renwyg in a week's time."

"You do not sound pleased," she said, barely able to concentrate with the way his touch was playing havoc with her senses.

Drawing the blanket up to her chin, he kissed the top of her head. "I am eager to see my nephews as well as Royce's wife. But I am not sure I am eager to return to England.

You know I must have an answer from my bishop. He is in London.''

"Will we go there?'' she asked, pulling away to watch his features tighten.

"I may have to, but you will not. Until the king requires you at court, you will stay with my family, where it is safer.''

"But if you go to London, I wish to come with you.''

"Non. You will remain behind.''

Gabby smiled at his stubborn expression. "It is not something we need decide now. We are not even in North Umberland yet. Shall we save our fight until it is unavoidable?''

The humor lighting his eyes bespoke his answer, and she caught a glimpse into his soul.

Then suddenly he stood, lifting her with him. "All arguments should end with such logic. I will bow to your judgment, little nun. We will disagree when the time comes and not before.''

Gabby smiled at the reminder of their changed circumstances. " 'Twill be an amusing story to tell our children, how we met.'' The moment the words left her mouth, her face colored. Why, oh why, had she said such an impertinent thing?

Guy chuckled. "It seems I will have to tell them, for you cannot even mention it without your face becoming the most lovely shade of red.''

" 'Tis cruel of you to tease me. Someday you will wish you had never made me feel so uncomfortable.''

"I will feel bad only if you are not by my side to enjoy the humor of the situation with me. I think I have been searching my whole life for you.''

She looked at him, really looked at him. Everything she ever wanted was before her. She cradled his face in her palms. "And if I should die tomorrow, Guy, I could not have known more happiness than I know now with you."

His face mirrored her seriousness as he replied, "Gabby, whatever happens, remember I love you. Can you do that? No matter what is said or done, know that my heart, such as it is, belongs to only you. If God commanded it I would lay down my life so that you would live."

"Guy, do not say such things."

"I not only say them, I vow them. I love you, Gabby, with my whole heart and soul. I will sacrifice whatever is necessary to be with you. You have my prayer and my promise of undying love."

Tears gathered in her throat. She had to swallow twice before speaking, but even then her voice cracked and she managed only to whisper. "I will keep your love safe in my heart."

"Remember, no matter what happens . . ." His eyes darkened as he gazed deeply into her own.

She covered his lips with her fingers. "I believe you," she vowed, withdrawing her hand.

A smile the likes of which she had never seen lit up his handsome face and eyes. "I will hold you to your promise."

"Do not worry, darling. I will always believe in you."

Hand in hand they walked over to her tent, then Guy drew her tenderly into his arms. When she felt his lips on hers, a jolt of heat shot through her. Her arms encircled his neck while she molded her body closer to his. His kiss created a fire deep within her that flared into a bonfire when he pulled her tighter into his embrace. Thrilled that the kiss affected him as much as it did her, her hands roamed freely over the thick ropey muscles of his arms and shoulders, kneading and caressing as she pressed against his chest. Feeling the urgent command of her body, her tongue slipped past his lips. When she grazed his teeth and felt the velvet texture within, she heard him groan, the husky sound sending waves of liquid fire through her. She wanted more, needed more, and was frustrated when he pulled away. "Guy?"

"Hush," he said, holding her still, his head resting against hers, his breathing labored. "Give me a moment, my love," he gasped.

"I am sorry I tempt you," she said with a sigh, "but it is hard for me to wait for the dispensation. You are an honorable man and I will try to be patient and respect your wishes."

Several moments passed before he kissed her gently, then lifted the tent flap and motioned her inside. "I will not be far if you need me," he whispered.

After he lowered the heavy material he stood, trying to get his emotions under control. Never had he wanted a woman so badly, and the bitter irony was that a lie kept them apart. Maybe it was a blessing in disguise, for if he consummated this marriage, he knew he could never give her up. This deception had him tied in knots. He turned to find his brother waiting for him a few feet away.

Royce motioned Guy to follow him. When they were far enough from the tent so as not to be overheard, Royce shook his head. "You are a fool. What will you do when William commands her return?"

"I am going to London to talk to the king. He does not have all the facts. I am confident that once he has time to study the problem, he will not force her to marry Quennel's man."

"Then you are a fool. William is the king; he will do what is best for his country and damn those who oppose him."

Guy clenched his fists. "It would be a death sentence for her. I nearly died protecting her from Quennel's treachery. He is a knave who hates her."

"What will you do if after hearing you out, William still commands you to hand her over to Quennel?"

Guy rubbed a hand over his cheek and sighed. "I do not know."

"You would make a traitor of yourself and anyone else you involve!"

"Do not worry, Royce. I would never implicate you."

"I would stand beside you and you do me a great dishonor by suggesting otherwise. But you needlessly court disaster. Take her to London with you and plead your case. If it becomes necessary, then you can develop a plan to rescue the maiden from her betrothed."

Guy thought about it for a minute. "Your plan has merit. It would allow me to deal with her uncle and betrothed."

"And you would stand more of a chance for victory."

Guy eyed his brother. There was only one problem. "She will hate me when she finds out my part in this."

"Tell her now," Royce urged.

"Non, I cannot." He could not bear the thought of losing her trust. He needed to find another way out of this coil he had woven.

Royce sighed. "You are making a mistake."

"I may very well be, but I have to do it this way." Guy smiled wryly. "Now I know what it must have been like when I tried to counsel you about Bethany."

"Perhaps she will have some ideas," Royce said jovially, then slapped Guy on the back. "Get some sleep. Tomorrow we head for Caithness. After Mactavish settles his business there, we ride for Renwyg." Royce's voice rang with warmth and pride at the mention of his home.

Guy smiled. His brother's marriage was his joy. Now, if only he could boast the same success.

Chapter Twelve

At midday they arrived in Caithness and traveled along the rugged shoreline until they reached a stone castle that seemed to sprout from the sea. Built on a peninsula, the fortress stood impenetrable and inhospitable, as huge waves crashed against the rock foundation, sending towering sprays of foam high into the air.

Gabby felt the hairs on the back of her neck rise. This would have been her home if Guy had not defeated Fenrir Gunn.

At the gate they were met by the captain of the guard.

"I am Laird Bram Mactavish. I have come for my clansmen, Brian and his son Angus. Laird Gunn's missive said they were in great need of assistance." Bram's deep voice carried over the pounding roar of the surf, and the gates were opened.

Inside the castle courtyard, green moss clung to the walls, and a damp, musty smell hung in the air.

"Laird Gunn directed me to take ye immediately to yer

men," the captain of the guard said, extending his hand for Mactavish to precede him.

"What about my lady?" Guy demanded of the soldier. "The ride was long and the journey difficult. She is tired and will need to rest."

Gunn's man shrugged. "My orders are to escort Laird Mactavish to his men."

Gabby shivered, but not from the cold. She welcomed Guy's comforting hug. "We will accompany the laird."

Though it seemed Gunn's soldier would argue the matter, he suddenly complied and turned for the stairs leading to the dungeons.

Gabby's insides roiled at the vile smell coming from below. A prickling of fear wound around her nerves, like wild ivy strangling a hedge. Laird Gunn had unusual accommodations for guests. She pressed closer to her husband as they descended the dimly lit steps.

When they reached the bottom her shocked gaze traveled to the poor wretches manacled to the wall. By the stench, more were dead than alive.

Moans too horrible to be human came from several cells. The guard unlocked the door of one and pointed. "The lad's in there."

Guy grabbed a torch and held it high as they entered the dank room where young Angus was kept. The lad lay in a pile of dirty straw.

Mactavish grabbed the boy and hauled him up by his tunic. "What happened to ye, boy? Speak!"

Though the boy had been sorely misused by someone's meaty fist, his spirit was not beaten. "My laird, ye should not have come. Laird Gunn will kill ye."

"Guy, help the boy," Gabby whispered.

"Mactavish must handle this."

Though Guy refused to interfere, she could see the anger in her husband's face. Angus's clothes were mere rags, and his bruises stood out from the deep cuts. He could be no older than Louis, yet when she looked into his eyes, his weary stare seemed to belong to an elderly man whose sight had blurred with time, regret, and sadness.

Mactavish released the lad. "Yer father is my friend. I have come to take ye both home."

The boy blinked, his eyes suspiciously moist. "Bless ye, Laird Mactavish, but I tell ye true, leave now, before ye find yerself on the end of a claymore."

"Why?" Bram asked.

All of Scotland watched as Gunn boasted to champion Mactavish's cause to free the Lady Bethany, and then lost. Defeated, his reputation suffered, and he vowed revenge. That is why he lured ye up here, Laird Mactavish."

Mactavish ran a hand through his hair and began to pace. "It appears I sorely misjudged the man."

Angus swayed like a man too far in his cups and Gabby rushed to his side, wrapping her arm around his waist gently to support him. "Rest," she urged, but started to lose her balance.

"Gabrielle," Guy admonished, taking the boy's weight from her and lowering him to the ground.

Angus grabbed Guy's arm. "Is she Lady Gabrielle Aumont?"

At Guy's nod, Angus shut his eyes and took a deep breath. "Fenrir's mood fouled after returning last week from the Campbell lists. Had he won the Lady Gabrielle, none would doubt his skill."

A bark of laughter rent the air, making everyone turn. There in the doorway stood a massive warrior with his sword drawn. "The fiasco of championing and losing Mactavish's cause was the day my woes began." Fenrir snarled, then his gaze traveled to Guy. "I had hoped to regain my status with Alec Campbell's lists, but who should defeat me but

Friar Guy''—he sneered the name—''brother to the Norman invader who caused my shame.''

Gabby's stomach tightened at the hatred in his voice. Her eyes widened as she watched him march into the room, leaving several guards in the doorway. Though she had not remembered his features, Fenrir Gunn was a thickset, muscular warrior. At the tournament he had seemed enormous, but in the tight confines of the dungeon he stood out like a giant in a cage.

Fenrir's foot nudged Angus. ''Unfortunately my bait is as stubborn as his sire proved to be. His father did not survive my hospitality.''

''Liar! I dinna believe ye,'' the boy croaked as Guy held him down.

''Ye will join him soon,'' Fenrir said, waving his hand in dismissal. ''But look what my trap has netted: not just Mactavish, but the Norman bastards as well. I could not be more pleased.''

'' 'Twas a fair fight,'' Mactavish protested.

''Aye, but when news spread of my defeat, I lost face with the clan, and they elected to follow my brother,'' he bellowed.

That is your own doing,'' Mactavish scoffed.

''I have planned my revenge for months,'' Fenrir went on as though Mactavish had not spoken, then pointed to Royce and Guy. ''But I never expected to settle the score so thoroughly.'' His arm swung in a wide arc, brandishing his sword with a disdainful flair. ''Ye now are at my mercy.''

''A charming host,'' Guy said, pulling Gabby close to his side.

Fenrir chuckled, but it was a cold, humorless sound. He sheathed his sword and turned to walk from the room, but at the doorway, he paused. ''At least see to yer lady's safety,'' Fenrir called back over his shoulder.

''What are you suggesting?'' Guy asked.

"Ye must die, nothing can change that. After yer death I will take her to wife. Her fortune and her gift of the Sight are most pleasing to me. If ye wish her to live, put her from ye now."

Gabby shook her head when she saw the inflexible expression on her husband's face. Tears blurred her vision as she wrapped her arms around his waist. "I will not! Do not even ask this of me."

"Wife, look at me." Guy lifted her chin when she refused. "You must do this. If the situation were reversed, would you not want my life spared?"

"I love you," she choked out.

His lips covered hers in a burning kiss of possession and regret. She clasped him in her embrace, longing to feel his warmth, and realizing this was the last time they would touch. Her chest tightened, knowing they had not made love and now never would. Her fingers traced a path over his face, as tears slipped down her cheeks.

Too soon he was pushing her away. "Go," he whispered.

She shook her head, and clung to him.

"Royce." His voice was hoarse.

When Royce touched her arm, she ignored him.

" 'Tis time, Gabrielle," Royce said.

"No," she said brokenly. "Guy."

While Royce pulled her to the door, she looked back over her shoulder at Guy's stoic features. With fists clenched and shoulders back, he stood motionless. His face looked etched in stone, his jaw firm, and expression set. All but his eyes. There she saw the raw pain he refused to show. Her heart breaking, she whispered, "Good-bye."

When the dungeon door slammed shut, she jumped. Her heart pounded in her ears as pure desperation flowed through her. Wild plans of rescue and escape flashed in her mind as Fenrir Gunn dragged her down the hall.

He shoved a cloth into her hand. "Dry yer face. Ye will

reassure his men that all is well. Tonight when they have drunk, my men will overpower them.''

"Will you drug them?" she questioned as she wiped her eyes.

"Dinna worry yerself about my affairs," Fenrir snapped. "Remember yer husband wishes ye to live, and to do so ye must follow my orders."

Gabby nodded, though she had no intention of obeying his orders. Her own life mattered not. She would bide her time and find a way to save Guy and the others.

In the great room, Royce and Bram's chief aides stood by the hearth. "My lady?" they questioned in unison.

"The men are with Angus and will be along directly," she said, racking her brain for some way to convey the truth.

"How long, my lady? Do you know if we will be spending the night?"

Fenrir's sharp-eyed warning could not be missed.

"I do not know." She looked at Vachel, the Norman, and her eyes lit on his silver cross. She had an idea. "But while we wait, would you say a prayer with me to give thanks?"

Fenrir stepped forward. "These men are tired. Dinna bother them, woman."

Vachel's head snapped up at the discourtesy. Without warning, he knelt, pulling his burly Scottish companion down to his knees with him. "A man is never too busy to give thanks for safe arrival, Laird Gunn."

Fenrir's face turned bright red at the chastisement. He had little choice but to join the Norman and Scot on their knees. To refuse would be suspect.

Fenrir knelt, and Gabby took a deep breath, hoping her ploy would work. When she started her prayer, he glared at her.

"I dinna ken Latin. Say it in our language," he warned.

Vachel intervened. " 'Tis the language of the Church,

heathen.'' His hand moved to his sword, the action not lost on Fenrir.

''My apologies,'' he said, begrudgingly.

Gabby sighed silently. The prayer she knew well, and scrambled to think of which Norman word she could insert that would not sound out of place. Only one came to mind, *embuscade,* meaning ambush, which if said haltingly sounded close to Latin. She repeated it throughout the prayer.

Vachel kept his head bowed, and she wondered if he had received her message.

He made the sign of the cross and kissed her hand. ''Thank you, my lady,'' he said, bowing respectfully. ''I expect Lord Royce and Laird Bram will send word when they are free.''

She nodded her head, frantically searching for a sign she could give, but none came to mind.

When the two soldiers left without showing any comprehension, her heart sank.

Fenrir smiled evilly. ''Ye were smart not to gainsay me.'' His fingers bit into her arm, but she refused to wince as he dragged her toward the stairs.

''Where are you taking me?''

''To the tower.''

''Please, I would ask that these last hours be spent with my husband.''

He shook his head. ''The future wife of Fenrir Gunn must show her loyalty.'' He laughed as he locked her in the shadowy room.

She shivered, wrapping her arms around herself for warmth, but the chill crawling up her spine came from fear, not cold.

She stumbled to the door and pulled the door handle, but the lock was solid. After banging on the door until her fist was sore and her energy spent, she sagged against the frame, then slid to her knees and entreated God's aid. She had failed. Guy would die.

* * *

Long after dusk had fallen, Vachel opened the dungeon door. ''My lord, the men await your orders.''

At Royce's questioning look, Vachel smiled. ''The Lady Gabrielle warned us of the trap.''

Guy pushed Royce aside to grab Vachel. ''My lady, how is she?'' he asked, twisting the man's tunic in his fists.

''Laird Gunn imprisoned her in the tower,'' Vachel said, pulling his tunic free. ''During the meal when he was busy impressing his troops, I sent a man for her.'' Vachel grinned and stepped aside.

Relief swept through Guy at the sight of his little nun. He opened his arms, and Gabby dashed into his embrace. God, but she felt right. He closed his eyes as his arms wrapped tightly around her, sheltering her next to his heart. ''Thank you,'' he whispered, knowing his prayers had been answered.

Angus moved to the center of the room. ''Laird Mactavish, Fenrir Gunn awaits the arrival of his brother's men. He did not expect ye to arrive with a Norman contingent. Yer only chance is to take him now.''

Mactavish turned to Royce's man. ''Can we take them?''

Vachel nodded. ''His forces are sparse and the majority of them are sotted.''

''While ye fight I will search for my father.'' Angus limped to the door, but Vachel laid a detaining hold on his shoulder. ''The Scots found your father. He was tied to the rack. Clearly he died rather than reveal the information Gunn sought.''

The boy shook his head in disbelief, ''He is not. We were only separated this morning.''

Guy let Gabby leave his embrace to offer comfort to the lad. She wrapped her arms around Angus, cradling his head on her shoulder. '' 'Tis all right, lad, let your grief out.''

Sobs of anguish filled the air as he clung to her.

When the plan was set Royce, Mactavish, and Vachel marched from the room. Guy hesitated long enough to pull Gabby into his arms and kiss her with such urgency that it robbed her of air. There was a primal savagery about this kiss that conveyed all the things left unsaid and unconsummated. Her legs buckled when he released her. After steadying her, he looked at Angus. "Take care of her, lad." Then he turned and ran after the others.

Gabby tried to follow, but young Angus held on to her arm. "Nay, my lady, ye would only distract him," he said solemnly, then moved to the door and closed it.

Her nerves felt raw, but she took a deep breath to still her fear. When Royce and Mactavish gave their war cry before they even cleared the dungeon, she flinched, but Angus reassured her that their men were ready.

Though they were deep in the bowels of the castle, muted sounds drifted through the dirt and stone. For over an hour the fight raged before the noise lessened.

When the gatekeeper's upper door opened, Angus stood in front of Gabby. Footsteps clattered down the steps leading to the dungeon. Their cell door slammed open, and Angus's eyes narrowed with determination as he faced Fenrir Gunn.

Chapter Thirteen

Gabby's heart pounded, her hands lightly touching Angus's arms.

"While yer friends are busy I will leave them a little taste of what to expect." Fenrir's daggers glinted dangerously in the dim light. "Which of ye is braver?"

Gabby stepped out from behind Angus and moved to his side. She would have shielded his body with hers, but he towered over her by a full head. " 'Tis a coward who would threaten a boy and a woman. But if this is the only way you will recover your good name, then by all means run me through. I shall endeavor not to struggle."

Fenrir's face flushed angrily. "I am no coward, woman."

Gabby pointed to the door leading to the fight, and nearly choked, seeing Mactavish standing at the top of the stairs. "Then your quarrel should be with the man who you think wronged you, not us," she managed to continue.

"Mactavish's clan will never let me near him," Fenrir snarled.

"I will meet ye face on," Mactavish said, making his presence known, then came toward his opponent with dagger drawn. "I need no clan to fight my battles."

Fenrir raised an eyebrow. "The fight must go against me if ye are back so soon."

"Aye, it does."

"Have done then," Fenrir snapped, charging forward up the steps with his weapon. "Ye have robbed me of my rightful place."

Mactavish easily parried the blow.

Fenrir's rage could be seen in his eyes. Hatred spurred the man on. "Ye will be with yer Maker soon."

The men danced up and down the stairs, slashing and hacking at one another. Though Mactavish had the greater experience, Fenrir's strength made the match an equal contest.

Suddenly one of Fenrir's soldiers appeared and immediately drew his sword.

"Look out," Gabby cried.

Her warning came just in time as Mactavish sidestepped the second attacker, but he could not hope to last against two opponents. Young Angus charged into the fray, saving Mactavish from a knife wound. Enraged, the soldier turned on the brave boy.

Gabby searched frantically for a weapon, but there was nothing in the dungeon but manacles. Angus choked and squirmed as the guard lifted him by his throat, squeezing the life from the boy. Gabby picked up a heavy leg-iron and charged forward, banging Fenrir's soldier on the head just as Angus lost consciousness. She rushed to hold the fallen lad, who drew a deep breath and clung to her.

All the while Mactavish continued to fight, trying to gain the upper hand but barely able to hold his own. Suddenly, Fenrir stumbled to the ground, but before Mactavish could deliver a blow, the man threw a handful of dirt into his eyes.

"Die!" Fenrir roared, jumping up to attack the blinded man. In that instant, Guy raced down the steps and jumped into the fray, fighting the northern Scot.

"Ye bested me once, but can ye again?" Fenrir challenged, and lunged forward, fighting like a man possessed, his wild strikes full of fury and rage, but not accuracy.

Unexpectedly, Guy dropped to one knee, and Gabby gasped. Fenrir charged the fallen man, and stabbed repeatedly. Guy parried every blow, then slipped his blade under Gunn's arm. The Scot slid to the ground, a surprised look on his face.

Gabby's cry of relief echoed in the air as she rushed over to her grime-covered husband and flung her arms around him.

"He killed my father," Angus said, staring down at the lifeless form. "I should have taken his life." In despair Angus walked over to the dead man and spit on the corpse.

Mactavish joined Angus and placed his arm over the lad's shoulder. "From this day on ye will be my son. Yer father, Brian, saved my life when we were lads. I now repay the debt."

Though the boy had tears in his eyes, he stood with dignity and nodded his assent.

Renwyg Castle stood like an impressive stone monolith in the vast fields. Gabby stared in awe as the sun's rays broke through a cloud and lit the imposing structure, making it gleam a burnished rose. As they rode through the gates and dismounted, a beautiful woman with flowing red hair and sparkling brown eyes rushed to meet Royce.

Guy's eyes twinkled at the sight of the woman in his brother's arms. When Royce set her free, Guy's arms opened to accept a greeting. Gabby felt an ugly twinge of jealousy as she watched the beauty in her husband's arms. Only a wench, she thought, would show such brazen affection for a man who was not her husband.

Laughing, the redheaded wench playfully slapped Guy, then pulled out of his arms. "Guy, I have been most anxious to meet the woman who stole your heart."

Guy smiled, turning around to introduce her. "Lady Bethany, this is my wife, Lady Gabrielle. Gabby, this is Royce's wife."

Royce's wife, not a leman, not a mistress, and certainly not a wench. Gabby felt so petty as she curtsied.

"Oh my, but she is truly a beauty. You do not deserve such an angel," Bethany said to Guy.

Not only beautiful, the woman is sweet. Gabby felt even worse, humbled by Bethany's sincerity.

"Come," Bethany said, pulling Gabby's hand.

As Gabby followed, she looked back over her shoulder at Guy, who smiled in approval.

"Do not look so worried," Lady Bethany said. "They will talk of war and intrigue, and we have more important things to discuss."

"Where are we going?" Gabby asked, looking around wide-eyed at the fine hall and lovely tapestries.

"To my apartments. Confidences need privacy, do you not agree?"

Gabby smiled. "You are like a whirlwind, Lady Bethany. I must catch my breath." She wanted to drink in the beauty of this castle after the hard journey.

"You will when we are safe from eavesdroppers." Bethany said, pulling her along through the great hall and up the stairs without a pause.

Gabby laughed despite herself. "Have you always had this much energy?"

"Nay, I had more before the twins were born."

"Twins?" Gabby said, surprised.

"Aye," she said, her eyebrow raised. "Did Guy not speak of his nephews?"

"He did not," she said, embarrassed to admit her husband's omission.

Bethany chuckled. "Never mind, we will speak about everything." She pulled Gabby through the main chamber doors. "I am so glad Guy found you. I told Royce that you must be an extraordinary woman to win Guy's heart. I can see I was right."

In less than a week Gabby had grown to love her sister-in-law, Bethany, and the twins, who were wonderful. Why, just looking at their sweet faces made Gabby long for a family of her own.

" 'Twas not always easy between Royce and me," Bethany said as she changed Bram's—or was it Lance's—clothes. "He once thought I was beneath his station."

"Beneath his station?" queried Gabby, admiring the other twin in his cradle. The baby held tightly on to her finger, his toothless smile warming her heart.

"Aye, I am a Saxon, and he the conquering Norman. It used to bother Royce greatly. He was determined to marry a Norman lady in order to reclaim his former status at court.

"Former status?"

"You do know of their circumstances?" Bethany asked frankly.

When Gabby shook her head, Bethany muttered, "Men," then laid the twin, who instantly protested, in the cradle. "Oh, Lance, why can you not be even-tempered like your brother?" she gently admonished the baby as she picked him back up and motioned Gabby to follow her into the other room. Shutting the door softly, Bethany motioned to Gabby to take a seat.

" 'Tis not necessary to explain, Bethany," Gabby said,

feeling as though she had put her new sister-in-law in an awkward position.

"Nonsense. Since you are part of the family, I will gladly tell you where the bones are buried." Bethany slowly walked, while patting her son's back to quiet him down. "Royce and Guy enjoyed a very privileged life until their father suddenly disclaimed parentage. Though their mother was a highborn aristocrat, and the de Bellemare name recognized everywhere, they were looked on as Lance Lemieux's by-blows."

Good God, Gabby thought as Bethany spoke. Guy was related to her betrothed, Bayard de Bellemare, and also to Louis's fostering family.

"They lost not only their father's love, but their way of life. Hence, Royce's desire to marry back into the aristocracy. Though I believe it was not status Royce sought, but a way to show his father he could succeed without him."

"You mean, Guy is a bastard, too?"

"Does it bother you? After all, you are a highborn lady."

Gabby considered the question fully. "Guy's bloodlines matter not to me."

Bethany smiled in approval.

"I had decided my calling to be a nun was not true the night before Louis ran away from the abbey. But when I went in search of my brother, I had no choice but to pretend to be a postulant," confided Gabby.

"I know. Life can be . . . complicated. We must sometimes do what in ordinary times we would never consider," Bethany agreed.

"But . . ." Tears misted Gabby's eyes.

"What is it?" Bethany asked.

"You are so understanding. I feared everyone would hate me for taking Guy away from the Church."

Bethany bit back the truth that she so wanted to reveal, and said only, " 'Twas Guy's decision."

"Forgive me," Gabby said. "I have no right to burden you with my fears."

Bethany sat down and patted her on the shoulder. "All will be put right," she sighed. "Have faith."

Gabby hiccuped. "I will. But sometimes I feel so guilty. Guy hesitates to talk about his life as a friar, especially now that he is leaving God's service. Bethany, I love him so. I want him to be happy."

"I promise you, Guy will get what he deserves!"

Bethany crossed her arms over her chest. "Royce, I insist, Guy tell Gabrielle the truth."

"Do you think I have not tried to talk some sense into him?" Royce asked. "I swear, since Guy has met this woman his common sense has fled."

"Love often causes such confusion."

"Whatever the reason, he is sorely lacking in judgment. I worry about him, Bethany."

"Perhaps it will help if I talk to him. I truly like Gabrielle and hate deceiving her."

"As do I." Royce nodded. "I fear he will lose the maiden if he does not handle the situation with more care."

Bethany's heart softened at Royce's concern. "Find Guy and send him to the great room," she said, running toward the hall.

"Very well, my dear, I will send him to you."

Watching idly as the servants laid out the midday meal, Bethany paced the long room four times before Guy entered. She turned around to look at her brother-in-law but before she could open her mouth, he spoke.

"I wish to take Gabrielle on a ride today. The weather has broken, and I think the outing will do her good. Will you and Royce join us?"

She drew a deep breath, knowing she would get much further with Guy if she agreed.

"A wonderful idea. I have not had an afternoon riding in Royce's company since the children were born."

"Good. I know Gabby needs a diversion—"

"Have you decided to tell her about your orders from the king?" Bethany broke in.

"Nay, I cannot. It may be for naught. William may change his mind."

"If he does not, will you confess your part to her?"

"I do not know. I cannot risk losing her."

Bethany shook her head. "You will if you are not honest with her. Gabrielle will feel betrayed."

"As much as I respect your opinion, dear sister, you will have to trust me in this."

"Oh! You are as stubborn and unreasonable as your brother."

Guy shook his head and walked over to the table to take a piece of bread. "I once thought you a sensible woman."

Bethany let out a sigh. "I will await your apology. I vow you will someday beg my forgiveness for your unconscionable attitude. Until then, I pray for your own good that you listen to my counsel."

"I always listen to you, Bethany, but I fear childbirth has addled your wits."

Royce walked in just as a bowl of stew was flung in his brother's face.

"I am sorry, Royce, but your brother was behaving like a boor," Bethany said, storming off.

Royce chuckled, enjoying the sight of his brother doused in gravy and meat, fighting off the hounds as they tried to get a tasty tidbit. His grin widened when he turned and watched the angry jaunt of his wife's hem as she marched from the room.

"I take it you tried to reason with my wife," Royce said, as he dragged a hound away from Guy's legs.

"A mistake, I admit," Guy said, knocking another hound away. "Perhaps I did not do you such a favor by playing matchmaker. If I ever knew this side of her nature existed, believe me, I would not have had a hand in your downfall."

Royce roared with laughter. "Do not judge my marriage when you have not yet dealt with yours."

"Then do not give me any more advice!"

Royce roared at the sullen command, not one bit put out by his brother's mood. "If I remember right, those are the same words I used when you tried to talk some sense into me about Bethany."

" 'Tis not the same."

"Nay, 'tis not. Now you are the one behaving like a spoiled child."

"Royce, I do not know why I ever considered you a man of great wisdom. 'Tis true as a warrior your prowess is unequalled, but when it comes to dealing with women, you are a rank recruit."

" 'Tis not I who is having the problem, brother. I have learned from experience."

Vachel entered the room, interrupting their conversation. "Cedric took this from the messenger," he said, and handed a missive to Royce. The royal seal was unmistakable. With foreboding, Royce opened it and scanned the script, then handed it to his younger brother.

Guy's stomach constricted. *God's teeth.* How could he return her to William? But how could he not? The command was clear, the script bold and strong. *"Return to London with the maiden."*

"Do not even contemplate it," Royce warned, guessing Guy's thoughts. "You must return her."

"Royce—"

"Go and plead your case before King William. If it will help, I would gladly add my voice to yours. Quennel Aumont will be discredited."

"But if William owes Quennel a boon, the debt will be repaid."

"You must see the king. You must try."

"If I am forced, I *will* disobey the king."

"Guy, you will be a hunted man. Where would you find asylum from William's wrath?"

"Enough! I will worry about that if and when it becomes necessary. Now let us take the ladies for a ride."

Guy started for the door, but was stopped by Royce's sudden bark of laughter. He turned and confronted his brother. "What jest is it this time, brother?"

"You must be in love. Look at yourself."

Guy looked down at his gravy-stained clothes and a sheepish grin broke out over his lips.

The day was unseasonably warm for late fall and a blessed relief from the snowstorm in northern Scotland two weeks earlier. Stirring from its autumn slumber, the land embraced the warmth. The near leafless trees, their black branches lifted to the sky, glistened in the early-afternoon light. A wet trail of hoof marks dotted the brown grass, and a mist rose quickly from the ground. Deer roamed the harvested fields, foraging for food as the deep earthy smell of tilled soil and fall vegetation filled the air.

The day was beautiful and calm. They rode for two hours until they neared the cliffs of the west, where the salt air cooled the shore and the tang of the sea could be tasted on the tongue. Gabby thought the estate marvelous. She looked over at Guy and found his gaze on her. Her cheeks blushed prettily and she brushed back the lustrous strands of hair that were blowing about her face. " 'Tis beautiful," she said.

"I know," he replied meaningfully.

It was while she was gazing into his midnight eyes that a wave of apprehension suddenly washed over her. She knew a vision was about to overcome her, and she looked helplessly at Guy. He immediately took her in his arms, pulling her off her mount onto his lap. Royce and Bethany turned and stared at them in surprise.

"My wife is blessed with the Sight," Guy explained

Gabby heard his voice as though from far away. He did not make excuses for her, nor did he pretend she was ill. For this alone, she would always love him dearly.

Her eyelids fluttered, and a vision surfaced. Swallowing back her anxiety and fear, she took several deep calming breaths in an effort to welcome the foresight. *The white mist unfolded, revealing faces that were frightening and almost distorted by the hard lines and taut muscles of determination. Unlike the gaunt features of the Norman peasants who had attacked them, these men were large and imposing and stared with a pitiless cold detachment.* The image faded.

"We are in grave danger," she whispered as she grabbed onto Guy's tunic. "All of us. We must return to the castle now."

Royce was about to speak when Bethany hushed him. "I think that would be an excellent idea." She pointed. "Royce, look."

Five armed men rode toward them.

"Bethany, take Lady Gabrielle back to the castle and alert the guard," Royce commanded.

Bethany turned her horse. "Come, Lady Gabrielle."

Gabby looked at Guy, unable to hide her worry and fear. "I do not want to leave you."

"Gabby, you must. I cannot fight and worry about your safety."

She understood. Without further argument, she remounted her horse and rode off with Bethany.

When they were halfway to the castle, an armed man suddenly rode out of the bushes. He grabbed Gabby from her horse and pulled her onto his saddle. Her scream alerted Bethany.

Bethany spun her mount and rode straight into the assailant's horse. He drew back his arm and viciously slammed his fist into Bethany's face, knocking her from her mount.

"No!" Gabby screamed.

Gabby wrestled against the captor's clutching hold while Bethany stirred on the ground. Fearing the soldier would try to trample Bethany beneath the horse's hooves, Gabby raked her nails down the man's face. "Save yourself, my lady," Gabby pleaded as Bethany struggled to her feet.

Cursing, the assailant turned his horse and galloped off toward the forest that sheltered the sea.

His grip bit into Gabby's waist, as she continued to struggle against him. His rotting breath hissed a warning. "Be still, woman, or you will taste the back of my hand." The image of Bethany being struck passed through Gabby's mind. She did not want to be rendered senseless. She had to think of an escape plan.

As soon as Vachel heard Lady Bethany's story, he mounted his horse and rode out of Renwyg in pursuit of the attackers. The castle forces split, half going in search of the Lady Gabrielle under Cedric's command, the other following Vachel to join the warlord and his brother.

Guy fought at his brother's back. The mercenaries were good, and all his skill was needed to fend off the attackers and hold his position. As the last man swooped forward, Guy felt a strange premonition. He suddenly knew Gabby was in peril. He fought like a demon, not only beating the mercenary back, but thrusting his sword deep within the man's chest.

"Thank God for Lady Gabrielle's premonition," Royce said, standing over the dead men. "With the timely warning we were able to send the ladies to safety."

Again, a feeling of trepidation overcame Guy. Gabby needed him. He knew it as surely as he knew day would follow night. "Gabby," he breathed, then looked sharply at Royce. "I think it was a diversion. A trap."

"Nay." Royce pointed to the fields. "There is the castle guard. Bethany and Gabrielle made it safely to the castle."

Though that made sense, Guy could not still his fear. And when the soldiers approached wearing grim expressions, he knew.

Vachel dismounted before the horse stopped and made his report.

Guy's guts twisted as he listened to an account of his wife's abduction.

Taking their place at the head of the patrol, Royce and Guy rode after Gabby's captor, but his trail disappeared near the rocky cliffs at the sea, where they found Cedric's men. Guy broke out in a sweat. What if a boat awaited the assailants and Gabby had been taken to sea? They would have no way to trace their direction.

Terror coursed through his veins as he thought of her helpless in Aumont's vile clutches. He could barely breathe for the fear. "Lord protect her," he whispered, feeling sick as he watched the waves crash against the rocks.

Royce sent soldiers out to search. Mercifully, a short time later, one returned, having located the trail. Relief surged through Guy. Thank God they had found them. But his relief was short-lived when he heard they were headed for the sea.

Guy pushed his horse to make the port before the tide came in and the boat could put out to sea. Dusk had fallen when they found an encampment at a river inlet. Lying on his belly, Guy peered through the foliage. His stomach tightened in fury as he saw Gabby shivering in a boat, while a company of war-hardened men sat around a small campfire.

Every nerve in Guy's body burned, and if Royce had not held him back he would have charged into the encampment and taken them on single-handedly.

"They will kill her if you attack."

Royce's warning helped to bring him under control.

Crawling back to a safe distance, Guy turned to his brother. "What is your plan?" he asked.

"We have to take them by surprise. These are no peasant farmers, but mercenaries."

"Agreed. How do we surprise them?"

Royce took hold of his brother's shoulders and narrowed his gaze. "We must send for a priest."

Chapter Fourteen

"Have you taken leave of your senses?" Guy asked.

"A cleric's robe can be fetched from the nearby church. Then you can enter the encampment as a friar and protect her when we attack," Royce said.

Guy rebelled at the delay. "If they are Quennel's men, they will know she was traveling with a friar."

"They may suspect you, but you must convince them you are simply a man of God. Even a seasoned warrior will hesitate before killing a man of the cloth."

Guy nodded his assent, knowing that every minute that passed with Gabby bound and terrified would be hell.

When the quarter moon rose in the night sky, Guy walked toward the assailants dressed as a friar. He knew Royce's men were in place, and his eyes scanned the area, taking note of their opponents' positions.

"Who goes there?" A burly warrior with an oversize girth pulled his sword from its sheath.

With a forced smile on his lips, Guy raised his hand. "Just a servant of the Lord going about his business. Do you have room at your fire for a cold and weary traveler?"

"Stay there, friar," the guard warned as his sword point touched Guy's chest.

Another man rose and went over to Gabby. Guy could see the gleam of the knife in the firelight as the attacker held the blade to her throat, but forced himself to look away.

"I am only a poor friar on a pilgrimage." He lifted his upturned hands heavenward as if evoking the Almighty.

"He has no weapons." The guard called to the others as he lowered his sword.

The warrior relaxed his hold on Gabby and motioned Guy forward with a wave of his hand. "Come farther into the light."

Seeing his wife's terrified expression, Guy's hands closed into tight fists at his side. When he stepped into the light, her eyes widened and relief swiftly swept over her features before she lowered her gaze. Guy walked steadily forward.

"You may warm yourself by the fire, but unless you have provisions, you will go hungry," the guard warned, stepping out of the boat.

Guy knew he would have to act now. Making the sign of the cross, his signal to Royce, Guy ran toward Gabby. At the same time Royce's men swarmed into the clearing, Gabby's guard rushed forward. Guy dived headlong into the man, and they wrestled in earnest on the wooden dock. The man drew his knife and sliced Guy's chest.

He sucked in his breath at the sharp, stinging pain, but instead of weakening him, his wound spurred him on, giving him added strength. When the weapon whistled through the air, Guy caught the guard's wrist and squeezed, forcing the knife from the man's hand. Locked together in mortal combat, neither released his hold as they rolled over the edge. A loud splash sounded as the icy water engulfed them, but

Guy managed to drive his fist into the man's face, rendering him unconscious.

He rose from the water and climbed onto the dock. Screams of agony echoed in the air as men were wounded or slain in the heat of battle. His gaze immediately sought Gabby, and his heart missed a beat. Three soldiers stood between them.

Guy rushed forward, throwing the first soldier who blocked his way into the water. The next man turned and was similarly dispatched. But the third soldier smiled, his sword drawn. Though the point of the blade was only inches from his chest, Guy tipped his head back, gave the blood-curdling Campbell war cry, and charged forward. Caught off guard, the soldier soon lost his weapon and fell beneath the fury of Guy's fist. Finally, his way clear, he jumped into the boat and took her in his arms, holding her as though he would never release her. Thankful that she was not injured, he silently cradled her, clutching her to his chest, unable to speak as he tried to absorb her terror.

The noise of the battle died away as he rocked her within his arms. Several long minutes passed when all he could do was whisper, "It is all right, *chérie*. You are safe now."

Royce touched his shoulder. "Although keeping a woman gagged is a treat for the ears, I think it would be chivalrous if you at least untied the lady's arms before you ravished her."

Guy grinned sheepishly at the jest, then gently slipped Gabby off his lap and freed her arms from the ropes. As he untied her legs, she reached behind her neck and pulled off the gag. "Oh Guy," she whispered before melting back into his arms for a kiss.

He had rescued her, but somehow she'd known that he would—she never doubted it. Knowing that her welfare meant more to him than his own, she realized that she trusted and loved him above all living things.

His lips moved on hers and suddenly all thoughts vanished. Lord, but this man had a magic. And she never wanted to be freed from his spell.

Gabby heard someone clear his throat and surfaced slowly. Royce stood over them with a pleased smile. "Brother, unless you are willing to entertain our men, I suggest you restrain your ardor." He extended his hand to help Gabby up. "My lady?"

She blushed and lowered her gaze. Reluctantly, she placed her hand in Royce's and allowed herself to be pulled upright, her eyes widening in surprise when he squeezed her hand in a comforting manner. There was a subtle difference in the way Royce looked at her. In truth, until now, she did not feel he had accepted her. But it was there now in his eyes, both respect and admiration. It surprised and warmed her.

"Do not worry about my oaf of a brother, Lady Gabrielle. In time I am sure he will make a decent husband."

Humor? Guy's stern brother, Royce, so solemn and brusque when they had met, now deigned to joke with her? How astonishing.

"I suppose anything is possible, my lord. I only hope your wife can say the same."

Royce roared at her wit. "You have chosen well, Guy."

Guy shot his brother a glare. "Do not take him seriously, Gabby. Mother despaired at his dull-wittedness and thought the sun rose and set upon myself. I am sure you will like her, and she you."

Gabby smiled at his silly antics.

She touched his face. "I am sure your mother loves both of you. But I can see why she would favor you. I do."

Guy's face beamed. It was as if she had handed him the riches of the world.

"You are right, brother. I have chosen well." He looked at Gabby, then back to his brother. "We will catch up with you, Royce."

Royce lifted Gabby's hand and deposited a kiss, then smiled at his brother. "There is a hut nearby I use while hunting, just a few leagues to the east. You need to get out of those wet clothes," he said, accepting two blankets from his man and handing them to Guy.

Gabby gratefully accepted Guy's help as he spread the woolen folds out and pulled the ends close about her neck before seeing to his own needs. Once he was cocooned in the wool, she fussed over him, worried he would take sick. If she was cold, he had to be freezing. She rubbed her hands over his arms and chest, trying to absorb the dampness and warm his chilled flesh.

Royce smiled. "I will make sure the area is secure, so your *night's sleep* will be uninterrupted. We will see you tomorrow."

He kissed her hard on the mouth. She trembled from the rough possession, then reveled when his savagery turned to tenderness. Passion heated her blood as his lips slanted over hers, touching, tasting, teasing a response.

When the kiss ended, he looked at her intensely, as though he were memorizing every feature on her face.

"What is it, Guy?"

"I thought I'd lost you. I could not bear that." He touched her face, his fingertips tracing her eyebrow, then softly drifted down to the line of her jaw before lightly caressing her lips. "I think you have become more important to me than is good. I cannot think of a world without you."

"For me the day would cease to have light if you did not reside in it. The night would be filled with terror instead of dreams. I, too, cannot picture a world without you."

"It would seem for better or worse, we are joined. Maybe our souls were destined to find each other. I know that I will never let you go."

His fierce words brought a smile to her lips. "Nor would I ever wish to leave you."

She sealed her words with a kiss. Gripping the edge of his blanket, she pressed closer into him, needing to feel his body as much as she wished him to be aware of hers. He groaned, a husky rumble from within his chest, and the sound sent shivers up her spine. When he ended the kiss, he drew a deep breath, then lifted her onto the horse and mounted behind her.

"Guy," she said suddenly, "I do not want to wait for the dispensation."

"We must."

"We are meant to be together. I wish to be with you as your wife."

Guy was humbled by her words. No one had ever loved him so unconditionally. He held her tight against his chest, wondering what to do. He knew if they made love, he would never be able to part from her. Swallowing the lump in his throat, he tried to form the words that would put her off. But he could not.

Selfishly, he wanted this moment and any other that would allow him to be with her. It was damn stupid, but he did not care. Let reality wait. Soon enough, he would have to take her to London and King William.

He knew that once he started this course it could not be changed. But she was his and, by God, he would have her. She was the single most important thing in his life. Everything else faded away.

"You are right, *chérie*. Nothing any church can say will unite us any closer than we are."

He felt her curl up closer to him, and his love for her seemed to burst into flower. There were things in his heart that he had never said to anyone before. Now he knew he could say them to her. He would hide no longer.

He would have this time with her.

The hut came into view, and though it looked forlorn and weathered, it represented a castle where he could be with his love. He needed nothing else.

All his life he had thought he searched for a place in the world. Now he knew his home resided within her embrace.

Gabby touched his face. Her beloved was perfect and a precious gift from God. She had not believed it possible to love someone so much, but it was. Guy meant more to her than her own life. She would gladly give up everything to see him safe.

"Come," he whispered.

She slid into his embrace, wrapping her arms about his neck, and settled comfortably against the huge, muscled chest. Resting her cheek on the warm skin, she heard the comforting rhythm of his heart.

He carried her into the hut and placed her carefully on her feet. "I will have the chill gone soon," he assured, wrapping his blanket around her. In the dim moonlight, he moved to the hearth and started a fire.

When a small flame caught he motioned her to the hearth. "Warm yourself while I tend to the horse and get more wood."

While he was gone she added more twigs and branches to the fire. The flames grew bright, and she opened her blanket, letting the warmth seep in. Guy returned, his arms laden with wood, and laughed ruefully. "Our first home is not much, my beloved."

She looked around at the bare surroundings and saw nothing of the shabbiness. " 'Tis enough, my love."

He stacked the chopped wood on the floor beside the

hearth, adding several logs end up to catch the flames. When he stood he pulled a pallet close to the fire. Then he took her into his arms. "You deserve every luxury, and I offer you this."

His voice held a touch of regret. Reaching up, she cradled his face between her palms. "I would rather be with you here than at court with anyone else."

It suddenly struck her that it was not mere words she had spoken. It was true. She could be happy with this man. How she wished they could walk away from their lives and become simple farmers. Till the land, raise their children, and take comfort in each other's love. But, alas, they were not free.

A cozy warmth spread through the hut, and she studied her lover's face in the soft firelight. Such handsome male perfection still awed her. Gently she traced her fingers over his brow, his lips, his jaw.

He caught one finger in his mouth and gave it a playful nip. "Woman," he growled, "I would have you for my wife." Her heart rejoiced that they would finally be together, that tonight he would hold nothing back. When he kissed her, she shivered, her lips clinging to his, yet relishing the forays his mouth would make to her ear, her neck.

He peeled back her gown, and she lowered her eyelashes, suddenly shy. When his fingers brushed away her soft linen smock she tingled as his touch caressed her bare skin, and with every slow, languid sweep of his hands, sensuous delight coursed through her as he removed each garment until none remained. He lifted her chin. "Look at me, Gabby."

Her gaze met his and she hoped, prayed, he understood the insecurity that assailed her.

"You are my love and my life." he said. "There is nothing to fear."

She swallowed the lump in her throat. " 'Tis hard. I love you, but . . ."

"There are no buts. You trust me, do you not?"

"Aye, with my life."

"Then trust me with your heart. I will never harm you."

Though she still felt anxious, the barriers that had naturally risen were lowered. Her gaze held his. "I am afraid, but not of you. Only of what is to happen."

"I will make it special," he said, cradling her face in his hands. "You are precious to me."

Gabby smiled, timorously, and reached out to untie the lacings on Guy's long clerical robe. Slipping off first the wet wool covering, then the soft linen underclothes, her fingers brushed the warm flesh beneath, and instantly desire flared in his eyes, darkening the midnight blue to black.

Guy's mouth covered hers in a slow, sultry kiss that stole her very breath away. Though a shy maiden, she responded to his sizzling heat. Nothing seemed more right. She belonged in his arms.

When his kiss ended, her hands caressed his broad shoulders, sliding down his arms and up to glide over his back. His flesh was warm and firm beneath her fingertips, and she was reminded of her rescue when the power and strength of his hard muscles had been loosed on her attacker.

Yet a man so strong and mighty could be so tender with her.

An ache began in her very core. His kiss sent messages of delight and desire, adding warmth to her already-heated flesh.

Guy instinctively knew how to touch her. His soft, feather-like caresses made her burn for him.

"You are taking my breath away," she whispered.

Guy's strained chuckle came from deep in his throat. " 'Tis nothing compared to what you do to me."

She wanted to please him, but did not know how and

refused to show her ignorance by asking. Instead, she imitated his movements. His groan filled her with excitement. Languidly, as slowly as his hands had stroked her flesh, she trailed her fingers over the hard ridges and firm valleys of his muscled chest and arms.

"Do not be afraid. Touch me," he whispered, guiding her hand lower.

She gasped at the size of his swollen member. Though she still thought it was too large for her to accommodate, she wrapped her hand around him and moved in the motion he showed her. His moan gave her a heady sense of power, and her fear suddenly dissolved. She stroked his firm shaft until he pulled her hand away and kissed her with a hunger that left her panting.

His hands worshiped her as though she were indeed a prized possession. With each sweeping caress, liquid fire raced through her veins.

"I love you," she whispered, and his lips devoured hers.

The kiss was not like the others. Where they had been passionate, this one was carnal.

With the heat and fire of his touch, she lost all thought.

His sensual demand never frightened, but only excited. The fire he ignited burned with an intensity that consumed her. She wanted, needed something she could not name.

"Guy, help me."

Still he stroked her body, learning every curve.

"Guy," she breathed, not able to stand the excitement building within her.

"Trust me," he whispered. His lips traveled to her breast, his tongue circling the peak before his teeth gently grazed the sensitive area.

Currents of white-hot desire streaked to her loins. When his mouth covered her other breast she cried out, her nails scoring his back.

His lips returned to hers for a scorching kiss, and a primitive rhythm played as his tongue darted in and out.

Her fingers raked through his dark hair, slipping down to his neck to knead the thick muscles on his shoulders. She arched against him as his lips left her mouth and nuzzled her neck. Then his hand dipped lower and slipped between her legs to stroke the swollen mound. ''No,'' She gasped, stilling his hand.

''Let me,'' he insisted, his voice hoarse.

When she released her hold, his lips covered hers, creating a scorching need with a purely sensual kiss, as his fingers once again stroked the tender folds, slipping inside to the same primitive rhythm his tongue kept.

Gabby was now breathing with difficulty; it seemed that only the hope and anticipation forced the air in and out of her lungs. She needed him, wanted him. ''Please,'' she whispered, urgently.

Perspiration dotted his brow, and the tendons on his arms stood out as he poised over her. ''My love, 'twill only hurt this once.'' Then he lowered his lips to her and kissed her passionately as slowly he eased into her.

The pressure was intense, and suddenly she became frightened, and tried to push him away.

Shaking with restraint, he stilled, and whispered against her lips, ''Trust me.''

She stopped struggling and returned his kiss. With one thrust he was inside, and pain knifed through her, but it lasted only moments before a rush of pleasure began. As though sensing her body's response, he moved with a slow rhythm that brought such pleasure and fulfillment that she could barely stand the joy.

''Guy,'' she moaned.

He covered her lips with a growl and continued the movement that brought her wonder beyond measure.

Suddenly, a million brilliant suns exploded within her,

sending her to heaven and giving her a glimpse of the stars. Seconds later, Guy joined her, his body lodged deep within her as they clung to each other, gasping for breath.

The rise and gentle descent from the heavens ended in the comfort and closeness of each other's embrace, and Gabby sighed in contentment.

Bethany met Royce in the stable the moment he returned. "Royce, your mother has arrived."

Nodding distractedly, Royce issued instructions to his men, then turned his attention to his horse.

Frustrated, Bethany followed him into the horse's stall and pulled on his arm. "Royce, did you hear me? I said your mother has arrived."

Royce looked at her, the light dawning in his eyes. He took a deep breath. "Poor Guy."

Chapter Fifteen

"I have wronged your half brothers greatly," Lance Lemieux said. Sadness etched deep lines and creases in his otherwise-handsome face. "Is it not ironic that we now need their help?"

"Father, you did not know they were your true blood when you disowned them."

"Be that as it may, I must set it right. Not until the birth of Royce's twins did I suspect the truth, and when Beltane confessed his part in the deception . . ." His voice trailed off as he remembered his violent confrontation with the base knight. He paced the deck, his hand on the rail of the ship bound for England.

"I wish you would take more time to recover from your illness," Rule said as he followed behind.

"Are you reluctant to see this breach repaired?" Lance asked, turning around to face his eldest son.

A more youthful image of his father, Rule's dark blue eyes and rugged features were tinged with anger for a moment, then he turned away to look at the sea. *"Non.* In truth, their mother was the only mother I knew.

When Royce and Guy were born, she still treated me as a beloved son, not as an outsider. It is unfortunate my mother's family spread the lies they did. All of us have suffered from that injustice. You, most of all."

"Non, 'twas your brothers, Royce and Guy, who suffered. They were only young boys when I so foolishly believed the false witness brought against their mother. In stung pride I disowned them. To lose their father's love and his name through no fault of their own—how frightened and angry they must have been."

" 'Tis said they hate the name Lemieux. Certainly they wear their mother's name with great pride. 'Twill not be easy to mend the rift, Father."

"Nothing of value is ever easily won." Lance slapped his son on the back, feeling better than he had in weeks. "Twins," he exclaimed, marveling at the good news. Male twins ran in his family, usually skipping a generation. "Royce's sons prove he is my seed."

Lance's eyes curiously scanned the deck of the ship, until a face he did not care for suddenly came into view. He touched Rule's arm to gain his attention and gestured toward their unwelcome sailing companion.

Rule stiffened. "God's teeth, what is Bayard de Bellemare doing on this vessel?"

Lance did not like the man. He was Royce and Guy's cousin, and a more evil man he had not met, unless it was Bayard's unsavory traveling companion, Quennel Aumont.

Lance continued to watch them as his son went to see about stowing their belongings. He remembered the night Gabrielle Aumont had taken her brother from the Lemieux Castle and fled Normandy to escape from Quennel. Lord help those poor children if Aumont was traveling to fetch them back to Normandy.

Quennel turned, and his eyes widened as he recognized Lance. He nudged Bayard de Bellemare, who also turned, his expression changing from indifference to dark disdain.

Bayard's hatred of Royce and Guy was no secret. A bastard's plight, Lance thought, grinding his teeth at the needless suffering caused by lies.

That Quennel and Bayard had joined forces boded ill for someone.

A nervous young woman joined Aumont and de Bellemare. Lance felt his heart skip a beat—she was the image of Royce and Guy's mother. There could be no doubt she was a de Bellemare. He searched his memory, this must be Liana, Bayard's little sister. Poor thing looked scared to death. If the stories he had heard about her brother and Aumont were true, then she had good reason to fear her traveling companions.

The day was fresh and clean and utterly wondrous, Gabby thought as they returned to Renwyg Castle. Guy loved her. How could the day not be glorious?

She wrapped her arms around Guy's waist and leaned into his chest. "Husband," she whispered.

He leaned down and stole a kiss from her lips as they entered the castle gates.

"I think I will like being your wife." She tried to comb her fingers through her hair, but he crushed the tangled tresses in his hands.

"You look beautiful." He kissed her again, thinking that the morning had been even more wonderful and passionate than the night before. "Like a woman who has been thoroughly made love to," he chuckled, then jumped off their horse and helped her down.

She blushed at the memory of their lovemaking. Unable to match his boldness, she simply drank in his devilish smile and knew she loved him. His arm slipped around her waist, and they walked up the steps.

When they entered the great room, Guy stopped short. "Mother!" he shouted.

"Mother?" Gabby sputtered.

"Guy," the petite dark-haired woman said. Leaving her sewing on the table, she rose to her feet. A demure smile slipped into place as she came to greet him, looking not at her son but his companion.

Gabby blushed under the subtle inspection. When Guy reached down and hugged his mother, Gabby took the opportunity to smooth back her hair. Then she noticed to her mortification what had drawn attention. Her fastenings were misaligned and she quickly retied them. After a night of lovemaking she looked every bit the ravished maiden.

After bestowing a kiss on his mother's cheek Guy turned to Gabby and took her trembling hand in his. "Lady Gabrielle, this is my mother, Lady Ambra de Bellemare," he said, making the first introduction. "Mother, please make the acquaintance of Lady Gabrielle Campbell Aumont de Bellemare."

Guy's mother narrowed her eyes. "You two are courting disaster by living in sin."

"Mother," Guy warned, as Gabby's face heated with embarrassment.

"I am old but not feeble," she reprimanded. "I understand you were married in a Druid rite. That will never do. Your marriage must be blessed in a Christian ceremony—let the papal dispensation follow." She pulled Gabby away from Guy's side. "My dear, I have learned from experience that whenever possible, one must always conform to society's rules." Still talking to Gabby she turned to shoot a look at Guy. "Until the wedding, Lady Gabrielle will stay with me."

When Guy stepped forward to protest, Ambra held up her hand.

"Do not even think it," she warned. "I am here, and you will show me the respect I deserve by honoring my wishes. Or would you like your wife to suffer the same fate as I?"

Guy flushed angrily. "That will not happen. I am not my father."

Alec Campbell, along with Ian and Louis, rode into Renwyg Castle long after the castle inhabitants had sought their rest. They were escorted to the great room and given mead while the master was summoned.

Yawning, Royce met a sleepy-eyed Guy in the hallway. "What catastrophe has brought them to our door?" Royce wondered.

Guy's exhaustion turned to apprehension. Pulling his tunic over his head, he brushed past Royce and took the steps two at a time until he reached the landing. Only Gabby's welfare would draw Louis out of hiding to join Alec in this unexpected visit.

The visitors' muted conversation stopped when Guy's footsteps echoed on the stone floor of the great room.

The men were covered in travel dust; they had obviously ridden long and hard.

"Greetings, Royce de Bellemare," Alec Campbell said.

"Laird Campbell, what brings you to my door at such an hour?" Royce walked to the trestle table and poured a cup of mead, offering the flagon to Guy as he took a seat.

"We have had unsettling news from Normandy. Quennel Aumont and his bridegroom for Gabrielle are en route to England."

"Are you sure?" Guy stared at the trio, hoping they were mistaken.

"Aye, our source is reliable."

Guy ran a hand through his hair. He had wanted to wait until he had talked to King William and received permission to marry Gabby. It would make the telling of his part in this fiasco so much easier if it had all ended happily. Now there was no choice, with Quennel Aumont on his way to England.

"Ye must marry my niece in the Christian faith to protect her from Quennel."

"*Oui,*" Guy agreed.

"*Who* is Quennel's choice?" Royce asked.

Louis stepped forward. "The prospective bridegroom is Bayard de Bellemare."

Guy looked at Royce, whose shock mirrored his own.

"Do you know him?" Louis asked.

"Aye, he is our cousin," Guy said.

Royce poured another goblet of mead and handed it to his brother. "Bayard is a man we have never liked. He has made it his personal business to cause us as much trouble as possible through the years."

Guy drained half of the goblet. "The wedding will be held before we leave for London." Bayard would take immense pleasure in torturing Gabby if he ever found out she was Guy's beloved."

"London?" Louis asked.

"King William wishes all of us to report in a fortnight."

"You cannot take Gabby to London," Louis argued, moving closer to make his point, but Alec silenced him and turned to Guy.

"I dinna ken why *ye* are being summoned." Nothing missed Alec's regard.

Guy slammed his tankard down, and met the Scotsman's glare straight on. "Because I was ordered by the king to bring Lady Gabrielle and her brother, Louis, out of the convent and back to London. I am no friar."

"I see," Alec said, his voice level.

"Deceitful cur," Louis cursed, lunging at Guy.

Alec held Louis back. "If the man meant to harm ye, he would have already betrayed ye."

His nephew subdued, Alec looked back at Guy. "Why did ye disobey yer orders?"

"Why do you think?" Guy snapped.

Alec smiled. "Have ye told the lass yet that ye love her? Or that ye were sent to betray her?"

"You go too far, Scotsman," Guy warned.

"Ah, the wee lassie does not know of yer part in this. I dinna envy ye when she learns of it."

Guy squared his shoulders. "I can handle my wife."

In the silence that followed, Royce poured mead for all and, forcing a smile, said, "Shall we toast the coming marriage?"

Everyone lifted their goblets but it was Louis who offered the toast. "To sweet, innocent Gabrielle, who has had to take care of all her loved ones. May she now be rewarded with the same unselfish devotion, and cherished with the same love that she has given so freely."

The reprimand was not lost on Guy. He watched his future brother-in-law over the rim of his goblet. The boy had grown up.

Guy raised his goblet in a toast of his own. "To my beloved, may she never know of the intrigue or my reluctant part in it. I would die before I let harm befall her." He downed his drink and noticed the boy's features had relaxed.

Eyes sparkling with amusement, Alec hoisted his goblet. "To a poor wee man who posed as a friar. He will need the Almighty's help if his secret is ever discovered."

Everyone but Guy drank to this toast.

When the men had drained their tankards, Alec turned to Royce. "Can ye give us quarters in the castle or the stable?"

"Since you are Guy's visitors, he can be inconvenienced."

Guy looked up. "Put them in my room for tonight. I will find them suitable quarters in the morning."

"I dinna care where ye sleep, Norman, but my niece willna sleep in a stable," Alec stated bluntly.

Royce chuckled. "Never fear, Campbell, your niece is not *now* sharing Guy's bed."

Guy glared at his brother.

"Ah," Alec said, turning to Guy. "A fight was it? Dinna worry, the lass will forgive ye. Her heart is kind."

" 'Twas not a fight," Guy grumbled.

" 'Twas our mother's untimely visit," Royce put in. "She insisted on propriety."

Alec laughed. "Women! They are a joy beyond measure, are they not? Well, lad, do not worry. We will tie the knot proper so none can stay ye from yer wife's bed."

As the men retired, Guy poured himself another drink, then strode out of the great room toward the stable. It would be a damn cold place to sleep tonight. But the bleak weather just might take his mind off the problems that beset him.

When the door shut behind Guy, a tiny woman sat up in the chair in which she had fallen asleep. The loud voices had intruded on her dreams, and embarrassed to be caught in her nightdress, she had remained still. Safely hidden beneath the fur robe, she had heard everything. Lady Ambra shook her head. "Guy, what have you gone and done now?"

As the occupants of Renwyg Castle lay peacefully on their pallets, a shady-looking figure crawled away from the knoll nearby.

"The boy is here," he whispered to his companion, "You must go and get reinforcements."

" 'Twill be several days before I can return."

"Hurry. We do not want to miss our opportunity to take him."

* * *

Gabby awoke in the dead of night, that silent time just before dawn. Her body was covered in perspiration and she knew her nightmare was no dream, but a warning of what was to come.

"Louis," she whispered.

Her brother's life was in peril, and the danger was very close. Throwing a blanket over her shift, she left Ambra's room in frantic search of Guy.

The stone floors were cold and she hurried her pace. Guy's room was down the corridor and to the left. The low-burning torches cast eerie shadows that slid along the wall, following her steps. A shiver ran up her spine and she hugged her wrap tighter about her shoulders.

Outside his door she carefully lifted the latch and peered inside. Though dark, the dying embers threw the room into heavy shadows. Guy lay on his side in the middle of the bed, a mound of fur covers blocking her view.

She tiptoed in and closed the door behind her. "Guy," she whispered, but silence met her ears.

Walking closer, she peered at the mound of bedclothes, but could not see him. "Guy?" she called out hesitantly.

When silence again met her ears, she moved next to the bed and nudged the lump beneath the hill of wolf pelts. "Guy."

Suddenly an arm snaked out from beneath the covers and grasped her wrist. A scream rose to her lips.

"What in God's good name are ye doing here at this hour?"

"Uncle Alec?" she squeaked in surprise as she met his gaze. "I am looking for Guy."

He chuckled. "I am proud to see ye respect our Druid rites, even if yer mother-in-law does not."

"Why are you here, Uncle Alec? Where is Guy?" Her

voice was unnaturally high as she clasped his hand. "Please, you must tell me."

"What is it, lassie?"

She took a deep breath, and nearly collapsed. "Louis is in trouble. We must find him."

Alec sat up and pointed to one of the two pallets on the floor by the hearth.

"Thank God," she whispered, seeing Louis sleeping peacefully next to his cousin. "My brother is in grave danger, Uncle. Please, you must get him away from here."

"Calm yerself, lassie, and tell me what has upset ye so. Is it the gift?"

"Aye," she said, wringing her hands together.

"Very well, lass." He patted her hands, stilling her nervousness. "Tell me what ye saw."

"There is danger to Louis, Ian, and a boy named Angus."

Alec rose from his pallet, taking care to cover himself from her view. When he had his blue-and-green kilt wrapped around his full girth he turned toward her. "Come, lass, 'tis important to recall every detail."

She drew a deep breath and allowed her uncle to guide her to a seat. He lit a candle, whose soft yellow glow chased away the gloom. After he poured a large tankard of ale and handed it to her, he took a seat in the chair opposite hers.

She raised an eyebrow at the amount of spirits he expected her to drink.

"Start at the beginning, lass," he prompted.

"I was sleeping when the Sight came upon me." When she noticed his skepticism, she rushed on, "Uncle Alec, it was not a dream. I swear it. I know the difference by now."

He merely nodded, and poured himself a goblet of ale.

"Ian, Louis, and Angus were bound and gagged. I know it occurred near here because I could see Renwyg Castle in the distance." She touched his arm. "Uncle Alec, they were taken during a celebration."

"A celebration, ye say?" He sat straight up and leaned closer. "What kind of celebration?"

"I do not know. But there were festivities of some kind."

"Like a wedding?"

"I do not know, perhaps a wedding or a feast day. The attackers were dressed as traveling troubadours."

A broad smile covered Alec's face. "Very good, lassie. I willna have trouble identifying them."

"Please take Louis and Ian and depart before this event occurs."

"Leave before yer wedding, lass? Are ye mad?"

"Wedding?" she whispered. "Oh my God." Then she downed the whole tankard.

"We have them," Ian said, as he and Louis returned with the maps from the armory. They assembled in the great room, ready to make plans for the security of Louis and Gabrielle.

Bethany bustled in with her arms laden with linen. "Royce, I am sorry, but you cannot stay here. I have a hall to prepare and servants to instruct."

She handed the linen to Maida, then stood like a little warlord with her hands on her hips and an uncompromising expression on her face.

When Royce rolled up the maps Guy shook his head in mock despair. "I never thought I would see the day when my brother the mighty warrior would meekly do his wife's bidding."

Only Louis and Ian guffawed. The Mactavish, who had just now arrived, glared at Guy.

" 'Twill be interesting to see how he handles his wife when she wishes to use a room to prepare for his honor," Mactavish said to Royce.

"I would tell her away," Guy said, making a shooing motion with his hands.

Royce roared, while Bethany scowled at the offender. "Guy de Bellemare, a wife is a woman, not a pet to command.

"Now, away with all of *you*," she said. "Be thankful Lady Gabrielle is being fitted for her wedding dress. It would be a pity if she heard your boorish comment and reconsidered agreeing to the marriage."

Bethany's father chuckled as he threw his arm over the shoulders of the young lad with him. "Bethany is a born leader. Watch her and learn, son."

"And who is this?" Bethany asked as the men walked toward the armory.

Mactavish and Angus turned back. "Angus, meet yer sister."

The lad respectfully nodded his head.

"Sister?" Bethany repeated.

"Angus saved my life. He is alone; therefore, I have taken him into my house. If he learns all I have to teach then he will, upon my death, lead the clan as my son."

"What of Bret?" she asked, worried about her half brother, who was visiting the Mactavish clan.

"Royce will make provisions for him."

"Oui, I will," Royce said, standing in the doorway to the armory.

"You knew?" she asked her husband.

"Oui."

Bethany shook her head. "You could have told me, husband."

"When was there time, wife?" He smiled and closed the door.

The men settled around a table as Alec stood up, the few dark braids among his wild mane swaying as he dramatically relayed what he was told.

"Are ye sure the girl has the gift?" Bram asked.

"Aye, she does," Alec said. "She saved our village."

Mactavish nodded. "I heard the tale."

"If she sees it, then it will come to pass," Louis added.

"Then we must prepare," Royce said. "I know most of the men of North Umberland. Mactavish can vouch for the Mactavish clansmen. Who else do we have to worry about?"

"My people will come," Alec Campbell said.

"*Oui*, but you will know them," Guy said.

"The Campbell clan will provide a guard for Louis, Ian, and Angus," Alec added.

"Who will guard Gabby?" Mactavish asked.

"Who else but Guy?" said Royce.

"Nay." Alec smiled, his eyes sparkling with amusement as he turned to Royce. "She needs someone with her both day and night."

Royce nodded in understanding. "Who would you like to see guarding her during the night? My mother?" he asked, enjoying Guy's distress.

"I will sleep outside her door," Guy said. He glared at each man who was enjoying his discomfort. "Not another word about the sleeping arrangements."

"Then it is settled." Alec chuckled as the others hid their grins. "Now all we have to do is set the trap for the assassins."

"Trap?" Royce asked.

"Aye. A stern reprisal will let others know that I will not tolerate any acts of aggression against my kin."

A knock on the door sounded, and, with Royce's permission, Cedric entered. "My lord," Cedric said, and bowed low.

"*Oui*, Cedric, what is it?"

"A message has come from Normandy," he said.

Royce held out his hand for the missive and the gray-haired guard looked uncomfortable.

"My lady has it."

"Bethany?" Royce questioned.

"Nay, Lady Ambra."

A sudden distressed cry drew Royce and the men from the armory into the great room. Ambra sat in the master's chair, the missive lying in her lap.

"Mother, what is it?" Royce reached for the open letter, but she grabbed it, cradling it close to her breast. Tears pooled in her eyes as her lips trembled. "Your father is coming to England."

The words knocked the wind from Guy's lungs. The pain of his father's betrayal resurfaced, exposing a childhood wound that had never healed.

" 'Tis good news, Guy." Alec slapped him on the back. "Ye can invite him to the wedding."

"Never," he growled.

Bethany jumped up. "Royce, 'tis the worst possible timing."

"Calm yourself, wife, and see to my mother. She has had a terrible shock."

But Gabrielle had already put a comforting arm around her future mother-in-law, while Guy fetched her a cup of wine.

"Do you think he will come to North Umberland?" Ambra whispered.

"Nay, mother. Rest your fears." Royce said.

He'd better not travel here, Guy thought. The only time he wanted to see Lance Lemieux was at his wake and not before.

Meats roasted slowly in the hearth. Sweets of all kinds filled an entire table with a guard posted to prevent anyone from sampling the wares before the wedding the next morn. Breads baked in the ovens, while candied fruits and nuts were dipped in a shiny, honey-coated glaze. Fresh rushes sprinkled with sweet-scented herbs were laid on the floor, and every inch of the castle had been scrubbed to perfection. Evergreen needles burned in the hearth, filling the air with a rich, pungent pine scent. At the evening meal every soldier, including Guy, agreed that the ladies had worked a miracle.

"Thank you, Guy," Bethany said. "But 'twas Lady Gabrielle who gave me the idea of burning the pine needles."

Guy beamed with pride as he put his arm over Gabby's shoulders and pulled her close to his side. "You are amazing."

"Truly, my lord, I did very little. 'Tis Lady Bethany who makes everyone move."

Guy laughed. "*Oui,* Bethany is like the center of a storm. I am glad you are not like her. 'Tis peace and tranquility I crave."

Banners and flags hung from the ceiling, denoting the clans friendly with the North Umberland house. William's crest and Royce's emblem hung together, the only Norman banners except for the one Gabby had sewn. None that entered the hall left without congratulating both ladies. They had indeed transformed the great room into a hall fit for royalty.

As Royce entered the great room, he stopped and looked around. " 'Tis not much, but I call it home."

Everyone laughed at his good humor. Soon others were noting the subtle change Lady Gabrielle's touch had wrought on all. Though quiet as a mouse, she affected everyone with her gentle, winning ways.

After the evening meal Lady Ambra excused herself and went straight to bed, while Bethany and Gabrielle retired to the master apartments. Bethany dismissed the servant watching the twins.

"What music are you planning, my lady?" Bethany asked Lady Gabrielle.

"I would have a mixture of Norman and Scottish."

Bethany smiled. "I thought as much."

"Then you are not offended?"

"How could I be? And even if I were, how could I, being married to a Norman, admit it?"

Gabby smiled, enjoying the wit and style of her pretty hostess. She could not have picked a better sister. "Thank you for everything."

"You will find that we Saxons are not as surly as Normans like to think."

"I have already found your Saxons to be a warm and loving people. Would that all Normans could claim the same."

Bethany stopped and stared at Gabby. "I can see what has attracted Guy. Your sincerity is genuine. Honesty, my dear, is your greatest charm. One does not expect anyone to be so genuine."

"I am far from what you think," Gabby denied, embarrassed by Bethany's glowing assessment.

"I will not argue the point. Now, my dear, let us proceed with the preparations. We could house family members in the armory, and build temporary lodging for the guests by the stable. What do you think?"

"I think you could run this castle without any help," Gabby said admiringly.

A bittersweet smile crossed Bethany's features. "I tried that once and found the running much smoother with a helpmate."

Gabby thought longingly of Guy. "I am very lucky that Guy de Bellemare wishes to marry me. I hope I can prove worthy of the honor he pays me."

Bethany frowned. "Gabby, he is human. Do not place him so high in your estimation that when he errs you cannot forgive him."

"I love him," she said simply.

"I know, but love is not worship. No man can live up to such expectations."

"Guy could," Gabby declared. "You do not know how honest and noble he is."

Bethany sighed. "You will have to learn for yourself that even a paragon of virtue can make mistakes. I hope it will not hurt too much."

"Nay! Guy would never hurt me."

Chapter Sixteen

That evening, several traveling minstrels arrived and waited to speak with the lady about her choice of music. They lingered in the courtyard, fighting off the chill breeze as best they could. Guy insisted Lady Gabrielle not be placed in danger.

A knock sounded on the master chamber door. Lady Bethany looked up from the selection of wares that she had been showing to Lady Gabrielle. "Come."

When Laird Mactavish swung the door open, the tallow candles flickered. Leaning against the doorframe, his long hair glowed a burnished copper from the hall torches.

"Lady Gabrielle, with yer permission, I would listen to the auditions of our musicians. Ye are busy with the wedding preparation, and I am a judge of Scottish music," he said.

"Should I come down?" She started to rise.

Mactavish waved her back in her seat. "There is no need. The men are familiar to us," he lied.

"Thank you, Laird Mactavish, but what of the Norman

music I also requested?'' she asked, while handing Bethany the ribbon she had chosen.

''I will let Guy choose,'' he said.

At Gabby's pleased nod, Bethany walked over to her father, and whispered. ''I know it is not the music that interests you, but the men who play it.''

''I have never doubted yer intellect, daughter, but keep it to yerself,'' he muttered softly. Then he looked to Gabrielle. ''Be about yer business my lady, and I shall be about mine.'' He smiled and closed the door.

When Mactavish joined Royce and Guy in the great room, he nodded, letting them know he was ready. ''Alec awaits, my lords.''

Guy moved around the table. ''In case the musicians are a diversion, we will make sure no one slips past and harms those within. After I am satisfied with security I will join you.'' Guy handed Mactavish a wicked-looking knife. ''I owe Campbell a weapon.''

Mactavish took the knife. ''Ye have good taste, Norman.'' He hid the sharp weapon beneath his red kilt.

Two Mactavish clansmen fell into step behind their laird when he entered the courtyard. Alec already stood in the bailey flanked by his clansmen as he studied the new arrivals. There were ten groups no one recognized.

''How will ye judge who is the impostor?'' Mactavish asked, joining Alec.

'' 'Twill be the man who canna play and canna sing.''

''We are in agreement.'' He handed Alec the knife. ''A gift from Guy, along with a reminder to exercise restraint. A live prisoner is needed.''

''I will handle it my way, the Scottish way.'' Alec smiled with sly intent as the knife disappeared beneath the blue-and-green Campbell plaid. ''Shall we proceed?''

''Aye,'' Mactavish chuckled.

''Ye there,'' Alec called out, pointing to a tall, pinched-face minstrel. When the man glanced around, Alec called again. ''Ye, by the stable, come and let us hear yer music.''

The musician looked embarrassed, but picked up his lute, rushed forward, and skidded to a stop before the Scotsman. ''What is your pleasure, my lord?''

''Can ye play any Scottish music, lad?''

''Nay, I know only the Norman.''

Alec crossed his arms, clearly displeased by the minstrel's limited selection. ''Let me hear it then.''

The musician played his piece, then bobbed his head and stepped back

''Next,'' Alec called out.

Several more musicians played. In a short time it became apparent that only a handful knew both Norman and Scottish tunes. After an hour just one band of musicians remained. Mactavish motioned the last group of troubadours forward.

''They dinna seem pleased,'' Alec whispered.

''Aye, it appears that they wish to avoid the audition,'' Bram agreed. Silently he nodded to his waiting man.

The burly minstrels lumbered forward, and Alec watched them closely. Their hands were not long and soft, but callused and large, and while their clothes appeared rough-worn, the material was fine.

The biggest man slowly raised his instrument and nodded to his companions, who in turn did the same. The raucous noise that resulted started the cat wailing.

Mactavish leaned forward to Alec. ''They are far from minstrels, but I think they do indeed know a tune. I would have them sing to it. What say ye?''

Alec nodded his head. His clansmen approached, tightening the circle surrounding the men.

Guy joined them, his gaze on the giant with the lute. ''A painful recital.'' He grabbed Alec's arm. ''Remember, I want them alive.''

"Aye, enough breath will remain to tell ye what ye wish to know."

Guy shook his head. The Scots were so bloody dramatic. Then he caught a glimmer of steel in all the clansmen's hands.

"Alive," Guy warned. "They are no good to me dead."

Guy reached the leader first, while the Scotsmen took hold of the other musicians. Cries of fear from the giant's companions filled the air, but he remained silent. Guy's hands circled the minstrel's thick neck.

"Tell me what I want to know and live, or refuse to answer and die."

The giant beneath his hands actually trembled. "My lord," he stammered, "I have done nothing."

"Who sent you? What was your mission? How many lie in wait?"

When silence met his ears, Guy released the man's throat and pulled out his sword. "You have chosen, then?"

The huge hulking captive dropped to his knees. "My lord, I have done nothing. Have mercy."

"Coward," Alec spit.

"Run him through," Mactavish ordered.

The man cringed when Guy drew his sword back, then suddenly exploded with fury. Like a wild bull, he lowered his head and charged Guy.

The force knocked Guy backwards, but he held on to the assailant, dragging him along. They wrestled on the ground, rolling back and forth for an advantage. Several punches were aimed at Guy's head, but he blocked them, returning as many blows to his opponent's face. Bruised and battered, the giant continued to struggle. But it was clear that the man was no soldier. Guy easily subdued him.

* * *

Gabby pretended to smother another yawn. Feigning fatigue was the only way to escape Bethany's watchful eye. Finally, Bethany bade her good night and Gabby made her way from the master chamber with haste. Ever since overhearing Bethany's whispered remark about the musicians, she had been trying to get away. The men were trying to protect her, of course. But she could identify the man posing as a minstrel.

At the base of the stairs she met Angus, Ian, and Louis.

"Where are you going?" Louis inquired as he barred her way.

"Guy sent for me," she lied, when she saw the Aumont look of determination. "I am going to identify the assailant." She folded her hands, knowing Louis would not defy Guy's order.

Louis raised an eyebrow, but said nothing, as Angus jumped forward and offered his arm. "Good, I am tired of hiding out."

Ian and Louis fell into step behind them.

Angus leaned forward as he opened the door and whispered, "They dinna believe ye."

"Do you?"

"Nay, but I willna let ye go alone," he said, escorting her to the circle of men.

"Uncle Alec," Gabby called out, then shuddered when she saw the beaten man in Guy's hold.

"Guy, they are innocent," she exclaimed, stunned by the musicians' terrified expressions and shocked by Guy's brutality.

Alec frowned at her untimely appearance and waved his hand. "Lass, we have the offenders."

She turned and studied the other minstrels by the wall. One man was hiding in the shadows and sliding along the wall, until he crossed a wedge of light thrown from an overhead torch.

"Nay, Uncle Alec. 'Tis he." She pointed to the first man who had auditioned, the one with the gaunt face. "He is the one."

The thin man quickly sprinted from the wall and off into the darkness.

Ian and Louis gave chase as orders were shouted to the gate guards.

The four terrified musicians were released. "Hard to believe these men made their livelihood playing those instruments," Alec said to Mactavish, as an elderly soldier picked up the dropped instrument.

"My lord, they are not bad," Cedric offered. "I expect they were just frightened." He handed the lute back to the timid musician as Guy joined Gabby.

" 'Twas not music, but noise," Alec accused the gray-haired Saxon.

"A Scotsman would not know the difference."

Guy chuckled at Cedric's insolent words while Ian and Louis dragged the accused minstrel back.

"Who do ye work for?" Alec questioned.

"I am innocent of any wrongdoing."

"Ye are not a bad minstrel. 'Twould be a pity if ye were to lose several fingers and be unable to play."

The man's face paled. "I did nothing wrong. I merely told a man when these boys practiced their sword fighting." He grabbed at Alec's hand, "Please my lord, I beg of you to hear me." He knelt down before the laird, two trails of tears inching down his cheeks. "I am just a poor minstrel, traveling from town to town to earn my keep."

"Leave him be," Mactavish commanded, disgusted by the unmanly display. " 'Tis obvious he is innocent. A musician would not risk his livelihood."

Gabby circled the man thoughtfully. Every instinct in her body screamed. She turned to her uncle Alec. "He is lying."

Alec considered her words, but Mactavish stepped forward. "Nay, lass, see how cowardly he is. He would give up the truth rather than suffer the loss of his fingers."

The minstrel gave a convincing performance as evidenced by the crowd's agreement. But she had seen him in her vision. She clenched her fists. "I tell you he is lying."

"Lass," Mactavish warned, at her tone.

She turned to Guy. "Please, I beg of you, believe me."

"Your uncle Alec—"

She reached out and touched Guy's arm. "I cannot explain how I know this is true. But you must believe me. I know this man is lying as surely as I know the sun will rise and set each day." Tears filled her eyes. "If you love and believe in me, then trust me now."

He stared long and hard at her, then nodded. "As you wish."

Grabbing the man by his tunic, he declared, "My lady believes you lie, and I always believe my lady." Then he dropped the man as though he were an unsightly troll. "Take him to the dungeon," Guy ordered Cedric.

The minstrel's face went red with rage. "That witch! Aye, I know more. But you will never pry the information from my lips. May the witch burn in hell, and you with her! Witch, witch," he screamed, and several soldiers turned and looked at her with worry in their eyes.

Gabby's face paled. Witchcraft was the most serious charge in all Christendom, one that could not be taken lightly. Guy stared down every curious expression as he placed his arm around Gabby and pulled her close.

"The rantings of a coward," he declared.

Several of the soldiers nodded in agreement, and those who had reservations did not voice them.

"I wonder if your uncle Quennel plans to discredit you," Guy said as he watched the crowd disperse.

Gabby shook her head. "That was not my vision. I am

not in danger, but these young men are. I cannot explain it. Please, they must be watched.''

"Lass," Alec said, "yer visions are not gospel. Some come true, and others do not. Rest yer mind and enjoy yer wedding. I swear to ye, we have the situation under control.''

Gabby looked at Guy and saw reassurance in his eyes. "I must give you the trust I myself sought,'' she acknowledged, then turned to the others. "You are right. I am over-wrought, no doubt due to the wedding preparations. I trust you all. Honestly, I do." She reached out and touched her brother's cheek. "I only worry for you.''

" 'Tis time ye let someone else worry," Ian advised.

"Yer husband will have a time of it,'' Alec said.

"Let her worry now and again, Guy," Louis teased. "She will need to keep in practice for your sons.''

Though her face blushed bright red, Gabby laughed, and the humor released her tension. "I do not know why I was blessed with such mutton-headed relatives," she quipped. "But I would not have it otherwise.''

The men chuckled as young Angus came forward. "My lady, I am not related to ye, but I am honored that ye concern yerself with my welfare." He lifted her fingers to deposit a gentle kiss on her hand.

Guy retrieved Gabby's hand from Angus's grasp. "Mac-tavish, this young whelp will cause you no end of trouble where the fair ladies are concerned. Tell him he should not be so free with his compliments, especially when the lady's intended can hear them.''

Angus grinned. "I would never compliment the lady with-out her husband or intended in audience. That would be a far worse transgression. But no one will stop me from expressing my gratitude.''

"Remember what I said: trouble," Guy repeated, only half in jest.

Gabby's smile was angelic. "Angus Mactavish, you are

very gallant. I shall treasure your good manners always, especially since you made my intended jealous.''

Angus beamed. ''If ever ye have need of my services again, my lady, I shall come.''

''Aye, he will be a handful where the ladies are concerned,'' Mactavish agreed, then good-naturedly cuffed his adopted son's shoulder.

Shortly after the break the fast meal the women walked back to the master chamber to finish hemming Gabby's wedding gown. Taking the last stitch, Bethany cut the thread and stood back to inspect her work.

'' 'Tis lovely,'' she said. ''Where is your girdle?''

Gabby reached for the matching belt.

''Wait,'' Bethany said. ''Maida, please open my chest and pull out the queen's gift.''

''Oh no,'' Gabby rushed to stop her hostess's generosity. ''You cannot.''

''A very wise woman once taught me to accept a gift gracefully. Queen Matilda simply refused to take no for an answer, and so do I.''

''*Oui,* Matilda is a strong-willed woman,'' Ambra said, rising to her feet. ''Excuse me for a moment, I left something in my room.''

When the door closed, Maida shook out the wedding girdle. The lovely embroidered sash fanned out before the ladies.

''But it is so beautiful,'' Gabby said, reverently touching the material.

''I was saving it for my daughter, but I fear with Royce as her sire, she will tower over me, and the girdle will be too short for her.'' Bethany sighed. ''I would be honored if you would wear my gift.''

Gabby swallowed the thickening in her throat and

accepted the girdle. She had been paid the highest compliment. "May I prove worthy of your kindness. You are truly
a good woman, and I am grateful. Thank you, Bethany."

Bethany ignored the compliment and turned to the servant.
"What scent have you chosen for the lady's bath, Maida?"

"Violets."

"Excellent." Bethany smiled. "Please send a maid for
the hot water, and we will begin."

When Maida opened the door to leave, Ambra entered
the room with a box under her arm. She opened the box
and pulled out the soft velvet pouch within. "Here, Gabrielle, these are yours to wear. They were a gift from my
beloved."

Gabby realized how much the admission cost, and she
hugged Ambra. The woman clung to her for a moment then
pulled away. Allowing Ambra time to collect herself, Gabby
opened the velvet bag and gasped. Inside the lined folds lay
a rope of pearls.

"You will wear them draped through your hair," Ambra
said. "That is how I always wished to say my vows.
Although I must confess, with your lovely ivory skin, jet-
black hair, and violet eyes, you will do them far more justice
then I ever could."

Gabby's face blushed at the compliment.

"She is right, you know," Bethany said. "Not only do
you have the face of an angel, but you behave like one."

Unaccustomed to praise, Gabby turned and quipped. "I
hope you remember that when your husband and mine
recount some of my earlier deeds."

A smile covered the lady's lips. "They already have.
But I found the stories filled with courage and love." She
chuckled at Gabby's groan. "You are indeed a woman of
substance and sparkle." Bethany turned away. She did not
add that her poor sister-in-law would need that courage when

she found out the deception played by her dear beloved. A sorrow entered her heart at the heartache ahead for her friend.

Ambra stepped up and hugged Gabrielle. ''We must hurry, today is your wedding day. And this ceremony will make those present forget the pagan rite.'' She took hold of Gabby's hand and held her gaze. ''I want your nuptials to be blessed by our Church and above reproach.''

On the morning of the wedding Friar John stood with Louis and Ian in the great hall awaiting the bride.

When Guy entered the room, he stood with his brother Royce before the man of God.

A hush stole over the room as Lady Gabrielle slowly descended the stairs.

Captivated by the vision, Guy's breath caught in his throat. With a slight tilt to her small chin, she seemed to float in a regal cloud of perfection. Her shiny ebony tresses were crowned by a halo of pure white pearls, and as she approached, the loving sparkle in her violet eyes, and the serene expression on her lips, captured his heart. This image of Gabby, open, vulnerable, and giving, would live in his memory forever.

Vachel nudged him in the arm, as Royce whispered, ''God Almighty, brother, she is a rare beauty.''

As Guy drank in her radiance, he suddenly knew that the rest of his life would not be nearly enough time to love this woman.

They were meant to be together, he thought, as she came and placed her hand in his. Together they turned and stepped before the cleric.

Guy knelt with her, refusing to release her hand. Before long the hall reverberated with the vigor of his vows; and her own, though soft and low, sounded clear and melodious to his ears. She was happy, and all within the reach of her voice knew it.

Guy knew he had no right to be so elated, but he was. And though Gabby might have trouble forgiving him when she learned the truth, she would, in time, see the right of what he had to do. Besides, she was tied to him in holy matrimony. They were forever bound.

When Friar John asked for the kiss of peace, Guy leaned down to comply and was stunned anew by the depth of love shining in his wife's eyes. Suddenly his life felt whole. She was his home, his heart. She completed his soul.

The kiss lasted much longer than the dear friar expected. Several times Friar John stepped forward and cleared his throat, but Guy ignored him. In his arms was the woman who had rescued him from every painful memory. It was not until Friar John touched his shoulder that Guy regretfully ended the kiss.

As soon as the friar pronounced them legally wed, Gabby was pulled from his side by Royce, who planted a hearty kiss on her lips, one that Guy did not like at all.

"But brother, I am merely returning the favor. Did you not kiss my lovely bride at my wedding?"

"*Oui,* but if I remember right, it was not done with such feeling."

"I am merely welcoming *my little sister* into the family."

Gabby smiled at Royce's jest. "The de Bellemares are never at a loss for charm."

At her answer Bethany laughed. "Yes, they are magnificent, are they not?" Then she whispered in Gabby's ear loud enough for the brothers to overhear. "Even if 'tis only in their own minds."

Royce's and Guy's smiles faded as they stared at their wives. "I think 'twould be a good idea to keep these two separated," Royce said. "Their humor is sorely distorted."

Guy's mother joined them, her two grandsons in her arms.

"Happiness, daughter," she said, kissing Gabrielle's cheek. Then she turned to Guy. " 'Tis always best to do the right and good deed. I am proud of you."

Guy lifted his wife's chin. "I know now why men lose their wits when they wed. And, my love, I have no regrets."

But he did. And the secret could destroy them.

After they had bidden a fond farewell to the wedding guests, Gabby stood before her husband in their private chamber. The moment the door shut, leaving the noise of the well-wishers behind, Gabby noticed a difference in her husband's mood. Though the Church had witnessed their vows, as Guy wished, did he now regret his decision? As the silence stretched between them, her anxiety grew. Guy had her heart and her soul. She had given both freely. Yet she knew something was wrong.

Without saying a word, he handed her a missive. Fear and concern clouded his blue eyes and the serious expression frightened her.

With dread her gaze traveled to the parchment. The king's order was clear. A sharp pain encircled her heart. They had known paradise, and now it was over. Reality had intruded.

"When will I have to return?"

"Soon."

She nodded. God had given her a brief moment of happiness. She would not repay his gift by asking for more. Her brother was safe, and she had had the pleasure and great good fortune of falling in love. That was far more than she had hoped for.

"What's wrong? Do you fear that I will be unable to keep you safe?"

"Nay. I have complete faith in you. But some things are not in our control. Though you wish it otherwise, there may be naught you can do."

He took her in his arms. "I would forfeit my life for your freedom."

Gabby quickly placed her fingers over his lips. "Do not ever say such a thing. Not even in jest." But she knew he meant every word in earnest. "I could not bear to live without knowing you were safe. My burdens are not yours."

"I have made them mine. Would you not do the same for me?"

"Aye, but it is different somehow."

"*Oui.* You think you can face this alone. I tell you, you cannot."

"Guy," she whispered, "I do not know what I have done to deserve you." She looked at him and knew that anything would be possible with this man. Suddenly, the fear of returning to face her uncle vanished. She knew Guy would protect her.

Strange that when her situation had seemed so hopeless, he entered her life. She could not think of the future without him. A smile lit her face. They would endure whatever was ahead together.

He took the parchment out of her hands. "Does your smile mean you trust me to care for you?"

"Aye," she sighed. "I trust you with my life."

Guy swallowed the bitter taste of deception. When she found out he was the messenger sent to deliver her from the convent to London, she would be devastated. He wanted to make their marriage a union of trust and honesty, but how could he when it was based on a lie? The unsteady foundation would crumble the moment she learned of his deceit. In his mind he pictured telling her everything, pictured her absolving him of his guilt with her angelic smile, opening her arms to him in full acceptance . . . Yet, when the moment came when he should speak, he was too afraid the truth might not bring the response he wished, and he remained silent.

Instead he took her lips with his in a scorching kiss. She pressed her body to his and he knew it would be some time before they spoke again. This he understood, this basic need and desire. This he could share with her.

His arms lifted her from the floor and hugged her to his chest. She laughed breathlessly as desire glowed in her eyes. God, she was beautiful. His lips covered hers once more in a searing kiss, leaving only to graze a trail from her jaw to her ear. He felt her tremble and reveled in her reaction.

"Husband," she whispered.

He chuckled, but his laughter died when she buried her face in his neck, nipping and nuzzling the sensitive skin. "Wife," he half whispered, half groaned, feeling the perspiration coat his brow as he carried her to the bed and lowered her to the mattress. He kissed her soft, willing lips, before withdrawing to undress.

Kneeling on the bed, she reached out her arms to him, urging him to hurry back to her embrace. Hastily, he tried to remove his tunic, but everything seemed knotted. She leaned forward, brushing his hands away, and undid the laces. A coy smile teased her mouth, as her passion-drugged gaze met his, then her fingers grazed his collarbone, slipping the material off his shoulders with slow, languid sweeps of her palms.

He took a deep breath and steeled himself for the slow exquisite pleasure when he saw the burning desire in her lovely eyes. This would be erotic torture, containing his ardor while his wife enflamed him.

She kissed his flesh, her lips savoring every inch of his chest. Her fingers raked his rib cage, greedily tracing every ridge and valley with a tantalizing scrape of her nails. When her tongue circled his nipple, laving attention, then her teeth tugged, he pushed her back, unable to stand the fire she had started.

His lips descended on hers, and she met his hunger with her own. He tugged and yanked at her ties, and seemed all thumbs. Again she pushed his hands away and slowly rose from the bed to remove her clothes with a languid seductiveness that took his breath away.

She moved sensually and gracefully, folding every piece as she preened and posed before the fire. By the time she reached her chemise, he had grown as hard as iron. The minx knew what she was doing to him. He stripped off his braies as she tormented his senses, removing the last bit of covering.

She was completely bare except for his ring. The gold caught the firelight, reflecting it with brilliant flashes as she stretched out her arms to him.

He leaped from the bed and into her welcoming embrace. The dreamy look in her eyes intoxicated him. His lips smothered hers, unable to quench his thirst for the taste of her essence.

Her hands slipped between them, and nearly drove him over the edge when her nails grazed his manhood. ''I remember when I peeked under the blanket and thought you possessed a weapon that was far too big for you ever to marry; I thought that was why you entered the Church.'' Playfully, a smile teased her lips as her fingers walked up his ribs. ''Perhaps I am the only woman who is up to it,'' she purred, leaning forward to kiss him.

Her arms wound around his neck, her fingers drifting through his hair. The little moans in her throat traveled through him like an intoxicating drug.

He lifted her in his arms and swung her around. ''I love you,'' he said, laughing.

''I know.'' She sighed, her hands moving enticingly over

his shoulders as she snuggled down against him, her breast rubbing against his chest.

"Love me," she whispered. "I have missed you."

The ache within him grew and he laid her down on the bed, using his hands and mouth to tease her as she had him. She moved beneath him, inviting with her body, but he held back, wanting her need as great as his.

Her body reacted to each caress with a fevered response. When his fingers slipped inside her she moaned, her nails digging into his back. "Please, Guy, I need you."

With a groan he drove deep into her. She held on to him, her arms and legs twining around him, and the rhythm that began carried them higher and higher. The firelight shone on their glistening bodies as they worshiped and adored one another. He loved her with an abandonment that he never dreamed existed, and she matched his passion with a tender ardor that touched his heart. Her cry of fulfillment preceded his by seconds. They clung to each other, in awe at the power of their lovemaking. She snuggled into his embrace and, never opening her eyes, drifted off to sleep in his arms.

Quennel Aumont paced the floor of William's castle. Finally the door opened and Bayard de Bellemare appeared, dressed in the finest linen, each finger bejeweled.

"What was so important, Quennel, that I must be interrupted at my pleasure?" Without looking up, Bayard adjusted the gold broach that held his mantle closed, then patted his thin brown hair into place.

"Ah, my friend. We will journey to northern England to recover the girl at last."

" 'Tis not the most auspicious beginning, a bride fleeing her intended." Bayard looked down his long, pinched nose, his nostrils flaring once as he sniffed in disdain.

Aumont did not miss the rebuke—again. *Damn the little*

bitch, he thought. "Bayard, she is merely maidenly. Surely you can understand that."

Without a hint of warning, Bayard crashed his fist onto the table. "I understand that she is making me a laughingstock. If I find your hand in this, I will kill you for the humiliation I have suffered."

Good, thought Aumont. *Bayard does not want to call off the wedding.* "Take your anger out on her, my friend, not me. You know why I wish to see this marriage contracted."

"When I have her within my reach, I will deal with the mademoiselle." His hands clenched into tight fists.

"We will leave tomorrow to fetch your unwilling bride." Quennel's elbow nudged Bayard's ribs. "Then you can show Gabrielle who is master."

A twisted smile covered Bayard's thin lips. *"Oui,* I will be ready. Is there any word about her brother?"

"He is also in North Umberland. Both of them were there for some festivities about to take place. If we hurry, we should have both my sister's dear children in hand."

"North Umberland?" Bayard said, his brow furrowing as he poured a tankard of ale.

"What troubles you, Bayard?"

"North Umberland is where my bastard cousins dwell. I do not wish to see them again." He fingered the scar by his left eye.

Quennel waved his hand in dismissal. "I doubt you will have occasion to see them."

"If I do, I will expect your support," Bayard warned. "They have haunted me since their birth. Why my grandfather did not reject them is beyond me."

"But they have no right to the land and titles you own."

"Non," Bayard agreed, then frowned. "But they still have my name. A name they did not earn."

Aumont did not remark that the de Bellemare name was now renowned thanks to the bastard sons' accomplishments, which kept their grandfather in close friendship with the king.

"*I* have the only right to carry that name," Bayard said, swallowing half a tankard.

"Exactly what did you do for King William that he will feel that way."

Bayard's eyes narrowed as he stared at Aumont. "I kept his land safe in Normandy. There was no insurrection by my serfs."

"That you did," Quennel agreed, knowing full well that there was no danger to the land at home.

"See that you remember it." Bayard wiped his sleeve across his mouth, then poured another tankard. "Or I am liable to tell the king of your plans."

Aumont smiled, enjoying toying with the man like he had when he kept his pets. Too bad none of the animals survived his little tortures. "That, sir, would be foolish, for it would implicate you as well. The king would be interested to know what you did with his tax tribute money. Would he not?"

Bayard de Bellemare's nervous laugh rang in the air. "Remember I have as much on you as you have on me," he blustered.

"Do not threaten me, de Bellemare."

" 'Tis not a threat, merely a promise. See that you back me if and when I need it." He finished his ale and tried to rise, but swaying back and forth, he gripped the table and slumped back in his chair. "My cousins always have a way of turning up at William's side."

Aumont smirked at the drunk. It was because the bastards served the king as his brave and loyal knights. But he dared not remind Bayard of the fact, and risk angering his already-volatile companion.

"To our journey." Aumont raised his cup.

Bayard met the toast. "To my betrothed, may she survive

the wedding night.'' He roared with laughter, then promptly passed out.

Aumont's snort was the only sound in the room.

Gabby would never live through the bedding. It would be a fitting end for that bitch. He raised his cup, drained the drink, then threw the vessel into the fireplace. What he had planned for her brother was even more fitting.

After listening to the two reports given, King William sighed heavily. ''Do not let Quennel Aumont or Bayard de Bellemare leave the castle.''

He turned and paced, thinking his plans through. He had sent for Guy de Bellemare, and knew he would come, but the marriage disturbed him.

''Send in Rule and Lance Lemieux,'' he said to his scribe.

When the servant returned, he held the door open for the men, then bowed to the king and left. Both men entered the room and took a seat. ''Your Majesty,'' said Lance, ''we have come on a grave errand. I have wronged my sons, Royce and Guy, by disowning them. There can be no doubt now that they are of my seed. I have come to take them back into the fold.''

''Would you feel so strongly if you did not need their support? Royce and Guy have become powerful lords, and their alliance would deter any threat to your lands.''

Lance's face grew red. *''Oui,* I would. Though I do not deny I need aid against my greedy neighbor, I do not expect it in return for my name.''

The king smiled. ''Lance, your sons are very stubborn men. Although I am for the reconciliation, I think you will have a hard time convincing them to listen. I do, however, have a plan that may help you.''

Both men leaned closer.

''Guy has married the very woman he was to escort here

to be given to her uncle Quennel Aumont. She was to marry Bayard de Bellemare.''

Lance's face paled. ''Good God, sire, you are not going to give the lady to Bayard?''

''I am going to do what is best for the kingdom. But you and Rule might use the opportunity to your advantage.''

The king outlined his plan.

''Are you mad?'' Rule couldn't help but exclaim, jumping up to face the king.

Lance's weary-eyed gaze met William's. ''I fear this plan will do more harm than good.''

William shrugged. ''Either way, it is your only chance to get your sons back.''

Chapter Seventeen

The weak winter sun shone threw the gray clouds as Gabby stepped out onto the porch and awaited the approach of her steed. They were heading to London today. Guy, along with an armed escort, would take her to the king.

She would not borrow heartache by thinking of what awaited her. Besides, she believed in the power of prayer. In the blink of an eye a miracle could appear.

Ambra gave her a kiss. "Take heart, daughter. My son will not let any harm befall you."

Gabby smiled. "I hope my child will bring me as much credit as yours does you."

"Safe journey, sister," Bethany said, embracing her next.

"I hope someday to acquire your charm and grace. I have never known a woman who can make motherhood, marriage, and management look so easy," Gabby said.

Bethany blushed prettily. "You must return to teach me your gentle demeanor," she said, then stepped back to make room for her husband.

Beaming with approval, Royce advanced and picked Gabby up clear off the ground. Giving her a bear hug, he deposited a kiss on her cheek. "My brother is a lucky man. You are a good and gentle lady," he said while setting her back on her feet.

Royce rejoined his family, and with an air of pride, he placed his arms around his wife and his mother. "Please return posthaste, Lady Gabrielle. My wife is sorely in need of tutoring."

Bethany kicked her big brute of a husband in the shin. As he bent to massage his leg, Gabby turned around to hide her amusement, and came face-to-face with her uncle Alec.

"Lass, I would go with ye, but Louis must be on his way to learn the art of a good fighting Scotsman. There, there, lass. Dinna fret. Ye have no need to fear now with a braw and bold husband at yer side." He leaned forward and brushed a kiss on her forehead. "We will see each other again."

She tried to swallow the knot forming in her throat. "Uncle Alec," she croaked, missing them already.

"Hush now. We will leave afore ye. Ian and Louis are bringing the horses. 'Tis best we be in Scotland by night."

She nodded her head in understanding.

Louis and Ian approached, leading a column of Scottish warriors. The spirited animals whinnied and pawed at the ground as Louis handed his reins to a soldier and separated from the group. He bounded up the stairs, taking the steps two at a time. Once again Gabby glimpsed her sire in his son.

He took her hands in his large ones. "I will miss you. If ever you need me, send for me."

She stood on the top of the landing and he two steps below, yet they met at eye level. "What a braw brother I have," she laughed, then sobered. "Father would have been proud of the man you have become."

He leaned forward to kiss her cheek. "Not as proud, I think, as he would be of the lady you are."

She felt her tears gather and turned to find that young Ian and Angus had joined them. "I shall miss you two also," she sniffed, unable to stem the lone tear that slipped down her cheek.

"Och," Angus said. "A pretty lassie should no cry." He leaned forward to brush the tear away, but Ian pushed his hand away.

"Leave be, Mactavish. 'Tis my cousin, not yers." Ian held her in a light embrace. "Dinna give these townsmen reason to think ye are weak when a courageous lass ye be," he said, and joined his party.

Through gathering tears she watched Louis, Ian, and Alec mount their horses and ride out of the castle with their clansmen. Guy offered his arm. "We should be away."

With her smile held firmly so she would not cry again and disgrace herself, she nodded.

After helping her mount her horse, Guy swung up into his saddle. He spared her a soft smile before he signaled the soldiers forward.

Gabby waved farewell and followed her husband from the courtyard. She was just outside the gate when the vision took hold. *The scent of danger lingered in the air, so strong and tangible it left an acrid taste in her mouth. Even stronger than the danger was a feeling of lost ideals and dreams. Words and faces flashed disjointedly through her mind.* Then the episode passed, leaving her chilled to the bone. When she looked up, Guy was watching her, a question in his gaze.

She swallowed. These were merely impressions, she adamantly told herself, but even so, an overwhelming despair washed over her. Images re-formed in her mind, and fragmented conversation replayed, each piece offering a frightening glimpse of the puzzle. The words formed in her mind, and without thought passed her lips. "Will you give me to my enemies for a reward?"

The shock on his features tore at her heart.

"Wife, I would die before I let harm befall you."

"But I saw a vision. In it I distinctly perceived betrayal and reward. Faces flashed before my eyes—your face."

He pulled her horse to the side of the road, letting the column of soldiers pass, then helped her dismount. In an instant his arms were around her. "Wife, the future is not set," he said earnestly. " 'Tis fear and apprehension that cloud your vision."

She felt the warmth of his embrace. How could she feel this loved by a man who would betray her? She must have made a mistake. She had to have made a mistake. Still . . .

"But the Sight has never failed me before," she cried.

"Your vision is merely an event that might occur. Did your uncle Alec not stop the musicians from harming Louis after you gave the warning? We will make our own future."

She wanted to believe him. God, she needed to believe him.

His hands moved up and down her back, massaging away the chills and creating exquisite warmth.

He was right. Her gift relied on interpretation, and she was human. Besides, had not the image of his eyes been with her since her earliest recollections? A harmful presence would not have become such an intimate part of her. Of that she was sure.

He lifted her chin and kissed her with such sweetness that she lost all desire, to think or reason. And for the first time in her life her heart overshadowed her intuitive insight. "You are right. My gift is not infallible," she murmured softly when their lips parted. "You would never betray us."

He crushed her against his chest until his heartbeat pounded in her ear. " 'Tis hard," she whispered. "I fear much, but I know you will not leave me at the king's mercy.

I give you my love and my life. My very being rests in your hands."

"And I swear I will protect you," he said fiercely.

At that moment she glanced up and caught a flicker of fear on his face. "What is it, Guy?"

" 'Tis nothing."

"You are such a poor liar. What troubles you? Do you share my fears?"

He looked down at her, regret shining in his dark eyes. "My fears are different than yours. Though I wish I could talk about them, I cannot."

His sincerity flooded her with warmth. "When you feel the time is right I will be here."

"You are more than I deserve, Gabrielle."

"I know," she teased, needing to lighten his mood. "In fact, my lord, with me as your wife, you will be hard-pressed to find a moment to yourself."

"Are you trying to tell me, madame, that I will never know peace?" he quipped, a grin tugging at his lips.

"Aye, my love. I shall wear you out day and night with my demands."

His eyes glinted knowingly. "And what demands would those be?"

She smiled mischievously. "Why, only that you be a most attentive and dutiful husband."

"A man could die from such demanding duty."

"Ah, but would he die happy, my lord?"

"Oui, my lady, he would die happy indeed."

Gabby's heart clenched in her breast. Guy was indeed a rare man, so full of laughter and love. "Thank you."

"For what?"

"For everything. For loving me."

" 'Twas a hardship, but I managed."

She chuckled as he gave her a quick kiss, then swung her back up on her mount, the vision forgotten. When they rejoined the soldiers, she felt a niggling of apprehension, but ignored it. She closed her eyes. "God protect us both," she whispered, then looked ahead. She would not cloud their future happiness with needless worries. There were far too many real problems to face to brood over imagined ones.

Gabby's gaze scanned the horizon. Though Royce's men would provide adequate escort, she still feared attack. "Guy, could we not stop at the abbeys along the way rather than making camp in the open?"

"Stop worrying, love. I have sworn to protect you, and I will do so with my life. Besides," he grinned, "do you really think Royce's men would make camp in a convent? The very thought would set these hardened warriors screaming with fear."

Despite her efforts, the edges of her lips began to twitch. "Guy, would you be serious? This is of great importance, yet you continue to jest."

"If you see me being earnest, dear wife, then 'tis time to worry."

"I never know what you will say or do. The next few years should prove interesting—until, of course, I figure you out."

He roared with laughter, earning him a hard rap on the arm. "Please, Guy. I do not think you understand what kind of man Quennel is. I fear he will try to harm those I love most."

Guy's features sobered. "I do understand. And I will not allow his evil to reach us or your brother. 'Tis a promise I give as our wedding gift, and you may hold me to it all the days of our lives."

She sighed. He was sincere, but she feared he just did not grasp the gravity of the situation. For the first time she wished her husband were truly a warrior instead of an ex-cleric with some military experience. She murmured a prayer that all his skill would return, then thought her entreaty in poor taste.

Deciding on another prayer, she looked heavenward. *Dear Lord, please send help. Your obedient servant, Gabby de Bellemare.*

Royce burst into his wife's chamber.

"Bethany, I must go to court. I will return as soon as possible. Your father will look out for you."

Bethany took the letter from her husband's hand and read it. "Oh, Royce. Your father and half brother are at court, and demand permission to travel here," she said, then looked up. "Does your mother know?"

"*Non.* 'Twill be kinder to keep it from her."

"Royce, she is not a child."

"I am well aware of my mother's strength. But wife, humor me in this, for I wish to keep the women in my life safe."

"I will honor your request." She sighed. "You must face your father, and help Guy to do the same." She smoothed his tunic and reached up to give her husband a kiss. "If not for the twins' tender age, I would accompany you."

" 'Tis happier I am that you are safely here."

Bethany hugged her husband. "Be careful. I know you have put the past to rest, but old wounds can still cause great pain."

" 'Tis my brother for whom I fear. Though he never shows it, our father's betrayal hurt him deeply." Then he kissed her soundly. "Do not fret. I promise I will keep safe."

She brushed away a wayward lock of hair that had fallen on his brow. "Best see that you keep that promise, Norman," she admonished.

"Always, little Saxon. I would not break my word to my loving, if sometimes disobedient, wife."

She chuckled. " 'Tis a wonder we ever matched."

" 'Twas destiny," Royce said, then took her in his arms and kissed her with the de Bellemare charm that left her breathless for more.

The early-morning air was cold and damp as Gabby lay quietly in her husband's arms inside their tent. The journey would be over in three days' time. They made little haste to London, and she wondered if deep in his heart Guy did not want to arrive. Even less so after Royce's late arrival last night, and Guy's orders that the names Lance and Rule Lemieux not be spoken. She recognized the name from her vision and understood his reluctance if his father was waiting at King William's court.

Nor did she have any desire to reach their destination. She was happy right where she was, she thought, as she gazed upon her husband's magnificent physique. She warmed to her very core, inspecting his massive chest, as ribbed and ridged as a breastplate of metal. The strength and solid firmness excited her. The pulsating warmth reminded her of his vulnerability and accessibility. Gently she stroked her hand down his side, savoring the feel of her husband's body.

"I could drive you wild for want of me," she whispered, feeling daring and playful.

Eyes still closed, Guy smiled. "Could you, after only such a short time of being wed?"

"Aye, I could," she chuckled, knowing her boast ridiculous. "Think of how crazed with passion you will be twenty years from now when I am truly experienced."

"Or even fifty years from now," he said as he finally opened his eyes and gazed into hers. "Aye. The possibilities are frightening."

Gabby ran her fingertip across his lower lip. "You are so good for me. I cannot remember when I was happier. You add laughter to my life."

He brushed a wisp of hair from her cheek. "And you add a reason to live to mine. I had no existence to speak of before you entered my life."

His words touched her very soul. Dropping her finger, she traced the line of his jaw. "I do not know why God has allowed me to be this happy, but I am grateful that he sent you to me. All the days of my life I will wonder why a man as handsome and fine as you would fall in love with me."

"Someday, my love, you will know I am the lucky one. When that day comes, I will rejoice. For we are both blessed, not one above the other. 'Twould be like saying I love you more than you love me. We love; that is enough."

Oh, how cherished he made her feel. She had no right to be so happy, and she prayed that God would let her linger in this state for as long as she lived. For in Guy's arms she had found paradise.

A warning sounded in her head, more fierce and frightening than the last vision. Overcome, she clutched his arms in a spasm of fear and her grip gouged nail marks into his flesh. This time it was clearer. They were all there: Guy, Louis, Royce and Bethany, her uncle Alec. Quennel Aumont, looking like a ghost. A man who leered at her. The king was presiding . . . it was a trial of some sort. Then the mist descended and she cried out in frustration. "No!"

Gabby felt Guy's arms enfold her, drawing her to his warmth, "What happened, my love? What is it?"

She tried to speak, but could only shudder with dread.

"Shh. We will talk of it later." He stroked her back, his hands as soothing as his voice and she allowed his confidence to travel through her, easing her panic.

When her tremors finally ceased, she looked up at him. "You cannot go to court," she said flatly.

"We have to."

"*I* have to go, but you do not." She grabbed hold of his arms. "Stay away, stay here where you are safe."

"Listen to yourself. Would you let me go alone into danger, or would you want to be at my side?"

"I would want to be at your side. But I fear for you. Never has the vision felt so strong."

"Whatever awaits us, my love, we will face together." His face seemed strained. "When we arrive at court, I will tell you about my life. There is something about my past I wish you to know, but I am not at liberty to speak of it now. Not until the matter is settled. Remember I have said this. Please, remember it."

"I will remember," she said, thinking that after he was released from his religious vows, he would understandably feel freer to speak of his past.

With a sigh of relief, he lifted a chain from his leather pouch, a heavy gold medallion dangling at the end.

He placed the necklace over her head. "Wear this as a reminder of my devotion and your promise to believe in me no matter what happens."

Apprehension pricked at her heart. "Aye, I will, but—"

Guy covered her lips and the fear subsided. When he deepened his kiss, her thoughts scattered.

Chapter Eighteen

When Guy entered William's court, he suddenly knew what it must be like for his beloved when she felt one of her premonitions. The hair on the back of his neck rose and the clammy feel of death stole over his skin.

His gaze traveled around the room, noting the familiar and unfamiliar faces. Then his blood froze. Standing by the king were his half brother, Rule, and their father. A sick feeling settled in his stomach. He had not expected them to be with the king. Next to them was his cousin, Bayard de Bellemare. When Gabby's grip on his arm tightened, he knew the man next to Bayard was her uncle Quennel, though his cold, lifeless eyes would have given him away.

When they passed abreast of Quennel's watchful gaze, Gabby's step faltered. Without giving pause Guy steadied her balance, and directed her toward the king.

"Guy de Bellemare and Lady Gabrielle. We are pleased at your arrival." King William spread his arms in welcome. "Thank you, Guy, for bringing the lady home."

Guy stepped forward. "My liege, we must talk in private."

"*Non,* there is no need. Your mission has been successful. Lady Gabrielle is here. I grant unto you the promised boon for your services, the land and castle in Lleyn."

The king's words, though softly spoken, echoed in the room like a death knell. Guy knew it was too late to explain.

He turned and read the stunned betrayal and hurt in Gabby's eyes.

Shaking her head in denial, she took a step back. "You were sent by the king to bring me to court?" she asked, unable to keep the pain from her voice.

Guy reached for her hand, but she pulled it from his grasp. "Were you?"

The king stepped between them. "*Oui,* my lady, I ordered Guy to pose as a friar in order to bring you out of the convent where you were hiding."

She stared blankly at the king. After several moments she nodded, then let her gaze traveled back to Guy.

"Then you are a mercenary, not a man of the cloth." Her voice was rigid with uncharacteristic disdain.

He ignored the anguish in her violet eyes, and turned to the king. "My liege, might I present Lady Gabrielle de Bellemare, my wife."

A collective gasp rose in the assembly.

"By His wounds," Quennel cursed. "Foul, most f—"

King William held up his hand, cutting off Quennel's words." "So you are married?"

"*Oui,* my liege, 'twas necessary."

A bright red stain burned Gabrielle's cheeks.

God's teeth, but he was making it worse. Guy moved toward her, and whispered, "Please, Gabby, remember your promise to trust me."

She did not respond, but her violet eyes shimmered with moisture.

"My liege, it has been a long trip. Might I see my lady to her quarters and then return?"

The king eyed her carefully. "I think not, Guy."

"I will kill you for this insult," Aumont swore, and Bayard de Bellemare added, "You slut."

At the insult, Guy spun around and stepped into his cousin's path. Bayard stumbled back. "You cannot undo what is done. The lady is my wife. If you cast one aspersion against her character, cousin, I will take you to task."

His face red with rage, Quennel Aumont stormed past Guy and Bayard and, before anyone could stop him, he slapped Gabby hard across the face.

"Bad form, Aumont," a solider called out, as William quickly stepped forward and put his arm protectively around Gabrielle.

Guy wheeled around. Enraged, he drove his fist into Aumont's smug smile, knocking him to the floor.

The court applauded as Aumont's features tightened in outrage and fury. William's guards held Guy back, while others reluctantly helped Aumont to his feet.

Struggling against his restrainers, Guy glared at Quennel. "I accuse you of the murders of Hamish and Blanchefleur Aumont, as well as attempting to assassinate Gabrielle and Louis Aumont."

"These are serious charges," the king counseled as he signaled his guards to relinquish their hold.

Guy straightened his tunic. *"Oui,* but I have had to hide all over Scotland and England to avoid his hired killers."

"I will look into the matter," the king said.

"Non!" Quennel bellowed. "I am the accused. I choose trial by combat."

William narrowed his eyes at Aumont's red-blotched face and sighed. "It is your right."

Aumont's gaze slanted around the crowd, a smile slipping across his thin lips. "Since I am no match for de Bellemare,

I choose a champion in my stead." He pointed to Bayard. "The man dishonored by the bedding of his betrothed. I choose Bayard de Bellemare."

"I will not fight for her," Bayard de Bellemare snarled, ignoring Quennel's glare. "I do not want another man's leavings. Let him keep the whore."

The scathing insult hung in the air. The court ladies covered their mouths, aghast at such crudity, while several knights grumbled their disgust.

"Bayard, you know you cannot best your cousin," one said loudly. "I think you decline not because of the lady, but because you cannot hope to win." The knight turned toward Lady Gabrielle and bowed to the accompaniment of rousing applause from his peers.

Rigid with anger, Bayard stormed out of the room, leaving Quennel behind, his eyes closed in dark, dangerous slits.

Gabby relaxed, and King William relinquished his hold on her shoulder and directed her to Guy.

Before Gabby had taken one step, a tall, dark, handsome knight emerged from the crowd. "I will fight for the honor of the maiden," Rule Lemieux declared.

Heads turned and silence again descended upon the hall. It was no secret that bad blood existed between these half brothers, but that a knave like Quennel might benefit was a shock.

"If you have need of my help, I will stand ready," Lance said.

Rule nodded.

"I will fight the man in combat." He came and stood toe-to-toe with his half brother. "Should you fail, not only is Aumont proved innocent of all charges, but I take the woman."

Guy's stomach tightened into knots. "My wife is not part of this. I will fight you anytime and anyplace you like, but not over my beloved."

Royce stepped out of the crowd and into the center of the floor. " 'Tis a strange request for an honorable man, do you not think, my liege?" Many in the assembly echoed his feelings out loud or shook their heads. What Rule proposed was very unorthodox. Bayard was the only man who had a prior claim to Gabby, and only he could include her as part of the contest. "Whatever animosity exists between us, Rule, do you really wish to hurt an innocent by taking her from the man she loves?"

"You mistake me, Royce. Lady Gabrielle's brother fostered at our castle. Had I known of her plight I would have offered my services then. I do so now," Rule replied, then he turned and walked over to Gabby. Lifting her hand, he deposited a slow, deliberate kiss on her palm.

Guy charged forward, but Royce blocked his path.

"Stay out of this, Royce," Guy warned.

Rule chuckled.

"Hold your tongue, Rule," Royce commanded.

"Do not push me, or you also will taste the edge of my sword," Rule warned.

"Enough," the king roared, eyes flashing. "We will take this discussion to my private chambers."

With every eye trained on them, the ensemble followed the king from the room.

Guy took Gabby's hand and wondered if the lack of warmth he felt was shock, anger, or fear.

"Trust me," he murmured.

When she looked up at him, the expression in her eyes chilled him. "You dare ask me for my trust! You Judas!" she spit.

He stopped and pulled her into a small alcove. "I will not give you up."

She drew a ragged breath. "You have already lost me."

Fear sliced through him, and he grabbed hold of her shoulders. "Does your wedding oath mean so little to you?"

"Unlike you, I have neither forgotten nor forsaken my marriage vows."

"If that is true, how can you give up when I am doing everything in my power to keep us together?"

She held up her hand to silence his argument. "Do you not know how powerful my uncle is? He will have me killed before you can put your grand scheme into effect. Thank God my brother was saved from your treachery."

She shook her head and a tear slipped down her cheek. "I trusted you with my heart and my life. Now, it would seem I will have to pay with both for my folly."

"You are my wife."

"Am I? The king may not recognize our marriage."

The thought had occurred to Guy of course but he refused to give it credence. "Nothing can come between us."

"You were bought for land, and I for love. 'Tis disheartening to know I came so cheap." She pulled free of his grasp. "What an easy conquest I must have been for someone with your experience. It should have cost you something, Guy."

Royce came back for them. "The king is waiting."

The moment Guy took her arm, Gabby pulled away, and ran ahead of him down the long corridor.

"God's teeth, Gabby, wait," Guy ground out, then chased her.

"Guy, do not lose your temper," Royce said, keeping pace. "You need to keep your wits about you."

When Guy caught up to Gabby, he captured her arm and swung her around into his embrace. Tears streamed down her face, and she tried to brush them away. His anger gone, he leaned down and tenderly kissed her lips. "Cry not, my beloved."

She tried to push him away but he crushed her to him as his lips moved over hers. She struggled, trying to end the kiss, but he knew the moment she surrendered. Her lips parted slightly, and his heart soared.

"God, I love you," he crooned, but she remained silent. To Royce, he said "Brother, I ask you to stand guard over my lady. She fears she will not live through the night."

" 'Tis done. No harm will befall her. But you had best think of an explanation that the king will accept."

"I need no explanation save the truth."

Royce shook his head. "We are talking about King William. You are in more trouble than you realize."

Guy smiled. "How much worse could it be?"

"Stop it, both of you," Gabby whispered, her voice strained.

"Do not worry, little sister, I will see to your safety."

"You two do not know who you toy with. 'Tis not the king you should fear but my villainous uncle. Not only will I be dead before morning, but so will both of you. I beg of you to leave here now and save yourselves."

"You hate me, but you would plead to save my life?" Guy arched an eyebrow. When she lowered her gaze, he spoke to Royce over her bowed head. "I think she still loves me."

"I would not have thought it possible, but it seems you are right. Best sharpen your fighting skills tonight."

Her head snapped up, her eyes flashing. "I swear your mother must have dropped you both on your heads when you were babes."

Guy took her into his arms, again. "I love you, Gabby. I always will. Lord knows I did not want to fall in love with you. But I did. And I swear to you, we will be together."

The king smiled on the way to his chambers. Bayard was just the coward he had predicted. All was going according to plan.

He had no doubt that Aumont was guilty as charged, but

he was within his rights to choose trial by combat and a champion. Thanks to the king's strategy it was Rule.

Like Guy, Rule was an excellent warrior. The match would be an even one. Though he did not like pitting knights he valued against each other, he had no choice. Fate would determine the outcome. And either way, his plan to mend the breach would be accomplished.

The king chuckled and silently applauded himself for having the wisdom of Solomon.

Inside the king's spartan chamber, Alec Campbell, Rule and Lance Lemieux, and Quennel Aumont waited at the large trestle table by the hearth. Gabby's heart lurched at seeing the confident expression on Quennel Aumont's face, but a measure of peace returned when she glanced at her uncle Alec. It was a welcome surprise to see him at the meeting.

The king motioned for her to take a seat at the table, a rare honor. The king raised his chalice and took a long sip.

"I have agreed to the contest to decide Aumont's guilt or innocence in the matter of the assassination attempts. It is his right. However, I now am faced with a more delicate matter." He leaned forward and poured Gabby a chalice of wine.

The goblet felt cold in her hands as she strangled the cup between her palms, unable to force a solitary swallow past her dry lips.

"Lady Gabrielle, if Guy de Bellemare wins you return to his side as his legal wife. If Rule Lemieux wins, you accompany him back to Normandy, and your marriage will be annulled."

Her heart pounded, and she forced her gaze to the king. "Have I no other options, my liege?"

The king sadly smiled and shook his head. "Would that there were one, my lady."

She took a healthy sip of wine. "I am to be regarded as a prize, and given to the man with the most prowess." Tears blurred her sight as she fought to hold them back. "I implore you, sire, to treat this matter differently."

"My lady, 'tis not possible. You have no family except an uncle you have fled. Your closest relative resides in Scotland. *Non,* this is truly the best way. Your land and titles will be held in trust by the crown until your brother comes of age and claims his position."

"What will happen to my people and their land?" she asked.

"Rest your fears, my lady. I will send a manager to care for the interests of my loyal subjects."

Aumont jumped to his feet, his chair clattering as it hit the floor. " 'Tis not necessary, my lord. I am capable of seeing to the estate."

"Do you not have your own estate, Lord Aumont?"

Aumont leaned forward on the table, the veins standing out on his forehead. *"Oui,* but—"

"Then I will hear no more of it. Loyal servant that you are to the crown, I would not think of taking advantage of your generosity. *Non,* I will send an unbiased overseer to serve the interest of these children." William then turned to Alec Campbell. "Does that meet with your approval, Laird Campbell?"

When Aumont pursed his lips, Campbell smiled. "Aye, I have nae problem with it."

"And you Lord Aumont?" The King raised an eyebrow.

"As Your Majesty desires. I am only concerned with justice," he said begrudgingly.

Relief soared through Gabby. The king's decision ended her uncle Quennel's scheme to control the Aumont estate. She took a deep breath, savoring the victory. Now, her people would be safe. Almost smiling, she glanced at Quennel, and the hatred in his gaze made her tremble.

King William turned to the two opponents. "I will give you this opportunity, gentlemen, to withdraw your suit. Guy de Bellemare, the challenge will be dropped if you rescind your accusation. Rule Lemieux, your championship will be unnecessary if Guy retracts his accusation."

Gabby's throat constricted and she began to feel light-headed. The king was giving them an out.

"What of the lady?" Guy asked.

"I will decide her fate."

Guy shook his head. "I will not withdraw my accusation. Quennel Aumont is guilty."

Fool, her mind screamed. He would risk her as part of the bargain? "Guy, no."

He looked at her as though he could not believe she challenged him. " 'Tis done."

At the harsh finality of his words, the room began to sway and the light blurred and dimmed. A soft cry passed her lips, and though she felt strong arms catching her as she slipped from awareness, she could not stop the cold empty void.

Guy carried his wife from the room, followed by most of the other players. Rule watched in silence as his half brothers departed. He held no animosity toward either of them, but he was committed to mend the family rift.

As the others left, Lance clasped his son's shoulder. "Rule, you are the son who had everything. Your half brothers have nothing. Why are you doing this?"

"I do not hate them. But Royce has been spoiling for a fight since he left Normandy. Now is the time to have done."

"Guy is the one you face."

"When, I defeat Guy, Royce will be honor-bound to see to me."

Lance raised an eyebrow. "You all share the same blood,

but until now I did not see you have the same shrewdness. Why not let them know you hold no malice toward them?''

''Royce will not believe me. He needs proof,'' Rule scoffed.

Lance sighed. ''He may someday come to tolerate you, Rule, but never me. I hurt his mother very badly when I turned them out.''

''Why, Father? Why did you do it?''

''Your mother's family thought I dishonored her memory by taking a mistress and having two sons by her. And so they schemed for years to discredit Ambra de Bellemare, and finally they succeeded.'' Lance drained his drink. ''God forgive me, I believed their lies.''

''I hold no animosity toward you for finding another woman after my mother's death, and, if anyone should, it would be me,'' Rule said, setting his untouched wine on the table.

''But you know what I sacrificed,'' Lance said, his eyes filled with sadness.

''*Oui*, and soon they will as well.''

Early the next morning Royce met Guy carrying the de Bellemare armor and colors. ''See you wear my armor today with pride,'' Royce said, handing him the expensive suit of mail.

''You worry overmuch, brother.'' Guy said lightly, but he knew Royce had just paid him the highest possible compliment by giving Guy his armor.

Unbidden an image of Gabby arose in his mind, watching the competition, her eyes huge with worry. ''Reassure Gabby, Royce.''

''You have to keep your mind on the contest,'' his brother answered. ''Do not underestimate Rule.''

But Guy saw that Royce was staring not at Rule, but his father.

"Royce," Guy snapped. " 'Tis you who should concentrate. Watch my back. I fear Aumont will make a move on Gabby. She had several frightening visions of this day."

Royce lifted the hauberk so Guy could slip into the coat of chain mail. *"Non,* I tell you the king has her well guarded. No attempts were made last night as she feared, and none will be made as long as she remains under William's protection. Rest your fears about Gabrielle and mind the task on hand."

"I have no fear of this contest," Guy said, shifting his shoulders so the heavy woven metal covering would fit comfortably. "In less than an hour my dreams will all be realized."

"I tell you, Rule is no fool. He is an experienced swordsman and a good soldier."

"And I am not?"

"Non. The only thing you suffer from is overconfidence. Everything in life has come too easy for you. Take care, little brother. Pride can be a more dangerous enemy than your opponent."

"I know what I know. Not only will I have Gabby without dispute, but I will ensure that her uncle can never harm her or her brother."

"Listen to me. Rule has a weakness. I have watched him before. In fact, I have done battle with him."

Guy's surprise could not be contained. "When?"

" 'Twas when you were in the seminary."

"Why?"

" 'Twas a matter of honor."

"Your erstwhile betrothed, Damiana?" Guy guessed, wondering why the bitch had fueled the animosity between these half brothers.

Royce nodded. "Now that she is gone, I can see the

damage that she did. It is too late for regrets. Remember this, however: Rule feints to his left when he attacks."

"I will remember."

"Godspeed, brother."

Guy accepted his brother's wish and his hand.

The area of battle was cleared, and a platform was erected for the king and his entourage to sit. Lesser nobles gathered around the roped-off area. The contest was with swords. The first to fall or yield would be the loser.

Rule looked the formidable warrior in his black dress. But Guy did not let the image intimidate him. He knew warfare was not only a test of skill but of wits. Guy took his place and chuckled deliberately.

"Black! Rule, you overstate your importance."

Rule's manner and stance hardened. "When this is over, Guy, you will wish you had not challenged me."

" 'Twas not you I challenged. I am surprised you let another use you for his purposes. You are rumored to be clever, but perhaps legend plays you false."

Rule smiled. " 'Tis a shame I must crush you. I rather like your insolence. But 'tis not Aumont I do this for."

"Who?" Guy asked, but just then the king gave his command.

"I am sorry, Guy, I must defeat you."

The fight was a study in nerves for Gabby. She could not believe the strength and energy expended by both men. After the first blow was countered, it was evident that this was a more than even match. The fight wore on most of the morning, with neither man gaining an upper hand. The king watched intently and several times patted her hand when Guy took an unusually hard blow. She wanted to close her eyes, but could not. Occasionally she slanted her gaze at Quennel, and the smile he wore tore at her.

Now she focused all her thoughts on Guy. She closed her eyes and whispered a fervent prayer. "Dear Lord, though you have favored him all his life, please do not forsake him now." She opened her eyes and drew a deep breath. Suddenly, as if her prayer had been audibly rejected, she knew he would lose. Her throat clogged with emotion. Damn the man. His arrogance had bartered away their future.

She watched Guy as though he moved in slow motion and knew the moment it would happen. His foot twisted, throwing him off-balance, and his leg crumpled. He went down without a blow being struck.

The king raised his hand and the contest was over. The trumpets blared and Gabby stood with the others, stunned at the outcome. She turned to the king, tears in her eyes, and he looked at her with understanding and compassion. " 'Tis over, Lady Gabrielle. I award you to Sir Rule."

Gabby swallowed the lump in her throat and bowed in deference to the king. She felt utterly empty. Quennel Aumont grabbed her arm and tried to pull her roughly from the platform. William's command stopped him. "I have given this woman over to Sir Rule's care. You have no more interest in the matter."

Aumont's features tightened in anger. He savagely flung her arm away. "I was merely delivering her to the victor," he snapped.

Rule's father stepped forward and offered the lady his arm. "My lady, if you will accompany me."

With vision blurred by tears, she watched Guy being lifted onto a plank to be carried off the field. Agony etched deep lines in his face. Suddenly, his eyes locked with hers. She read in them not the pain of his body, but his spirit. He had never lost before. He was more stunned than she.

Her sight of Guy was blocked as Rule approached. He knelt before the king and received his due, then turned to Gabby.

"My lady." He bent low over her hand.

Tears fell down her cheeks as she met his gaze.

He should have been furious over her tears, but if he was he did not reprimand her. Instead, he took her hand from his father's and led her away.

Surprisingly her legs moved, taking her away from her husband, her life. But the moment they left the field the darkness engulfed her. She fought it, but the pain was too great.

Rule caught her as she fell and carried her toward the castle.

"This is not right, son. She belongs with Guy."

"Father, there are many things that are not right in this world. Rest your fears. I do not have dishonorable intentions toward the lady."

"What are you planning?"

Gabby stirred in his arms. Rule looked down at her delicate features. She was truly lovely, and for a moment he let his thoughts wonder to the delights of such a winsome creature. Then his mind cleared. He knew what he wanted, what they must do.

"The slate must be wiped clean. Family business must be put in order if any of us are to know peace."

"You risk much. Royce and Guy would kill either of us on sight."

"Not with Lady Gabrielle in our possession. They will hear us out."

Chapter Nineteen

Guy moaned as an excruciating pain shot up his ankle, and almost thrashed the healer who was wrapping it tightly.

"Easy," Royce said.

Royce's compassion compounded Guy's suffering, and he could not look his brother in the eye. Worse than the pain was the knowledge that he had lost his wife over a challenge. In his arrogance, he had agreed to the idiotic terms. The truth stood out like a shameful cloak for all to see. Never had he known such heartache.

"Royce, go after her. I will follow as soon as this leg is bandaged. Do not let Rule spend time alone with her."

Royce pushed Guy back on the table. "Are you mad? The king has given her to him."

Guy grabbed his brother's tunic front, pulling him near. "Listen to me. I will kill that dog if he dares to touch my lady. You must follow them. Impede their progress so I can catch them."

''What then? You are in no position to fight,'' Royce argued.

''I will offer him my land. A trade for my beloved.''

''Guy,'' Royce said, running his hand through his hair. ''Rule did not fight for land, nor Quennel, nor even Gabrielle. He fought for one reason. To settle the score with us. I told you not to underestimate him.''

Guy leaned his head back against the table, and closed his eyes. Lord, the thought of his half brother with Gabby drove him near senseless. He clenched his teeth and sat up, then pushed the healer away. ''I will go after him.''

''Non,'' the king said, drawing everyone's attention to the tent opening. William pulled the flap down behind him as he entered. ''You will not chase after Rule.''

For the first time in his life Guy knew a rage so strong, so consuming that he could have killed the monarch.

''I have annulled your marriage.''

''What?'' Guy bellowed, barely able to refrain from attacking William.

Eyes narrowed, William held up several papers. ''However, the formalities will take a week. Until then, the lady will have her own quarters. Perhaps while you are recovering you will use the time to meditate on a plan. Since you cannot defeat Rule, I suggest you find out what he wants before making stupid offers that might incense him.''

Guy tried to stand. But streaks of fiery pain shot up his leg, and he collapsed, his ankle unable to support his weight. When he was lifted back onto the table, he grabbed the tankard of spirits the healer offered him and quaffed the brew. William made sense, but in his misery Guy was having trouble accepting the wisdom.

Royce approached William. ''Then you know why Rule is here.'' His statement was suddenly filled with meaning.

''Oui, I do.'' He nodded, his gaze unflinching.

Royce turned to Guy. "I fear we have been pawns in the king's game."

" 'Twas necessary," William said. "I want you to solve the problem with Rule, as you have eliminated the problem of Aumont."

"At what cost, sire?" Guy asked glumly, as he lay down to let the healer finish his work.

"Guy, in truth, I have never seen you act without thought before. This lady has indeed bewitched you."

"The lady you have denied me, sire," he said, resting his arm over his eyes.

The king sighed. "It is unfortunate that you lost the contest. However, the lady is safe for the time being. You and Royce will have to meet with your father and half brother to work this out."

Royce's jaw clenched, while Guy rolled onto his side and glared at the king.

"You heard me, Guy."

"Here is my family," Guy said to the king. "I have no other brother, and no father whom I recognize."

"Recognize him or not, you will meet with the man."

"Why?" Guy asked, dreading the response.

"Because that is the only way you will get your lovely bride back," William said, then turned to Royce. "If you care for your brother you will both do this."

"How long have you had this planned?" Guy asked.

The king cleared his throat. "Longer than you would like to know. I have been investigating Aumont for months. I am glad Louis is safe. With Alec Campbell as his protector, I know he is in good hands. As to his sister, Gabrielle, her fate lay undecided. I feared my plans might run into some problem. However, you did not let me down."

"Guy and Royce, you had best act soon. I can delay their departure for only one week."

"As you wish, sire," Guy said. "But from now on, if

you want something of us, just ask. You need not go to such lengths to test our loyalty.''

"But it would not be nearly so interesting. Take heart, Guy, I have never doubted your loyalty, not even when I walked into this room and you wished to strangle me.''

"Running you through with a sword would be more accurate.''

William raised an eyebrow at the candor. "I will keep that in mind, Guy. See you work this out.''

When the king left, Guy gazed at his brother. Though Royce believed he had put the past to rest, meeting with the father who had abandoned them would open old wounds. It certainly had for Guy.

Gritting his teeth, Guy sat up. "If there were any other way, Royce, I would not ask this of you.''

"I know.'' Royce offered his shoulder for Guy to lean on. "You once did what was in my best interest, and I can do no less.''

Guy clasped his brother's arm. "We will see this to the end.''

Furious Quennel Aumont stormed back and forth within the confines of his room. "By his wounds,'' Quennel swore as he threw a good chalice into the burning hearth. How dare William tell him to return to Normandy. In one blow the monarch had stripped him of any hope to rule the Aumont estates. He would never listen to a bastard impersonating as a king. And he was not alone in his feelings. He would return home, but he would find others and band together to defeat William. In the meantime he had a score to settle with his niece and nephew.

Quennel laughed wickedly. In a year's time, who knows, he might even be king of England.

* * *

Rule sat in his chamber, his hand soaking in a bowl of warm water, while Lance sat by the hearth, staring silently into the fire. His sire was old and tired and needed so little to bring him peace. If it was the last thing Rule did, he had vowed to end his father's suffering. It was a shame an innocent had to be used to bring it about. But it was necessary. And besides, he had saved her from her uncle's treachery.

A knock at the door interrupted Rule's thoughts, and he bid the person enter. There in the doorway, looking hesitant and guarded, stood Guy's lovely wife.

"Come in."

She entered slowly, her gait conveying her misery. "Sir, I understand that I am now your responsibility."

He could see what the words cost her, and he admired her courage. There was a quiet dignity about her.

"Why?" he said, his hand waving her to take a seat. "Do you have a boon to ask of me?"

"I do." She moved closer, but did not sit. The beauty of her features were not lost on him.

"My brother is in hiding in Scotland. I know you have won me fairly, and I will not contest it, if I have your vow that you will not aid my uncle Quennel in searching for and harming my brother."

"You do me a great disservice, madame to imply that I would harm your sibling."

" 'Tis a bargain I offer, sir, not an insult," she replied. "After all, I do not know you."

He considered her words, then stood up and walked around her. He watched her stiffen at his assessment and knew her pride would not allow her to bend meekly before him. In truth, he had not thought much about the maiden. She had merely been a means to an end.

Yet she stood before him with admirable spirit, forcing him to acknowledge her. Her chin lifted, and he did not miss the quivering of her lips. Without his willing it his hand reached out and touched the soft skin of her cheek. Her eyelids slid shut, and though she remained still, the rapid pulse beating in her neck gave away her distress.

"My lady," he said brusquely, more affected than he cared to admit.

She opened her eyes, and he saw a sparkling sheen. "Aye, my lord."

"Do you love your husband?"

He glimpsed a combination of raw pain and longing in her gaze before she quickly looked away. "*Aye,* my lord," she whispered. "More than he loves me."

The simple response touched him deeply. "Then could you not love another?"

"Rule." The elder Lemieux stood, capturing his son's attention. "Lady Gabrielle has naught to fear from you," he said purposefully. "Ease her misery."

"My lady, my sire has the right of it. I will accept your word, and in return give you my vow. Are we so agreed?"

Her eyes lowered. "Aye, we are my lord."

As she turned to leave, he touched her hand. "You will be ready to travel when the king gives his approval?"

She took a deep breath. "I have given my word."

"*Oui,* you have, but will you keep it?"

"Now, sir, you insult me."

"My apologies. But as you say, I do not know you."

"I have given you my word in return for your vow. I shall not betray my family."

He nodded, seeing that beneath her words was a deeper reason. He saw her to the door, and as soon as it closed behind her, his father pounded his fist on the table.

"What in God's name has Quennel done to that child to

make her fear him so? Good God, she would agree to anything for her brother's sake.''

Rule stroked his beard. ''And what have we done to her? Thank God it was I who won, and not one of Quennel's knaves.''

''If it had been one of his paid assassins, I doubt Guy would have been defeated. He is too good a warrior.''

''True. But now there is also another problem we must contemplate.''

''What is that?''

''For her brother's sake, she will keep her vow, and Guy will not understand her disloyalty. A king's order must be obeyed, but Guy's pride will be injured that she does so willingly.''

Gabby felt the blood drain from her face as she left Rule's chamber. Trembling, she leaned against the wall and let herself sink to the floor.

She had settled the matter. Her brother would be safe. She thought of Guy, and a sharp, piercing pain sliced through her heart.

She would not think of the future. It was too painful and lonely a proposition to know the man of your dreams would not share your destiny.

But he had thrown away their love.

Despair filled her at his arrogance. She wanted to rail against him, then stopped herself. It was done. He had made his decision and lost her. She stood, drawing a deep calming breath in a desperate attempt to keep her wits about her, and she forced herself to continue down the cold dark hallway, wondering if her life would always be this bleak.

A hand abruptly reached out, covered her mouth, and pulled her back against a hard-muscled chest.

A scream froze in her throat, and she struggled in her unknown assailant's arms.

''What business sees my wife and half brother together?''

Elation soared through her at the sound of Guy's wonderful voice. But it was short-lived when his words penetrated her mind.

He spun her around. "Answer me!"

"I went to Rule to tell him I will do his bidding if he keeps my brother safe."

The anger, rage, and disgust that filled Guy showed on his features. She tried to pull away but he would not allow it.

"You sold yourself!"

"Guy, I am foresworn. I must protect my family."

"Do love and honor mean nothing to you?"

"Honor! You speak to me of honor, friar?"

He did not even flinch at the rebuke. He pulled her closer. "How can you go to another man after what we have shared?" he asked, his lips a mere breath from her.

She tried to resist the desire that immediately flared. If she kissed him she would be lost.

"You promised to protect me and my family."

"And I will."

"You bartered me away, Guy. I no longer believe in you."

"Stop! I will purchase your freedom."

"You speak as though I am no more than a bag of grain to be bought and sold."

"You intentionally misunderstand."

"Nay, I do not."

"I will protect you."

"Rule will protect me."

"I will not permit it."

"You have no say. Through your foolishness, I now belong to another."

Guy's handsome features hardened into a rigid mask. "You want this? You wish to go to Rule?"

"I have no choice."

He pulled her closer yet. "Damn you. You will never forget the nights in my arms. When he takes you in his embrace, you will remember my kiss, not his." He bent down and covered her lips with his.

At the touch of his mouth, she knew he was right. Her arms crept around his neck and savored their last kiss, a kiss filled with all the passion and possessiveness in their souls.

"Take your hands from my property!"

The harsh order tore them apart.

A band of soldiers held torches, but Gabby did not need the light to recognize Rule's voice.

Guy held on to her shoulders, defying the order, daring the man to action. "She is my wife," he snapped angrily. "You can have the marriage annulled, but that will not change the fact that she belongs to me."

Gabby swallowed down her pain. "No, I do not."

Rule stepped forward and pulled her free of Guy. "Should the time ever come that you again take a wife, make sure you do not treat her so lightly."

Guy lunged forward, but his ankle gave way, refusing to support his attack. He fell to the floor, cursing his half brother. As he struggled to his feet, Gabby shrank back. She could not bear his pain.

"Look at me, Gabby," Guy demanded. When her gaze locked with his she felt his misery as her own. But there was nothing she could do.

Slowly she looked away, and turned to leave, then suddenly remembered her ring and turned back with tears misting her eyes. She pulled the ring off her finger and handed it to Guy.

"Keep my ring and my love, for I have no use for either," she whispered as her gaze met his.

Then she tore free of the crowd of men and ran to her

room. Once the door shut she threw herself on the bed and wept uncontrollably. This ache would never heal and the hurt never fade. Although she had pledged herself to another, her heart and love would forever belong to Guy.

Chapter Twenty

"See this, Verdon." The king handed over the documents that Bayard's sister, Liana, had smuggled to him. "Quennel is guilty of killing his sister and brother-in-law. In his own hand he penned to Bayard this vile account of each murder." William shook his head at the grisly account of cutting off Hamish's finger to retrieve the Aumont ring.

"Order his arrest. I now have the proof that I lacked before to bring him to trial. Quennel will serve as an example that murdering one's relatives to inherit will not be condoned during my reign."

The advisor shook his head. "Guy's allegations were right. 'Twas bad luck that Rule volunteered as Quennel's champion."

The king denied that assessment with a shake of his head. "Nothing happens by chance. Believe it or not, this will serve the kingdom well. Quennel will be brought to justice. And the proud and fine name of Lemieux will survive the de Bellemare rift and grow stronger."

The advisor bowed in silent salute, acknowledging the wisdom of his liege, and exited just as the queen was entering the room.

"Will, I am worried about Gabby."

Ah, his wife had taken quite a liking to the woman. Not that he could blame her. Gabby was sweet, kind, and loyal. He also admired her selfless devotion to duty.

"Does the maid ail?"

"*Non,* but I fear her unhappiness is in part our fault. Is there nothing you can do to help her plight?"

"Matilda, my love, I promise you within a fortnight all will be well."

His little wife stared up at him with a hint of suspicion in her eyes. "Will, have you been rearranging lives again?"

"*Oui,* 'twill be no time at all until the fair Gabrielle and the sad but wiser Guy are reunited."

"I should have known not to worry. Someday, Will, I hope you tire of this game."

"A king *rules* his subjects, Matilda."

"I know, but I have never liked it."

He put his arms around her. "How was I so lucky to fall in love with you?"

She chuckled. "You mean you have not figured that out?"

At her mischievous laugh he looked at her. "What do you mean, wife?"

"I rearranged a few lives myself."

"Never," he roared.

Her eyes sparkled. "*Oui,* 'twas easy. You were half in love with me the day we met."

He stared at her in wonder. "You mean you, and not I, did the pursuing?" He was shocked.

"Let us say I allowed you to catch me."

He laughed and pulled her tightly to his chest. "Rest your fears about yon couple. That is exactly what Gabby shall do to Guy."

* * *

At the sound of their echoing footsteps, Gabby could not fail to know they arrived, but refused to look at Guy or Royce. She stared off into the tapestries, seemingly oblivious to the proceedings. A private audience had been arranged and the room's huge size seemed to dwarf everything and magnify every sound.

The king handed Guy the annulment paper to sign. Without reading it, he handed it back unsigned.

The king smiled. " 'Tis not necessary," he said, taking the paper and writing in Guy's name "My lady, your signature is all that is required."

Gabby accepted the paper and read it over.

Guy held his breath, hoping she also would refuse to sign it. He needed that small sign that she, too, clung to their bond. But she signed it without a moment's hesitation. *Damn her,* he thought, his chest hurting painfully. In all the time he stood before the king willing her to look at him, she had not once glanced his way.

He needed to touch her. Every inch of him screamed to take her into his arms and make her admit her love.

"Gabby," Guy pleaded, his voice harsh with raw emotion.

Slowly she raised her head. He saw the tears in her eyes.

"Aye?"

"It is not over."

A tear overspilled, and she looked away, whispering, "It is for us."

The king's voice filled the room. "Let everyone present know that by the Church's authority Gabrielle Aumont is no longer wed to Guy de Bellemare, and has on this day become the possession of Rule Lemieux."

Gabby's shoulders visibly sagged with the pronouncement, but she did not look up.

Guy limped forward. "Rule, I have a parcel of land and a castle. I will deed them to you for the lady."

Rule looked Guy straight in the eye. *"Non,* 'tis not to my liking."

Guy's mouth dropped open. "Are you mad? Why not?"

" 'Tis not what I want."

Stunned, Guy could not find his voice. He heard Royce grit out, "What is it you want, Rule?"

"I will discuss the lady's future at Renwyg Castle in the presence of your family. There and only there is where we will meet, and I will make my wishes known."

"Never," Royce hissed.

"As you wish, brother," Rule said, taking Gabrielle's arm.

"Royce!" Guy grabbed his brother's arm and matched his steely-eyed glare. "You must agree to his demands. Would you deny me my chance at happiness?"

Royce pulled his arm free and tersely nodded his head. With his eyes mere slits and his lips tightly drawn, Royce faced his half brother. "You will be welcome in my home."

Rule nodded his head, "We will leave at once for North Umberland, but we will not travel in your company. William has granted my boon. Our party will leave first, so no trap can awaits us." Still holding Gabby's arm, he turned.

Royce stiffened at the insult.

"One moment," Guy said to Rule, even while he stared at Gabby. "You will not touch the lady until this matter is resolved."

Rule glanced back at him. "My father will act as my chaperon, and none will challenge his word."

Lance Lemieux nodded his head. "The lady will have nothing to fear from us. You have my word on it."

"Your word," Guy sneered at the offer. "I remember your promise to another lady, and that one was broken without thought of the consequences."

Lance's anger rose as his face flushed a deep red.

"I will have the king's man, Verdon, with us. Is that to your liking?"

"*Oui.* I shall know that the lady's honor is not in danger."

Quennel Aumont paced the ridge. Court had been a defeat, and he silently glowered. Damn Rule Lemieux and his own agenda. That was another score to settle, but later. First his nephew and his niece. He needed information and he had come to Renwyg Castle to get it. His men in Scotland could not locate Louis. Laird Campbell had hidden the boy well.

Quennel turned at the sound of approaching steps.

"My Lord, there is no news of the boy," Rowland said.

Quennel stared at his soldier until the man looked uncomfortable.

"But, Laird Campbell is journeying to North Umberland to see his niece."

"Is that all?" Quennel did not allow his excitement to show.

"*Non,* my lord. King William has sent a man to Normandy to order your return to court."

"For what reason?"

"I do not know."

Quennel dismissed the man and began pacing back and forth. Ignoring the king's command could be fatal, but he would not enter the lion's den without some assurance he would not be the meal.

For the time being he had a good excuse. William thought Quennel had returned to Normandy as ordered. He would simply pretend news of the summons had not reached him. Quennel smiled. When he laid eyes on the king again, Gabby and Louis would be dead. Time was on his side.

He turned his attention to the castle. Now, how would he infiltrate the structure and gain information? He studied the stone building. The castle defense could not be breached without an army, and even then, it would take weeks to scale the walls. He needed a plan that would yield immediate entry into the Norman stronghold.

A group of traveling minstrels approached the gate and it swung open, but not before Quennel hit upon his idea. The entertainers gained easy entry. He called to Rowland and the man hurried back.

"*Oui*, my lord."

"I have discovered our way in."

Lance shook his head, watching Verdon ride away to answer the King's summons. "Guy will be furious," he mumbled, holding the reins of the three horses.

"Please, forgive me, my lord. I think the sickness has passed," Gabby said, lifting her head gingerly.

Rule felt totally inadequate. What would he do with a sick woman on his hands? He looked over her head to his father, sending a silent plea.

"My lady, what malady do you think has beset you?" Lance asked.

" 'Tis nothing more than exhaustion. I am so sorry to trouble you." She pushed away from Rule and suddenly staggered.

His arm went around her, again. "We will stop for the evening," he said, though he did not want to stop when they were in a hurry to reach North Umberland. Royce and Guy were only a day's ride behind them. But he could not ask the woman to continue on when she was so poorly disposed.

Her eyes were glossy with moisture. He prayed she did not start bawling. How he hated that. A man just did not have a defense against a woman's tears, and he resented anything that placed him at a disadvantage.

She gave him a watery smile and wiped the moisture from her eyes. "I have never been sick before. You are very kind to humor my illness."

"My lady, 'tis you who are kind. We did not mean to set a pace that would exhaust you," Rule replied.

"Why are we going to North Umberland?" she suddenly asked, trying to take her mind off the terrible wave of nausea that engulfed her.

"We have heard certain stories, and wish to see if they are true," Rule said, thinking of the news of Royce's twins.

"Stories!" she gasped. "This was done because of stories?" But before Rule could answer, the world began to spin and the black mist of night engulfed her.

Rule caught her in his arms. "Lord, but she is ill."

"Non," Lance said. "I believe she is with child."

"God, I hope not. Guy will be in enough of a rage."

"True. And we have not enamored him to us. For the lady's sake, I hope he believes the babe his."

"Why would he not?" Rule asked.

Lance looked years older when he faced his son. "Why indeed? After all, he is his father's son. My jealousy destroyed my life."

"Guy would not be so foolish, Father." Rule motioned up ahead. "Is that a cave? I think we should find a shelter."

"Our pace will be much slower tomorrow. I would not risk my grandchild," Lance said, pulling the reins of the horses.

Rule nodded. His stubborn father would also benefit from the slower pace. Lance refused to let his limitations interfere with his life, and he resented anyone who suggested caution. Since his illness, the sire he loved had faced his personal failings and in doing so, had come face-to-face with the truth. Family is a man's immortality. Nothing else lasts, and nothing else has meaning.

Lance looked at his son. "You and your brothers are all I have to show for a lifetime of success."

"Father, you have a legacy any man would envy," Rule said, carrying Gabrielle up the long incline to the cave.

"Do I?"

"*Oui.* You have twin grandsons to carry on your name."

Lance agreed as he looked at the lady, "And I will have more grandchildren if the lady takes care. We will have to be extremely gentle with this little flower to ensure she blossoms."

"I wonder if Guy suspects?" Rule asked.

"I doubt it," Lance said. "Surely he would have died before relinquishing his family."

"He has not yet given up," Rule warned, as he stood at the entrance of the cave.

"*Oui.* A true Lemieux." Lance chuckled, tying their horses up.

"I wonder how I will feel when the day arrives that I look forward to a son?" Rule said, peeking into the dark cave.

" 'Twill be the happiest day of your life. When you hold God's greatest miracle in your arms, you know what it is to glimpse heaven." Lance brushed by him to gather some wood for a fire, and soon sat feeding the soft flame.

"A man must see his past clearly to enjoy his future," he said thoughtfully. Your brothers have never come to terms with it. If for no other reason, I would see them find peace. I owe them that much."

"Father, all will be put right when we reach North Umberland. They will have to listen to you."

"Perhaps. I only hope God allows me the wisdom and patience to set right the wrong I did." He sighed. "I was a fool. I would not have my sons bear the burden of my folly. Before I die I would see all three of the Lemieux brothers united."

"We will be, Father. There is more at stake than merely us," he said pointedly as he looked at Gabby. She lay in his arms oblivious to their words.

"She will be our key. As much as I hate to use her, the love Guy bears her will see this through. A man will cross seas and climb mountains for love. She is our edge."

Rule nodded as he placed her carefully on the pallet Lance had made. Then he noticed the medallion that had slipped from her tunic. "Look, Father." He pointed to the exact copy of his own medallion.

"I gave each of my sons that gold medallion." Lance chuckled, his eyes alight with hope at the shiny medal stamped with the Lemieux crest. "Mayhap our reconciliation will be easier than we think."

Chapter Twenty-One

Midmorning brought foul weather. Dark clouds masked the sun, and nasty winds swirled about, carrying the hint of moisture that would soon fall.

"We cannot travel in this," Rule said to his father.

Lance studied the pale features of the woman in their company, then nodded.

"Please, you need not change your plans for me," Gabby said, edging her horse closer to the men. "I can travel."

Rule hid the smile that threatened his lips. *"Non,* we always rest during a storm."

"Oui," Lance said. He dismounted and helped Gabby from her horse.

Rule pointed to a deserted hut and took the reins from his father. "At this pace Royce and Guy will arrive in North Umberland long before we do."

"It might just serve our purpose to have the whelp wondering where we are." Lance laughed.

Gabby whirled about. "What game are you about?" She

stepped closer to the gray-haired man. "You seem intent on making Guy suffer."

"Non, my lady, you misunderstand. I will upbraid the man, but not for the reasons you think."

"Think? I do not know what to think. Why are you doing this? It is obvious neither of you is interested in me. And I have seen you are not willing to carry out Quennel's bidding. Yet, you have some reason for keeping me."

"My lady, I only wish I could tell you but I cannot. You must trust us," Lance said. "No harm will come to you."

"Will you vow on all you hold holy that harm will not come to Guy?"

"That is up to him." Rule shrugged.

Gabby's eyes remained on the father. He felt the intensity of her gaze, and for the first time since they traveled together he knew without doubt or reservation that she loved his son. Her determined look spoke of her feeling more eloquently than words. She would without hesitation protect her beloved from harm.

Lance took a deep breath. "My lady, Guy will not suffer by my hand. His only danger lies in his wounded pride, but I think now he will listen to reason."

The relief on her face filled him with satisfaction. He did not want to harm this flower. She was one of those rare human beings who did good rather than preached it.

The party of mercenaries lay belly down in the meadow, their dark, heavy cloaks covering their heads in a weak attempt at protection from the downpour. Nestled among the green weeds, they looked like a pond of sleeping turtles, not peeping their heads out except at an occasional traveler.

Their orders were clear. Laird Campbell would travel this route on his way to North Umberland. They would kidnap the laird and demand Louis Aumont as ransom.

The pantomime they had performed a week ago at Renwyg Castle had allowed them to garner all the information they needed, and also provided an excellent opportunity. As fate would have it the castle needed a farrier, and fortunately one of their men had trained as a blacksmith. Now along with the ten men left behind to watch Renwyg, they had one man inside the castle. After leaving those soldiers in North Umberland, the rest of Aumont's army now waited in Scotland on Mactavish land for their unsuspecting victim.

Quennel smiled in satisfaction. His plan was foolproof. He could not be accused of any foul play. Right now, he was believed to be on his way back to his own estates in Normandy.

He could not hope to take Gabrielle until she and her champion, Rule, traveled abroad. But Louis he must have; the boy would not return to Normandy for many years. Once his nephew was eliminated, the Aumont estates and all the wealth of the demesne would fall to him as the only male heir. He could dispose of the wretched girl at his convenience.

Gabby arrived in North Umberland tired, weak, and long overdue. They rode into Renwyg a week and a half after Guy and Royce. The relentless nausea she had suffered served her poorly. Guy, Royce, and Bethany all ran to the stable to meet her. Her appearance brought an immediate reaction from Guy.

"What the hell have you done to her?" Guy demanded as he marched by her and stood toe to toe with his half brother in the middle of the barn.

"We have done nothing," Rule said, handing his reins to the stablemaster.

"You expect me to believe that?" Guy scoffed.

Listlessly, Gabby trailed after Guy and pulled on his sleeve but he was too angry to listen.

"Where have you been all this time? We left after you and arrived before you. What dalliance have you been up to?"

"Guy, please," Gabby softly entreated. "Your brother and father are delayed because I fell ill. They would have been here long before you if they had not a care to my well-being."

He finally turned to her. His face remained an angry mask, but he did relax, slightly, his stance now challenging instead of confrontational. "What, pray tell, afflicted you that you could not travel?"

The nasty tone in his question tore at her heart.

"I do not know," she said. This was not the time to tell him of her suspicions. "But I was truly too poorly disposed to travel."

His cold midnight gaze reflected condemnation and suspicion.

The reason for his harshness suddenly dawned on her. "Do you question my honor?" she asked. "Or do you question theirs?"

When he remained silent, staring at her as though he could see into her soul, she turned away. A tight band encircled her heart. The pain of a lover's mistrust was nearly unbearable.

With a snort of disgust, Rule stepped forward and grabbed Guy's arm. "You arrogant fool. The lady is telling the truth. You may not believe us, but you should never doubt her integrity."

Guy pulled free of the hold. " 'Tis not her I mistrust but you," he snarled.

"Have done, boy." Lance moved into Guy's path. "Your lady is without guile. She has not played you false."

"Look at her clothes, her hair, and," he grabbed her chin, tilting it up, "her face." So, Gabby thought, a swollen lip along with her rumpled and travel-stained tunic and her windblown hair, would convict her.

"She was scratched when a swaying tree branch clipped her face," Lance said, his gaze lingering on her.

Guy's eyes narrowed. "Really? And where is Verdon?"

Lance looked uncomfortable. "Verdon returned to London at the king's request."

"Convenient."

" 'Tis the truth."

"Why in God's name should I believe you?" he snapped, grabbing his father's tunic. His anger erupted into a storm Gabby had never seen. "You deserted us! I do not believe you capable of one honest act."

Rule tried to come between the two, but Royce held him back as Bethany took Gabby's arm.

"You are a fool, son. You would make the same mistake I did."

"Liar!"

"I doubted your mother's fidelity by believing the lies I was told by Beltane. Not until Royce's twins were born did I question the explanation given; then I confronted Beltane and he confessed the deception. I realized my folly, and I knew the truth. You *are* my sons. I abandoned you. 'Twas the sorriest mistake of my life, and now you are about to dishonor your lady with the same unfounded accusations."

"You don't know what you're talking about," Guy spit.

"Prove it. Tell the lady that you could never doubt her love."

Gabby saw the angry frustration flit across Guy's expression and knew he was remembering how willingly she had accepted Rule. His honor and pride had been sorely bruised, but so had hers.

So much of their future hinged on this moment that she willed him with all of her heart to give his trust unconditionally.

But he did not. He wavered long enough to show doubt lived in his heart.

"Fool," Lance snarled, pushing free. "We are late arriving because great care had to be taken to bring your lady here. She is with child. Your child!"

The pronouncement stunned everyone. Gabby's eyes filled with tears, and she lowered her head. But Guy did not even look at her.

"You dare to play your games here," he shouted at his father. "You who abandoned your family dare to criticize me. I will, in time, be a father. But this trick suits your deceitful nature. And a man who would lie to further his selfish cause damns his soul."

"I care little where the Almighty sends me. I had hoped to right a terrible wrong. Nothing more. God will have his say with my soul no matter what you decide. But take care, Guy, you are more like me than you admit."

With a growl Guy launched himself at his father and the two men went crashing to the ground.

Rule tried to intervene, but Lance yelled for him to stay out of it.

Shrugging, Rule joined Royce to watch the struggle with a mixture of resigned acceptance and divided loyalties.

Bethany clasped Gabby's hand and murmured, "Royce could never imagine forgiving his father until our sons were born. Now his attitude is softening toward his sire. But it would seem Guy carried the scars hidden. He must mend this breach, Gabby. Let it happen."

"He never told me," Gabby moaned, despairing that Guy had hidden this hurt from her.

The men rolled around the courtyard, throwing fists amid flying dirt and straw, wrestling for control.

She felt sick watching father and son fight. Her stomach heaved, and the dizziness returned. "Stop it," she cried.

Hearing her pitiful plea, Rule and Royce broke up the

fight by pulling the men apart. Gabby stumbled into their midst and stood between Guy and his father.

"You should be ashamed and you call yourselves grown men. A pity you cannot set a better example for the youth of this castle. 'Tis time to bury the hurt and bridge the years of anger. Do it now."

Breathing heavily, Guy jerked his shoulders free of Royce's hold. But before he could speak, she went on.

"I had hoped that my child would have as his father a man full-grown."

As Lance slipped free of Rule's grasp and smiled at her reprimand of Guy, she turned on him. "If you are indeed their sire, then there is little hope for this line."

Lance's eyes widened, then he blustered in disbelief until Rule and Royce burst out in laughter.

Suddenly, Ambra appeared on the castle steps. As she slowly descended the stairs, the men fell silent from her solemn stare. When her gaze settled on Rule, her expression softened. "Rule, you have grown into a fine man."

"Thank you, Mother," he said, bowing before her. "I have missed you."

She nodded, glanced briefly at Lance, then turned to Gabby.

"You are right, childishness must indeed be a family trait," Ambra said, as she took Gabby's arm and walked away without a backward glance.

"We have behaved badly," Lance said. He turned to his sons. "I suggest we go inside and talk this over until it is at last put to rest."

Gabby paced back and forth in Bethany's room. "I have never lost my temper like that before," she said distraught. "How unworthy you must think me."

"Nay. In fact I am very proud of you. They were behaving

like spoiled little boys.'' Bethany looked at her sideways. "Admit it, Gabby, it felt good to speak your mind. Did it not?''

She had to concede a taste of assertiveness felt immensely satisfying. "Yes, but I hope I do not make a practice of emotional outbursts.''

Bethany chuckled. "Though I doubt you would under normal circumstances, I am afraid that outbursts are a symptom of pregnancy you will not escape.''

Though Ambra smiled, her face was still white from her encounter with Lance, and her hands trembled as she took hold of Gabby's.

"Although Guy is my son, and I love him, he is a man, and they are blind to their own tender emotions.''

Gabby smiled. "I am afraid I do not possess your wisdom.''

"Nonsense. Time will take care of insight. But you possess something far greater. Courage. You kept your family safe and served your name well. 'Tis not easy being a woman in a man's world. We have to abide by rules not of our own making and laws that do not consider us equal. I am proud to know you and pleased to call you daughter.''

Gabby felt an immense sense of worth and belonging. "Thank you, Ambra.'' She looked toward the door. "I cannot stand this waiting,'' she said, irritated that her fate was being decided while she was relegated to her room.

Ambra smiled. " 'Tis frustrating, my dear, but that is how it has always been done. Though I must confess, I have always found it amazing that we who labor hours in childbirth, teach and raise our babies, cook and clean for our husbands, and run a household while the men are away, are rewarded for our efforts by being treated like children.''

Gabby wrapped her arms around the tiny little woman's waist. "You are right. If I am to have a child, then I refuse to be treated like one.''

* * *

Even as she descended the stairs, Gabby knew she breached all etiquette by intruding on the meeting held downstairs. Lord forgive her, but she was about to challenge convention.

Angry voices came from the hall below, and she paused at the heated words. She sank to her knees and peeked over the balustrade into the room. Her heart skipped a beat. Guy stood with his feet braced apart and his hands balled into tight fists. Royce held much the same stance as Rule. Both men's faces were drawn. Lance was the only one who seemed relaxed.

" 'Tis time to set the record straight," Lance said, pouring a tankard of ale.

"That time has passed," Guy said. " 'Tis too late now."

Rule raised an eyebrow. "Listen to our father, Guy, or you may never know the comfort of the lovely Gabby."

Guy charged toward him, stopping inches from Rule's nose to stare him down. "How dare you threaten me?"

Rule was not intimidated. "We must end the animosity and unite the family. We are out of time."

"Enough," Lance said, leaning forward with difficulty.

"Why now?" Guy asked, catching the slip.

Lance's gaze darted to Guy. "I will not explain."

"You will explain or there will be no truce."

With a terse nod, Lance leaned back in the chair, gripping his chest. Rule brought a chalice of cool water, adding medicine to the liquid before handing it to his father. "Drink it slowly, Father."

When Lance had finished his drink he drew a deep breath and motioned the men closer. "Guy, Royce, our very existence is in danger. Our neighbor is encroaching on our land. Rule is fighting a battle alone, and needs the added support of a powerful family. If you do not join forces with him, he will lose everything.''

"What of you?" Guy asked.

"I can no longer give aid. This cursed ailment I have comes and goes, and because my health is failing, I no longer hold an important position at court.'' It was evident that admission cost the man dearly, but the truth was written on his face. He was old and weak and could no longer help Rule.

"Why should we support him?"

"The truth,'' Lance gasped, trying to rise, pausing midway and collapsing back into the chair. "Open acceptance and a division of my estate.''

Royce's mouth dropped open, while Guy stared at Lance in disbelief.

"After all these years you will claim us as your flesh and blood?'' Guy turned to Royce. "I do not believe him. 'Tis a trick.''

"Non," Lance interrupted, his voice raw with emotion. "I will right the wrong grievously done to you years ago.''

"I believed you once; I will not trust you again,'' Royce said.

"I swear to you on all I hold holy I will announce before the whole kingdom that you and Guy are my sons and equal to Rule.''

"You do not know what it is to swear on all you hold holy.'' Guy snapped. "You left all of us alone in a hostile world. Mother defied her family to be with you, and when you cast her out her own family treated her with contempt.''

"Hate me, Guy, but not Rule; he needs your support. I will keep my word. And as proof I do here and now give each of you titles to the land the king has settled on me for quelling the last uprising.''

Royce took the paper and together with Guy looked it over.

"You are giving us everything detailed here?"

"Oui, for you and your families."

Royce rubbed his chin in contemplation. " 'Twas hard to put the past from my mind. I am glad 'tis now laid to rest without bitterness." He offered his hand to his father. "I will offer Rule my support."

"What of our mother?" Guy snapped to Royce.

Lance's expression softened. "If she would forgive me, I would love her to my dying day. But after my betrayal, that is truly unlikely."

A lump formed in Gabby's throat, and she pitied Lance. He had learned too late the value of what he had lost. He looked old and tired as he held out his hand to Guy.

"Will you take my hand and let go of the past, Guy? Or will you hold on to your hate?"

Gabby held her breath waiting for Guy to decide. "Please," she whispered, "let the hate go."

After what seemed like an eternity, Guy extended his hand. *"Oui,* I will help, but not for your sake, for Rule's."

Joy surged through Gabby. It was a start.

"You both must know that the villain will stop at nothing to gain our ancestral home."

"What is it you require of us?" Royce asked, pouring everyone a chalice of wine.

"I need your public support. If you back our position I do not think you will need to lead troops. The knave will back down. He is a bully and only harms those weaker than himself."

Rule raised his glass. "To my brothers."

"To forgiveness," Royce joined.

"To family," Lance saluted as his gaze proudly took in each and every son.

"To victory," Guy toasted.

"Once united we will be a formidable force. You have earned the king's favor," Rule said.

"What of my wife?" Guy asked.

"Nice of you to remember," Gabby whispered.

"I only wished to help. If I had not come forward, Quennel would have recruited another. I was relieved I could save her."

Guy's surly expression showed he was still stinging over the loss.

"You fought valiantly, but I am the eldest brother. It would be like fighting yourself with five years more experience."

Put so diplomatically, Guy's pride was eased.

Still, her foolish husband needed a lesson for his behavior. Straightening her shoulders to take on the whole Lemieux family, Gabby stepped into the room.

"Guy, have you worked out the problem?" she called out sweetly.

"*Oui,* my love." He held out his hand for her to join him. "Rule has given up all his rights where you are concerned."

Gabby strolled about, refusing to come to her husband's side. "Am I now free?"

"*Oui,*" he said, studying her curiously.

"Good, now I will tell you what *I* wish, since no one in this room bothered to ask me."

Four mouths dropped open at her soft-spoken announcement.

"Wife, how dare you?" Guy recovered his wits first.

She blinked at his shout. "By the king's decree I am no longer married. What, then, will I tell my child?"

"Our child," Guy corrected.

"*Non,* we are not married," she said, trailing her finger along the table edge as she slanted a glance at him. " 'Tis my child."

"We will marry, immediately."

His smug smile irritated her, but she forced herself to remain calm.

"What makes you think I will even consider marrying a man who wagers his wife away on a whim? My child needs more security than that."

"Gabby," Guy warned.

"Do not take that tone with me, sir. I am not a child."

Guy advanced on her, his face red as his brothers and father moved out of the way and whispered among themselves.

Gabby rounded on the men. "You think this is humorous?"

When every face sobered, she sighed and softened her voice. "Perhaps you can counsel yon fool," she said, pointing to Guy. "For there will be no marriage until I have his assurance our family's security will come first."

Guy stood before her, clenching and unclenching his fists.

"Gabby, think you well what you say."

Though he towered over her, she folded her hands and met his angry gaze. "I know what I ask of you, Guy. Admit you were wrong and I will count the matter done. I will not bend on this." She turned and left the room.

Guy's voice rang out in the hall. "Come back here!"

She ignored it, and heard Rule counsel Guy. "Take heart, Guy, breeding women are often unreasonable. It will pass."

"Pass?" Guy questioned. "What of now?"

"She will wed you when she realizes how foolish she is," Royce said.

"I will not," she fumed as she started climbing the stairs.

"You do not know Gabby," Guy warned. "She is not one given to rash statements."

"Brother, you do not know women," Royce said. "I have found that Bethany will not speak to me if I have angered her. Lord, but I hate that.

"My experience with women is this. Once they are with child they change. They cannot help it. Your mother, sweet mademoiselle though she was, could, during her pregnancies, be capable of the most fiendish tempers over nothing.''

"You act the fools. I tell you Gabby is not like that."

Indeed, Gabby thought. Halfway up the stairs she glanced and noticed Bethany and Ambra listening near the rail. Bethany's lips were pursed tight while Ambra face was deeply flushed.

Gabby reached the top of the stairs, and saw both women bursting with silent laughter. "You heard?" When both nodded she took each woman's arm in hers and headed for the bedchamber. "Men," she said.

After the others went to bed Guy sat alone, contemplating his follies. He had never thought that he would lose the challenge. Never. If for a moment he had thought there was a chance of defeat, he would never have agreed to Rule's terms. He had the best intentions, but that did not stop it from recoiling into disaster. It was a lesson well learned. He would not forget it. To prove to Gabby that he was wiser now would be the difficulty. Still, he believed in his heart that she loved him, that even in her anger she would forgive him. He knew he would forgive her, if the situation were reversed.

He sighed deeply. He missed her. This time of separation seemed like the limbo the monks spoke of. Limbo existed for lost souls, and without her he was indeed hopeless and forlorn. She had become his reason to rise in the morning and lie down at night. The day existed because she was in it.

He went up to bed, knowing that this purgatory was well earned. In the morning he would set things aright.

*   *   *

The news came at dawn. A messenger had roused the castle, and the men quickly gathered in the great room. Bethany and Gabby, each holding one of the twins, pushed through the tight circle.

"The Scotsman, Alec Campbell, has been taken prisoner," the messenger was saying. "A ransom has been demanded: Alec Campbell's life in exchange for the lad, Louis Aumont. The Campbell clan wishes their laird back."

"Dear God," Gabby said, meeting Guy's gaze.

Chapter Twenty-Two

The look on her face haunted him. Hopelessness clouded her violet eyes.

He had taken her into a light embrace trying to offer comfort. But the warmth he shared did not assuage the cold fear in her expression.

"You will make no more bargains," Gabby exclaimed. "You cannot trade my uncle for my brother."

"That is not for you to decide," a strong voice declared.

Guy felt her nails dig into his arm as Louis appeared, standing tall and determined before them. He had returned not as a boy, but as a man.

"Then I will go." Gabby wrestled to be free of Guy's embrace.

"*Non.*" The chorus echoed around the room as everyone refused her suggestion.

Royce and Louis moved away from them to the trestle table where they talked in hushed tones with the soldiers.

Guy's arms pulled her up against his chest when she tried to follow.

"I will take care of him," he whispered in her ear. He felt every curve of her body through her thin night smock. And he ached to be alone with her. The sweet smell of violets drifted to him, and he knew the soft subtle scent would haunt him forever.

"So that Uncle Quennel will kill you, also?" she murmured.

"Trust us, Gabby. We can take care of this."

She shook her head.

"Trust me, then," Guy whispered, trying and needing to reach her.

She turned in his arms. Her beautiful eyes, wet with unshed tears, shimmered like a rare amethyst. "I have always trusted you. I always will."

Her heartfelt words of belief humbled him. He truly did not deserve her. But he silently vowed that he would never again disappoint her.

With gentle tenderness, he cradled her face, his thumbs lightly stroking her skin. "Someday, my love, I will be worthy of your devotion. I know you are still angry with me. I am sorry." He caressed her cheek, and felt the petal softness of her skin. Trailing a finger down her jaw, he lifted her chin, and kissed her, hungry for her yielding mouth beneath his. When he finished tasting the wondrous sweet nectar of her lips, he closed his eyes and rested his head against hers.

"Will you marry me," he asked.

Her answer was lost in a sob as two giant tears spilled over her dark lashes and trickled down her cheeks.

He drew her to an alcove, away from the watchful eyes. "Will you consent to be my wife, again? That is, if you have forgiven me."

"Will you trust me, unconditionally?" she asked.

"Trust?" he asked confused.

"*Oui*. Trust! No more secrets can exist between us."

"I swear to you, I will never again keep anything from you. Even William could not hold me to secrecy. And," he said reading the hurt she had suffered when he doubted her faithfulness, "I will never question your fidelity again."

She wrapped her arms around his neck and kissed him.

He felt the fire and passion in her kiss and nearly lost his mind as her body moved against his.

"Gabby? Is that a yes?" he gasped, pulling free of her embrace.

"If we had time, I would marry you now." Her gaze lowered. "Forgive me, husband. Though I was hurt, I should not have tried to teach you a lesson. 'Twas unbecoming and foolish, and I regret it."

"Do not worry about the lesson. I deserved it. 'Tis enough that I know you love me."

"I never stopped loving you," she said, then removed the golden chain from around her neck and offered it to him. "You bade me to wear this to remember your pledge. I now ask the same of you."

Guy smiled. Though she had returned his ring when the king had annulled their marriage, she had kept his gift. He reverently placed it back over her head, repeating what he had said when he first gave her the medallion. "Remember, believe in me."

"Take care," she whispered. "You hold my heart and my hope within your hands."

He kissed her again and turned to leave. Then he paused and turned back. "Do not worry. I will keep Louis safe."

She smiled. "Keep yourself safe, too. I could not bear it if you did not return."

That was how he left her. The glistening tears exposed her longing, along with her love. A man could die happy knowing such a woman awaited him. But he had no intentions of dying.

Royce had sent for reinforcements from his father-in-law, Mactavish. Unfortunately, even though a missive was sent informing William of their dire straits, he would not have time to send men.

As they rode toward Quennel's meeting place, only once did Guy allow the memory of his woman to play about his mind, before he turned to the business at hand. The picture of her lying soft and warm after their lovemaking, stirred his senses: her lips kiss-swollen, parted and beckoning, her eyes heavy-lidded, with a lazy, dreamy-eyed glow as she gazed at him. Such a recollection was enough to see him through hell and back. Then Guy put all thoughts of his love and his home from his mind. He had to concentrate when he went into battle.

Gabby turned the golden medallion over and over in her hand.

The hours passed with dreadful agony, and she knew this would be the longest wait of her life.

A Scotsman from the clan Campbell and one from the clan Mactavish came to stay at Renwyg. Each man was a sour-looking rough warrior, and she felt the censure of their gaze. No doubt they blamed her for putting their kin in danger. Though they never voiced it, she could hear the silent condemnation in their attitude and manner.

Whether it was the soldiers' condemnation, or more likely her own brand of self-flagellation, guilt ate at her. Though she tried to find chores to occupy her every moment, the fear and remorse accompanied her through the long day and sleepless night.

By the second night she knew she must do something. While she was deciding her course of action, a soldier appeared at the gates. He carried a missive from her uncle Alec.

Cedric, the silver-haired Saxon guard, brought the note to the great hall where the women were sewing.

Gabby read the note, demanding her presence at the exchange site. Though she knew her uncle Alec would never endanger her, she could only imagine the horrible pressure brought to make him write such a note. With her throat hurting from the emotions held in check, she turned to Bethany.

"I am going to the meeting place."

"I will not permit it. And I am in charge," Bethany said, surprising Gabby with her strength and purpose.

But the intimidation only served to stiffen Gabby's resolve. "I am leaving, and whether you say yea or nay, I will go."

Bethany studied her for a long moment. "I think Guy does not know the woman he has married. Being good of heart does not make one weak."

Gabby sighed. "He thinks I am helpless?"

Ambra abruptly stood up, spilling the threads onto the floor. "He cares enough to try to protect you. There is much to be said for that." When she walked to the window, Bethany and Gabby exchanged glances.

Gabby followed Ambra and placed a hand on her arm. "I am just as worried about them as you."

Ambra turned with tears in her eyes. "I am sorry. I did not mean to snap. I fear the shock of seeing Lance after so many years has rattled me."

"I know," Gabby said, walking her mother-in-law back to the table and helping her pick up the thread.

Bethany read the note. "I think it is a trap. I do not believe any Scotsman would put his own in danger.'' She handed the note to the Campbell man.

'' 'Tis not my laird's script,'' he said, his tone adamant.

Understanding suddenly dawned, and Gabby paced. "Uncle Quennel is setting a trap for me so in one swift blow he can rid himself of any burdens or claims to the estate.''

"Perhaps," Bethany said, "he is setting a trap for your husband.''

Gabby's blood froze in her veins. Of course! If she went, she would be the bait. She would not foolishly endanger Guy. She would trust him.

"You cannot go," Bethany said again, her expression worried.

"I know." Gabby patted Bethany's shoulder, then reread the note. "Why not *use* the messenger?" Gabby held up her hand to forestall Ambra's interruption. "Perhaps we can set a trap of our own.''

Shifting her sewing aside, Bethany leaned forward. "What, pray tell, do you have in mind?''

Gabby immediately took a seat. '' 'Tis a bit dangerous, but this is my idea. We set a trap for Quennel Aumont, with me as the bait. He will never face Guy's army. Coward that he is, he will let others fight while he is safe. If he thinks I am vulnerable, he will come.''

The fire in the hearth burned hot, but Gabby felt a distinct chill. Comfort and security would have to wait. Her beloved and her family needed her more than ever.

'' 'Twill be a risky scheme at best, and there is no way to let the men know, but I will sanction the plan.'' Bethany called her man, Cedric, forward. "Lady Gabrielle wishes to send a message to Quennel Aumont that will immediately elicit a response.''

Cedric nodded his head, waiting for the rest.

"You will inform yon soldier waiting outside the gate that Lady Gabrielle cannot travel. Tell him she is with child."

Cedric bowed, and moved off as Ambra exclaimed with shock. Gabby drew her mother-in-law's cold hands in her warm ones.

"Uncle Quennel will not be able to leave the country until he takes care of this detail. He will come for me. My child poses more of a threat to him than I do."

"Guy will never forgive you for this," Ambra warned.

"Mayhap, but I must do what I know is right. Ambra, you do not strike me as a timid woman."

"I am not. But I would never have considered defying my lord and master." She paused, then said, "Mayhap, I have much to learn from my new daughters."

"Tell her the rest, Gabby," Bethany urged.

"I know Uncle Quennel; he will not engage our soldiers. I hope they rescue Uncle Alec, but I think Quennel will hold him as a hostage until he is free of this land."

"With the men gone, the castle guards must serve double duty. I will see to the preparation of the castle, and to your clever trap," Bethany said with excitement, then turned to her mother-in-law. "Ambra, would you like to look in on the twins or come with me?"

Ambra momentarily considered the question, then grinned. "I think I shall come with you. I have much to learn. And I believe it is not too late for me to master new ideas."

Left alone, except for the two Scottish guards who followed her everywhere, Gabby sat down at the trestle table. She wanted so badly to help her husband, but he never listened to her. She knew Quennel was a coward. He would never meet an adversary out in the open if he could attack without warning.

She was so worried about her loved ones she did not hear the two dour-faced Scotsmen until they each took a seat beside her. Her hand fluttered to her mouth, stifling a startled gasp. Like two distant shadows they had always kept their distance; now they joined her as though they approved and accepted her.

"My lady, ye must get ye rest if ye are with child," the man with the thick red beard said, while the other man nodded in agreement.

She had not expected concern, nor a sympathetic smile.

"How can you care about me? If not for my family, no one would be in danger."

" 'Tis not yer fault, my lady. 'Tis that of an evil man driven by greed and hate. Dinna worry, he will be stopped. But ye must take care of the bairn within ye."

"You do not blame me?" she asked stunned.

"Nay, lass, 'tis the stupid Normans and their stupid families that allow such men power. 'Tis no different in Scotland, but the villains last a wee bit briefer in the bonny hills."

She smiled hearing the Scottish boast that warmed her heart. She loved the moors, and the people who lived there were her father's clan. "I will try to take care of the bairn. Ye are right, we need more lads like him and his father to protect the land for all."

The Scotsman smiled at her brogue. "Ye understand, lassie."

She did indeed understand. Their dour mien was directed against the situation, not her. Bless them. They cared not only about her and her child, but about the right of it. They were braw men who on this day had earned a place in her heart.

"What be your names?"

"I am known as Kay and this oversize giant answers to the name of Sim."

She hugged them each in turn. "I shall remember your names."

"We have been sent to protect ye, my lady, and we will do so with our very lives."

" 'Tis an honor I do not deserve. Thank you."

She went to bed knowing that no harm would befall her with those two giants standing guard.

Camped on the Scottish moors, Quennel's army knew that when the Normans attacked it would be a fight to the death. Their loyalty had been paid for. Still, the spirit leaves even the most mercenary of men when their commander retreats before a sword has been raised.

After seeing the arrival of Guy's army, Quennel knew the odds were against him. With only the help of his servant, Perrin, Quennel dragged a bound and gagged Alec with him on his trek to North Umberland. He had left several soldiers back at Renwyg and sent word to be ready. Perrin complained loud and long about the hardship as he carried the supplies. Quennel ignored the catamite and concentrated on the journey. He had never expected two clans to band together and support the de Bellemares. Damn his niece. He would see her in Hades.

All he had wanted was the home and land that by rights belonged to him. Now, because of her defiance, he had run afoul of the king. No one would have investigated the death of his niece and nephew. But she had gained the attention of William and the support of Norman lords and Scottish lairds. Damn her to hell and back. He would this day seek his revenge. If not for the bitch's friends, he would have traded Alec for Louis. It was too late to capture his dream. But he would see the vixen dead. She would arrive in hell long before him, and he would take great pleasure in her suffering.

That night he stared over the campfire at the surly Scotsman, Alec Campbell. "Tomorrow, heathen, you and your precious niece will be together in agony. I want her to watch you die before I end her life.'' The pronouncement did not even make the man flinch, and his stoicism irritated Quennel.

"Did you not hear me?'' He ripped the gag from the man's mouth.

Alec's level stare never wavered. " 'Tis best ye hope ye are strong enough to end my life. For if any breath exists in this body, ye will be the one in hell.''

"I do not fear you,'' Quennel snapped. "But I cannot understand why you do not fear me.''

"I dinna fear death, because I dinna fear damnation.''

"I do not think God looks kindly on heathens,'' Quennel snarled.

Alec chuckled. "I am not afraid to stand before my God and hear his judgment. Can ye say the same?''

Quennel rubbed his forehead, wiping away the sudden perspiration. "I have nothing to fear.''

"A man who would plot the execution of his niece and nephew for coin and no doubt did away with his own sister and her husband for the same end. Aye, ye will fear his wrath. Only God can forgive ye, and without remorse there is neither salvation nor deliverance. Ye will suffer the torment of the damned.''

"I wish to hear no more of your superstitious prattle,'' he snapped, quickly gagging the Scot.

Suddenly, he had an idea. All this talk of judgment and God had given him a brilliant inspiration. "Perrin,'' he bellowed.

When the boy came running, Quennel pulled him away from the Scot. "Bring me my parchment and ink. When I am through with my missive, you will go to London and deliver it to my friend, Bishop Barton, along with this purse of coin.'' He hefted a heavy bag of gold and gave the pouch to the boy. "I want this in his hand in one week." Quennel wrote out a message, then handed Perrin the sealed letter. "Go, and mind you watch for brigands."

Quennel watched the boy gallop out of camp. "Damnation indeed." He chuckled.

Guy looked over the battlefield where the mercenaries camped, and listened as his companions offered various strategies. Their biggest concern was finding out where Alec was, for once the battle began his life would be forfeited.

Louis stepped forward. "I can sneak into their camp disguised as a squire. No one will take notice of me. I can easily find the information out."

"Non," Guy said curtly, causing Lance and Mactavish to raise an eyebrow. "I promised your sister to keep you safe. This man wishes to kill you. Would you walk into his den?"

Louis bristled, but said nothing more as the men decided to attack the next day at midday. But as soon as he could slip away, he changed into squire's clothes of tunic and tights, mussed his hair, and moved toward the enemy lines.

Once inside the enemy camp he took a deep breath to fortify his courage, then walked around as though he belonged.

With the feigned assurance of youth he wandered through the area. Acquiring a drink, he sipped the brew sparingly to listen and watch the men.

Two burly men sat down at the fire after their watch and poured themselves a generous horn of ale. They talked in hushed tones which grew louder as their brew disappeared.

"Quennel, that cowardly vermin! Leaving us here to meet his foes, and taking the Scot."

"He is a weak, sniveling lord. I pity his targets."

"I know. The girl does not suspect his game. He will have her easily."

Louis had heard enough and eased away from the fire, heading toward the woods as fast as he could. He had to reach their lines. Gabby's and Alec's lives were in the balance.

Chapter Twenty-Three

At eventide Quennel gazed upon Renwyg Castle filled with elation. He knew, as no one else could, that his time of revenge had come. *Stupid bitch, setting a trap for me.* He looked down at the bodies of the soldiers who had lain in wait, then at the babies the blacksmith had sneaked through the hidden passage.

"Twas easy, my lord. They guard the Lady Gabrielle more than these mites."

Quennel roughly took one of the twins, causing the baby to wail, and thrust him into a cart.

Alec strained against his bonds. "I will kill ye! And if not me, then be sure the de Bellemares and the Lemieuxes will hunt ye down and cut ye to tiny pieces, fodder for the pigs."

"*Non.* No one will pursue me as long as I have these little ones at my mercy."

* * *

The gatekeeper sent for the mistress of the castle.

"He took the bait," Gabby said, wrapping the mantle tight against her body. Bethany huddled close to her side, fighting the frigid wet wind as they walked out on to the battlements.

Gabby felt her sister-in-law's hand slip into hers as they leaned over the high stone wall. An icy rain bit into her face as she stared down. At the base of the castle stood Quennel, with a wagon and several soldiers.

"Gabrielle Aumont, if you do not accompany me, I will kill my hostages," he yelled with hands cupped by his mouth, then wiped the rain from his face, and added, "Do you want that on your conscience?"

"Are the men in place?" Gabby whispered to Bethany.

"Aye."

"See it done."

Bethany raised her hand to give the men the signal.

"Lady Campbell, how do your boys fare?" Quennel asked.

Cold fingers of fear gripped Gabby's spine as she stayed Bethany's hand. "Not the twins."

"He lies," Bethany said, but still sent a man to check on her babies.

Through the rain, they could see two bundles being lifted from the cart. "I have your sons, Lady Bethany!" Quennel lowered the first covering, and Gabby held her breath. It was definitely a baby, but it was too far away to identify.

As Quennel lowered the other covering, revealing a second child, Cedric ran back, followed by Ambra, with tears streaming down her face. Their expressions confirmed that the twins were missing.

Bethany moaned and swayed as Gabby caught her about the waist.

"Send Lady Gabrielle out or these poor little whelps will meet with an unfortunate accident," Quennel demanded.

Gabby did not hesitate. "I must go, or Quennel will kill them."

Bethany grabbed her arm. "I will come with you."

"As will I," Ambra said, quietly.

Gabby started to protest, but one look at both mothers' determined expressions made her fall silent and nod. She leaned over the side of the walkway. "I will come out, with Lady Bethany and Lady Ambra. They will return the twins to safety."

Quennel whipped off the hood of the man next to him, revealing Alec Campbell. "If you delay, the babies will look like this."

"Uncle Alec," Gabby cried at the sight of his bruised and bloody face. Tears filled her eyes, blurring his image as she swallowed her emotion. Blinking the moisture away, she squared her shoulders and turned to Bethany. "We must hurry," she said, her voice husky.

Quennel moved his prisoners back to the grove of trees, and Gabby felt a measure of assurance. The castle guards were there.

"I am ready." As Gabby made her way across the courtyard, her body guards, appeared.

"You cannot come."

To her surprise, they didn't argue, but each offered her a weapon.

Gabby placed the dagger within the folds of her cloak, then fitted the dirk into her girdle.

"Thank you," she whispered past the lump in her throat. Neither was considered a weapon by a man, but she felt armed to the teeth.

At the gate she took a deep breath and steeled herself to meet Quennel. He would not meet her as an equal. But it did not matter; she was through running. The time had come to face her destiny.

After the castle's gate opened, she stepped out with Bethany and Ambra, moving slowly into the field in the direction Quennel had taken.

What he did not know was his little niece was no longer a victim, and never would be again.

She had just turned and left sight of the castle when her uncle sprang from the bushes. He grabbed her by the shoulders and pulled her face close to his, his breath sour, his eyes glazed.

"I have you now, you little bitch," he growled.

She looked at him with a coolness she had seen Guy practice many times.

"Do you?" she inquired.

His expression registered his shock. He had expected a timid rabbit, but instead found a lioness.

"You and your precious Scot will die together. I have no intention of letting him go."

"I never expected you to."

"Then why did you come?" he asked as he dragged her into his camp.

The minute they entered the encampment, Ambra and Bethany ran to the twins, scooping them into their arms. But Quennel's men blocked their retreat.

"You have no need of the children," Gabby protested, seeing the women detained.

"They will leave when I have Louis." He flung her away and walked over to the fire.

Gabby went to her uncle Alec, who was tied by the campfire. His eyes wide and woeful as he shook his head in regret. Then at a distance she saw the slain bodies of the castle guards who had waited to intercept Quennel.

Terror surged through her, but she refused to show it, as she silently counted Quennel's soldiers. Ten. They had been more than enough to slay Bethany's unsuspecting guard.

"I am surprised your Sight did not warn you." Quennel's voice in her ear made her jump, and in that instant his hands went around her throat. "It has been a long time coming. But"—he squeezed tighter then released her—"be assured your death will be slow."

Gasping, she fell to her knees, but in an instant he was hauling her to her feet again.

"First I will teach you to set a trap for me!" The force of his backhand sent her crashing to the ground once more. Thoughts spinning, ears ringing, she tried to stand, but reeled with dizziness and lost her balance.

Quennel grabbed her hair and yanked her forward.

Pain exploded in her head when his fist smashed her cheek.

Suddenly, a horse burst through the brush and into the clearing. Quennel spun around, dragging her with him.

"De Bellemare," Quennel swore.

"Guy," she whispered, as the de Bellemare men charged into the camp.

Guy jumped from his horse before it had finished running. "Let her go, Quennel."

A queer laughter filled the air. "Would you run her through to get to me?" For a moment there was silence. "Drop your weapon," Quennel ordered.

When she thought Guy would comply, Gabby sank her teeth into Quennel's arm.

He yelped, cursing violently as he threw her aside, and drew his sword to face Guy. "Today you will meet your Maker. You have interfered for the last time."

As Guy advanced, Royce, Rule, and Lance drew their weapons. They were sorely outnumbered.

Guy's sword met Quennel's blade. Steel crashed against steel and the sound tolled the ringing of battle, distinct and unforgettable.

Gabby watched the fight with rising trepidation, and suddenly she was in the mist. *Guy lay motionless in the dirt, a sword wound in his stomach. The only movement came*

from the blood that poured from his body into the earth.
The terrible picture faded and was replaced by the sight of
Quennel driving his sword toward Guy. "No," she
screamed, and jumped forward, barely managing to take
hold of her uncle's cloak and drag him backward. He turned
halfway toward her and wrapped his arm around her neck.

She struggled with all her strength, trying to gain her
freedom as her mind screamed in protest. Guy was on his
feet, but now he battled not one swordsman but three. To
Gabby's horror, blood stained his white smock.

Suddenly, Lance finished off his opponents and charged
over the dead bodies to help. His sword raised, he stood
back to back with Guy. Father and son were a formidable
team as they fended off the swordsmen.

Royce and Rule gained the advantage and took on the
remaining guards.

Gabby heard Guy shout her name just as she managed to
break her uncle's hold.

But Quennel's sharp nails bit into her arm as he jerked
her back toward him. Her hand closed on her dirk, and,
keeping his gaze locked with hers, she said, "There's unfin-
ished business between you and me."

His smirk made her shudder. Such evil should not exist.

"I hear you are with child. I will see you and your brat
in hell."

Her hand protectively covered her stomach. "Hell is your
destination, not mine."

He raised his hand to strike her and she saw her father's
ring. With a surge of determination she embedded her blade
deep into his ribs. He looked nothing less than stunned.

"You will no longer harm me or those I love!" she
shouted.

Quennel stumbled back and fell to the ground. "You,
you . . ."

He spit out blood and wiped it with his sleeve, staring at it as though he did not recognize it.

"A woman. A woman has seen my end." He looked at her, then a slow thin smile appeared. "It is not over, witch. I will reach out from the grave and pull you into hell."

The words were garbled as he choked on his own blood, and the raspy sound of his uneven breathing filled the air with the cold hiss of death.

At the threat, a chill passed through her, but watching him pitch forward, she felt not a shred of remorse or pity. It was over. She reached down and removed her father's ring.

Numbly, she stumbled over the slick ground to her uncle and untied his hands. His voice seemed to come to her from far away as the ringing in her ears grew deafening.

Her gaze sought her beloved. Guy took one step toward her, then collapsed. "Guy," she gasped as hot tears stung her cheeks. Nearby her she heard the muffled sounds of Ambra and Bethany, but slowly their voices receded as she sank into the darkness.

Her uncle Alec caught her in his arms. As he looked down at his niece he knew that his brother had sired a true Campbell. "Dear God," he said, knowing she deserved his loyalty and his life. He would not soon forget her sacrifice. He picked up the ring she had dropped.

"Dinna worry, little lass, the lad will be all right."

Now he saw that Lance lay wounded next to Guy. "Rule," he called, "run to the castle for help."

Ambra handed Royce his son, then knelt down before Lance and Guy. "Help me, Bethany," she cried, checking each wound as tears streamed down her cheeks.

Bethany handed Royce his other son, and sank down beside Guy, while Ambra tended Lance.

Alec lifted Gabby into his arms and started toward the

castle even as the guards rushed out of the gates, his own clansmen included.

"'Twas a poor job ye made of it," he rebuked Sim, sending the Norman soldiers to fetch Guy and Lance.

"My laird, she is an honorable little lady," Sim replied.

"Aye, and one to whom we all owe our gratitude. For today she slew a man who should never have been born. My brother's daughter, like his son, is a brave and bonny child," he said.

Alec carried her into the castle and looked around uncertainly, wondering where to place the lady.

Bethany ran in after Alec, her face pinched and white as Royce followed, carrying their sons. "Put Gabrielle up in my room," she said.

Following her orders, Alec carried Gabby through the great hall. Whispered voices asked the questions of how and why, and by the time Gabrielle lay in bed, those who hovered no longer were curious but concerned.

Downstairs, the great oak doors swung open once more as Lance and Guy were carried in. "Put the injured men in the great room, where I can treat them." Ambra said, directing the litter carriers.

Bethany sighed, hearing Ambra's voice below. The wounded men would be in capable hands. She turned back to her patient and, rinsing a linen cloth in cool water, bathed Gabrielle's face.

Her eyelids fluttered, then lifted.

"What has happened?" Gabby asked, confused by the concerned faces hovering above her.

Bethany let out a shaky laugh. "You slay your horrible uncle, then ask us what has happened?"

Gabby tried to sit up, but Bethany held her down. "You must rest. You will need all your strength to withstand your husband's wrath."

Gabby's memory suddenly returned and her eyes filled

with an avalanche of tears. "Guy is dead!" The words choked her.

"Dead? Nay, he is wounded. Ambra and Maida are treating him now in the great room."

"Wounded?" Relief swept through her and she pushed Bethany away. "I must go to him."

"Nay, you are too weak." Bethany struggled, but could not hold Gabrielle down.

In the great room Guy was agitated. "Let me up, woman. I must see Gabby. Get thee out of my way."

But the stubborn cook continued to minister to him, while asking Ambra if she needed any potions to treat Lance's wound.

"Do you have trouble hearing?" Guy bellowed at the cook.

Royce stepped up to the table and spoke to Rule. "Hold Guy down."

"Brother, I will surely box your ears. Let me up."

Lance bent forward from his table, his hand holding Ambra's over his heart. "You must be treated, son. Then you can go to your sweet wife. I am told she is resting and in no danger."

Guy relaxed slightly. "Thank you, Father. You saved my life." Then he brushed the bandages aside, disturbing Maida's handiwork. "Now someone carry me up the stairs so I can be with Gabby."

A small crowd had gathered around the table to hold Guy down.

Royce shook his head as he looked up over the small circle surrounding Guy and saw Gabby, her face alight with happiness, running down the steps.

He chuckled. "Why would we carry you up to yon lady?"

"Royce, I swear sometimes you are as dense as the wood outside. I love her and must be near her."

When Royce ignored his request, Guy's eyes narrowed.

"Now," he bellowed as he threw the healing tray aside. "I will go to my woman and we will not be separated again."

Gabby broke through the crowd. "Guy, lie down. You are wounded and need care."

"There you are. These dull-witted louts would not let me up." His eyes took on a dreamy look and he instantly relaxed. "Will you marry me?"

Gabby grabbed a cloth from Maida and tried to stem the blood. "Maida, help me. He has ripped open his wound and is losing so much blood."

"Will you marry me?" he said his voice growing agitated.

"Yes, yes. Now be quiet and let me treat this."

"You are not just saying that because I am close to death?"

She grabbed his tunic and fairly lifted his shoulders clear off the pallet. "You are not close to death. Do you hear me? Never will you say that again in my presence. I will marry you because I love you. Now lie back and let me tend your wound."

Guy leaned back, a contented look on his face. "See, Royce, I told you she was an angel."

Chapter Twenty-Four

"Do you think they have healed?" Rule asked Royce as he gestured with his tankard toward Guy and Lance at the end of the table.

"Aye, a man needs his strength and stamina if he is to please a maiden through the night." Royce smiled, watching the red stain creep up his brother's face.

"Guy is healed." Louis grinned, his father's jeweled ring glistening in the firelight as he raised his chalice in a mock salute. "How could he not be with my sister ordering him not to die."

Guy chuckled at the reminder of his little nun demanding he recover, then turned to Lance. "You also had gentle ministrations."

"*Oui*. Ambra poured out her love, thinking I was close to death." Lance softly sighed, his eyes misted by memory. "Thank God for my wound."

Alec handed Lance a tankard of ale. "I wonder if congratulations or condolences are in order. Proposing marriage on the spot to Lady Ambra had the rashness of youth.''

"*Non.* I have wasted too many years." Lance raised his tankard.

"But if ye have too many years, there be a maiden's disappointment," Angus added, laughing at the outrage on the older man's face.

"Too old is it, whelp!" Lance bellowed, turning to Mactavish. "You best teach the lad some respect, Mactavish. Too old, bah!" His eyes narrowed at the boy. "You best learn, lad, that unlike the battlefield, when you unsheathe your weapon in the bedroom, speed is neither expected, nor valued."

A roar of laughter erupted, and several more ribald comments were made to father and son.

Guy slapped his father on the back, "Never mind. They only envy us our good fortune."

Ian raised his chalice. "To the bridegrooms, Lance and Guy. Tonight is their last night as free men."

A chorus of toasts filled the air as servants heaped more food and wine onto the table.

Gabby awoke early to the crisp morning air and inhaled deeply. Her wedding day. Again. Well, the third time should be charmed.

She looked over at Ambra, expecting to find her still asleep. Instead she lay awake, tension furrowing her fine brow. " 'Tis only normal to be nervous on your wedding day," Gabby said.

Ambra shook her head. "You are not."

"You must remember 'tis my third trip to the altar, and only your first."

"After all these years, I fear Lance will find me old and

not as desirable as he once did.'' She sighed and threw back the covers.

Gabby reached over and took hold of Ambra's hands. ''All you have to do is look at the man to see he is besotted with you. Let the fears go and enjoy your happiness.''

A smile lit the older woman's eyes. ''I have always loved that man. Even when I wished it otherwise I could not change the fact that my heart belonged to him.''

''Close your eyes,'' Gabby admonished, then released Ambra's hands to retrieve the borrowed pearls she had worn at her wedding. ''You must wear these today, your wedding day.''

Ambra's eyes filled with tears as she cupped the jewels in her hand. ''Though I am the mother of two grown men, I feel like a blushing bride. Love is truly a miracle.''

The whole assembly gasped when two beautiful brides appeared on the balcony. Ambra wore Lance's pearls, and a light tunic of ivory, the soft delicate color enhancing her lovely complexion. A glow of happiness melted the years of strain away, leaving a beautiful, blushing bride. In contrast to Ambra's subdued appearance, Gabby looked striking and dramatic. Her stark white linen tunic was pure and plain except for the finely embroidered mistletoe adorning the rolled neckline. Even her hairstyle was severe. Instead of long, flowing hair worn loose as custom dictated, her tresses were braided and shaped into a coronet atop her head. The only jewelry she wore was a shiny gold medallion that hung from a long, thick gold chain.

Guy's throat constricted when he looked at Gabby. He had never seen such a lovely woman. Her dark amethyst eyes sparkled and when she moistened her lips, his insides tightened in response. She was a rare jewel and far more than he deserved. His breath caught at the sight of his medallion around her neck, marking her as his. At his pleased surprise, an answering smile crossed her lips. Then his sweet, little angel flashed him a saucy wink as she passed before him to take her place.

When Ambra joined Lance, all four knelt before the cleric.

Gabby's hand slipped into Guy's. When her fingers touched his, he felt warm, safe, complete. He finally understood the precious gift God had bestowed.

Like the sweet song of a harp was Gabby's promise to love, honor, and obey. The simple certainty in her voice moved him, and for a moment he lost himself, staring at her. The priest nudged him to say the vows and his hands actually shook as he lifted hers for a soft kiss. "I vow that I will love, honor, and cherish you all the days of my life," he promised.

When the friar turned to his parents Guy leaned down and whispered, "I would restate my vows every day of our life, if only to see the loving expression shining in your eyes."

Then the friar blessed them and Guy's lips covered hers in the kiss of peace. He had all a man could hope for, and her devotion humbled him. *Thank you,* he silently whispered.

The cleric shook their hands. Then Lance and Ambra congratulated them. Ambra hugged her son. "I do not know who I am happier for, you or me."

He kissed her cheek and accepted his father's hand. Lance's grip was firm "Today I have gained a wife and a family. I am blessed to be given another chance," he said huskily.

The rest of the family rushed forward. His brothers spared no mercy as they kissed his little wife and hugged their mother. "Be good to her," Louis told Guy. "She loves you more than you deserve."

Guy gripped Louis's hand. "I am aware of how lucky I am."

Louis smiled and made way for the villagers as the family moved in behind the happy couple.

Guy looked around at all the smiling faces as he hugged Gabby to his side. He had never felt this peace. He could not wait to start their life in Wales. He longed for the challenges that awaited them. "I will build you a castle fit for a queen," he said.

She blushed. "Wherever you call home will be my castle."

Good wishes abounded as the crowd moved toward the feasting tables, and the dancers and entertainers filled the hall with merriment and music.

Wine and ale flowed freely. Gabby's face was flushed. She had been whisked away from Guy to dance with Rule, Royce, Lance, and Alec before being returned to her husband.

Her eyes were sparkling, her cheeks rosy. "Come dance with me," she cried, pulling him to the middle of the floor. She laughed at his pained expression. " 'Tis easy, I will teach you," she said.

Guy chuckled. "I can dance well enough, my love, but I think the wine has gone to your feet," he teased.

She made a face, then laughed. "Then teach me, my lord," she said softly, seductively, while melting into his embrace.

The moment her soft form met his, he forgot his surroundings. When his lips touched hers, the music faded, and his senses were aware of nothing but her. She gave a throaty purr as the kiss deepened and she wrapped her arms around his neck, her fingers teasing his nape. He crushed her in his arms, kissing her with a need that frightened him.

She answered his passion with her own, until he tore his lips from hers. "We need to cool our blood." He looked around and drew a deep breath. God, she was more potent than any wine he had ever drunk.

"I will try," she responded, as breathless as he.

He chuckled. "Let us stay only until the feasting is over, then make our good-byes."

Suddenly the music came to a halt. Guy looked up and his blood froze.

An armed guard had entered.

All heads turned as the room grew quiet.

It was the king's own guard, followed by William, himself.

The king's strained features boded ill. Instinctively, Guy pushed Gabby a little behind him as William approached and handed him a missive. Guy recognized the church seal and opened the letter, as Royce and his family crowded around. His hand shook as the words jumped off the page. "Sire," he exclaimed, "you must stop this madness."

William shook his head, his expression grim. "I cannot."

"Husband, what is it?" asked Gabby softly.

They could make a run for it, Guy thought, but then he saw the king's soldiers fanning out against the walls. Damn William's foresight. Besides, Gabby could never survive as an outlaw in her present, delicate condition.

He swallowed. "We are ordered back to London."

"Why?"

His jaw tightened. "It seems Quennel died too late. He had already started the proceedings for a trial."

A puzzled frown marred her lovely features. "A trial?"

"Show her," William ordered. When Guy did not comply, William snatched the missive and handed it to Gabby.

Her face drained of all color. "No," she breathed. "How can this be?"

"Quennel wrote his old friend, Bishop Barton, offering the Church all of his estate on his death, a huge recompense for an investigation." The king took her hand in his. "Unfortunately I learned of the plot too late to intervene. All I could do, my lady, was insist the trial be held in my castle."

"Will you preside?" she asked.

He drew a deep breath. *"Non.* A Church tribunal oversees all trials for witchcraft."

Heresy and witchcraft drew big crowds. The solemn air of the church tribunal descended on those present like a cold mist from the moors.

Dressed in white, Gabby stood on a small raised dais before the church hierarchy. The church tribunal consisted of Bishop Barton and his four attendants, who sat behind a long table. With almost a pretentious posturing, Bishop Barton leaned forward every time he put a question to her. "How long have you practiced witchcraft and the dark powers?"

"Dark powers?" she questioned.

"Your visions."

Guy held his breath. *Lie,* his mind screamed, knowing how ruthless the Church could be in its search for heretics.

Gabby squared her shoulders and raised her eyes to meet the condemning stares. "Are you to be my judge? I thought the Bible says, judge not lest you be judged."

At the crowd's murmur of agreement the bishop banged his fist on the table for silence. His eyes narrowed at her. "It is my sacred duty. Rout out the heretics among us."

A chill passed through Guy at the cold announcement.

Bishop Barton studied the crowd, then pointed his finger at Gabby. "How long have you practiced witchcraft and the dark powers?" he repeated.

"Sorceress," a woman screamed, inciting several others to chant witch.

Though the bishop did not silence the disturbance, William did. "I cannot hear the lady's answer." He turned to the bishop. "Justice is your first consideration, I believe. If so, order is necessary."

Stinging from the king's reprimand, the bishop glared at Gabby. "Answer the question."

"I, like you, have been given special talents by my creator. I will not apologize nor explain them to you."

Guy's mouth hung open. Why had she chosen this minute to be a tigress? Guy closed his eyes. *Gabby, love, hear my thoughts. Meekness will serve you much better.*

Tension hung in the air as one thick-browed, bald priest leaned forward. "Do you dare to reprimand this tribunal?"

Tears glistened in her eyes, yet she stood straight before the censure of the clerics. "I do not challenge you on Church doctrine. I do, however, challenge your right to test my innocence. Our Savior stood on trial himself but never did he judge another, not even Judas. He taught forgiveness. I see none in your eyes. Therefore, I do not recognize the power of this court."

When Guy saw the red-faced judges draw back in horror at her answer, he jumped to his feet. "She is innocent, and naturally distraught by these proceedings. The lady is with child. Her responses are bound to be emotional. I beg the court's leniency." He walked over to his wife and placed his arm around her in a show of support. "Good Fathers, Lady Gabrielle spent years in a convent considering her calling. Can you not see an angel here?"

"There is still the question of her power. We must know if she sees visions."

Guy nodded his head and turned to his wife. "Lie," he whispered.

She shook her head slowly and reached out to touch his cheek. "I am not guilty of what they accuse."

Her soft words struck him harder than a mighty opponent's blow.

"I have seen visions since I was a small child. They have harmed no one. God does not send these images without reason. And I believe it is not our place to question Him. I no more wanted this gift than one would wish for the plague. But His ways are often mysterious and beyond our understanding."

"You admit of your own free will that you have visions?"

"Aye, I do."

Guy inwardly groaned.

The clerics conferred. Minutes dragged until their murmurs ceased, and Bishop Barton stood up. "It is the decision of this court that you will at noon tomorrow be taken to the courtyard and forced to walk the trial of coals. Only if there is a sign from God will we know you are innocent of these charges."

The sentence hit Guy like a roar of storm waves crashing against the shore. *"Non,"* he shouted, and pulled out his sword.

Several armed guards rushed toward him. Though he could not hope to succeed against so many, he would have tried if his sweet wife had not stepped in front of him.

"Stop this madness. Or would you make me watch your death?" Moving closer she whispered. "I could not bear it. I need your strength now more than ever. Please, help me in this."

Her words touched his very soul. With a groan, his arms went around her and he held her close. God, how he loved her.

The guards ripped her from his arms. With fists clenched, but held tightly at his side, he honored her wishes, and watched them take her away. Not dragged like a frightened child, but escorted like a queen.

When the doors closed behind her, he turned defiantly

toward the tribunal. "My wife is innocent of anything evil. Those who know her will attest to her goodness."

Bishop Barton steepled his fingers before his mouth, but they failed to cover his sneer. "We will see tomorrow how good she is."

Royce and Rule stepped up and grabbed Guy's arms to hold him back from throttling the sanctimonious priest.

Guy knew there was no mercy in the man's heart. The other judges seemed approachable, but did not question the bishop's authority.

Guy allowed his family to pull him away, knowing that Royce, ever the strategist, would surely have a plan to rescue Gabby.

Once free of the crowd and in the hallway he turned to his brother. "What think you?"

"I think you had better get down on your knees and pray for a miracle."

"I will not accept that. There has to be a way to extricate her."

"I have gone over the defenses. Rescue is impossible. I have even met with William. He will not interfere in the Church's affairs."

Guy had never faced defeat such as this. Not even losing to Rule had given him this hopeless feeling. He smashed his fist into his hand as the others crowded around.

"What is yer plan?" Alec asked.

Guy looked up. "I am without a plan. Do you have a suggestion?"

"Get the lass to me and I will hide her among the clans, where no man will ever know of her whereabouts again," Alec said.

"The rescue is the problem." Guy raked his fingers through his hair, then looked wearily at the Scotsman. "What do you suggest?"

"Kill the bastards that would think she is guilty," Alec replied.

"That will not be easy," Guy said, thinking the Scots reduced everything to the simplest solution.

"I dinna have a problem taking a cleric's life."

"Do you think I do?" Guy asked.

A door closed down the hall and the Mactavish and Angus hurried toward them.

"I have bad news, Guy," Mactavish said as he and Angus joined them. "Tell them what ye overheard, lad."

"After ye left, I followed the bishop. He told the jailer if there is any disturbance tonight to kill Lady Gabrielle. Bishop Barton will sleep outside Gabby's door. He will personally direct the guards."

Royce shook his head. "Does anyone have an idea?"

"Perhaps a diversion would help," said Bethany. "I could disguise myself as a peasant and take her a meal."

"Non," Royce bellowed.

"Listen, I could—"

"Non, you would only succeed in getting yourself hurt along with Gabby."

"Let her tell her idea, Royce," Guy insisted.

"I could drug the bishop and the guards. Then you could rescue her. With the guards incapacitated, they could not harm her."

Hope shone in every pair of eyes at her suggestion.

" 'Tis so simple it could work," Alec said.

"I agree, but you will not deliver the drug," Royce insisted.

"Could I do it?" a shy voice piped up. "No one will suspect me." A beautiful girl stepped forward from the darkened alcove, and it was clear Louis could not take his eyes from her.

"My name is Liana de Bellemare and I would very much like a chance to do this. I tried to help earlier when I learned about Aumont's horrible plan. He and my brother, Bayard, behaved abominably, and I am ashamed of their actions. I wished the lady no harm, but there was little I could do without incurring my brother's wrath.

"Please," she beseeched. "Let me."

Guy nodded his head as Louis stepped forward and took the lady's hand and kissed it. "You are very brave."

Her cheeks blushed and she curtsied to Louis. "My lord, I meant no harm to your family. Would that I was stronger and dared to defy my brother earlier, your sister would not have endured this ordeal. Pray forgive my weakness."

"You were an innocent pawn, much like my sister. There is no reason to ask my forgiveness."

Liana smiled, and Louis tucked her arm in his, then said to Guy. "I will escort the lady to the kitchen, where we can prepare a potion for the guards."

Guy felt relieved for the first time. *She will be in my arms tonight,* he thought. "I'm afraid both of you will suffer for your parts in this," he said to his brothers.

"I have been taking care of you for years," Royce said. "Now should be no different."

Rule gripped his arm. "I will stand by you."

Guy nodded as his mother stepped forward. "I worried you would never be able to trust and put the pain of betrayal to rest. In her you have found your salvation. Do not worry about us; we will weather whatever comes."

"Besides," she added, placing her hand in Lance's, "Our families are powerful; William will not want to alienate us. Though he must appear upset, I feel little will come of it."

Lance cleared his throat. "I will do whatever you wish of me, son."

Though Guy wanted to hold on to a lingering resentment,

he remembered his sweet wife's words. "In forgiveness there is life." Guy clasped his sire's arm, feeling the bitterness of the past permanently slip away. "Thank you, Father."

With the handshake the healing had begun, and Guy realized that Gabby had brought peace to his family.

The guards and the bishop were asleep thanks to the drug. Guy, Royce, and Louis quietly stepped up the staircase and over the sleeping bishop's body, while the others stood watch below.

Guy searched the fat cleric's robe, retrieved the key and entered the cell. Royce held the torch up, letting the light fill the room. The soft glow slipped across the floor and spilled over her. She was asleep on a cot.

Guy grinned at Louis and rushed over to awaken her.

Before he had reached her a voice rang out. "De Bellemares, you will forfeit your lives and the lady's if you do not drop your weapons now."

Guy spun around, ready to fight to the death until he saw Gabby standing in the doorway held by two soldiers.

With a curse, he turned back and looked closely at the woman lying on the cot. It was Liana. Apparently, she had been drugged.

"What now?" Guy asked Bishop Barton.

The cleric shook his head. "The only hope your wife has is God." He lifted his arm to the soldiers. "Lock them all up. I want no more trouble from her family."

Guy saw the fear in his wife's eyes. He could not leave her. But when he started to struggle a knife appeared at his wife's throat.

"I love you," she said softly. "Have faith, my darling. Do not worry."

"Bishop Barton, let me be with her tonight," Guy begged.

"She needs to repent in solitude."

Tears formed in her eyes but she said nothing.

"You filthy, sanctimonious pig," Guy shouted.

"Guy." Gabby's gentle voice captured his attention. "It is all right. I will be fine."

As always, when her thoughts and prayer should be for herself, others held her attention. He struggled and shouted her name as they dragged him from her. Uncaring of the blows he suffered as the guards delivered him to his cell, a tortured cry ripped from his soul. If she should perish, his life would cease to have meaning. He would die, too.

Alone in his cell he fell to his knees, begging God to save her, making promise after promise to do good deeds. But as the night passed he feared his prayers went unanswered.

In the morning they dragged him from his cell and led him outside into the courtyard. There they tied him to a pole as they prepared a bed of coals before him. Ten feet long the pit stretched. The smoke drifted into his face, and tears streamed down his cheeks.

It took all morning to get the coals red-hot, and he knew she would never survive this ordeal. "God have mercy on her," he whispered. But the heavens were calm, and silence met his plea.

At noon they brought Gabby from the tower cell along with his family. The crowd had grown, and he could hear their macabre curiosity as the gates were opened and the peasants swarmed into the yard, but his eyes remained fixed on Gabby. As fragile as a delicate flower, she stood in simple grace, her beauty undeniable, her courage unassailable. Her gaze met his, and he swallowed his fear. Never had he seen such unwavering strength or dignity. He knew he would feel every painful step.

"Cleric," he bellowed when the bishop entered the courtyard. "Let me do the test."

Bishop Barton's beady eyes narrowed until they almost

disappeared. "The test is for your wife. You cannot stand in her place."

He strained against his bonds, the rope cutting into his flesh. "But she is with child. What manner of man would let a woman suffer this fate? What manner of God would ask this of her?"

"Be careful, de Bellemare, you are dangerously close to blasphemy," Bishop Barton warned.

A harsh laugh sprang from his lips. "You, Bishop, are dangerously close to losing your immortal soul. If God does not punish you, I will."

The cleric's face turned bright red. "Do not threaten me."

" 'Tis not a threat but a promise."

While Guy struggled futilely against his restraints, the cleric smiled and walked away.

When he had ascended the raised platform, and lifted his hand, calling for attention, the crowd fell silent.

"This woman has been accused of witchcraft. This test will determine her innocence—or her guilt."

The gathering of Saxons and Normans erupted in a calliope of noise. The bishop continued to speak and gesture, working the crowd into a frenzy.

Royce and Rule stepped out from the crowd and shouted to be heard "Would the Church accept a donation to see this woman free?" said Royce.

"*Non,* but I might consider it in exchange for your brother's freedom."

Perspiration covered Guy when he realized they were doomed. She would be tortured, and there was nothing he could do. He could not bear it. "Take me, let her live," he silently begged.

The bishop again called for order. "We will proceed."

The soldiers led Gabby to the pit.

"Lady Gabrielle, do you have anything to say?" Bishop

Barton yelled from his lofty position as the crowd hung on every word.

"Just the Lord's Prayer," she responded evenly, but though her voice was quiet, every ear strained to hear her response. She closed her eyes and began the prayer. Her family joined in, their voices loud and solemn. The volume grew as all the villagers added their voices.

When the prayer ended she turned to the cleric. "I am ready."

His expression had grown darker at the support she so easily garnered. "Begin," he ordered.

"No," Guy yelled. "You cannot do this." His gaze met hers and he held on to her sweet image. He struggled wildly to get to her, gasping for breath.

"I love you," she mouthed.

His chest tightened when she turned away and faced the pit. As Gabby stood before the steaming heat, the sun suddenly grew dim. Several frightened women screamed, while others looked toward the sun, then covered their faces. " 'Tis a sign," a cry went up, "a sign from God!"

They all fell to their knees. "Spare us, spare us," they chanted. Then a babble of voices were raised. "Release the lady, she is innocent. Release the lady, or God will punish us."

The bishop blustered and postured. "Nonsense," he chided his flock and glared up at the sun. " 'Tis nothing but a cloud. Look and see, 'tis nothing." But the villagers would not heed him. He kept looking up at the sky, pointing and commanding them to look. Suddenly, he screamed. Falling to his knees and covering his eyes, he cried, "Dear God, I am blind."

The villagers trembled at God's retribution.

William stepped forth. "The lady is innocent!" he declared. "We will set her free."

A soldier cut Guy's bindings and with rawhide strips still dangling from his wrists, he ran and took Gabby in his arms, whispering a prayer of thanks to his Maker. The sign had come, and not a moment too soon.

Epilogue

Wales

"Guy," Gabby cried out in her sleep, waking slowly from her nightmare.

He could not speak as he drew her into his arms. He felt the rapid beat of her heart, inhaled her violet scent, and stroked the soft smooth skin of her face.

His own fears surfaced as he relived her terror and his throat choked with emotion. His lips lightly grazed hers as he drew her closer, wanting, needing to comfort and assuage all the horror, pain, and terror.

Her eyelashes fluttered open as his lips smothered hers. Relief surged through him at her response. He lost himself to the sheer bliss of her tender passion. He kissed her again, savoring every taste, and touch. Their breath mingled, and the sweet sensuous intimacy heated his blood. He would never get enough of her. Yet as frantic as his kiss had been, she had gentled him. He wondered if he offered or drew comfort as he pulled away from her and rested his head against her forehead.

"I have learned that you could be taken from me in a heartbeat, and so I cherish the moments we have together. The most precious seconds in my life are those that we share. Your laughter, love, and even your tears give my life meaning. But I wish it had not needed such terror to make me realize it."

She caressed his cheek. "I would suffer all the agonies of life to have the miracle of meeting and falling in love. Guy, I would change nothing."

The lump in his throat grew. "I do not deserve you. But I will spend the rest of my life thanking God for you. I promise you, my lady, you will never regret that meeting." He pulled her close and kissed her. There was no way that he could give his thanks other than to share his love.

She pulled away and cradled his face. "You are the answer to my prayers," she whispered.

"And you, my love, are the fulfillment of God's promise."